W9-BXZ-129

FRANK MILDMAY

<u>OR</u>

The Naval Officer

NAUTICAL FICTION
PUBLISHED BY McBOOKS PRESS

BY ALEXANDER KENT
Midshipman Bolitho
Stand into Danger
In Gallant Company
Sloop of War
To Glory We Steer
Command a King's Ship
Passage to Mutiny
With All Despatch
Form Line of Battle!
Enemy in Sight!
The Flag Captain
Signal—Close Action
The Inshore Squadron

BY CAPTAIN FREDERICK MARRYAT
Frank Mildmay <u>OR</u> *The Naval Officer*
The King's Own
Mr Midshipman Easy
Newton Forster <u>OR</u> *The Merchant Service*
Snarleyyow

BY NICHOLAS NICASTRO
The Eighteenth Captain

BY W. CLARK RUSSELL
Wreck of the Grosvenor
Yarn of Old Harbour Town

BY RAFAEL SABATINI
Captain Blood

BY MICHAEL SCOTT
Tom Cringle's Log

BY A.D. HOWDEN SMITH
Porto Bello Gold

FRANK MILDMAY

OR THE NAVAL OFFICER

by
Captain Frederick Marryat

CLASSICS OF NAUTICAL FICTION SERIES

McBOOKS PRESS
ITHACA, NEW YORK

Copyright © 1998 by McBooks Press

All rights reserved, including the right to reproduce this book or any portion thereof in any form or by any means, electronic or mechanical, without the written permission of the publisher. Requests for such permissions should be addressed to: McBooks Press, 908 Steam Mill Road, Ithaca, NY 14850.

Book and cover design by Paperwork.
Cover painting is a detail from *The Hero of Trafalgar* by W.H. Overend, 1891.
Courtesy of Peter Newark's Military Pictures.
Edited by Patricia Zafiriadis
Glossary by Alexander G. Skutt

Library of Congress Cataloging-in-Publication Data

Marryat, Frederick. 1792-1848.
    [Frank Mildmay]
    Frank Mildmay, or, The naval officer / by Frederick Marryat.
       p. cm. — (Classics of nautical fiction series : no. 1)
    "First published in 1829. This text is based on the 1895 edition of the novels of Captain Marryat edited by R. Brimley Johnson and published by J.M. Dent and Co. in London and Little, Brown and Co. in Boston"—T.p. verso.
    ISBN 0-935526-39-0 (pbk.)
    1. Great Britain—History, Naval—19th century—Fiction. 2. Sea stories. gsafd. I. Title. II. Title: Frank Mildmay. III. Title: Naval officer. IV. Series.
PR4977.F73 1997
823'.7—DC21   97-3123
                                                           CIP

Frank Mildmay or The Naval Officer was first published in 1829. This text is based on the 1895 edition of *The Novels of Captain Marryat* edited by R. Brimley Johnson and published by J.M. Dent and Co. in London and Little, Brown and Co. in Boston. Corrections were made for consistency and clarity, but most of the original spelling and punctuation remains intact.

Distributed to the book trade by:
Login Trade, 1436 West Randolph, Chicago, IL 60607, 312-432-7600.

Additional copies of this book may be ordered from any bookstore or directly from McBooks Press, 908 Steam Mill Road, Ithaca, NY 14850. Please include $3.00 postage and handling with mail orders. New York State residents must add 8% sales tax. All McBooks Press publications can also be ordered by calling toll-free 1-888-BOOKS11 (1-888-266-5711).

Visit the McBooks Press website at http://www.McBooks.com.

Printed in the United States of America

9 8 7 6 5 4 3 2

PREFACE

ENGLAND'S greatness as a world power in the sixteenth through nineteenth centuries was based on her nautical might. The Royal Navy and the merchant fleet were the tools that built and maintained the British Empire.

England fought wars against the Spanish, the Dutch, and other European powers, forming and breaking alliances, but its epic military struggle was against France. For more than 125 years, from 1689 to 1815, England and France waged a series of wars. This almost ceaseless conflict was the first to attain a truly global scale. A tale of enmity that often involved other nations, its "chapters" bear names such as the Nine Years War, the War of the Spanish Succession, the War of the Austrian Succession, the Seven Years War (the American subchapter was called the French and Indian War), the War of American Independence, and the Napoleonic Wars.

Safe at home, the British citizenry eagerly read the newspapers and broadsheets that described the numerous naval campaigns and battles. Noble sea captains and brave sailors were celebrated in stories and popular songs. Perhaps the most popular British hero was the legendary rear-admiral, Sir Horatio Nelson. Nelson died in 1805 at the moment of his greatest victory—the Battle of Trafalgar—and became a figure of mythic proportion.

Another great hero was Captain Lord Cochrane. The adventurous Cochrane became famous when his ship, the *"Flying Pallas,"* captured four richly laden Spanish galleons off the Azores, and the prize-money made every member of his crew a rich man. In 1806, a fourteen-year-old midshipman, Frederick Marryat, signed on with Lord Cochrane's next command, the frigate *Impérieuse*. Marryat made lieutenant in 1814. The next year he was promoted to commander. From 1820 to 1822 Marryat commanded the sloop

Beaver which, among other duties, cruised off St. Helena, in the South Atlantic, to guard against Napoleon's escape from his second forced exile from France. He rose to captain and his later posts included an appointment as Senior Naval Officer in Burma. Because of Frederick Marryat's successes in Asia, the Crown bestowed upon him the C.B. (Companion, Order of the Bath), a high honor. Altogether, Captain Marryat saw action in fifty battles.

In 1829, Marryat was still serving in the Royal Navy as captain of the *Ariadne* when he wrote his first novel, *Frank Mildmay or The Naval Officer*. He had previously published a book of ship's flag signals and a polemic calling for the abolition of the impressment of sailors. Marryat's fiction was such a success that he quit the Navy to devote himself to writing. Over a nineteen-year writing career, Marryat authored 22 novels or books of stories. His early writings were nearly all set on or around the sea. Most of his later works were adventure stories intended for young people. He journeyed to America and, in 1839, published a widely read, six volume, rather acerbic account of his travel experiences. Marryat died in 1848 at the age of 56.

Marryat's writing followed notable examples of the sea-story genre by Daniel Defoe and Sir Walter Scott. In turn, his writing influenced Herman Melville and Joseph Conrad and—in our time—C.S. Forester, Alexander Kent, and Patrick O'Brian. What made Marryat different than some of the aforementioned writers was that he lived the adventures about which he wrote. Marryat had skylarked in the rigging with other midshipmen, he had heard the roar of the cannon, and he had commanded a surging man-of-war into battle. Lord Cochrane, the first naval captain under whom Marryat served, was the model for Forester's Horatio Hornblower and O'Brian's Jack Aubrey. But Marryat was there first. His Midshipman Jack Easy was the first fictional character modeled after Lord Cochrane.

Patrick O'Brian's phenomenally popular "Aubrey/Maturin" series of historical novels has reawakened interest in this venerable genre of English literature—nautical fiction. As readers explore this realm, they will find that Marryat is still well worth reading. His value is not just in the perfectly authentic lore of the navy of wooden ships, present in every page of his books. Marryat's sharp wit, love of word play, sense of irony, and interest in the strange and the scandalous are evident throughout his works.

ALEXANDER G. SKUTT

PREFATORY NOTE

by R. BRIMLEY JOHNSON *from the 1895 edition*

"WE do not intend to review our own work; if we did it justice we might be accused of partiality, and we are not such fools as to abuse it. We leave that to our literary friends who may have so little taste as not to appreciate its merits. Not that there would be anything novel in reviewing our own performances—that we have discovered since we have assumed the office of editor; but still it is always done *sub rosa,* whereas in our position we could not deny our situation as editor and author. Of *Peter Simple,* therefore, we say nothing, but we take this opportunity of saying a few words to the public. . . . *The Naval Officer* was our first attempt, and its having been our first attempt must be offered in extenuation of its many imperfections; it was written hastily, and before it was complete we were appointed to a ship. We cared much about our ship and little about our book. The first was diligently taken care of by ourselves, the second was left in the hands of others to get on how it could. Like most bantlings put out to nurse, it did not get on very well. As we happen to be in a communicative vein, it may be as well to remark that, being written in the autobiographical style, it was asserted by friends, and believed in general, that it was a history of the author's life. Now, without pretending to have been better than we should have been in our earlier days, we do most solemnly assure the public that had we run the career of vice of the hero of the *Naval Officer,* at all events we should have had sufficient sense of shame not to have avowed it. Except the hero and heroine, and those parts of the work which supply the slight plot of it as a novel, the work in itself is materially true, especially in the narrative of sea adventure, most of which did (to the best of our recollection) occur to the author. We say to the best of our recollection, as it behooves us to be careful. We have not forgotten the snare in which Chamier found himself by asserting in his preface that his narrative was fact. In *The Naval Officer* much good material was thrown away; but we intend to write it over again some day of these days, and *The Naval Officer,* when corrected, will be so improved that he may be permitted to stand on the same shelf with *Pride and Prejudice* and *Sense and Sensibility.**

"The confounded licking we received for our first attempts in the critical notices is probably well known to the reader—at all events we have not forgotten it. Now, with some, this severe castigation of their first offense would have had the effect of their never offending again; but we felt that our punishment was rather too severe; it produced indignation instead of contrition, and we determined to write again in spite of all the critics in the universe; and in the due course of nine months we produced *The King's Own.* In *The Naval Officer* we had sowed all our wild oats; we had *paid off* those who had ill-treated us, and we had no further personality to indulge in. *The King's Own,* therefore, was wholly fictitious in characters, in plot, and in events, as have been its successors. *The King's Own* was followed by *Newton Forster, Newton Forster* by *Peter Simple.* These are *all* our productions. Reader, we have told our tale."

This significant document was published by Captain Marryat in the *Metropolitan Magazine* 1833, of which he was at that time the editor, on the first appearance of *Peter Simple,* in order, among other things, to disclaim the authorship of a work entitled the *Port Admiral,* which contained "an infamous libel upon one of our most distinguished officers deceased, and upon the service in general." It repudiates, without explaining away, certain unpleasant impressions that even the careful reader of today cannot entirely avoid. Marryat made Frank Mildmay a scamp, I am afraid, in order to prove that he himself had not stood for the portrait; but he clearly did not recognize the full enormities of his hero, to which he was partially blinded by a certain share thereof. The adventures were admittedly his own, they were easily recognized, and he had no right to complain of being confounded with the insolent young devil to whom they were attributed. It would, however, be at once ungracious and unprofitable to attempt any analysis of the

---

* *The improvement was never made.—ED.*

points of difference and resemblance; any reader will detect the author's failings by his work; other coincidences may be noticed here.

It has been said, in the general introduction, that Marryat's cruises in the *Impérieuse* are almost literally described in Frank Mildmay. We have also independent accounts of certain personal adventures there related.

The episode, chap. iv., of being bitten by a skate—supposed to be dead—which is used again in *Peter Simple* came from Marryat's own experience; and he declared that he ran away from school on account of the very indignity—that of being compelled to wear his elder brother's old clothes—which Frank Mildmay pleads as an excuse for sharing at least the sentiments of Cain. Marryat, again, was trampled upon and left for dead when boarding an enemy (see chap. v.); he saved the midshipman who had bullied him, from drowning, though his reflections on the occasion are more edifying than those recounted in chap. v. "From that moment," he says, "I have loved the fellow as I never loved a friend before. All my hate is forgotten. I have saved his life." The defense of the castle of Rosas, chap. vii., is taken straight from his private logbook, while Marshall's *Naval Biography* contains an account of his volunteering during a gale to cut away the mainyard of the *Aeolus*, which scarcely pales before the vigorous passage in chap. xiv.:—

"On the 30th of September, 1811, in lat. 40° 50' N., long. 65° W. (off the coast of New England), a gale of wind commenced at S.E., and soon blew with tremendous fury; the *Aeolus* was laid on her beam ends, her topmasts and mizzenmasts were literally blown away, and she continued in this extremely perilous situation for at least half an hour. Directions were given to cut away the main yard, in order to save the mainmast and right the ship, but so great was the danger attending such an operation considered, that not a man could be induced to attempt it until Mr Marryat led the way. His courageous conduct on this occasion excited general admiration, and was highly approved of by Lord James Townsend, one of whose company he also saved by jumping overboard at sea."

The edition of 1873 contained a brief memoir of the author, by "Florence Marryat," frequently reprinted.

Frank Mildmay, originally called *The Naval Officer; or, Scenes and*

Adventures in the Life of Frank Mildmay, is here printed from the first edition published in 1829 by Henry Colborn, with the following motto on the title page—

> *My muse by no means deals in fiction;*
> *She gathers a repertory of facts,*
> *Of course with some reserve and slight restriction,*
> *But mostly traits of human things and acts.*
> *Love, war, a tempest—surely there's variety;*
> *Also a seasoning slight of lubrication;*
> *A bird's-eye view, too, of that wild society;*
> *A slight glance thrown on men of every station.*
>
> "DON JUAN"

CHAPTER I

These are the errors, and these are the fruits of misspending our prime youth at the schools and universities, as we do, either in learning mere words, or such things chiefly as were better unlearned.

MILTON

MY FATHER was a gentleman, and a man of considerable property. In my infancy and childhood I was weak and sickly, but the favourite of my parents beyond all my brothers and sisters, because they saw that my mind was far superior to my sickly frame, and feared they should never raise me to manhood; contrary, however, to their expectations, I surmounted all these untoward appearances, and attracted much notice from my liveliness, quickness of repartee, and impudence: qualities which have been of much use to me through life.

I can remember that I was both a coward and a boaster; but I have frequently remarked that the quality which we call cowardice in a child, is no more than implying a greater sense of danger, and consequently a superior intellect. We are all naturally cowards: education and observation teach us to discriminate between real and apparent danger; pride teaches the concealment of fear, and habit renders us indifferent to that from which we have often escaped with impunity. It is related of the Great Frederick that he misbehaved the first time he went into action; and it is certain that a novice in such a situation can no more command all his resources than a boy when first bound apprentice to a shoemaker can make a pair of shoes. We must learn out trade, whether it be to stand steady before the enemy, or to stitch a boot; practice alone can make a Hoby or a Wellington.

I pass on to my schooldays, when the most lasting impressions are made. The foundation of my moral and religious instruction had been laid with care by my excellent parents; but, alas! from the time I quitted the paternal roof not one stone was added to the building, and even the traces of what existed were nearly obliterated by the deluge of vice which threatened soon to overwhelm me. Sometimes, indeed, I feebly, but ineffectually endeavoured to stem the torrent; at others, I suffered myself to be borne along with all its fatal rapidity. I was frank, generous, quick, and mischievous; and I must admit that a large portion of what sailors call "devil" was openly displayed, and a much larger portion latently deposited in my brain and bosom. My ruling passion, even in this early stage of life, was pride. Lucifer himself, if he ever was seven years old, had not more. If I have gained a fair name in the service, if I have led instead of followed, it must be ascribed to this my ruling passion. The world has often given me credit for better feelings, as the source of action, but I am not writing to conceal, and the truth must be told.

I was sent to school to learn Latin and Greek, which there are various ways of teaching. Some tutors attempt the *suaviter in modo,* my schoolmaster preferred the *fortiter in re;* and, as the boatswain said, by the "instigation" of a large knotted stick, he drove knowledge into our skulls as a caulker drives oakum into the seams of a ship. Under such tuition, we made astonishing progress; and whatever my less desirable acquirements may have been, my father had no cause to complain of my deficiency in classic lore. Superior in capacity to most of my schoolfellows, I seldom took the pains to learn my lesson previous to going up with my class: "the master's blessing," as we called it, did occasionally descend on my devoted head, but that was a bagatelle; I was too proud not to keep pace with my equals, and too idle to do more.

Had my schoolmaster being a single man, my stay under his care might have been prolonged to my advantage; but unfortunately, both for him and for me, he had a helpmate, and her peculiarly unfortunate disposition was the means of corrupting those morals over which it was her duty to have watched with the most assiduous care. *Her* ruling passions were suspicion and avarice, written in legible characters in her piercing eyes and sharp-pointed nose. She never supposed us capable of telling the truth, so we very naturally never gave ourselves the trouble to cultivate a useless virtue, and seldom resorted to it unless it answered our purpose better than a lie. This propensity of Mrs Higginbottom converted our candour and honesty into deceit and fraud. Never believed, we cared little about the accuracy of our assertions; half-starved, through her meanness and parsimony, we were little scrupulous as to the ways and means provided we could satisfy our hunger; and thus we soon became as great adepts in the elegant accomplishments of lying and thieving, under her tuition, as we did in Greek and Latin under that of her husband.

A large orchard, fields, garden, and poultry-yard attached to the establishment, were under the care and superintendence of the mistress, who usually selected one of the boys as her prime minister and confidential adviser. This boy, for whose education his parents were paying some sixty or eighty pounds per annum, was permitted to pass his time in gathering up the windfalls; in watching the hens, and bringing in their eggs, when their cackling throats had announced their safe accouchement; looking after the broods of young ducks and chickens, *et hoc genus omne;* in short, doing the duty of what is usually termed the odd man in the farmyard. How far the parents would have been satisfied with this arrangement, I leave my readers to guess; but to us who preferred the manual to mental exertion, exercise to restraint, and any description of cultivation to that of cultivating the mind, it suited extremely well; and accordingly no place in the gift of government was ever the object of such solicitude and intrigue, as was to us schoolboys the situation of collector and trustee of the eggs and apples.

I had the good fortune to be early selected for this important post, and the misfortune to lose it soon after, owing to the cunning and envy of my schoolfellows and the suspicion of my employers. On my first coming into office, I had formed the most sincere resolutions of honesty and vigilance; but what are good resolutions, when discouraged on the one hand by the revilings of suspicion, and assailed on the other by the cravings of appetite? My morning's collection was exacted from me to the very last nut, and the greedy eyes of my mistress seemed to inquire for more. Suspected when innocent, I became guilty out of revenge; was detected and dismissed. A successor was appointed, to whom I surrendered all my offices of trust, and having perfect leisure, I made it my sole business to supplant him.

It was an axiom in mathematics with me at that time, though not found in Euclid, that wherever I could enter my head, my whole body might follow. As a practical illustration of this proposition, I applied my head to the arched hole of the hen house door, and by scraping away a little dirt, contrived to gain admittance, and very speedily transferred all the eggs to my own chest. When the new purveyor arrived, he found nothing but "a beggarly account of empty boxes;" and his perambulations in the orchard and garden, for the same reason were equally *fruitless*. The pilferings of the orchard and garden I confiscated as droits; but when I had collected a sufficient number of eggs to furnish a nest, I gave information of my pretended discovery to my mistress, who, thinking she had not changed for the better, dismissed my successor, and received me into favour again. I was, like many greater men, immediately reinstated in office when it was discovered that they could not do without me. I once more became chancellor of the hen roost and ranger of the orchard, with greater power than I had possessed before my disgrace. Had my mistress looked half as much in my face as she did into my hatful of eggs, she would have read my guilt; for at that unsophisticated age I could blush, a habit long since discarded in the course of my professional duties.

In order to preserve my credit and my situation, I no longer contented myself with windfalls, but assisted nature in her labours, and greatly lightened the burthen of many a loaded fruit-tree; by these means, I not only gratified the avarice of my mistress at her own expense, but also laid by a store for my own use. On my restoration to office, I had an ample fund in my exchequer to answer all present demands; and by a provident and industrious anticipation, was enabled to lull the suspicions of my employers, and to bid defiance to the opposition. It will readily be supposed that a lad of my acuteness did not omit any technical management for the purpose of disguise; the fruits which I presented were generally soiled with dirt at the ends of the stalks, in such a manner as to give them all the appearance of "*felo de se*," i.e. fell of itself. Thus, in the course of a few months, did I become an adept of vice, from the mismanagement of those into whose hands I was intrusted to be strengthened in religion and virtue.

Fortunately for me, as far as my education was concerned, I did not long continue to hold this honourable and lucrative employment. One of those unhappy beings called an usher peeped into my chest, and by way of acquiring popularity with the mistress and scholars, forthwith denounced me to the higher powers. The proofs of my peculation were too glaring, and the amount too serious to be passed over; I was tried, convicted, condemned, sentenced, flogged, and dismissed in the course of half an hour; and such was the degree of turpitude attached to me on this occasion, that I was rendered for ever incapable of serving in that or any other employment connected with the garden or farm; I was placed at the bottom of the list, and declared to be the worst boy in the school.

This in many points of view was too true; but there was one boy who bade fair to rival me on the score of delinquency; this was Tom Crauford, who from that day became my most intimate friend. Tom was a fine spirited fellow, up to everything; loved mischief, though not vicious; and was ready to support me in everything through thick and thin; and truly I found him sufficient employment. I threw off all disguise, laughed at any suggestion of reform, which I considered as not only useless, but certain of subjecting me to ridicule and contempt among my associates. I therefore adopted the motto of some great man "to be rather than seem to be." I led in every danger; declared war against all drivellers and half-measures; stole everything that was eatable from garden, orchard, or hen house, knowing full well that whether I did so or not, I should be equally suspected. Thenceforward all fruit missed, all arrows shot into pigs, all stones thrown into windows, and all mud spattered over clean linen hung out to dry, were traced to Tom and myself; and with the usual alacrity of an arbitrary police, the space between apprehension and punishment was very short—we were constantly brought before the master, and as regularly dismissed with "his blessing" till we became hardened to blows and to shame.

Thus, by the covetousness of this woman, who was the grey mare, and the folly of the master, who, in anything but Greek and Latin, was an ass, my good principles were nearly eradicated from my bosom, and in their place were sown seeds which very shortly produced an abundant harvest.

There was a boy at our school lately imported from the East Indies. We nick-named him Johnny Pagoda. He was remarkable for nothing but ignorance, impudence, great personal strength, and, as we thought, determined resolution. He was about nineteen years of age. One day he incurred the displeasure of the master, who, enraged at his want of comprehension and attention, struck him over the head with a knotted cane. This appeal, although made to the least sensitive part of his frame, roused the indolent Asiatic from his usual torpid state. The weapon, in the twinkling of an eye,

was snatched out of the hand, and suspended over the head of the astonished pedagogue, who, seeing the tables so suddenly turned against him,
made the signal for assistance. I clapped my hands, shouted "Bravo! lay on,
Johnny—go it—you have done it now—you may as well be hanged for a
sheep as a lamb;" but the ushers began to muster round, the boy hung aloof,
and Pagoda, uncertain which side the neutrals would take, laid down his
arms, and surrendered at discretion.

Had the East Indian followed up his act by the application of a little
discipline at the fountain-head, it is more than probable that a popular com-
motion, not unlike that of Mas' Aniello would have ensued; but the time was
not come: the Indian showed a white feather, was laughed at, flogged, and
sent home to his friends, who had intended him for the bar; but foreseeing
that he might, in the course of events, chance to cut a figure on the wrong
side of it, sent him to sea, where his valour, if he had any, would find more
profitable employment.

This unsuccessful attempt of the young Oriental, was the primary cause
of all my fame and celebrity in afterlife. I had always hated school; and this,
of all others, seemed to me the most hateful. The emancipation of Johnny
Pagoda convinced me that my deliverance might be effected in a similar
manner. The train was laid, and a spark set it on fire. This spark was supplied by the folly and vanity of a fat French dancing-master. These Frenchmen are ever at the bottom of mischief. Mrs Higginbottom, the master's wife,
had denounced me to Monsieur Aristide Maugrebleu as a *mauvais sujet;* and
as he was a creature of hers, he frequently annoyed me to gratify his patron-
ess. This fellow was at that time about forty-five years of age, and had much
more experience than agility, having greatly increased his bulk by the roast
beef and ale of England. While he taught us the rigadoons of his own country, his vanity induced him to attempt feats much above the cumbrous weight
of his frame. I entered the lists with him, beat him at his own trade, and he
beat me with his fiddle-stick, which broke in two over my head; then,
making one more glorious effort to show that he would not be outdone,
snapped the tendon Achilles, and down he fell, *hors de combat* as a dancing-
master. He was taken away in his gig to be cured, and I was taken into the
school-room to be flogged.

This I thought so unjust that I ran away. Tom Crauford helped me to
scale the wall; and when he supposed I had got far enough to be out of

danger from pursuit, went and gave information, to avoid the suspicion of having aided and abetted. After running a mile, to use a sea phrase, I hove to, and began to compose, in my mind, an oration which I intended to pronounce before my father, by way of apology for my sudden and unexpected appearance; but I was interrupted by the detested usher and half a dozen of the senior boys, among whom was Tom Crauford. Coming behind me as I sat on a stile, they cut short my meditations by a tap on the shoulder, collared and marched me to the right about in double quick time. Tom Crauford was one of those who held me, and outdid himself in zealous invective at my base ingratitude in absconding from the best of masters, and the most affectionate, tender, and motherly of all school-dames.

The usher swallowed all this, and I soon made him swallow a great deal more. We passed near the side of a pond, the shoals and depths of which were well known to me. I looked at Tom out of the corner of my eye, and motioned him to let me go; and, like a mackerel out of a fisherman's hand, I darted into the water, got up to my middle, and then very coolly, for it was November, turned round to gaze at my escort, who stood at bay, and looked very much like fools. The usher, like a low bred cur, when he could no longer bully, began to fawn; he entreated and he implored me to think on "my papa and mamma; how miserable they would be, if they could but see me; what an increase of punishment I was bringing on myself by such obstinacy." He held out by turns coaxes and threats; in short, everything but an amnesty, to which I considered myself entitled, having been driven to rebellion by the most cruel persecution.

Argument having failed, and there being no volunteers to come in and fetch me out of the water, the poor usher, much against his inclination, was compelled to undertake it. With shoes and stockings off, and trousers tucked up, he ventured one foot into the water, then the other; a cold shiver reached his teeth, and made them chatter, but, at length, with cautious tread he advanced towards me. Being once in the water, a step or two farther was no object to me, particularly as I knew I could but be well flogged after all, and I was quite sure of that, at all events, so I determined to have my revenge and amusement. Stepping back, he followed, and suddenly fell over head and ears into a hole, as he made a reach at me. I was already out of my depth, and could swim like a duck, and as soon as he came up, I perched my knees on his shoulders and my hands on his head, and sent him souse under a second time, keeping him there until he had drunk more water than any horse that ever came to the pond. I then allowed him to wallow out the best way he could; and as it was very cold, I listened to the entreaties of Tom and the boys who stood by, cracking their sides with laughter at the poor usher's helpless misery.

Having had my frolic, I came out, and voluntarily surrendered myself to my enemies, from whom I received the same mercy, in proportion, that a Russian does from a Turk. Dripping wet, cold, and covered with mud, I was first shown to the boys as an aggregate of all that was bad in nature; a lecture was read to them on the enormity of my offense, and solemn denunciations of my future destiny closed the discourse. The shivering fit produced by the cold bath was relieved by as sound a flogging as could be inflicted, while two ushers held me; but no effort of theirs could elicit one groan or sob from me; my teeth were clenched in firm determination of revenge: with this passion my bosom glowed, and my brain was on fire. The punishment, though dreadfully severe, had one good effect—it restored my almost suspended animation; and I strongly recommend the same remedy being applied to all young ladies and gentlemen who, from disappointed love or other such trifling causes, throw themselves into the water. Had the miserable usher been treated after this prescription, he might have escaped a cold and rheumatic fever which had nearly consigned him to a country churchyard, in all probability to reappear at the dissecting room of St. Bartholomew's Hospital.

About this time Johnny Pagoda, who had been two years at sea, came to the school to visit his brother and schoolfellows. I pumped this fellow to tell me all he knew: he never tried to deceive me, or to make a convert. He had seen enough of a midshipman's life, to know that a cockpit was not paradise; but he gave me clear and ready answers to all my questions. I discovered that there was no schoolmaster in the ship, and that the midshipmen were allowed a pint of wine a day. A man-of-war, and the gallows, they say, refuse nothing; and as I had some strong presentiment from recent occurrences, that if I did not volunteer for the one, I should, in all probability, be pressed for the other, I chose the lesser evil of the two, and having made up my mind to enter the glorious profession, I shortly after communicated my intention to my parents.

From the moment I had come to this determination, I cared not what crime I committed, in hopes of being expelled from the school. I wrote scurrilous letters, headed a mutiny, entered into a league with the other boys to sink, burn and destroy, and do all the mischief we could. Tom Crauford had the master's child to dry nurse: he was only two years old: Tom let him fall, not intentionally, but the poor child was a cripple in consequence of it for life. This was an accident which under any other circumstances we should have deplored, but to us it was almost a joke.

The cruel treatment I had received from these people, had so demoralized me, that those passions—which under more skilful or kinder treatment, had either not been known, or would have lain dormant, were roused into full and malignant activity: I went to school a good-hearted boy, I left it a savage. The accident with the child occurred two days before the commencement of the vacation, and we were all dismissed on the following day in consequence. On my return home I stated verbally to my father and mother, as I had done before by letter, that I was resolved to go to sea. My mother wept, my father expostulated. I gazed with apathy on the one, and listened with cold indifference to the reasoning and arguments of the other; a choice of schools was offered to me, where I might be a parlour boarder, and I was to finish at the University, if I would but give up my fatal infatuation. Nothing, however, would do; the die was cast, and for the sea I was to prepare.

What fool was it who said that the happiest time of our lives is passed at school? There may, indeed, be exceptions, but the remark cannot be generalized. Stormy as has been my life, the most miserable part of it (with very little exception) was passed at school; and my mind never received so much injury from any scenes of vice and excess in afterlife, as it did from the shameful treatment and bad example I met with there. If my bosom burned with fiend-like passions, whose fault was it? How had the sacred pledge, given by the master, been redeemed? Was I not sacrificed to the most sordid avarice, in the first instance, and almost flayed alive in the second, to gratify revenge? Of the filthy manner in which our food was prepared, I can only say that the bare recollection of it excites nausea; and to this hour, bread and milk, suet pudding, and shoulders of mutton, are objects of my deep-rooted aversion. The conduct of the ushers, who were either tyrannical extortioners, or partakers in our crimes—the constant loss of our clothes by the dishonesty or carelessness of the servants—the purloining our silver spoons, sheets, and towels, when we went away, upon the plea of "custom"—the charges in the account for windows which I had never broken, and books which I had never received—the shameful difference between the annual cost promised by the master, and the sum actually charged, ought to have opened the eyes of my father.

I am aware how excellent many of these institutions are, and that there are few so bad as the one I was sent to. The history of my life will prove of what vital importance it is to ascertain the character of the master and mistress as to other points besides teaching Greek and Latin, before a child is intrusted to their care. I ought to have observed, that during my stay at this school, I had made some proficiency in mathematics and algebra.

My father had procured for me a berth on board a fine frigate at Plymouth, and the interval between my nomination and joining was spent by my parents in giving advice to me, and directions to the several tradesmen respecting my equipment. The large chest, the sword, the cocked hat, the half-boots, were all ordered in succession; and the arrival of each article either of use or ornament was anticipated by me with a degree of impatience which can only be compared to that of a ship's company arrived off Dennose from a three years' station in India, and who hope to be at anchor at Spithead before sunset. The circumstance of my going to sea affected my father in no other way than it interfered with his domestic comforts by the immoderate grief of my poor mother. In any other point of view my choice of profession was a source of no regret to him. I had an elder brother, who was intended to have the family estates, and who was then at Oxford, receiving an education suitable to his rank in life, and also learning how to spend his money like a gentleman. Younger brothers are, in such cases, just as well out of the way, particularly one of my turbulent disposition: a man-of-war, therefore, like *another piece of timber,* has its uses. My father paid all the bills with great philosophy, and made me a liberal allowance for my age.

The hour of departure drew near; my chest had been sent off by the Plymouth wagon, and a hackney coach drew up to the door, to convey me to the White Horse Cellar. The letting down of the rattling steps completely overthrew the small remains of fortitude which my dearest mother had reserved for our separation, and she threw her arms around my neck in a frenzy of grief. I beheld her emotions with a countenance as unmoved as the figure-head of a ship; while she covered my stoic face with kisses, and washed it with her tears. I almost wondered what it all meant, and wished the scene was over.

My father helped me out of this dilemma; taking me firmly by the arm, he led me out of the room: my mother sank upon the sofa, and hid her face in her pocket-handkerchief. I walked as slowly to the coach as common decency would permit. My father looked at me, as if he would inquire of my very inward soul whether I really did possess human feelings? I felt the meaning of this, even in my then tender years; and such was my sense of propriety, that I mustered up a tear for each eye, which, I hope, answered the intended purpose. We say at sea, "When you have no decency, sham a little," and I verily believe I should have beheld my poor mother in her coffin with less regret than I could have foregone the gay and lovely scenes which I anticipated.

How amply has this want of feeling towards a tender parent been re-called to my mind, and severely punished, in the events of my vagrant life!

CHAPTER II

Injuries may be atoned for and forgiven; but insults admit of no compensation. They degrade the mind in its own esteem, and force it to recover its level by revenge.

JUNIUS

THERE are certain events in our lives poetically and beautifully described by Moore, as "green spots in memory's waste." Such are the emotions arising from the attainment, after a long pursuit, of any darling object of love or ambition; and although possession and subsequent events may have proved to us that we had overrated our enjoyment, and experience have shown us "that all is vanity," still, recollection dwells with pleasure upon the beating heart, when the present only was enjoyed, and the picture painted by youthful and sanguine anticipation in glowing and delightful colours. Youth only can feel this; age has been often deceived—too often has the fruit turned to ashes in the mouth. The old look forward with a distrust and doubt, and backward with sorrow and regret.

One of the red-letter days of my life, was that on which I first mounted

the uniform of a midshipman. My pride and ecstasy were beyond description. I had discarded the school and schoolboy dress, and, with them, my
almost stagnant existence. Like the chrysalis changed into a butterfly, I flut-
tered about as if to try my powers and felt myself a gay and beautiful creature, free to range over the wide domains of nature, clear of the trammels
of parents or schoolmasters; and my heart bounded within me at the
thoughts of being left to enjoy at my own discretion, the very acme of all the
pleasure that human existence could afford; and I observe that in this, as in
most other cases, I met with that disappointment which usually attends us.
True it is, that in the days of my youth, I did enjoy myself. I was happy for
a time, if happiness it could be called; but dearly have I paid for it. I contracted a debt, which I have been liquidating by instalments ever since; nor
am I yet emancipated. Even the small portion of felicity that fell to my lot
on this memorable morning was brief in duration, and speedily followed by
chagrin.

But to return to my uniform. I had arrayed myself in it; my dirk was
belted round my waist; a cocked hat, of an enormous size, stuck on my
head; and, being perfectly satisfied with my own appearance, at the last
survey which I had made in the glass, I first rang for the chambermaid,
under pretence of telling her to make my room tidy, but, in reality, that she
might admire and compliment me, which she very wisely did; and I was fool
enough to give her half a crown and a kiss, for I felt myself quite a man. The
waiter, to whom the chambermaid had in all probability communicated the
circumstance, presented himself, and having made a low bow, offered the
same compliments, and received the same reward, save the kiss. Boots
would, in all probability, have come in for his share, had he been in the way,
for I was fool enough to receive all their fine speeches as if they were my
due, and to pay for them at the same time in ready money. I was a gudgeon
and they were sharks; and more sharks would soon have been about me,
for I heard them, as they left the room, call "boots" and "ostler," of course
to assist in lightening my purse.

But I was too impatient to wait on my captain and see my ship—so I
bounced down the stairs, and, in the twinkling of an eye, was on my way
to Stonehouse, where my vanity received another tribute, by a raw recruit
of marine raising his hand to his head, as he passed by me. I took it as it
was meant, raised my hat off my head, and shuffled by with much self-

importance. One consideration, I own, mortified me—this was that the *natives* did not appear to admire me half so much as I admired myself. It never occurred to me then, that middies were as plentiful at Plymouth Dock, as black boys at Port Royal, though, perhaps, not of so much value to their masters. I will not shock the delicacy of my fair readers by repeating all the vulgar alliterations with which my noviciate was greeted, as I passed in review before the ladies of North Corner, who met me in Fore Street. Unsophisticated as I then was, in many points, and certainly in this, I thought them extremely ill-bred. Fortunately for me, the prayers of a certain description of people never prevail, otherwise I should have been immediately consigned to a place, from which, I fear, all the masses of France and Italy would not have extricated me.

I escaped from these syrens without being bound to the mast, like Ulysses; but, like him, I had nearly fallen a victim to a modern Polyphemus; for though he had not one eye in the middle of his forehead, after the manner of his prototype, yet the rays from both his eyes meeting together at the tip of his long nose, gave him very much that appearance. Ignorance, sheer ignorance, in this, as in many other cases, was the cause of my disaster. A party of officers, in full uniform, were coming from a court-martial. "Oh ho!" said I, "here come some of us." I seized my dirk in my left hand, as I saw they held their swords, and I stuck my right hand into my bosom as some of them had done. I tried to imitate their erect and officer-like bearing; I put my cocked hat on fore and aft, with the gold rosette dangling between my two eyes, so that in looking at it, which I could not help doing, I must have squinted. And I held my nose high in the air, like a pig in a hurricane, fancying myself as much an object of admiration to them as I was to myself. We passed on opposite tacks, and our respective velocities had separated us to the distance of twenty or thirty yards, when one of them called out to me in a voice evidently cracked in His Majesty's service— "Hollo, young gentleman, come back here."

I concluded I was going to be complimented on the cut of my coat, to be asked the address of my tailor, and to hear the rakish sit of my hat admired. I now began to think I should hear a contention between the lords of the ocean, as to who should have me as a sample middy on their quarterdecks; and I was even framing an excuse to my father's friend for not joining his ship. Judge then of my surprise and mortification, when I was thus accosted in an angry and menacing tone by the oldest of the officers—

"Pray, sir, what ship do you belong to?"

"Sir," said I, proud to be thus interrogated, "I belong to His Majesty's ship, the *Le*——" (having a French name I clapped on both the French and English articles, as being more impressive).

"Oh, you do, do you?" said the veteran with an air of conscious superiority; "then you will be so good as to turn round, go down to Mutton Cove, take a boat, and have your person conveyed with all possible speed on board of His Majesty's ship the *Lee*," (imitating me); "and tell the first lieutenant it is my order that you be not allowed any more leave while the ship is in port; and I shall tell your captain he must teach his officers better manners than to pass the port-admiral without touching their hats."

While this harangue was going on, I stood in a circle, of which I was the centre, and the admiral and the captains formed the circumference. What little air there was their bodies intercepted, so that I was not only in a stew, but stupefied into the bargain.

"There, sir, you hear me—you may go."

"Yes, I do hear you," thinks I; "but how the devil am I to get away from you?" for the cruel captains, like schoolboys round a rat-trap, stood so close that I could not start. Fortunately, this my blockade, which they no doubt intended for their amusement, saved me for that time. I recollected myself, and said, with affected simplicity of manner, that I had that morning put on my uniform for the first time; that I had never seen my captain, and never was on board a ship in all my life. At this explanation, the countenance of the admiral relaxed into something that was meant for a smile, and the captains all burst into a loud laugh.

"Well, young man," said the admiral—who was really a good-tempered fellow, though an odd one—"well, young man, since you have never been at sea, it is some excuse for not knowing good manners; there is no necessity now for delivering my message to the first lieutenant, but you may go on board your ship."

Having seen me well-roasted, the captains opened right and left, and let me pass. As I left them I heard one say, "Just caught—marks of the dogs, teeth in his heels, I warrant you." I did not stop to make any reply, but sneaked away, mortified and crest-fallen, and certainly obeyed this the first order which I had ever received in the service, with more exactness than I ever did any subsequent one.

During the remainder of my walk, I touched my hat to every one I met. I conferred the honour of a salute on midshipmen, master's mates, sergeants of marines, and two corporals. Nor was I aware of my over complaisance, until a young woman, dressed like a lady, who knew more of the navy than I did, asked me if I had come down to stand for the borough? Without knowing what she meant, I replied, "No."

"I thought you might," said she, "seeing you are so d——d civil to everybody."

Had it not been for this friendly hint, I really believe I should have touched my hat to a drummer.

Having gone through this ordeal, I reached the inn at Plymouth, where I found my captain, and presented my father's letter. He surveyed me from top to toe, and desired the pleasure of my company to dinner at six o'clock. "In the mean time," he said, "as it is now only eleven, you may go aboard, and show yourself to Mr Handstone, the first lieutenant, who will cause your name to be entered on the books, and allow you to come back here to dine." I bowed and retired. And on my way to Mutton Cove was saluted by the females, with the appellation of Royal Reefer (midshipman), and a Biscuit Nibbler; but all this I neither understood nor cared for. I arrived safely at Mutton Cove, where two women, seeing my inquiring eye and span-new dress, asked what ship they should take "my honour" to, I told them the ship I wished to go on board of.

"She *lays* under the *Obelisk*," said the elder woman, who appeared to be about forty years of age; "and we will take your honour off for a shilling."

I agreed to this, both for the novelty of the thing, as well as on account of my natural gallantry and love of female society. The elder woman was mistress of her profession, handling her scull (oar) with great dexterity; but Sally, the younger one, who was her daughter, was still in her noviciate. She was pretty, cleanly dressed, had on white stockings, and sported a neat foot and ankle.

"Take care, Sally," said the mother; "keep stroke, or you will catch a crab."

"Never fear, mother," said the confident Sally; and at the same moment, as if the very caution against the accident was the cause of it, the blade of her scull did not dip into the water. The oar meeting no resistance, its loom, or handle, came back upon the bosom of the unfortunate Sally, tipped her backwards—up went her heels in the air, and down fell her head into the bottom of the boat. As she was pulling the stroke oar, her feet almost came in contact with the rosette of my cocked hat.

"There now, Sally," said the wary mother; "I told you how it would be— I knew you would catch a crab!"

Sally quickly recovered herself, blushed a little, and resumed her occupation.

"That's what we calls catching a crab in our country," said the woman. I replied that I thought it was a very pretty amusement; and I asked Sally to try and catch another; but she declined; and, by this time, we had reached the side of the ship.

Having paid my naiads, I took hold of the man-rope, as I was instructed by them, and mounted the side. Reaching the gangway, I was accosted by a midshipman in a round jacket and trousers, a shirt none of the cleanest, and a black silk handkerchief tied loosely round his neck.

"Who did you want, sir?" said he.

"I wish to speak with Mr Handstone, the first lieu-tenant," said I. He informed me that the first lieutenant was then gone down to frank the letters, and, when he came on deck, he would acquaint him with my being there.

After this dialogue, I was left on the larboard side of the quarter-deck to my own meditations. The ship was at this time refitting, and was what is usually called in the hands of the dockyard, and a sweet mess she was in. The quarter-deck carronades were run fore and aft; the slides unbolted from the side, the decks were covered with pitch fresh poured into the seams, and the caulkers were sitting on their boxes, ready to renew their noisy labours as soon as the dinner-hour had expired. The middies, meanwhile, on the starboard side of the quarter-deck, were taking my altitude, and speculating as to whether I was to be a messmate of theirs, and what sort of a chap I might chance to be—both these points were solved very speedily.

The first lieutenant came on deck; the midshipman of the watch presented me, and I presented my name and the captain's message.

"It is all right, sir," said Mr Handstone. "Here, Mr Flyblock, do you take this young gentleman into your mess; you may show him below as soon as you please, and tell him where to hang his hammock up."

I followed my new friend down the ladder, under the half deck, where sat a woman, selling bread and butter and red herrings to the sailors; she had also cherries and clotted cream, and a cask of strong beer, which seemed to be in great demand. We passed her, and descended another ladder, which brought us to the 'tween-decks, and into the steerage, in the forepart of which, on the larboard side, abreast of the mainmast, was my future residence—a small hole, which they called a berth; it was ten feet long by six, and about five feet four inches high; a small aperture, about nine inches square, admitted a very scanty portion of that which we most needed, namely, fresh air and daylight. A deal table occupied a very considerable extent of this small apartment, and on it stood a brass candle-stick, with a dip candle, and a wick like a full-blown carnation. The table-cloth was spread, and the stains of port wine and gravy too visibly indicated, like the midshipman's dirty shirt, the near approach of Sunday. The black servant was preparing for dinner, and I was shown the seat I was to occupy. "Good Heaven!" thought I, as I squeezed myself between the ship's side and the mess-table; "and is this to be my future residence?—better go back to school; there, at least, there is fresh air and clean linen."

I would have written that moment to my dear, broken-hearted mother, to tell her how gladly her prodigal son would fly back to her arms; but I was prevented doing this, first by pride, and secondly by want of writing materials. Taking my place, therefore, at the table, I mustered up all my philosophy; and, to amuse myself, called to mind the rejections of Gil Blas, when he found himself in the den of the robbers, "Behold, then, the worthy nephew of my uncle, Gil Perez, caught like a rat in a trap."

Most of my new associates were absent on duty; the 'tween-decks was crammed with casks and cases, and chests, and bags, and hammocks; the noise of the caulkers was resumed over my head and all around me; the stench of bilge-water, combining with the smoke of tobacco, the effluvia of gin and beer, the frying of beef-steaks and onions, and red herrings—the pressure of a dark atmosphere and a heavy shower of rain, all conspired to oppress my spirits, and render me the most miserable dog that ever lived. I had almost resigned myself to despair, when I recollected the captain's invitation, and mentioned it to Flyblock. "That's well thought of," said he;

"Murphy also dines with him; you can both go together, and I dare say he will be very glad of your company."

A captain seldom waits for a midshipman, and we took good care he should not wait for us. The dinner was in all respects one "on service." The captain said a great deal, the lieutenants very little, and the midshipmen nothing at all; but the performance of the knife and fork, and wine-glass (as far as it could be got at), were exactly in the inverse ratio. The company consisted of my own captain, and two others, our first lieutenant, Murphy, and myself.

As soon as the cloth was removed, the captain filled me out a glass of wine, desired I would drink it, and then go and see how the wind was. I took this my first admonitory hint in its literal sense and meaning; but having a very imperfect idea of the points of the compass, I own I felt a little puzzled how I should obtain the necessary information. Fortunately for me, there was a weather-cock on the old church-steeple; it had four letters, which I certainly did know were meant to represent the cardinal points. One of these seemed so exactly to correspond with the dial above it, that I made up my mind the wind must be West, and instantly returned to give my captain the desired information, not a little proud with my success in having obtained it so soon. But what was my surprise to find that I was not thanked for my trouble; the company even smiled and winked at each other; the first lieutenant nodded his head and said, "Rather green yet." The captain, however, settled the point according to the manners and customs, in such cases, used at sea. "Here, youngster," said he, "here is another glass for you; drink that, and then Murphy will show you what I mean." Murphy was my chaperon; he swallowed his wine—rather *à gorge déployée;* put down his glass very energetically, and, bowing, left the room.

When we had got fairly into the hall, we had the following duet:— "What the h—— brought you back again, you d——d young greenhorn? Could not you take a hint, and be off, as the captain intended? So I must lose my wine for such a d——d young whelp as you. I'll pay you off for this, my tight fellow, before we have been many weeks together."

I listened to this elegant harangue, with some impatience, and much more indignation. "I came back," said I, "to tell the captain how the wind was."

"You be d——d," replied Murphy: "do you think the captain did not know how the wind was? and if he had wanted to know, don't you think he would have sent a sailor like me, instead of such a d——d lubberly whelp as you?"

"As to what the captain meant," said I, "I do not know. I did as I was bid—but what do you mean by calling me a whelp? I am no more a whelp than your-self!"

"Oh, you are not, a'n't you?" said Murphy, seizing me by one of my ears, which he pulled so unmercifully that he altered the shape of it very considerably, making it something like the leeboard of a Dutch schuyt.

This was not to be borne; though, as I was but thirteen, he seventeen, and a very stout fellow, I should rather not have sought an action with him. But he had begun it: my honour was at stake, and I only wonder I had not drawn my dirk, and laid him dead at my feet. Fortunately for him, the rage I was in, made me forget I had it by my side: though I remembered my uniform, the disgrace brought upon it, and the admiration of the chamber-maid, as well as the salute of the sentinel, all which formed a combustible in my brain. I went off like a flash, and darted my fist (the weapon I had been most accustomed to wield) into the left eye of my adversary, with a force and precision which Crib would have applauded. Murphy staggered back with the blow, and for a moment I flattered myself he had had enough of it.

But no—alas, this was a day of disappointments! he had only retreated to take a spring; he then came on me like the lifeguards at Waterloo, and his charge was irresistible. I was upset, pummelled, thumped, kicked, and should probably have been the subject of a coroner's inquest had not the waiter and chambermaid run in to my rescue. The tongue of the latter was particularly active in my favour: unluckily for me, she had no other weapon near her, or it would have gone hard with Murphy. "Shame!" said she, "for such a great lubberly creature to beat such a poor, little, innocent, defence-less fellow as that. What would his mamma say to see him treated so?"

"D——n his mamma, and you too," said Pat, "look at my eye."

"D——n your eye," said the waiter: "it's a pity he had not served the other one the same way; no more than you deserve for striking a child; the boy is game, and that's more than you are; he is worth as many of you, as will stand between this and the iron chair at Barbican."

"I'd like to see him duck'd in it," said the maid.

While this was going on, I had resumed my defensive attitude. I had never once complained, and had gained the good-will of all the bystanders, among whom now appeared my captain and his friends. The blood was streaming from my mouth, and I bore the marks of discipline from the superior prowess of my enemy, who was a noted pugilist for his age, and would not have received the hit from me, if he had supposed my presumption would have led me to attack him. The captain demanded an explanation. Murphy told the story in his own way, and gave anything but the true version. I could have beaten him at that, but truth answered my purpose better than falsehood on this occasion; so, as soon as he had done, I gave my round unvarnished tale, and, although defeated in the field, I plainly saw that I had the advantage of him in the cabinet. Murphy was dismissed in disgrace, and ordered to rusticate on board till his eye was bright.

"I should have confined you to the ship myself," said the captain, "but the boy has done it for me, you cannot appear on shore with that black eye."

As soon as he was gone, I was admonished to be more careful in future. "You are," said the captain, "like a young bear; all your sorrows are before you; if you give a blow for every hard name you receive, your fate in the service may be foreseen: if weak you will be pounded to a mummy—if strong, you will be hated. A quarrelsome disposition will make you enemies in every rank you may attain; you will be watched with a jealous eye, well knowing, as we all do, that the same spirit of insolence and overbearing which you show in the cockpit, will follow you to the quarter-deck, and rise with you in the service. This advice is for your own good; not that I interfere in these things, as everybody and everything finds its level in a man-of-war; I only wish you to draw a line between resistance against oppression, which I admire and respect, and a litigious, uncompromising disposition, which I despise. Now wash your face and go on board. Try by all means to conciliate the rest of your messmates, for first impressions are everything, and rely on it, Murphy's report will not be in your favour."

This advice was very good, but had the disadvantage of coming too late for that occasion by at least half an hour. The fracas was owing to the captain's mismanagement, and the manners and customs of the navy at the beginning of the nineteenth century. The conversation at the tables of the higher ranks of the service in those days, unless ladies were present, was generally such as a boy could not listen to without injury to his better feelings. I was therefore "hinted off;" but with due respect to my captain, who is still living; I should have been sent on board of my ship and cautioned against the bad habits of the natives of North Corner and Barbican; and if I could not be admitted to the mysterious conversation of a captain's table, I should have been told in a clear and decided manner to depart, without the needless puzzle of an innuendo, which I did not and could not understand.

I returned on board about eight o'clock, where Murphy had gone before me, and prepared a reception far from agreeable. Instead of being welcomed to my berth, I was received with coldness, and I returned to the quarter-deck, where I walked till I was weary, and then leaned against a gun. From this temporary alleviation, I was roused by a voice of thunder, "Lean off that gun." I started up, touched my hat, and continued my solitary walk, looking now and then at the second lieutenant, who had thus gruffly addressed me. I felt a dejection of spirits, a sense of destitution and misery, which I cannot describe. I had done no wrong, yet I was suffering as if I had committed a crime. I had been aggrieved, and had vindicated myself as well as I could. I thought I was among devils, and not men; my thoughts turned homeward. I remembered my poor mother in her agony of grief, on the sofa; and my unfeeling heart then found that it needed the soothings of affection. I could have wept, but I knew not where to go; for I could not be seen to cry on board of ship. My pride began to be humbled. I felt the misery of dependence, although not wanting pecuniary resources; and would have given up all my prospects to have been once more seated quietly at home.

The first lieutenant came on board soon after, and I heard him relating my adventure to the second lieutenant. The tide now evidently turned in my favour. I was invited down to the gun-room, and having given satisfactory answers to all the questions put to me, Flyblock was sent for, and I was once more placed under his protection. The patronage of the first lieutenant, I flattered myself would have ensured me at least common civility for a short time.

I had now more leisure to contemplate my new residence and new associates; who, having returned from the duty of the dock-yard, were all assembled in the berth, seated round the table on the lockers, which paid "the double debt" of seats and receptacles; but in order to obtain a sitting, it was requisite either to climb over the backs of the company, or submit to "high pressure" from the last comer. Such close contact, even with our best friends, is never desirable; but in warm weather, in a close, confined air, with a manifest scarcity of clean linen, it became particularly inconvenient. The population here very far exceeded the limits usually allotted to human beings in any situation of life, except in a slave ship. The midshipmen, of whom there were eight full-grown, and four youngsters, were without either jackets or waistcoats; some of them had their shirt-sleeves rolled up, either to prevent the reception or to conceal the absorption of dirt in the region of the wristbands. The repast on the table consisted of a can or large blackjack of small beer, and a Japan bread-basket full of sea-biscuit. To compensate for this simple fare, and at the same time to cool the close atmosphere of the berth, the table was covered with a large green cloth with a yellow border, and many yellow spots withal, where the colour had been discharged by slops of vinegar, hot tea, &c., &c.; a sack of potatoes stood in one corner, and the shelves all round, and close over our heads, were stuffed with plates, glasses, quadrants, knives and forks, loaves of sugar, dirty stockings and shirts, and still fouler table-cloths, small tooth-combs, and ditto large, clothes brushes and shoe brushes, cocked hats, dirks, German flutes, mahogany writing-desks, a plate of salt butter, and some two or three pairs of naval half-boots. A single candle served to make darkness visible, and the stench had nearly overpowered me.

The reception I met with tended in no way to relieve these horrible impressions. A black man, with no other dress than a dirty check shirt and trousers, not smelling of amber, stood within the door, ready to obey all and any one of the commands with which he was loaded. The smell of the towel he held in his hand, to wipe the plates and glasses with, completed my discomfiture; and I fell sick upon the seat nearest at me. Recovering from this, without the aid of any "ministering angel," I contracted the pupils of my eyes, and ventured to look around me. The first who met my gaze, was my recent foe; he bore the marks of contention by having his eye bound up with brown paper and a dirty silk pocket-handkerchief; the other was quickly turned on me; and, with a savage and brutal countenance, he swore and denounced the severest vengeance on me for what I had done. In this, he was joined by another ill-looking fellow, with large whiskers.

I shall not repeat the elegant philippics with which I was greeted. Suffice it to say that I found all the big ones against me, and the little ones neuter; the caterer supposing I had received suitable admonition for my future guidance, and that I was completely bound over to keep the peace—turned all the youngsters out of the berth. "As for you, Mr Fistycuff," said he, addressing himself to me, "you may walk off with the rest of the gang, so make yourself scarce, like the Highlander's breeches."

The boys all obeyed the command in silence, and I was not sorry to follow them. As I went out he added, "So, Mr Rumbusticus, you can obey orders, I see, and it is well for you; for I had a biscuit ready to shy at your head." This affront, after all I had suffered, I was forced to pocket; but I could not understand what the admiral could mean, when he said that people went to sea "to learn manners."

I soon made acquaintance with the younger set of my messmates, and we retreated to the forecastle as the only part of the ship suitable to the nature of the conversation we intended to hold. After one hour's deliberation, and notwithstanding it was the first night I had ever been on board a ship, I was unanimously elected leader of this little band. I became the William Tell of the party, as having been the first to resist the tyranny of the oldsters, and especially of the tyrant Murphy. I was let into all the secrets of the mess in which the youngsters were placed by the captain to be instructed and kept in order. Alas! what instruction did we get but blasphemy? What order were we kept in, except that of paying our mess, and being forbidden to partake of those articles which our money had purchased? My blood boiled when they related all they had suffered, and I vowed I would sooner die than submit to such treatment.

The hour of bed-time arrived. I was instructed how to get into my hammock, and laughed at for tumbling out on the opposite side. I was forced to submit to this pride of conscious superiority of these urchins who could only boast of a few months' more practical experience than myself, and who, therefore, called me a greenhorn. But all this was done in good nature; and after a few hearty laughs from my companions, I gained the centre of my suspended bed, and was very soon in a sound sleep. This was only allowed to last till about four o'clock in the morning; when down came the head of my hammock, and I fell to the deck, with my feet still hanging in the air, like poor Sally, when she caught the crab. Stunned and stupefied by the fall, bewildered by the violent concussion and the novelty of all around me, I continued in a state of somnambulism, and it was some minutes before I could recollect myself.

The marine sentinel at the gun-room door seeing what had happened, and also espying the person to whom I was indebted for this favour, very kindly came to my assist-ance. He knotted my lanyard, and restored my hammock to its place; but he could not persuade me to confide myself again to such treacherous bedposts, for I thought the rope had broken; and so strongly did the fear of another tumble possess my mind, that I took a blanket, and lay down on a chest at some little distance, keeping a sleepless eye directed to the scene of my late disaster.

This was fortunate; for not many minutes had elapsed, when Murphy, who had been relieved from the middle watch, came below, and seeing my hammock again hanging up, and supposing me in it, took out his knife and cut it down. "So then," said I to myself, "it was you who invaded my slumbers, and nearly dashed my brains out, and have now made the second attempt." I vowed to Heaven that I would have revenge; and I acquitted myself of that vow. Like the North American savage, crouching lest he should see me, I waited patiently till he had got into his hammock, and was in a sound sleep. I then gently pushed a shot-case under the head of his hammock, and placed the corner of it so as to receive his head; for had it split his skull I should not have cared, so exasperated was I, and so bent on revenge. Subtle and silent, I then cut his lanyard: he fell, and his head coming in contact with the edge of the shot-case, he gave a deep groan, and there he lay. I instantly retreated to my chest and blanket, where I pretended to snore, while the sentinel, who, fortunately for me, had seen Murphy cut me down the first time, came with his lanthorn, and seeing him apparently dead, removed the shot-case out of the way, and then ran to the sergeant of marines, desiring him to bring the surgeon's assistant.

While the sergeant was gone, he whispered softly to me, "Lie still; I saw the whole of it, and if you are found out, it may go hard with you."

Murphy, it appeared, had few friends in the ship; all rejoiced at his accident. I laid very quietly in my blanket while the surgeon's assistant dressed the wound; and, after a considerable time, succeeded in restoring the patient to his senses: he was, however, confined a fort-night to his bed. I was either not suspected, or, if I was, it was known that I was not the aggressor. The secret was well kept. I gave the marine a guinea, and took him into my service as *valet de place*.

And now, reader, in justice to myself, allow me to make a few remarks.

They may serve as a palliative, to a certain degree, for that unprincipled career which the following pages will expose. The passions of pride and revenge, implanted in our fallen natures, and which, if not eradicated in the course of my education, ought, at least, to have lain dormant as long as possible, were, through the injudicious conduct of those to whom I had been entrusted, called into action and full activity at a very early age. The moral seeds sown by my parents, which might have germinated and produced fruit, were not watered or attended to; weeds had usurped their place, and were occupying the ground which should have supported them; and at this period, when the most assiduous cultivation was necessary to procure a return, into what a situation was I thrown? In a ship crowded with three hundred men, each of them, or nearly so, cohabiting with an unfortunate female, in the lowest state of degradation; where oaths and blasphemy interlarded every sentence; where religion was wholly neglected, and the only honour paid to the Almighty was a clean shirt on a Sunday; where implicit obedience to the will of an officer, was considered of more importance than the observance of the Decalogue; and the Commandments of God were in a manner abrogated by the Articles of War—for the first might be broken with impunity, and even with applause, while the most severe punishment awaited any infraction of the latter.

So much for the ship in the aggregate; let us now survey the midshipmen's berth. Here we found the same language and the same manners, with scarcely one shade more of refinement. Their only pursuits when on shore were intoxication and worse debauchery, to be gloried in and boasted of when they returned on board. My captain said that everything found its level in a man-of-war. True; but in a midshipman's berth it was the level of a savage, where corporal strength was the *sine quâ non,* and decided whether you were to act the part of a tyrant or a slave. The discipline of public schools, bad and demoralizing as it is, was light, compared to the tyranny of a midshipman's berth in 1803.

A mistaken notion has long prevailed, that boys derive advantages from suffering under the tyranny of their oppressors at schools; and we constantly hear the praises of public schools and midshipmen's berths on this very account—namely, "that boys are taught to find their level." I do not mean to deny but that the higher orders improve by collision with their inferiors, and that a young aristocrat is often brought to his senses by receiving a sound thrashing from the son of a tradesman. But he that is brought up a slave, will be a tyrant when he has the power; the worst of our passions are nourished to inflict the same evil on others which we boast of having suffered ourselves. The courage and daring spirit of a noble-minded boy is rather broken down by ill-usage, which he has not the power to resist, or, surmounting all this, he proudly imbibes a dogged spirit of sullen resistance and implacable revenge, which become the bane of his future life.

The latter was my fate; and let not my readers be surprised or shocked, if, in the course of these adventures, I should display some of the fruits of that fatal seed, so early and so profusely sown in my bosom. If, on my first coming into the ship, I shrank back with horror at the sound of blasphemy and obscenity—if I shut my eyes to the promiscuous intercourse of the sexes, it was not so long. By insensible degrees, I became familiarised with vice, and callous to its approach. In a few months I had become nearly as corrupt as others. I might indeed have resisted longer; but though the fortress of virtue could have held out against open violence, it could not withstand the undermining of ridicule. My young companions, who, as I have observed, had only preceded me six months in the service, were already grown old in depravity; they laughed at my squeamishness, called me "milksop" and "boarding-school miss," and soon made me as bad as themselves. We had not quite attained the age of perpetration, but we were fully prepared to meet it when it came.

I had not been two days on board, when the youngsters proposed a walk into the main top. I mounted the rigging with perfect confidence, for I was always a good climber; but I had not proceeded far, when I was overtaken by the captain of the top and another man, who, without any ceremony or preface, seized me by each arm, and very deliberately lashed me fast in the rigging. They laughed at my remonstrance. I asked what they meant, and the captain of the top said very civilly taking off his hat at the same time, "that it was the way all gemmen were sarved when they first went aloft; and I must pay my footing as a bit of a parkazite." I looked down to the quarter-deck for assistance, but every one there was laughing at me; and even the very little rogues of midshipmen who had enticed me up were enjoying the joke. Seeing this was the case, I only asked what was to pay. The captain of the top said a seven shilling bit would be thought handsome.

This I promised to give, and was released on my own recognizances. When I reached the quarter-deck I paid the money.

Having experienced nothing but cruelty and oppression since I had been on board, I sorely repented of coming to sea; my only solace was seeing Murphy, as he lay in his hammock, with his head bound up. This was a balm to me. "I bide my time," said I; "I will yet be revenged on all of you;" and so I was. I let none escape: I had them all in their turns, and glutted my thirst for revenge.

I had been three weeks on board; when the ship was reported ready for sea. I had acquired the favour of the first lieutenant by a constant attention to the little duties he gave me to perform. I had been put into a watch, and stationed in the fore-top, and quartered at the foremast guns on the main deck. I was told by the youngsters that the first lieutenant was a harsh officer, and implacable when once he took a dislike; his manners, however, even when under the greatest excitement, were always those of a perfect gentleman, and I continued living on good terms with him. But with the second lieutenant I was not so fortunate. He had ordered me to take the jolly-boat and bring off a woman whom he kept; I remonstrated and refused, and from that moment we never were friends.

Murphy had also recovered from his fall, and returned to his duty; his malice towards me increased, and I had no peace or comfort in his presence. One day he threw a biscuit at my head, calling me at the same time a name which reflected on the legitimacy of my birth, in language the most coarse and vulgar. In a moment all the admonitions which I had received, and all my sufferings for impetuosity of temper, were forgotten; the blood boiled in my veins, and trickled from my wounded forehead. Dizzy, and almost sightless with rage, I seized a brass candlestick, the bottom of which (to keep it steady at sea) was loaded with lead, and threw it at him with all my might; had it taken effect as I intended, that offence would have been his last. It missed his head, and struck the black servant on the shoulder; the poor man went howling to the surgeon, in whose care he remained for many days.

Murphy started up to take instant vengeance, but was held by the other seniors of the mess, who unanimously declared that such an offence as mine should be punished in a more solemn manner. A mock trial (without adverting to the provocation I had received) found me guilty of insubordination "to the oldsters," and setting a bad example to the youngsters. I was sentenced to be *cobbed* with a worsted stocking, filled with wet sand. I was held down on my face on the mess-table by four stout midshipmen; the surgeon's assistant held my wrist, to ascertain if my pulse indicated exhaustion; while Murphy, at his own particular request, became the executioner. Had it been any other but him, I should have given vent to my agonizing pain by screams, but like a sullen Ebo, I was resolved to endure even to death, rather than gratify him by any expression of pain. After a most severe punishment, a cold sweat and faintness alarmed the surgeon's assistant. I was then released, but ordered to mess on my chest for a fortnight by myself. As soon as I was able to stand, and had recovered my breath, I declared in the most solemn manner, that a repetition of the offence should produce the action for which I had suffered, and I would then appeal to the captain for justice; "and," said I, turning to Murphy, "it was I who cut down your hammock, and had very nearly knocked out your brains. I did it in return for your cowardly attack on me; and I will do it again, if I suffer martyrdom for it; for every act of tyranny you commit I will have revenge. Try me now, and see if I am not as good as my word." He grinned, and turned pale, but dared do no more, for he was a coward.

I was ordered to quit the berth, which I did, and as I went out, one of the mates observed, that I was "a proper malignant devil, by G——."

This violent scene produced a sort of cessation from hostilities. Murphy knew that he might expect a decanter at his head or a knife in his side, if I was provoked; and that peace which I could not gain from his compassion, I obtained from his fears. The affair made a noise in the ship. With the officers in the gun-room I lost ground, because it was misrepresented. With the men I gained favour, because they hated Murphy. They saw the truth, and admired me for my determined resistance.

Sent to Coventry by the officers, I sought the society of the men. I learned rapidly the practical part of my duty, and profited by the uncouth criticism of these rough warriors on the defective seamanship of their superiors. A sort of compact was made between us: they promised that whenever they deserted, it should not be from my boat when on duty, and I promised to let them go and drink at public-houses as long as I could spare them. In spite, however, of this mutual understanding, two of them violated their faith the night before we went to sea, and left the boat of which I had charge; and as I had disobeyed orders in letting them go to a public-house, I was, on my return to the ship, dismissed from the quarter-deck, and ordered to do my duty in the fore-top.

CHAPTER III

The might of England flush'd
  To anticipate the same;
And her van the fleeter rush'd
  O'er the deadly space between.
"Hearts of Oak!" our captains cried; when each gun
  From its adamantine lips
  Spread a death-shade round the ships,
  Like the hurricane eclipse
  Of the sun.

CAMPBELL

CONSIDERING my youth and inexperience, and the trifling neglect of which I was accused, there are few, even of the most rigid disciplinarians, who will not admit that I was both unjustly and unkindly treated by the first lieutenant, who certainly with all my respect for him, had lent himself to my enemies. The second lieutenant and Mr Murphy did not even conceal their feelings on the occasion, but exulted over my disgrace.

The ship was suddenly ordered to Portsmouth, where the captain, who had been on leave, was expected to join us, which he did soon after our arrival, when the first lieutenant made his reports of good and bad conduct during his absence. I had been about ten days doing duty in the fore-top, and it was the intention of Mr Handstone, to which the captain seemed not disinclined, to have given me a flogging at the gun, as a gratuity for losing the men. This part of the sentence, however, was not executed. I continued a member of the midshipmen's mess, but was not allowed to enter the berth: my meals were sent to me, and I took them solus on my chest. The youngsters spoke to me, but only by stealth, being afraid of the oldsters, who had sent me to the most rigid Coventry.

My situation in the fore-top was nearly nominal. I went aloft when the hands were called, or in my watch, and amused myself with a book until we went below, unless there was any little duty for me to do, which did not appear above my strength. The men doated on me as a martyr in their cause, and delighted in giving me every instruction in the art of knotting and splicing, rigging, reefing, furling, &c., &c.; and I honestly own that the happiest hours I had passed in that ship were during my seclusion among these honest tars.

Whether my enemies discovered this or not, I cannot say; but shortly after our arrival I was sent for by the captain into his own cabin, where I received a lecture on my misconduct, both as to my supposed irritable and quarrelsome disposition, and also for losing the men out of the boat. "In other respects," he added, "your punishment would have been much more severe but for your general good conduct; and I have no doubt, from this little well-timed severity, that you will in future conduct yourself with more propriety. I therefore release you from the disgraceful situation in which you are placed, and allow you to return to your duty on the quarter-deck."

The tears which no brutality or ill-treatment could wring from me, now flowed in abundance, and it was some minutes before I could recover myself sufficiently to thank him for his kindness, and to explain the cause of my disgrace. I told him, that since I had joined the ship I had been treated like a dog; that he alone had been ignorant of it, and that he alone had behaved to me with humanity. I then related all my sufferings, from the moment of that fatal glass of wine up to the time I was speaking. I did not conceal the act of cutting down Murphy's hammock, nor of throwing the candlestick at his head. I assured him I never gave any provocation; that I never struck without being first stricken. I said, moreover, that I would never receive a blow or be called an improper name without resenting it, as far as I was able. It was my nature, and if killed, I could not help it. "Several men have run away," said I, "since I came into the ship and before, and the officers under whose charge they were only received a reprimand, while I, who have just come to sea, have been treated with the greatest and most degrading severity."

The captain listened to my defence with attention, and I thought seemed very much struck with it. I afterwards learnt that Mr Handstone had received a reprimand for his harsh treatment of me; he observed, that I should one day turn out a shining character, or go to the devil.

It appeared pretty evident to me, that however I might have roused the pride and resentment of the senior members of the mess by my resistance to arbitrary power, that I had gained some powerful friends, among whom was the captain. Many of the officers admired that dogged, "don't care," spirit of resistance which I so perseveringly displayed, and were forced to admit that I had right on my side. I soon perceived the change of mind by the frequency of invitations to the cabin and gun-room tables. The youngsters were proud to receive me again openly as their associate; but the oldsters regarded me with a jealousy and suspicion like that of an unpopular government to a favourite radical leader.

I soon arranged with the boys of my own age a plan of resistance, or rather of self-defence, which proved of great importance in our future warfare. One or two of them had nerve enough to follow it up: the others made fair promises, but fell off in the hour of trial. My code consisted of only two maxims: the first was always to throw a bottle, decanter, candlestick, knife, or fork, at the head of any person who should strike one of us, if the assailant should appear too strong to encounter in fair fight. The second was, never to allow ourselves to be unjustly defrauded of our rights; to have an equal share of what we paid equally for; and to gain by artifice that which was withheld by force.

I explained to them that by the first plan we should ensure civility, at least; for as tyrants are generally cowards, they would be afraid to provoke that anger which in some unlucky moment might be fatal to them, or maim them for life. By the second, I promised to procure them an equal share in the good things of this life, the greater part of which the oldsters engrossed to themselves: in this latter we were much more unanimous than the former, as it incurred less personal risk. I was the projector of all the schemes for forage, and was generally successful.

At length we sailed to join the fleet off Cadiz, under the command of Lord Nelson. I shall not pretend to describe the passage down Channel and across the Bay of Biscay. I was seasick as a lady in a Dover packet, until inured to the motion of the ship by the merciless calls to my duties aloft, or to relieve the deck in my watch.

We reached our station, and joined the immortal Nelson but a few hours before that battle in which he lost his life and saved his country. The history of that important day has been so often and so circumstantially related, that

I cannot add much more to the stock on hand. I am only astonished, seeing the confusion and *invariable variableness* of a sea-fight, how so much could be known. One observation occurred to me then, and I have thought of it ever since with redoubled conviction; this was, that the admiral, after the battle began, was no admiral at all; he could neither see nor be seen; he could take no advantage of the enemy's weak points or defend his own; his ship, the *Victory,* one of our finest three-deckers, was, in a manner, tied up alongside a French eighty-gun ship.

These observations I have read in some naval work, and in my mind they receive ample confirmation. I could not help feeling an agony of anxiety (young as I was) for my country's glory, when I saw the noble leaders of our two lines exposed to the united fire of so many ships. I thought Nelson was too much exposed, and think so now. Experience has confirmed what youthful fancy suggested; the enemy's centre should have been *macadamized* by our seven three-deckers, some of which, by being placed in the rear, had little share in the action; and but for the intimidation which their presence afforded, might as well have been at Spithead. I mean no reflection on the officers who had charge of them: accidental concurrence of light wind and station in the line, threw them at such a distance from the enemy as kept them in the back ground the greater part of the day.

Others, again, were in enviable situations, but did not, as far as I could learn from the officers, do quite so much as they might have done. This defect on our part being met by equal disadvantages, arising from nearly similar causes, on that of the enemy, a clear victory remained to us. The aggregate of the British navy is brave and good; and we must admit that in this day "when England expected every man to do his duty," there were but few who disappointed their country's hopes.

When the immortal signal was communicated, I shall never, no, never, forget the electric effect it produced through the fleet. I can compare it to nothing so justly as to a match laid to a long train of gunpowder; and as Englishmen are the same, the same feeling, the same enthusiasm, was displayed in every ship; tears ran down the cheeks of many a noble fellow when the affecting sentence was made known. It recalled every past enjoyment, and filled the mind with fond anticipations which, with many, were never, alas! to be realised. They went down to their guns without confusion;

and a cool, deliberate courage from that moment seemed to rest on the countenance of every man I saw.

My captain, though not in the line, was no niggard in the matter of shot, and though he had no real business to come within range until called by signal, still he thought it his duty to be as near to our ships engaged as possible, in order to afford them assistance when required. I was stationed at the foremost guns on the main deck, and the ship cleared for action; and though on a comparatively small scale, I cannot imagine a more solemn, grand, or impressive sight, than a ship prepared as ours was on that occasion. Her noble tier of guns, in a line gently curving out towards the centre; the tackle laid across the deck; the shot and wads prepared in ample store (round, grape, and canister); the powder-boys, each with his box full, seated on it, with perfect apparent indifference as to the approaching conflict. The captains of guns, with their priming boxes buckled round their waists; the locks fixed upon the guns; the lanyards laid around them; the officers, with their swords drawn, standing by their respective divisions.

The quarter-deck was commanded by the captain in person, assisted by the first lieutenant, the lieutenant of marines, a party of small-arm men, with the mate and midshipmen, and a portion of seamen to attend the braces and fight the quarter-deck guns. The boatswain was on the forecastle; the gunner in the magazine, to send up a supply of powder to the guns; the carpenter watched and reported, from time to time, the depth of water in the well; he also walked round the wings or vacant spaces between the ship's side and the cables, and other stores. He was attended by his mates, who were provided with shot-plugs, oakum, and tallow, to stop any shot-holes which might be made.

The surgeon was in the cockpit with his assistants. The knives, saws, tourniquets, sponges, basins, wine and water, were all displayed and ready for the first unlucky patient that might be presented. This was more awful to me than anything I had seen. "How soon," thought I, "may I be stretched, mangled and bleeding, on this table, and have occasion for all the skill and all the instruments I now see before me!" I turned away, and endeavoured to forget it all.

As soon as the fleet bore up to engage the enemy, we did the same, keeping as near as we could to the admiral, whose signals we were ordered to repeat. I was particularly astonished with the skilful manner in which this was done. It was wonderful to see how instantaneously the same flags were displayed at our mast-heads as had been hoisted by the admiral; and the more wonderful this appeared to me, since his flags were rolled up in round balls, which were not broken loose until they had reached the mast-head, so that the signal officers of a repeater had to make out the number of the flag during its passage aloft in disguise. This was done by the power of good telescopes, and from habit, and sometimes by anticipation of the signal that would be next made.

The reader may perhaps not be aware that among civilised nations, in naval warfare, ships of the line never fire at frigates, unless they provoke hostility by interposing between belligerent ships, or firing into them, as was the case in the Nile, when Sir James Saumarez, in the *Orion,* was under the necessity of sinking the Artemise, which he did with one broadside, as a reward for her temerity. Under this *pax in bellum* sort of compact we might have come off scot-free, had we not partaken very liberally of the shot intended for larger ships, which did serious damage among our people.

The two British lines running down parallel to each other, and nearly perpendicular to the crescent line of the combined fleets, was the grandest sight that was ever witnessed. As soon as our van was within gun-shot of the enemy, they opened their fire on the *Royal Sovereign* and the *Victory;* but when the first-named of these noble ships rounded to, under the stern of the *Santa Anna,* and the *Victory* had very soon after laid herself on board the *Redoubtable,* the clouds of smoke enveloped both fleets, and little was to be seen except the falling of masts, and here and there, as the smoke blew away, a ship totally dismasted.

One of these proved to be English, and our captain, seeing her between two of the enemy, bore up to take her in tow: at the same time, one of our ships of the line opened a heavy fire on one of the French line-of-battle ships, unluckily situated in a right line between us, so that the shot which missed the enemy sometimes came on board of us. I was looking out of the bow port at the moment that a shot struck our ship on the stern between wind and water. It was the first time I had ever seen the effect of a heavy shot; it made a great splash, and to me as I then thought, a very unusual noise, throwing a great deal of water in my face. I very naturally started back, as I believe many a brave fellow has done. Two of the seamen quartered at my guns laughed at me. I felt ashamed, and resolved to show no more such weakness.

This shot was very soon succeeded by some others not quite so harmless: one came into the bow port, and killed the two men who had witnessed my trepidation. My pride having been hurt that these men should have seen me flinch, I will own that I was secretly pleased when I saw them removed beyond the reach of human interrogation. It would be difficult to describe my feelings on this occasion. Not six weeks before, I was the robber of hen-roosts and gardens—the hero of a horse-pond, ducking an usher—now suddenly, and almost without any previous warning or reflection, placed in the midst of carnage, and an actor of one of those grand events by which the fate of the civilised world was to be decided.

A quickened circulation of blood, a fear of immediate death, and a still greater fear of shame, forced me to an involuntary and frequent change of position; and it required some time, and the best powers of intellect, to reason myself into that frame of mind in which I could feel as safe and as unconcerned as if we had been in harbour. To this state I at last did attain, and soon felt ashamed of the perturbation under which I had laboured before the firing began. I prayed, it is true: but my prayer was not that of faith, of trust, or of hope—I prayed only for safety from imminent personal danger; and my orisons consisted of one or two short, pious ejaculations, without a thought of repentance for the past or amendment for the future.

But when we had once got fairly into action, I felt no more of this, and beheld a poor creature cut in two by a shot with the same indifference that at any other time I should have seen a butcher kill an ox. Whether my heart was bad or not, I cannot say; but I certainly felt my curiosity was gratified more than my feelings were shocked, when a raking shot killed seven and wounded three more.

I was sorry for the men, and, for the world, would not have injured them; but I had a philosophic turn of mind; I liked to judge of causes and effects; and I was secretly pleased at seeing the effect of a raking shot.

Towards four P.M. the firing began to abate, the smoke cleared away, and the calm sea became ruffled with an increasing breeze. The two hostile fleets were quiet spectators of each other's disasters. We retained possession of nineteen or twenty sail of the line. Some of the enemy's ships were seen running away into Cadiz; while four others passed to windward of our fleet, and made their escape. A boat going from our ship to one near us, I jumped into her, and learned the death of Lord Nelson, which I communicated to the captain, who, after paying a tribute to the memory of that great man, looked at me with much complacency. I was the only youngster that had been particularly active, and he immediately despatched me with a message to a ship at a short distance. The first lieutenant asked if he should not send an officer of more experience. "No," said the captain, "he shall go; the boy knows very well what he is about!" and away I went, not a little proud of the confidence placed in me.

Further details of this eventful day are to be found recorded in our national histories; it will, therefore, be needless to repeat them here. When I met my messmates at supper in the berth, I was sorry to see Murphy among them. I had flattered myself that some fortunate shot would have for ever divested me of any further care on his account; but his time was not come.

"The devil has had a fine haul to-day!" said an old master's mate, as he took up his glass of grog.

"Pity you, and some others I could name, had not been in the net!" thinks I to myself.

"I hope plenty of the lieutenants are bowled out!" said another; "we shall stand some chance then of a little promotion!"

When the hands were turned up to muster, the number of killed amounted to nine, and wounded to thirteen.

When this was made known, there seemed to be a general smile of congratulation at the number fallen, rather than of their regret for their loss. The vanity of the officers seemed tickled at the disproportionate slaughter in a frigate of our size, as compared to what they had heard the ships of the line had suffered.

I attended the surgeon in the steerage, to which place the wounded were removed, and saw all the amputations performed, without flinching; while men who had behaved well in the action fainted at the sight. I am afraid I almost took a pleasure in observing the operations of the surgeon, without once reflecting on the pain suffered by the patients. Habit had now begun to corrupt my mind. I was not cruel by nature; I loved the deep investigation of hidden things; and this day's action gave me a very clear insight into the anatomy of the human frame, which I had seen cut in two by shot, lacerated by splinters, carved out with knives, and separated with saws!

Soon after the action, we were ordered to Spithead, with duplicate despatches. One morning I heard a midshipman say, "he would do his old father out of a new kit." I inquired what that meant, was first called a greenhorn for not knowing, and then had it explained to me. "Don't you know," said my instructor, "that after every action there is more canvas, rope, and paint, expended in the warrant-officer's accounts than were destroyed by the enemy?"

I assented to this on the credit of the informer, without knowing whether it was true or false, and he proceeded. "How are we to have white hammock-clothes, skysail masts, and all other finery, besides a coat of paint for the ship's sides every six weeks, if we don't expend all these things in action, and pretend they were lost overboard, or destroyed? The list of defects are given in to the admiral, he signs the demand, and the old commissioner must come down with the stores, whether he will or not. I was once in a sloop of war, when a large forty-four-gun frigate ran on board of us, carried away her jib-boom, and left her large fine-weather jib hanging on our foreyard. It was made of beautiful Russia duck, and to be sure, didn't we make a gang of white hammock-cloths, fore and aft, besides white trousers for the men? Well now, you must know, that as we make *Uncle George* suffer for the stores, so I mean to make dad suffer for my traps. I mean to lose my chest overboard with all my 'kit,' and return home to him and the old woman just fit for the fashion."

"And do you really mean to deceive your father and mother in that way?" replied I, with much apparent innocence.

"Do I? to be sure I do, you flat. How am I to keep up my stock, if I don't make the proper use of an action like this that we have been in?"

I took the hint: it never once occurred to me, that if I had fairly and candidly stated to my parents that my stock of clothes were insufficient for my appearance as a gentleman on the quarter-deck, that they would cheerfully have increased it to any reasonable extent. But I had been taught artifice and cunning; I could tell the truth where I thought it served my purpose, as well as a lie; but here I thought deception was a proof at once of spirit and of merit; and I resolved to practise it, if only to raise myself a trifling degree in the estimation of my unworthy associates. I had become partial to deception from habit, and preferred exercising my own ingenuity in outwitting my father, to obtaining what I needed by more straight-forward and honourable measures.

The ship needed some repairs, and by the indulgence of the captain, who was pleased with my conduct, I, who required so much instruction in the nature and cause of her defects, was allowed to be absent while they were made good. By this oversight, I lost all that improvement which I should have gained by close attention to the unrigging or shipping of the ship; the manner of returning her stores; taking out her masts and ballast, and seeing her taken into dock; the shape of her bottom, and the good or bad qualities which might be supposed to accelerate or retard her movements. All this was sacrificed to the impatience of seeing my parents; to the vainglory of boasting of the action in which I had been present; and, perhaps, of being encouraged to tell lies of things which I never saw, and to talk of feats which I never performed. I loved effect; and I timed the moment of my return to my father's house (through a correspondence with my sister) to be just as a large party had sat down to a sumptuous dinner. I had only been absent three months, it is true; but it was my first cruise, and then "I had seen so much, and been in such very interesting situations."

CHAPTER IV

'Twill be time to go home. What shall I say I have done? It must be a very plausive invention that carries it. I find my tongue is too foolhardy.

SHAKESPEARE

REACHING the well known mansion of my father, I knocked softly at the front door, was admitted, and, without saying a word to the servant, rushed to the head of the dining room table, and threw my arms round my mother's neck, who only screamed, "Good heavens, my child!" and fell into hysterics. My father, who was in the very midst of helping his soup, jumped up to embrace me and assist my mother. The company all rose, like a covey of partridges: one lady spoiled a new pink satin gown by a tip of the elbow from her next neighbour, just as a spoonful of soup had reached "the rosy portals of her mouth;" the little spaniel "Carlo" set up a loud and incessant bark; and in one minute the whole comely arrangement of the feast was converted into anarchy and confusion.

Order was, however, soon restored: my mother recovered her composure—my father shook me by the hand—the company all agreed that I was a very fine, interesting boy—the ladies resumed their seats, and I had the satisfaction to observe that my sudden appearance had not deprived them of their appetites. I soon convinced them that in this particular, at least, I also was in high training. My midshipman's life had neither disqualified nor disgusted me with the luxuries of the table; nor did I manifest the slightest backwardness or diffidence when invited by the gentlemen to take wine. I answered every question with such fluency of speech, and such compound interest of words, as sometimes caused the propounder to regret that he had put me to the trouble of speaking.

I gave a very florid description of the fight; praised some admirals and captains for their bravery, sneered at others, and accused a few of right down misconduct. Now and then, by way of carrying conviction into my auditors, very souls, I rammed home my charges with an oath, at which my father looked grave, my mother held up her finger, the gentlemen laughed, and the ladies all said with a smile, "Sweet boy!—what animation!—what sense!—what discernment!" Thinks I to myself, "You are as complete a set of gulls as ever picked up a bit of biscuit!"

Next morning, while my recent arrival was still warm, I broke the subject of my chest to my father and mother at breakfast; indeed, my father, very fortunately for me, began by inquiring how my stock of clothes held out.

"Bad enough," said I, as I demolished the third egg, for I still had a good appetite at breakfast.

"Bad enough!" repeated my father, "why you were extremely well fitted with everything."

"Very true, sir," said I; "but then you don't know what a man-of-war is in clearing for action; everything not too hot or too heavy is chucked overboard with as little ceremony as I swallow this muffin. 'Whose hat-box is this?' 'Mr Spratt's, sir.' 'D——n Mr Spratt, I'll teach him to keep his hat-box safe another time; over with it'—and away it went over the lee gangway. Spratt's father was a hatter in Bond Street, so we all laughed."

"And pray, Frank," said my mother, "did your box go in the same way?"

"It kept company, I assure you. I watched them go astern, with tears in my eyes, thinking how angry you would be."

"Well, but the chest, Frank, what became of the chest? You said that the Vandals had some respect for heavy objects, and yours, I am sure, to my cost, had very considerable specific gravity."

"That's very true, sir; but you have no notion how much it was lightened the first day the ship got to sea. I was lying on it as sick as a whale— the first lieutenant and mate of the lower deck came down to see if the men's berths were clean; I, and my Noah's ark, lay slap in the way—'Who have we here?' said Mr Handstone. 'Only Mr Mildmay, and his chest, sir,' said the sergeant of marines, into whose territory I acknowledged I had made very considerable incroachments. 'Only!' repeated the lieutenant, 'I thought it had been one of the big stones for the new bridge, and the owner of it a drunken Irish hodman.' I was too sick to care much about what they said."

"You forget your breakfast," said my sister.

"I'll thank you for another muffin, and another cup of coffee," said I.

"Poor fellow!" said my mother, "what he must have suffered!"

"Oh! I have not told you half yet, my dear mother; I only wonder I am alive."

"Alive, indeed!" said my Aunt Julia; "here, my dear, here is a small trifle to help you to replenish the stock you have lost in the service of your country. Noble little fellow! what should we do without sailors?"

I pocketed the little donation—it was a ten-pounder; finished my breakfast, by adding a slice of ham and half a French roll to the articles already shipped, and then continued my story. "The first thing Mr Handstone said, was, that my chest was too big; and the next thing he said, was, 'tell the carpenter I want him. Here, Mr Adze, take this chest; reduce it one foot in length, and one in height.' 'Ay, ay, sir,' said Adze; 'come, young gentleman, move off, and give me your key.' Sick as I was, I knew remonstrance or prayer were alike useless, so I crawled off and presented my key to the carpenter, who very deliberately unlocked, and as expeditiously unloaded all my treasure. The midshipmen all gathered round. The jars of preserves and the cakes of gingerbread which you, my dearest mother, had so nicely packed up for me, were seized with greediness, and devoured before my face. One of them thrust his filthy paw into a pot of black currant jelly, which you gave me for a sore throat, and held a handful of it to my mouth, knowing at the same time that I was ready to be sea-sick in his hand."

"I shall never bear the sight of jelly again," said my sister.

"The nasty brutes!" said my aunt.

"Well," I resumed, "all my nice things went; and, sick as I was, I wished them gone; but when they laughed and spoke disrespectfully of you, my dear mother, I was ready to fly up and tear their eyes out."

"Never mind, my dear boy," said my mother, "we will make all right again."

"So I suppose we must," said my father; "but no more jelly and ginger-bread, if you please, my dear. Proceed with your story, Frank."

"Well, sir, in half an hour my chest was ready for me again; but while they were about it, they might have taken off another foot, for I found ample space to stow what the plunderers had left. The preserve jars, being all empty, were given of course to the marines; and some other heavy articles being handed away, I was no longer puzzled how to stow them. After this, you know, sir, we had the action, and then chest and bedding and all went to the ———."

"Do they throw all the chests and bedding overboard on these occasions?" said my father, with a cool and steady gaze in my face, which I had some trouble in facing back again.

"Yes; always everything that is in the way, and my chest was in the way, and away it went. You know, sir, I could not knock down the first lieutenant: they would have hanged me at the yard-arm."

"Thank Heaven, you did not, my love," said my mother; "what has happened can be repaired, but that could never have been got over. And your books, what is become of them?"

"All went in the lump. They are somewhere near the entrance of the Gut of Gibraltar—all lost except my Bible: I saved that, as I happened to be reading it in my berth the night before the action!"

"Excellent boy!" exclaimed my mother and aunt both together; "I am sure he speaks the truth."

"I hope he does," said my father, drily; "though it must be owned that these sea-fights, however glorious for Old England, are very expensive amusements to the parents of young midshipmen, unless the boys happen to be knocked on the head."

Whether my father began to smell a rat, or whether he was afraid of putting more questions, for fear of hearing more fibs, I know not, but I was not sorry when the narrative was concluded, and I dismissed with flying colours.

To my shame be it spoken, the Bible that assisted me so much in my mother's opinion, had never but once been opened since I had left home, and that was to examine if there were any bank-notes between the leaves, having heard of such things being done, merely to try whether young gentlemen did "search the Scriptures."

My demands were all made good. I believe with the greater celerity, as I began to grow very tiresome; my sea manners were not congenial to the drawing-room. My mother, aunt, and sister, were very different from the females I had been in the habit of seeing on board the frigate. My oaths and treatment of the servants, male and female, all conspired to reconcile the family to my departure. They therefore heard with pleasure that my leave was expired; and, having obtained all I wanted, I did not care one pin how soon I got clear of them; so when the coach came to the door, I jumped in, drove to the Golden Cross, and the next morning rejoined my ship.

I was received with cheerfulness and cordiality by most of my shipmates, except Murphy and some of his cronies; nor did one feeling of regret or compunction enter my mind for the lies and hypocrisy with which I had deceived and cheated my parents. The reader will probably be aware that except the circumstance of reducing the size of my chest, and the seizure and confiscation of my jars and gingerbread, there was scarcely a vestige of truth in my story. That I had lost most of my things was most true; but they were lost by my own carelessness, and not by being thrown overboard. After losing the key of my chest, which happened the day I joined, a rapid decrease of my stock convinced the first lieutenant that a much smaller package might be made of the remainder, and this was the sole cause of my chest being converted into a razée.

My fresh stock of clothes I brought down in a trunk, which I found very handy, and contrived to keep in better order than I had formerly done. The money given me to procure more bedding, I pocketed: indeed I began to grow cunning. I perceived that the best-dressed midshipmen had always the most pleasant duties to perform. I was sent to bring off parties of ladies who came to visit the ship, and to dine with the captain and officers. I had a tolerably good address, and was reckoned a very handsome boy; and though stout of my age, the ladies admitted me to great freedom, under pretence of my being still a dear little darling of a middy, and so perfectly innocent in my mind and manners. The fact is, I was kept in much better order on board my ship than I was in my father's house—so much for the habit of discipline; but this was all outside show. My father was a man of talent, and knew the world, but he knew nothing of the navy; and when I had got him out of his depth, I served him as I did the usher: that is, I soused him and his company head over heels in the horse-pond of their own ignorance. Such is the power of local knowledge and cunning over abstruse science and experience.

So much assurance had I acquired by my recent success in town, that my self-confidence was increased to an incredible degree. My apparent candour, impudence, and readiness gave a currency to the coinings of my brain which far surpassed the dull matter-of-fact of my unwary contemporaries.

Of my boyish days, I have now almost said enough. The adventures of a midshipman, during the first three years of his probationary life, might, if fully detailed, disgust more than amuse, and corrupt more than they would improve; I therefore pass on to the age of sixteen, when my person assumed an outline of which I had great reason to be proud, since I often heard it the subject of encomium among the fair sex, and their award was confirmed even by my companions.

My mind kept pace with my person in every acquirement save those of morality and religion. In these, alas! I became daily more and more deficient, and for a time lost sight of them altogether. The manly, athletic frame, and noble countenance, with which I was blessed, served to render me only more like a painted sepulchre—all was foul within. Like a beautiful snake, whose poison is concealed under the gold and azure of its scales, my inward man was made up of pride, revenge, deceit, and selfishness, and my best talents were generally applied to the worst purposes.

In the knowledge of my profession I made rapid progress, because I delighted in it, and because my mind, active and elastic as my body, required and fed on scientific research. I soon became an expert navigator and a good practical seaman, and all this I acquired by my own application. We had no schoolmaster; and while the other youngsters learned how to work a common day's work from the instruction of the older midshipmen, I, who was no favourite with the latter, was rejected from their coteries. I determined, therefore, to supply the deficiency myself, and this I was enabled to do by the help of a good education. I had been well grounded in mathematics, and was far advanced in Euclid and algebra, previous to leaving school: thus I had a vast superiority over my companions.

The great difficulty was to renew my application to study, after many months of idleness. This, however, I accomplished, and after having been one year at sea, kept a good reckoning and sent in my day's work to the captain. The want of instruction which I first felt in the study of navigation, proved in the end of great service to me: I was forced to study more intensely, and to comprehend the principles on which I founded my theory, so that I was prepared to prove by mathematical demonstration, what others could only assert who worked by "inspection."

The pride of surpassing my seniors, and the hope of exposing their ignorance, stimulated me to inquiry, and roused me to application. The books which I had reported lost to my father, were handed out from the bottom of my chest, and read with avidity: many others I borrowed from the officers, whom I must do the justice to say, not only lent them with cheerfulness, but offered me the use of their cabin to study in.

Thus I acquired a taste for reading. I renewed my acquaintance with the classic authors. Horace and Virgil, licentious but alluring, drove me back to the study of Latin, and fixed in my mind a knowledge of the dead languages, at the expense of my morals. Whether the exchange were profitable or not, is left to wiser heads than mine to decide; my business is with facts only.

Thus, while the ungenerous malice of the elder midshipmen thought to have injured me by leaving me in ignorance, they did me the greatest possible service, by throwing me on my own resources. I continued on pretty nearly the same terms with my shipmates to the last. With some of the mess-room officers I was still in disgrace, and was always disliked by the oldsters in my own mess; with the younger midshipmen and the foremast men I was a favourite. I was too proud to be a tyrant, and the same feeling prevented my submitting to tyranny. As I increased in strength and stature, I showed more determined resistance to arbitrary power: an occasional turn-up with boys of my own size (for the best friends will quarrel), and the supernumerary midshipmen sent on board for a passage, generally ended in establishing my dominion or insuring for me a peaceable neutrality.

I became a scientific pugilist, and now and then took a brush with an oldster; and although overpowered, yet I displayed so much prowess, that my enemies became cautious how they renewed a struggle which they perceived became daily more arduous; till at last, like the lion's whelp, my play ceased to be a joke, and I was left to enjoy that tranquillity, which few found it safe or convenient to disturb. By degrees the balance of power was fairly established, and even Murphy was awed into civil silence.

In addition to my well known increase in personal strength, I acquired a still greater superiority over my companions by the advantage of education; and this I took great care to make them feel on every occasion. I was appealed to in all cases of literary disputation, and was, by general consent, the umpire of the steerage. I was termed "good company,"—not always to the advantage of the possessor of such a talent; for it often tends, as it did with me, to lead into very bad company. I had a fine voice, and played on one or two instruments. This frequently procured me invitations to the gun-room, and excuses from duty, together with more wine or grog than was of service to me, and conversation that I had better not have heard.

We were ordered on a cruise to the coast of France; and as the junior port-admiral had a spite against our captain, he swore by —— that go we should, ready or not ready. Our signal was made to weigh, while lighters of provisions, and the powder-hoy with our powder, were lying alongside— the quarter-deck guns all adrift, and not even mounted. Gun after gun from the *Royal William* was repeated by the *Gladiator,* the flag-ship of the harbour-admiral, and with our signal to part company.

The captain, not knowing how the story might travel up by telegraph to London, and conscious, perhaps, that he had left a little too much to the first lieutenant, "tore the ship away by the hair of the head"—unmoored, bundled everything in upon deck out of the lighters—turned all the women out of the ship, except five or six of the most abandoned—and, with a strong northerly wind, ran down to Yarmouth Roads, and through the Needles to sea, in a state of confusion and disaster which I hope never to see again.

The rear-admiral, Sir Hurricane Humbug, stood on the platform looking at us (I was afterwards told), and was heard to exclaim, "D——n his eyes" (meaning our captain), "there he goes at last! I was afraid that that fellow would have grounded on his beef bones before we should have got him out!"

"The more haste the less speed," is oftener true in naval affairs than in any other situation of life. With us it had nearly proved fatal to the ship. Had we met with an enemy, we must either have disgraced the flag by running away, or been taken.

No sooner clear of the Needles than night came on, and with it a heavy gale of wind at north-north-west. The officers and men were at work till four in the morning, securing the boats, booms, and anchors, clearing the decks of provisions, and setting up the lower rigging, which by the labour of the ship, had begun to stretch to an alarming degree; by great exertion this was accomplished, and the guns secured before the gale had increased to a hurricane.

About nine the next morning, a poor marine, a recruit from Portsmouth, unfortunately fell overboard; and though many brave fellows instantly jumped into one of the quarter-boats, and begged to be lowered down to save him, the captain, who was a cool calculator, thought the chance of losing seven men was greater than that of saving one, so the poor fellow was left to his fate. The ship, it is true, was hove to; but she drifted to leeward much faster than the unfortunate man could swim, though he was one of the best swimmers I ever beheld.

It was heart-breaking to see the manly but ineffectual exertions made by this gallant youth to regain the ship; but all his powers only served to prolong his misery. We saw him nearly a mile to windward, at one moment riding on the top of the mountainous wave, at the next, sinking into the deep valley between, till at last we saw him no more! His sad fate was long deplored in the ship. I thought at the time that the captain was cruel in not sending a boat for him; but I am now convinced, from experience, that he submitted only to hard necessity, and chose the lesser evil of the two.

The fate of this young man was a serious warning to me. I had become, from habit, so extremely active, and so fond of displaying my newly-acquired gymnastics, called by the sailors "sky-larking" that my speedy exit was often prognosticated by the old quarter-masters, and even by the officers. It was clearly understood that I was either to be drowned or was to break my neck; for the latter I took my chance pretty fairly, going up and down the rigging like a monkey. Few of the topmen could equal me in speed, still fewer surpass me in feats of daring activity. I could run along the topsail yards out to the yard-arm, go from one mast to the other by the stays, or down on deck in the twinkling of an eye by the topsail halyards; and, as I knew myself to be an expert swimmer, I cared little about the chance of being drowned; but when I witnessed the fate of the poor marine, who I saw could swim as well, if not better than myself, I became much more cautious. I perceived that there might be situations in which swimming could be of no use; and however beloved I might have been by the sailors, it was evident that, even if they had the inclination, they might not always have the power to relieve me: from this time, I became much more guarded in my movements aloft.

A circumstance occurred shortly after we got to sea which afforded me infinite satisfaction. Murphy, whose disposition led him to bully every one whom he thought he could master, fixed a quarrel on a very quiet, gentle-manly young man, a supernumerary midshipman, who had come on board for a passage to his own ship, then down in the Bay of Biscay. The young man, resenting this improper behaviour, challenged Murphy to fight, and the challenge was accepted; but as the supernumerary was engaged to dine with the captain, he proposed that the meeting should not take place till after dinner, not wishing to exhibit a black eye at the captain's table. This was considered by Murphy as an evasion; and he added further insult by saying that he supposed his antagonist wanted Dutch courage, and that if he did not get wine enough in the cabin, he would not fight at all.

The high-spirited youth made no reply to this insolence; but, having dressed himself, went up to dinner; that over, and after the muster at quarters, he called Mr Murphy into the steerage, and gave him as sound a drubbing as he ever received in his life. The fight, or set-to, lasted only a quarter of an hour, and the young supernumerary displayed so much science, and such a thorough use of his fists, as to defy the brutal force of his opponent, who could not touch him, and who was glad to retreat to his berth, followed by the groans and hisses of all the midshipmen, in which I most cordially joined.

After so clear a proof of the advantages of the science of self-defence, I determined to acquire it; and, with the young stranger for my tutor, I soon became a proficient in the art of boxing, and able to cope with Murphy and his supporters.

There was a part of my duty which, I am free to confess, I hated—this was keeping watch at night. I loved sleep, and, after ten o'clock, I could not keep my eyes open. Neither the buckets of water which were so liberally poured over me by the midshipmen, under the facetious appellation of "blowing the grampus," nor any expostulation or punishments indicted on me by the first lieutenant could rouse my *dormant* energies after the first half of the watch was expired. I was one of the most determined votaries of Somnus; and for his sake, endured every sort of persecution. The first lieutenant took me into his watch, and tried every means, both of mildness and coercion, to break me of this evil habit. I was sure, however, to escape from him, and to conceal myself in some hole or corner, where I slept out the remainder of the watch; and the next morning, I was, as regularly, mastheaded, to do penance during the greater part of the day for my deeds of darkness. I believe that of the first two years of my servitude, one-half of my waking hours, at least, were passed aloft.

I took care, however, to provide myself with books, and, on the whole, was perhaps better employed than I should have been in my berth below. Handstone, though a martinet, was a gentleman; and as he felt a great interest in the young officers in the ship, so he took much pains in the instruction and improvement of them. He frequently expostulated with me on the great impropriety of my conduct; my answer invariably was, that I was as sensible of it as he could be, but that I could not help it; that I deserved all the punishment I met with, and threw myself entirely on his mercy. He used frequently to call me over to the weather side of the deck, when he would converse with me on any topic which he thought might interest or amuse me. Finding I was tolerably well read in history, he asked my opinion, and gave me his own with great good sense and judgment; but such was the irresistible weight of my eyelids, that I used, when he was in the midst of a long dissertation, to slip down the gangway-ladder and leave him to finish his discourses to the wind.

Now, when this occurred, I was more severely punished than on any other occasion; for, to the neglect of duty, I added contempt both of his rank and the instruction he was offering to me. His wrath was also considerably increased when he only discovered my departure by the tittering of the other midshipmen and the quarter-master at the conn.

One evening, I completed my disgrace with him, though a great deal might be said in my own favour. He had sent me to the fore-topmast head, at seven o'clock in the morning, and very unfeelingly, or forgetfully, kept me there the whole day. When he went off deck to his dinner, I came down into the top, made a bed for myself in one of the top-gallant studding sails, and, desiring the man who had the look-out to call me before the lieutenant was likely to come on deck, I very quietly began to prepare a sacrifice to my favourite deity, Somnus; but as the look-out man did not see the lieutenant come up, I was caught napping just at dusk, when the lieutenant came on deck, and did me the honour to remember where he had left me. Looking at the fore-topmast head, he called me down.

Like Milton's devils, who were "found sleeping by one they dread," up I sprung, and regained my perch by the topsail-tie, supposing, or rather hoping, that he would not see me before the mast, in the obscurity of the evening; but he was too lynx-eyed, and had not presence of mind enough *not* to see what he should not have seen. He called to the three men in the top, and inquired where I was? They replied at the mast-head, "What!" exclaimed Handstone, with an oath; "did I not see him this moment, go up by the topsail-tie?"

"No, sir," said the men; "he is now asleep at the mast-head."

"Come down here, you lying rascals, every one of you," said the lieutenant, "and I'll teach you to speak the truth!"

I, who had by this time quietly resumed my station, was ordered down along with them; and we all four stood on the quarter-deck, while the following interrogations were put to us:—

"Now, sir," said the first lieutenant to the captain of the top, "how dare you tell me that that young gentleman was at the mast-head, when I myself saw him 'shinning' up by the topsail-tie?"

I was sorry for the men, who, to save me, had got themselves into jeopardy; and I was just going to declare the truth, and take the whole odium upon myself, when, to my utter astonishment, the man boldly answered, "He was at the mast-head, sir, upon my honour."

"Your honour!" cried the lieutenant, with contempt; then, turning to the other men, he put the same question to them both in succession, and received the same positive answers; so that I really began to think I had been at the mast-head all the time, and had been dreaming I was in the top. At last, turning to me, he said, "Now, sir, I ask you, on your honour, as an officer and a gentleman, where were you when I first hailed?"

"At the mast-head, sir," said I.

"Be it so," he replied; "as you are an officer and a gentleman, I am bound to believe you." Then turning on his heels, he walked away in a greater rage than I ever remember to have seen him.

I plainly perceived that I was not believed, and that I had lost his good opinion. Yet, to consider the case fairly and impartially, how could I have acted otherwise? I had been much too long confined to the mast-head—as long as a man might take to go from London to Bath in a stagecoach; I had lost all my meals; and these poor fellows, to save me from further punishment, had voluntarily exposed themselves to a flogging at the gangway by telling a barefaced falsehood in my defence. Had I not supported them, they would certainly have been flogged, and I should have lost myself with every person aboard; I therefore came to that paradoxical conclusion on the spot, namely, that, as a man of honour and a gentleman, I was bound to tell a lie in order to save these poor men from a cruel punishment.

I am sensible that this is a case to lay before the bench of bishops; and though I never pretended to the constancy of a martyr, had the consequences been on myself alone, I should have had no hesitation in speaking the truth. The lieutenant was to blame, first, by too great a severity; and, secondly, by too rigid an inquiry into a subject not worth the trouble. Still my conscience smote me that I had done wrong; and when the rage of the lieutenant had abated, so as to insure the impunity of the men, I took the earliest opportunity of explaining to him the motives for my conduct, and the painful situation in which I stood. He received my excuses coldly, and we never were friends again.

Our captain, who was a dashing sort of a fellow, contrived to brush up the enemy's quarters, on the coast of France. On one of our boat expeditions, I contrived to slip away with the rest; we landed, and surprised a battery, which we blew up, and spiked the guns. The French soldiers ran for their lives, and we plundered the huts of some poor fishermen. I went in with the rest, in hopes of finding plunder, and for my deserts caught a Tartar. A large skait lay with its mouth open, into which I thrust my fore-finger, to drag him away; the animal was not dead, and closing his jaws, divided my finger to the bone—this was the only blood spilt on the occasion.

Though guilty myself, I was sorry to see the love of plunder prevail so extensively among us. The sailors took away articles utterly useless to them;

and, after carrying them a certain distance, threw them down for others equally useless. I have since often reflected how justly I was punished for my fault, and how needlessly we inflicted the horrors of war on those inoffensive and unhappy creatures.

Our next attempt was of a more serious nature, and productive of still greater calamity to the unoffending and industrious, the usual victims of war, while the instigators are reposing in safety on their down beds.

CHAPTER V

My life is spanned already;

.   .   .   .   .   .

Go with me, like good angels, to my end.

"HENRY VIII."

Danger, like an ague, subtly taints
Even then when we sit idly in the sun.

"TROILUS AND CRESSIDA."

I HAD never been able to regain the confidence and esteem of the first lieutenant since the unfortunate affair of the mast-head. He was certainly an excellent and a correct officer, too much so to overlook what he considered a breach of honour. I, therefore, easily reconciled myself to a separation, which occurred very soon after. We chased a ship into the Bay of Arcasson, when, as was customary, she sought safety under a battery; and the captain, according to our custom, resolved to cut her out.

For this purpose, the boats were manned and armed, and every preparation made for the attack on the following morning. The command of the expedition was given to the first lieutenant, who accepted of it with cheerfulness, and retired to his bed in high spirits, with the anticipation of the honour and profit which the dawn of day would heap upon him. He was proverbially brave and cool in action, so that the seamen followed him with confidence as to certain victory. Whether any ill-omened dreams had disturbed his rest, or whether any reflections on the difficult and dangerous nature of the service had alarmed him, I could not tell; but in the morning we all observed a remarkable change in his deportment. His ardour was gone; he walked the deck with a slow and measured pace, apparently in deep thought; and, contrary to his usual manner, was silent and melancholy, abstracted, and inattentive to the duties of the ship.

The boats prepared for the service were manned; the officers had taken their seats in them; the oars were tossed up; the eyes of the young warriors beamed with animation, and we waited for Mr Handstone, who still walked the deck, absorbed in his own reflections. He was at length recalled to a sense of his situation by the captain, who, in a tone of voice more than usually loud, asked him if he intended to take the command of the expedition? He replied, "most certainly;" and with a firm and animated step, crossed the quarter-deck, and went into his boat.

I, following, seated myself by his side; he looked at me with a foreboding indifference; had he been in his usual mood, he would have sent me to some other boat. We had a long pull before we reached the object of our intended attack, which we found moored close in shore, and well prepared for us. A broadside of grape-shot was the first salute we received. It produced the same effect on our men as the spur to a fiery steed. We pulled alongside, and began to scramble up in the best manner we could. Handstone in an instant regained all his wonted animation, cheered his men, and with his drawn sword in his hand; mounted the ship's side, while our men at the same time poured in volleys of musketry, and then followed their intrepid leader.

In our boat, the first alongside, eleven men, out of twenty-four, lay killed or disabled. Disregarding these, the lieutenant sprang up. I followed close to him; he leaped from the bulwark in upon her deck, and, before I could lift my cutlass in his defence, fell back upon me, knocked me down in his fall, and expired in a moment. He had thirteen musket-balls in his chest and stomach.

I had no time to disengage myself before I was trampled on, and nearly suffocated by the pressure of my shipmates, who, burning to gain the prize, or to avenge our fall, rushed on with the most undaunted bravery. I was supposed to be dead, and treated accordingly, my poor body being only used as a stop for the gangway, where the ladder was unshipped. There I lay fainting with the pressure, and nearly suffocated with the blood of my brave leader, on whose breast my face rested, with my hands crossed over the back of my head, to save my skull, if possible, from the heels of my friends, and the swords of my enemies; and while reason held her seat, I could not help thinking that I was just as well where I was, and that a change of position might not be for the better.

About eight minutes decided the affair, though it certainly did seem to me, in my then unpleasant situation, much longer. Before it was over I had fainted, and before I regained my senses the vessel was under weigh, and out of gunshot from the batteries.

The first moments of respite from carnage were employed in examining the bodies of the killed and wounded. I was numbered among the former, and stretched out between the guns by the side of the first lieutenant and the other dead bodies. A fresh breeze blowing through the ports revived me a little, but, faint and sick, I had neither the power nor inclination to move, my brain was confused; I had no recollection of what had happened and continued to lie in a sort of stupor, until the prize came alongside of the frigate, and I was roused by the cheers of congratulation and victory from those who had remained on board.

A boat instantly brought the surgeon and his assistants to inspect the dead and assist the living. Murphy came along with them. He had not been of the boarding party; and seeing my supposed lifeless corpse, he gave it a slight kick, saying, at the same time, "Here is a young cock that has done crowing! Well, for a wonder, this chap has cheated the gallows."

The sound of the fellow's detested voice was enough to recall me from the grave, if my orders had been signed. I faintly exclaimed, "You are a liar!" which, even with all the melancholy scene around us, produced a burst of laughter at his expense. I was removed to the ship, put to bed, and bled, and was soon able to narrate the particulars of my adventure; but I continued a long while dangerously ill.

The soliloquy of Murphy over my supposed dead body, and my laconic reply, were the cause of much merriment in the ship: the midshipmen annoyed him by asserting that he had saved my life, as nothing but his hated voice could have awoke me from my sleep of death.

The fate of the first lieutenant was justly deplored by all of us; though I cannot deny my Christian-like acquiescence in the will of Providence in this, as well as on a former occasion, when the witnesses of my weakness had been removed for ever out of my way. As I saw it was impossible to regain his good opinion, I thought it was quite as well that we should part company. That he had a strong presentiment of his death was proved; and though I had often heard these instances asserted, I never before had it so clearly brought home to my senses.

The prize was called *L'Aimable Julie,* laden with coffee, cotton, and indigo; mounted fourteen guns; had, at the commencement of the action, forty-seven men, of whom eight were killed, and sixteen wounded. The period of our return into port, according to our orders, happened to coincide with this piece of good fortune, and we came up to Spithead, where our captain met with a hearty welcome from the admiral.

Having delivered his "butcher's bill," *i.e.* the list of killed and wounded, together with an account of our defects, they were sent up to the Admiralty; and, by return of post, we were ordered to fit foreign: and although no one on board, not even the captain, was supposed to know our destination, the girls on the Point assured us it was the Mediterranean; and this turned out to be the fact.

A few days only were spent in hurried preparation, during which I continued to write to my father and mother. In return I received all I required, which was a remittance in cash. This I duly acknowledged by a few lines as the ship was unmooring. We sailed, and soon after arrived without accident at Gibraltar, where we found general orders for any ship that might arrive from England to proceed and join the admiral at Malta. In a few hours our provisions and water were complete; but we were not in so much haste to arrive at Malta as we were to quit Gibraltar—hugging the Spanish coast, in hopes of picking up something to insure us as hearty a welcome at Valette as we found on our last return to Portsmouth.

Early on the second morning of our departure we made Cape de Gaete. As the day dawned we discovered four sail in the wind's eye, and close in shore. The wind was light, and all sail was made in chase. We gained very little on them for many hours, and towards evening it fell calm. The boats were then ordered to pursue them, and we set off, diverging a little from each other's course, or, as the French would say, *déployée,* to give a better chance of falling in with them. I was in the gig with the master and, that being the best running boat, we soon came up with one of the feluccas. We fired musketry at her: but having a light breeze, she would not bring-to. We then took good aim at the helmsman, and hit him. The man only shifted the helm from his right hand to his left, and kept on his course. We still kept firing at this intrepid fellow, and I felt it was like wilful murder, since he made no resistance, but steadily endeavoured to escape.

At length we got close under the stern, and hooked on with our boat-hook. This the Spaniards unhooked, and we dropped astern, having laid our oars in; but the breeze dying entirely away, we again pulled up alongside, and took possession. The poor man was still at the helm, bleeding profusely. We offered him every assistance, and asked why he did not surrender sooner. He replied that he was an old Castilian. Whether he meant that an earlier surrender would have disgraced him, or that he contemplated, from his former experience, a chance of escape to the last moment, I cannot tell. Certain it is that no one ever behaved better; and I felt that I would have given all I possessed to have healed the wounds of this patient, meek, and undaunted old man, who uttered no complaint, but submitted to his fate with a magnanimity which would have done credit to Socrates himself. He had received four musket-balls in his body, and, of course, survived his capture but a very few hours.

We found to our surprise that this vessel, with the three others, one of which was taken by another of our boats, were from Lima. They were single-masted, about thirty tons burthen, twelve men each, and were laden with copper, hides, wax, and cochineal, and had been out five months. They were bound to Valentia, from which they were only one day's sail when we intercepted them. Such is the fortune of war! This gallant man, after a voyage of incredible labour and difficulty, would in a few hours have embraced his family, and gladdened their hearts with the produce of honest industry and successful enterprise; when, in a moment, all their hopes were blasted by our legal murder and robbery; and our prize-money came to our pockets with the tears, if not the curses, of the widow and the orphan!

From some information which the captain obtained in the prize, he was induced to stand over towards the Balearic Islands. We made Ivica, and stood past it; then ran for Palma Bay in the island of Majorca; here we found nothing, to our great disappointment, and continued our course round the island.

An event occurred here, so singular as scarcely to be credible; but the fact is well attested, as there were others who witnessed it beside myself.

The water was smooth, and the day remarkably fine; we were distant from the shore more than a mile and a quarter, when the captain, wishing to try the range of the main deck guns, which were long eighteen-pounders, ordered the gunner to elevate one of them and fire it towards the land. The gunner asked whether he should point the gun at any object. A man was seen walking on the white sandy beach, and as there did not appear to be the slightest chance of hitting him, for he only looked like a speck, the captain desired the gunner to fire at him; he did so, and the man fell. A herd of bullocks at this moment was seen coming out of the woods, and the boats were sent with a party to shoot some of them for the ship's company.

When we landed we found that the ball had cut the poor man in two; and what made the circumstance more particularly interesting was, that he was evidently a man of consequence. He was well dressed, had on black breeches and silk stockings; he was reading Ovid's Metamorphoses, and still grasped the book, which I took out of his hand.

We have often heard of the miraculous powers ascribed to a chance shot, but never could we have supposed that this devilish ball could have gone so far, or done so much mischief. We buried the remains of the unfortunate gentleman in the sand; and having selected two or three bullocks out of the herd, shot them, skinned and divided them into quarters, loaded our boat, and returned on board. I had taken the book out of the hand of the deceased, and from his neck a small miniature of a beautiful female. The brooch in his shirt I also brought away; and when I gave an account to the captain of what had happened, I offered him these articles. He returned them all to me, desired me to keep them until I could see any of the friends of the deceased, and appeared so much distressed at the accident, that we never mentioned it afterwards; and in the course of the time we were together, it was nearly forgotten. The articles remained in my possession unnoticed for many years.

Two days after, we fell in with a vessel of suspicious appearance; and it being calm, the boats were sent in chase. They found her, on their approach, to be a xebeque, under French colours; but these they very soon hauled down, and showed no others. As we came within hail, they told us to keep off, and that if we attempted to board they should fire into us. This was not a threat likely to deter a British officer, and particularly such fire-eaters as ours. So to it we went, and a desperate struggle ensued, the numbers being nearly equal on both sides; but they had the advantage of their own deck and bulwarks. We got on board, however, and in a few minutes gained possession, with a loss, on our side, of sixteen; and on that of our opponent's of twenty-six, killed and wounded.

But great was our sorrow and disappointment when we discovered that we had shed the blood of our friends, while we had lost our own. The vessel, it appeared, was Gibraltar privateer; they took us for French, our boats being fitted with thoels and grummets for the oars, in the French fashion; and we supposed them to be French from their colours and the language in which they hailed us. In this affair we had three officers killed or wounded, and some of our best men. The privateer was manned by a mixed crew of all nations, but chiefly Greeks; and although ostensibly with a commission signed by the Governor of Gibraltar, were no doubt little scrupulous as to the colours of any vessel they might encounter, provided she was not too strong for them.

After this unfortunate mistake we proceeded to Malta: the captain expecting a severe rebuke from his admiral, for his rashness in sending away his boats to attack a vessel without knowing her force. Fortunately for him, the admiral was not there; and before we met him, the number of prizes we had taken were found sufficient in his eyes to cover our multitude of sins, so the affair blew over.

While we lay in Malta Harbour, my friend Murphy fell overboard one night, just after all the boats were hoisted in; he could not swim, and would have been drowned if I had not jumped overboard and held him up until a boat was lowered down to our assistance. The officers and ship's company gave me more credit for this action than I really deserved. To have saved any person under such circumstances, they said, was a noble deed; but to risk my life for a man who had always, from my first coming into the ship, been my bitterest enemy, was more than they could have expected, and was undoubtedly the noblest revenge that I could have taken. But they were deceived—they knew me not: it was my vanity, and the desire of oppressing my enemy under an intolerable weight of obligation, that induced me to rush to his rescue; moreover, as I stood on the gangway witnessing his struggles for life, I felt that I was about to lose all the revenge I had so long laid up in store; in short, I could not spare him, and only saved him, as a cat does a mouse, to torment him.

Murphy acknowledged his obligations, and said the terrors of death were upon him; but in a few days forgot all I had done for him, consummated his own disgrace, and raised my character on the ruins of his own. On some frivolous occasion he threw a basin of dirty water in my face as I passed through the steerage; this was too good an opportunity to gratify my darling passion. I had long watched for an occasion to quarrel with him; but as he had been ill during our passage from Gibraltar to Malta, I could not justify any act of aggression. He had now recovered, and was in the plenitude of his strength, and I astonished him by striking the first blow.

A set-to followed; I brought up all my scientific powers in aid of my strength and the memory of former injuries. I must do him the justice to say he never showed more game—but he had everything to contend for; if I was beaten I was only where I was before, but with him the case would have been different. A fallen tyrant has no friends. Stung to madness by the successful hits I planted in his face, he lost his temper, while I was cool; he fought wildly, I stopped all his blows, and paid them with interest. He stood forty-three rounds, and then gave in with his eyes bunged up, and his face so swollen and so covered with blood, as not to be known by his friends if he had had any.

I had hardly a mark; most of our midshipmen were absent in prizes, but the two seniors of our berth, an old master's mate past promotion, and the surgeon's assistant, who had held my wrist when I was cobbed, were present as the supporters of Murphy during the combat. I always determined whenever I gained a battle to follow it up. The shouts of victory resounded in the berth—the youngsters joined with me in songs of triumph, and gave great offence to the trio. The young Esculapius, a white-faced, stupid, pockmarked, unhealthy-looking man, was fool enough to say, that although I had beaten Murphy, I was not to suppose myself master of the berth. I replied to this only by throwing a biscuit at his head, as a shot of defiance; and, darting on him before he could get his legs from under the table, I thrust my fingers into his neckcloth, which I twisted so tightly, that I held him till he was nearly choked, giving his head at the same time two or three good thumps against the ship's side.

Finding that he grew black in the face, I let him go, and asked if he required any further satisfaction, to which he replied in the negative, and from that day he was always dutiful and obedient to me. The old superannuated mate, a sturdy merchant seaman, seemed greatly dismayed at the successive defeats of his allies, and I believe would have gladly concluded a separate peace. He had never offered to come to the assistance of the doctor, although appealed to in the most pitiable gestures.

This I observed with secret pleasure, and would the more willingly have given him a brush, as I saw he was disinclined to make the attempt. I was, however, determined to be at the head of the mess. At twelve o'clock that night I was relieved from the first watch, and coming down, I found the old mate in a state of beastly intoxication. Thus he went to his hammock, and fell asleep. While he lay "dormant," I took a piece of lunar caustic, which I wetted, and drew stripes and figures all over his weather-beaten face, increasing his natural ugliness to a frightful degree, and made him look very like a New Zealand warrior. The next morning, when he was making his toilet, my party were all ready prepared for the *éclaircissement*. He opened his little dirty chest, and having strapped an old razor, and made a lather in a wooden soap-box, which bore evident marks of the antique, he placed a triangular piece of a looking-glass against the reclining lid of the chest, and began the operation of shaving. His start back with horror, when he beheld his face, I shall never forget: it outdid the young Roscius, when he saw the ghost of Hamlet. Having wetted his forefinger with his tongue, the old mate tried to remove the stain of the caustic, but the "d——d spot" still remained, and we, like so many young imps, surrounded him, roaring with laughter.

I boldly told him that he bore my marks as well as Murphy and the doctor; and I added, with a degree of cruel mockery which might have been spared, that I thought it right to put all my servants in black to-day. I asked whether he was contented with the arrangement, or whether he chose to appeal against my decree; he signified that he had no more to say.

Thus, in twenty-four hours, I had subdued the great allies who had so long oppressed me. I immediately effected a revolution; dismissed the doctor from the office of caterer—took the charge on myself, and administered the most impartial justice. I made the oldsters pay their mess which they had not correctly done before; I caused an equal distribution of all luxuries from which the juniors had till then been debarred; and I flatter myself I restored, in some degree, the golden age in the cockpit. There were no more battles, for there was no hope of victory on their part, nor anything to contend for on mine. I never took any advantage of my strength, further than to protect the youngsters. I proved by this that I was not quarrelsome, but had only struggled for my own emancipation—that gained, I was satisfied. My conduct was explained to the captain and the officers; and being fully and fairly discussed, did me great service. I was looked upon with respect, and treated with marks of confidence, not usual towards a person so young.

We left Malta, expecting to find our commander-in-chief off Toulon; but it seldom happens that the captain of a frigate is in any hurry to join his admiral, unless charged with despatches of importance. This not being our case, we somehow or other tumbled down the Mediterranean before a strong Levanter, and then had to work back again along the coast of Spain and France. It is an ill wind, they say, that blows nobody good; and we found it so with us; for off Toulon, in company with the fleet, if we did take prizes they became of little value, because there were so many to share them. Our captain, who was a man of the most consummate *ruse de guerre* I ever saw or heard of, had two reasons for sending his prizes to Gibraltar. The first was, that we should, in all probability, be sent down there to receive our men, and have the advantage of the cruise back; the second, that he was well aware of the corrupt practices of the admiralty-court at Malta.

All the vessels, therefore, which we had hitherto captured, were sent to Gibraltar for adjudication, and we now added to their number. We had the good fortune to take a large ship laden with barilla, and a brig with tobacco and wine. The charge of the last I was honoured with: and no prime minister ever held a situation of such heavy responsibility with such corrupt supporters. So much was the crew of the frigate reduced by former captures and the unlucky affair with the Maltese privateer, that I was only allowed three men. I was, however, so delighted with my first command, that, I verily believe, if they had only given me a dog and a pig I should have been satisfied.

The frigate's boat put us on board. It blew fresh from the eastward, and I instantly put the helm up, and shaped my course for the old rock. The breeze soon freshened into a gale; we ran slap before it, but soon found it necessary to take in the top-gallant sails. This we at last accomplished, one at a time. We then thought a reef or two in the topsails would be acceptable; but that was impossible. We tried a Spanish reef, that is, let the yards come down on the cap: and she flew before the gale, which had now increased to a very serious degree. Our cargo of wine and tobacco was, unfortunately, stowed by a Spanish and not a British owner. The difference was very material to me. An Englishman, knowing the vice of his countrymen, would have placed the wine underneath, and the tobacco above. Unfortunately it was, in this instance, the reverse, and my men very soon helped themselves to as much as rendered them nearly useless to me, being more than half seas over.

We got on pretty well, however, till about two o'clock in the morning, when the man at the helm, unable to wake the other two seamen to fetch him a drop, thought he might trust the brig to steer herself for a minute, while he quenched his thirst at the wine-cask: the vessel instantly broached to, that is, came with her broadside to the wind and sea, and away went the *mainmast* by the board. Fortunately, the *foremast* stood. The man who had just quitted the helm had not time to get drunk, and the other two were so much frightened that they got sober.

We cleared the wreck as well as we could, got her before the wind again, and continued on our course. But a British sailor, the most daring of all men, is likewise the most regardless of warning or of consequences. The loss of the mainmast, instead of showing my men the madness of their indulgence in drink, turned the scale the opposite way. If they could get drunk with two masts, how much more could they do so with one, when they had only half as much sail to look after? With such a rule of three, there was no reasoning; and they got drunk, and continued drunk during the whole passage.

Good luck often attends us when we don't deserve it:

"The sweet little cherub that sits up aloft,"

as Dibdin says, had an eye upon us. I knew we could not easily get out of the Gut of Gibraltar without knowing it; and accordingly, on the third day after leaving the frigate, we made the rock early in the morning, and, by two o'clock, rounded Europa Point. I had ordered the men to bend the cable, and, like many other young officers, fancied it was done because they said it was, and because I had ordered it. It never once occurred to me to go and see if my orders had been executed; indeed, to say the truth, I had quite as much as I could turn my hand to: I was at the helm from twelve o'clock at night till six in the morning, looking out for the land; and when I ordered one of the men to relieve me, I directed him how to steer, and fell into a profound sleep, which lasted till ten o'clock; after which I was forced to exert the whole of my ingenuity in order to fetch into the Bay, and prevent being blown through the Gut; so that the bending of the cable escaped my memory until the moment I required the use of the anchor.

As I passed under the stern of one of the ships of war in the Bay, with my prize colours flying, the officer on deck hailed me, and said I "had better shorten sail." I thought so too, but how was this to be done? My whole ship's company were too drunk to do it, and though I begged for some assistance from his Majesty's ship, it blew so fresh, and we passed so quick, that they could not hear me, or were not inclined. Necessity has no law. I saw among the other ships in the bay a great lump of a transport, and I thought she was much better able to bear the concussion I intended for her than any other vessel; because I had heard then, and have been made sure of it since, that her owners (like all other owners) were cheating the government out of thousands of pounds a year. She was lying exactly in the part of the Bay assigned for the prizes; and as I saw no other possible mode of "bringing the ship to anchor," I steered for "the lobster smack," and ran slap on board of her, to the great astonishment of the master, mate, and crew.

The usual expletives, a volley of oaths and curses on our lubberly heads, followed the shock. This I expected, and was as fully prepared for as I was for the fall of my foremast, which, taking the foreyard of the transport, fell over the starboard quarter and greatly relieved me on the subject of short-ening sail. Thus, my pretty brig was first reduced to a sloop and then to a hulk; fortunately, her bottom was sound. I was soon cut clear of the trans-port, and called out in a manly voice, "Let go the anchor."

This order was obeyed with promptitude: away it went sure enough; but the devil a cable was there bent to it, and my men being all stupidly drunk, I let my vessel drift athwart-hawse of a frigate; the commanding officer of which, seeing I had no other cable bent, very kindly sent a few hands on board to assist me; and by five o'clock I was safely moored in the Bay of Gibraltar, and walked my quarter-deck as high in my own estimation as Columbus, when he made the American islands.

But short, short was my power! my frigate arrived the next morning. The captain sent for me, and I gave him an account of my voyage and my disasters; he very kindly consoled me for my misfortune; and so far from being angry with me for losing my masts, said it was wonderful, under all circumstances, how I had succeeded in saving the vessel. We lay only a fortnight at Gibraltar, when news arrived that the French had entered Spain, and very shortly after orders came from England to suspend all hostilities against the Spaniards. This we thought a bore, as it almost annihilated any chance of prize-money; at the same time that it increased our labours and stimulated our activity in a most surprising manner, and opened scenes to us far more interesting than if the war with Spain had continued.

We were ordered up to join the admiral off Toulon, but desired to look into the Spanish port of Carthagena on our way, and to report the state of the Spanish squadron in that arsenal. We were received with great politeness by the governor and the officers of the Spanish fleet lying there. These people we found were men of talent and education; their ships were mostly dismantled, and they had not the means of equipping them.

CHAPTER VI

PAR. *You give me most egregious indignity.*
LAF. *Ay, with all my heart; and thou art worthy of it.*

"ALL'S WELL THAT ENDS WELL."

NATURALLY anxious to behold a country from which we had hitherto been excluded for so many years, we all applied for leave to go on shore, and obtained it. Even the seamen were allowed the same indulgence, and went in parties of twenty and thirty at a time. We were followed and gaped at by the people; but shunned at the same time as "hereticos." The inns of the town, like all the rest of them in Spain, have not improved since the days of the immortal Santillana—they were all more or less filled with the lowest of the rabble, and a set of bravos, whose calling was robbery, and who cared little if murder were its accompaniment. The cookery was execrable. Garlic and oil were its principal ingredients. The olla podrida, and its constant attendant, the tomato sauce, were intolerable, but the wine was very well for a midshipman. Whenever we had a repast in any of these houses, the bravos endeavoured to pick a quarrel with us; and these fellows being always armed with stilettos, we found it necessary to be equally well prepared; and whenever we seated ourselves at a table, we never failed to display the butts of our pistols, which kept them in decent order, for they are as cowardly as they are thievish. Our seamen, not being so cautious or so well provided with arms, were frequently robbed and assassinated by these rascals.

I was, on one occasion, near falling a victim to them. Walking in the evening with the second master, and having a pretty little Spanish girl under my arm, for, to my shame be it spoken, I had already formed an acquaintance with the frail sisterhood, four of these villains accosted us. We soon perceived, by their manner of holding their cloaks, that they had their stilettos ready. I desired my companion to draw his dirk, to keep close to me, and not to let them get between us and the wall. Seeing that we were prepared, they wished us *"buenos noches"* (good night); and, endeavouring to put us off our guard by entering into conversation, asked us to give them a cigar, which my companion would have done, had I not cautioned him not to quit his dirk with his right hand, for this was all they wanted.

In this defensive posture we continued until we had nearly reached the plaza or great square, where many people were walking and enjoying themselves by moonlight, the usual custom of the country. "Now," said I to my friend, "let us make a start from these fellows. When I run, do you follow me, and don't stop till we are in the middle of the square."

The manoeuvre was successful; we out-ran the thieves, who were not aware of our plan, and were encumbered with their heavy cloaks. Finding we had escaped, they turned upon the girl, and robbed her of her miserable earnings. This we saw, but could not prevent; such was the police of Spain then, nor has it improved since.

This was the last time I ventured on shore at night, except to go once with a party of our officers to the house of the Spanish admiral, who had a very pretty niece, and was *liberale* enough not to frown on us poor heretics. She was indeed a pretty creature: her lovely black eyes, long eyelashes, and raven hair, betrayed a symptom of Moorish blood, at the same time that her ancient family-name and high good-breeding gave her the envied appellation of *Vieja Christiana*.

This fair creature was pleased to bestow a furtive glance of approbation on my youthful form and handsome dress. My vanity was tickled. I spoke

French to her: she understood it imperfectly, and pretended to know still less of it, from the hatred borne by all the Spaniards at that time to the French nation.

We improved our time, however, which was but short; and, before we parted, perfectly understood each other. I thought I could be contented to give up everything, and reside with her in the wilds of Spain.

The time of our departure came, and I was torn away from my Rosaritta, not without the suspicions of my captain and shipmates that I had been a too highly favoured youth. This was not true. I loved the dear angel, but never had wronged her; and I went to sea in a mood which I sometimes thought might end in an act of desperation: but salt water is an admirable specific against love, at least against such love as that was.

We joined the admiral off Toulon, and were ordered by him to cruise between Perpignan and Marseilles. We parted from the fleet on the following day, and kept the coast in a continued state of alarm. Not a vessel dared to show her nose out of port: we had her if she did. Batteries we laughed at, and either silenced them with our long eighteen-pounders, or landed and blew them up.

In one of these little skirmishes I had very nearly been taken, and should, in that case, have missed all the honour, and glory, and hairbreadth escapes which will be found related in the following pages. I should either have been sabred in mere retaliation, or marched off to Verdun for the remaining six years of the war.

We had landed to storm and blow up a battery, for which purpose we carried with us a bag of powder, and a train of canvas. Everything went on prosperously. We came to a canal which it was necessary to cross, and the best swimmers were selected to convey the powder over without wetting it. I was one of them. I took off my shoes and stockings to save them; and, after we had taken the battery, I was so intent on looking for the telegraphic signal-box, that I had quite forgotten the intended explosion, until I heard a cry of "Run, run!" from those outside who had lighted the train.

I was at that moment on the wall of the fort, nearly thirty feet high, but sloping. I jumped one part, and scrambled the other, and ran away as fast as I could, amidst a shower of stones, which fell around me like an eruption of Vesuvius. Luckily I was not hit, but I had cut my foot in the leap, and was

in much pain. I had two fields of stubble to pass, and my shoes and stockings were on the other side of the canal—the sharp straw entered the wound,
and almost drove me mad, and I was tempted to sit down and resign myself
to my fate.

However, I persevered, and had nearly reached the boats which were
putting off, not aware of my absence, when a noise like distant thunder
reached my ears. This I soon found was cavalry from Cotte, which had come
to defend the battery. I mustered all my strength, and plunged into the sea
to swim off to the boats, and so little time had I to spare, that some of the
enemy's chasseurs, on their black horses, swam in after me, and fired their
pistols at my head. The boats were at this time nearly a quarter of a mile
from the shore; the officers in them fortunately perceived the cavalry, and
saw me at the same time: a boat laid on her oars, which with great difficulty
I reached, and was taken in; but so exhausted with pain and loss of blood,
that I was carried on board almost dead; my foot was cut to the bone, and
I continued a month under the surgeon's care.

I had nearly recovered from this accident, when we captured a ship,
with which Murphy was sent as prize-master; and the same evening a schooner, which we cut out from her anchorage. The command of this latter vessel
was given to me—it was late in the evening, and the hurry was so great that
the keg of spirits intended for myself and crew was not put on board. This
was going from one extreme to the other; in my last ship we had too much
liquor, and in this too little. Naturally thirsty, our desire for drink needed not
the stimulus of salt fish and calavances, for such was our cargo and such was
our food, and deeply did we deplore the loss of our spirits.

On the third day after leaving the frigate, on our way to Gibraltar, I fell
in with a ship on the coast of Spain, and knew it to be the one Murphy
commanded, by a remarkable white patch in the main-topsail. I made all
sail in chase, in hopes of obtaining some spirits from him, knowing that he
had more than he could consume, even if he and his people got drunk
every day. When I came near him, he made all the sail he could. At dusk
I was near enough almost to hail him, but he stood on; and I, having a
couple of small three-pounders on board, with some powder, fired one of
them as a signal. This I repeated again and again; but he would not bring
to; and when it was dark, I lost sight of him, and saw him no more until we
met at Gibraltar.

Next morning I fell in with three Spanish fishing-boats. They took me for a French privateer, pulled up their lines, and made sail. I came up with them, and, firing a gun, they hove to and surrendered. I ordered them alongside; and, finding they had each a keg of wine on board, I condemned that part of their cargo as contraband; but I honestly offered payment for what I had taken. This they declined, finding I was *"Ingles,"* too happy to think they were not in the hands of the French. I then gave each of them a pound of tobacco, which not only satisfied them, but confirmed them in the newly-received opinion among their countrymen, that England was the bravest as well as the most generous of nations. They offered everything their boat contained; but I declined all most nobly, because I had obtained all I wanted; and we parted with mutual good will, they shouting, "Viva Ingleterre!" and we drinking them a good passage in their own wine.

Many days elapsed before we reached Gibraltar: the winds were light, and the weather fine; but as we had discovered that the fishing-boats had wine, we took care to supply our cellar without any trouble from the excise; and, from our equitable mode of barter, I had no reason to think that his Majesty King George lost any of his deserved popularity by our conduct. When we reached Gibraltar, I had still a couple of good kegs wherewith to regale my messmates; though I was sorry to find the frigate and the rest of her prizes had got in before us. Murphy, indeed, did not arrive till the day after me.

I was on the quarter-deck when he came in; and, to my astonishment, he reported that he had been chased by a French privateer, and had beat her off after a four hours' action—that his rigging had suffered a good deal, but that he had not a man hurt. I let him run on till the evening. Many believed him; but some doubted. At dinner, in the gun-room, his arrogance knew no bounds; and, when half drunk, my three men were magnified into a well-manned brig, as full of men and guns as she could stuff!

Sick of all this nonsense, I then simply related the story as it had occurred, and sent for the quarter-master, who was with me, and who confirmed all my statement. From that moment he was a mark of contempt in the ship. Every lie was a Murphy, and every Murphy a liar. He dared not resent this scorn of ours; and found himself so uncomfortable, that he offered no objection to the removal proposed by the captain; his character followed him, and he never obtained promotion. It is a satisfaction to me to reflect that I not only had my full revenge on this man, but that I had been the instrument of turning him out of an honourable profession which he would have disgraced.

This was no time for frigates to be idle; and if I chose to give the name of mine and my captain, the naval history of the country would prove that ours, of all other ships, was one of the most distinguished in the cause of Spanish freedom. The south of Spain became the theatre of the most cruel and desolating war. Our station was off Barcelona, and thence to Perpignan, the frontier of France, on the borders of Spain. Our duty (for which the enterprising disposition of our captain was admirably calculated) was to support the guerilla chiefs; to cut off the enemy's convoys of provisions, either by sea or along the road which lay by the sea-shore; or to dislodge the enemy from any stronghold he might be in possession of.

I was absent from the ship on such services three and four weeks at a time, being attached to a division of small-arm men under the command of the third lieutenant. We suffered very much from privations of all kinds. We never took with us more than one week's provision, and were frequently three weeks without receiving any supply. In the article of dress, our "catalogue of negatives," as a celebrated author says, "was very copious;" we had no shoes nor stockings—no linen, and not all of us had hats—a pocket-handkerchief was the common substitute for this article; we clambered over rocks, and wandered through the flinty or muddy ravines in company with our new allies, the hardy mountaineers.

These men respected our valour, but did not like our religion or our manners. They cheerfully divided their rations with us, but were always inexorable in their cruelty to the French prisoners; and no persuasion of ours could induce them to spare the lives of one of these unhappy people, whose cries and entreaties to the English to intercede for, or save them, were always unavailing. They were either stabbed before our faces, or dragged to the top of a hill commanding a view of some fortress occupied by the French, and, in sight of their countrymen, their throats were cut from ear to ear.

Should the Christian reader condemn this horrid barbarity, as he certainly will, he must remember that those people were men whose every feeling had been outraged. Rape, conflagration, murder, and famine had everywhere followed the step of the cruel invaders; and however we might lament their fate, and endeavour to avert it, we could not but admit that the retaliation was not without justice.

In this irregular warfare, we sometimes revelled in luxuries, and at others were nearly starved. One day, in particular, when fainting with hunger, we met a fat, rosy-looking capuchin: we begged him to show us where we might procure some food, either by purchase or in any other way; but he neither knew where to procure any, nor had he any money: his order, he said, forbade him to use it. As he turned away from us, in some precipitation, we thought we heard something rattle, and as necessity has no law, we took the liberty of searching the padre, on whose person we found forty dollars, of which we relieved him, assuring him that our consciences were perfectly clear, since his order forbade him to carry money; and that as he lived among good Christians, they would not allow him to want. He cursed us; but we laughed at him, because he had produced his own misfortune by his falsehood and hypocrisy.

This was the manner in which the Spanish priests generally behaved to us; and in this way we generally repaid them when we could. We kept the plunder—converted it into food—joined our party soon after, and supposed the affair was over; but the friar had followed us at a distance, and we perceived him coming up the hill where we were stationed. To avoid discovery we exchanged clothes, in such a manner as to render us no longer cognizable. The friar made his complaint to the guerilla chief, whose eyes flashed fire at the indignant treatment his priest had received; and it is probable that bloodshed would have ensued had he been able to point out the culprits.

I kept my countenance though I had changed my dress, and as he looked at me with something beyond suspicion, I stared him full in the face, with the whole united powers of my matchless impudence, and, in a loud and menacing tone of voice, asked him in French if he took me for a brigand.

This question, as well as the manner in which it was put, silenced, if it did not satisfy, the priest. He seemed to listen with apparent conviction to the suggestion of some of our people, that he had been robbed by another party, and he set out in pursuit of them. I was quite tired of his importunities, and glad to see him depart.

As he turned away, he gave me a very scrutinizing look, which I returned with another, full of well dissembled rage and scorn. My curling hair had been well flattened down with a piece of soap, which I had in my pocket, and I had much more the appearance of a Methodist parson than a pickpocket.

Some time previous to this, the frigate to which I belonged had been ordered on other services; and as I had no opportunity of joining her, I was placed, *pro tempore,* on board of another.

But as this has already spun out its length; I shall refer my reader to the next for further particulars.

CHAPTER VII

The shout
Of battle now began, and rushing sound
Of onset
'Twixt host and host but narrow space was left.

MILTON

FROM the deservedly high character borne by the captain of the frigate which I was ordered to join, he was employed by Lord Collingwood on the most confidential services; and we were sent to assist the Spaniards in their defence of the important fortress of Rosas, in Catalonia. It has already been observed that the French general, St Cyr, had entered that country and, having taken Figueras and Gerona, was looking with a wistful eye on the castle of Trinity, on the south-east side, the capture of which would be a certain prelude to the fall of Rosas.

My captain determined to defend it, although it had just been abandoned by another British naval officer, as untenable. I volunteered, though a supernumerary, to be one of the party, and was sent: nor can I but acknowledge that the officer who had abandoned the place had shown more than a sound discretion. Every part of the castle was in ruins. Heaps of crumbling stones and rubbish, broken gun-carriages, and split guns, presented to my mind a very unfavourable field of battle. The only advantage we appeared to have over the assailants was that the breach which they had effected in the walls was steep in its ascent, and the loose stones either fell down upon them, or gave way under their feet, while we plied them with every kind of missile: this was our only defence, and all we had to prevent the enemy marching into the works, if works they could be called.

There was another and very serious disadvantage attending our locality. The castle was situated very near the summit of a steep hill, the upper part of which was in possession of the enemy, who were, by this means, nearly on a level with the top of the castle, and, on that eminence, three hundred Swiss sharpshooters had effected a lodgment, and thrown up works within fifty yards of us, keeping up a constant fire at the castle. If a head was seen above the walls, twenty rifle-bullets whizzed at it in a moment, and the same unremitted attention was paid to our boats as they landed.

On another hill, much to the northward, and consequently, further inland, the French had erected a battery of six 24-pounders. This agreeable neighbour was only three hundred yards from us; and, allowing short intervals for the guns to cool, this battery kept up a constant fire upon us from daylight till dark. I never could have supposed, in my boyish days, that the time would arrive when I should envy a cock upon Shrove Tuesday; yet such was my case when in this infernal castle. It was certainly not giving us fair play; we had no chance against such a force; but my captain was a knight-errant, and as I had volunteered, I had no right to complain. Such was the precision of the enemy's fire, that we could tell the stone that would be hit by the next shot, merely from seeing where the last had struck, and our men were frequently wounded by the splinters of granite with which the walls were built, and others picked off like partridges, by the Swiss corps on the hill close to us.

Our force in the castle consisted of a hundred and thirty English seamen and marines, one company of Spanish, and another of Swiss troops in Spanish pay. Never were troops worse paid and fed, or better fired at. We all pigged in together; dirty straw and fleas for our beds; our food on the same scale of luxury; from the captain downwards there was no distinction. Fighting is sometimes a very agreeable pastime, but excess "palls on the sense:" and here we had enough of it, without what I always thought an indispensable accompaniment, namely, a good bellyful; nor did I conceive how a man could perform his duty without it; but here I was forced, with many others, to make the experiment, and when the boats could not land, which was often the case, we piped to dinner *pro formâ,* as our captain liked regularity, and drank cold water to fill our stomachs.

I have often heard my poor old uncle say that no man knows what he can do till he tries; and the enemy gave us plenty of opportunities of displaying our ingenuity, industry, watchfulness, and abstinence. When poor Penelope wove her web, the poet says—

"The night unravelled what the day began."

With us it was precisely the reverse: the day destroyed all the labours of the night. The hours of darkness were employed by us in filling sandbags, and laying them in the breach, clearing away rubbish, and preparing to receive the enemy's fire, which was sure to recommence at daylight. These avocations, together with a constant and most vigilant watch against surprise, took up so much of our time that little was left for repose, and our meals required still less.

There was some originality in one of our modes of defence, and which, not being *secundum artem,* might have provoked the smile of an engineer. The captain contrived to make a shoot of smooth deal boards, which he received from the ship: these he placed in a slanting direction in the breach, and caused them to be well greased with cook's slush; so that the enemies who wished to come into our hold, must have jumped down upon them, and would in an instant be precipitated into the ditch below, a very considerable depth, where they might either have remained till the doctor came to them, or, if they were able, begin their labours *de novo.* This was a very good bug-trap; for, at that time, I thought just as little of killing a Frenchman as I did of destroying the filthy little nightly depredator just mentioned.

Besides this slippery trick, which we played them with great success, we served them another. We happened to have on board the frigate a large quantity of fishhooks; these we planted, not only on the greasy boards, but in every part where the intruders were likely to place their hands or feet. The breach itself was mined, and loaded with shells and hand-grenades; masked guns, charged up to the muzzle with musket-balls, enfiladed the spot in every direction. Such were our defences; and, considering that we had been three weeks in the castle, opposed to such mighty odds, it is surprising that we only lost twenty men. The crisis was now approaching.

One morning, very early, I happened to have the look-out. The streak of fog which during the night hangs between the hills in that country, and presses down into the valleys, had just begun to rise, and the stars to grow more dim above our heads, when I was looking over the castle-wall towards the breach. The captain came out and asked me what I was looking at. I told him I hardly knew; but there did appear something unusual in the valley, immediately below the breach. He listened a moment, looked attentively with his night-glass, and exclaimed, in his firm voice, but in an undertoned manner, "To arms!—they are coming!"

In three minutes every man was at his post; and though all were quick, there was no time to spare, for by this time the black column of the enemy was distinctly visible, curling along the valley like a great centipede; and, with the daring enterprise so common among the troops of Napoleon, had begun in silence to mount the breach. It was an awful and eventful moment; but the coolness and determination of the little garrison was equal to the occasion.

The word was given to take good aim, and a volley from the masked guns and musketry was poured into the thick of them. They paused—deep groans ascended! They retreated a few paces in confusion, then rallied, and again advanced to the attack; and now the fire on both sides was kept up without intermission. The great guns from the hill fort, and the Swiss sharp-shooters, still nearer, poured copious volleys upon us, and with loud shouts cheered on their comrades to the assault. As they approached and covered our mine, the train was fired, and up they went in the air, and down they fell buried in the ruins. Groans, screams, confusion, French yells, British hurras rent the sky! The hills resounded with the shouts of victory! We sent them hand-grenades in abundance, and broke their shins in glorious style. I must say that the French behaved nobly, though many a tall grenadier and pioneer fell by the symbol in front of his warlike cap. I cried with rage and excitement; and we all fought like bull-dogs, for we knew there was no quarter to be given.

Ten minutes had elapsed since the firing began, and in that time many a brave fellow had bit the dust. The bead of their attacking column had been destroyed by the explosion of our mine. Still they had re-formed, and were again half-way up the breach when the day began to dawn; and we saw a chosen body of one thousand men, led on by their colonel, and advancing over the dead which had just fallen.

The gallant leader appeared to be as cool and composed as if he were at breakfast; with his drawn sword he pointed to the breach, and we heard him exclaim, *"Suivez moi!"* I felt jealous of this brave fellow—jealous of his being a Frenchman; and I threw a lighted hand-grenade between his feet— he picked it up, and threw it from him to a considerable distance.

"Cool chap enough that," said the captain, who stood close to me; "I'll give him another;" which he did, but this the officer kicked away with equal *sang froid* and dignity. "Nothing will cure that fellow," resumed the captain, "but an ounce of lead on an empty stomach—it's a pity, too, to kill so fine a fellow—but there is no help for it."

So saying, he took a musket out of my hand, which I had just loaded— aimed, fired—the colonel staggered, clapped his hand to his breast, and fell back into the arms of some of his men, who threw down their muskets, and took him on their shoulders, either unconscious or perfectly regardless of the death-work which was going on around them. The firing redoubled from our musketry on this little group, every man of whom was either killed or wounded. The colonel, again left to himself, tottered a few paces further, till he reached a small bush, not ten yards from the spot where he received his mortal wound. Here he fell; his sword, which he still grasped in his right hand, rested on the boughs, and pointed upwards to the sky, as if directing the road to the spirit of its gallant master.

With the life of the colonel ended the hopes of the French for that day. The officers, we could perceive, did their duty—cheered, encouraged, and drove on their men, but all in vain! We saw them pass their swords through the bodies of the fugitives; but the men did not even mind that—they would only be killed in their own way—they had had fighting enough for one breakfast. The first impulse, the fiery onset, had been checked by the fall of their brave leader, and *sauve qui peut,* whether coming from the officers or drummers, no matter which, terminated the affair, and we were left a little time to breathe, and to count the number of our dead.

The moment the French perceived from their batteries that the attempt had failed, and that the leader of the enterprise was dead, they poured in an angry fire upon us. I stuck my hat on the bayonet of my musket, and just showed it above the wall. A dozen bullets were through it in a minute: very fortunately my head was not in it.

The fire of the batteries having ceased, which it generally did at stated periods, we had an opportunity of examining the point of attack. Scaling-ladders, and dead bodies lay in profusion. All the wounded had been re-moved, but what magnificent "food for powder" were the bodies which lay before us!—all, it would seem, picked men; not one less than six feet, and some more: they were clad in their grey *capots,* to render their appearance more *sombre,* and less discernible in the twilight of the morning: and as the weather was cold during the nights, I secretly determined to have one of those great coats as a *chère amie* to keep me warm in night-watches. I also resolved to have the colonel's sword to present to my captain; and as soon as it was dark I walked down the breach, brought up one of the scaling-ladders, which I deposited in the castle; and having done so much for the king, I set out to do something for myself.

It was pitch dark. I stumbled on: the wind blew a hurricane, and the dust and mortar almost blinded me; but I knew my way pretty well. Yet there was something very jackal-like, in wandering about among dead bod-ies in the night-time, and I really felt a horror at my situation. There was a dreadful stillness between the blasts, which the pitch darkness made pecu-liarly awful to an unfortified mind. It is for this reason that I would ever discourage night-attacks, unless you can rely on your men. They generally fail: because the man of common bravery, who would acquit himself fairly in broad daylight, will hang back during the night. Fear and Darkness have always been firm allies; and are inseparably playing into each other's hands. Darkness conceals Fear, and therefore Fear loves Darkness, because it saves the coward from shame; and when the fear of shame is the only stimulus to fight, daylight is essentially necessary.

I crept cautiously along, feeling for the dead bodies. The first I laid my hand on, made my blood curdle. It was the lacerated thigh of a grenadier, whose flesh had been torn off by a hand-grenade. "Friend," said I, "if I may judge from the nature of your wound, your great coat is not worth having." The next subject I handled, had been better killed. A musket-ball through his head had settled all his tradesmen's bills; and I hesitated not in becoming residuary legatee, as I was sure the assets would more than discharge the undertaker's bill; but the body was cold and stiff, and did not readily yield its garment.

I, however, succeeded in obtaining my object; in which I arrayed my-self, and went on in search of the colonel's sword; but here I had been anticipated by a Frenchman. The colonel, indeed, lay there, stiff enough, but his sword was gone. I was preparing to return, when I encountered, not a dead, but a living enemy.

"Qui vive?" said a low voice.

"Anglois, bête!" answered I, in a low tone: and added, *"mais les corsairs ne se battent pas."*

"C'est vrai," said he; and growling, *"bon soir,"* he was soon out of sight. I scrambled back to the castle, gave the countersign to the sentinel, and showed my new great coat with a vast deal of glee and satisfaction; some of my comrades went on the same sort of expedition, and were rewarded with more or less success.

In a few days the dead bodies on the breach were nearly denuded by nightly visitors; but that of the colonel lay respected and untouched. The heat of the day had blackened it, and it was now deprived of all its manly beauty, and nothing remained but a loathsome corpse. The rules of war, as well as of humanity, demanded the honourable interment of the remains of this hero; and our captain, who was the very flower of chivalry, desired me to stick a white handkerchief on a pike, as a flag of truce, and bury the bodies, if the enemy would permit us.

I went out accordingly, with a spade and a pick-axe; but the *tirailleurs* on the hill began with their rifles, and wounded one of my men. I looked at the captain, as much as to say, "Am I to proceed?" He motioned with his hand to go on, and I then began digging a hole by the side of a dead body, and the enemy, seeing my intention, desisted from firing. I had buried several, when the captain came out and joined me, with a view of reconnoitring the position of the enemy. He was seen from the fort, and recognized; and his intention pretty accurately guessed at.

We were near the body of the colonel, which we were going to inter; when the captain, observing a diamond ring on the finger of the corpse, said to one of the sailors, "You may just as well take that off: it can be of no use to him now." The man tried to get it off, but the rigidity of the muscle after death prevented his moving it. "He won't feel your knife, poor fellow," said the captain;" and a finger more or less is no great matter to him now: off with it."

The sailor began to saw the finger-joint with his knife, when down came a twenty-four pound shot, and with such a good direction that it took the shoe off the man's foot, and the shovel out of the hand of another man. "In with him, and cover him up!" said the captain.

We did so; when another shot not quite so well directed as the first, threw the dirt in our faces, and ploughed the ground at our feet. The captain then ordered his men to run into the castle, which they instantly obeyed; while he himself walked leisurely along through a shower of musket-balls from those cursed Swiss dogs, whom I most fervently wished at the devil, because, as an aide-de-camp, I felt bound in honour as well as duty to walk by the side of my captain, fully expecting every moment that a rifle-ball would have hit me where I should have been ashamed to show the scar. I thought this funeral pace, after the funeral was over, confounded nonsense; but my fire-eating captain never had run away from a Frenchman, and did not intend to begin then.

I was behind him, making these reflections, and as the shot began to fly very thick, I stepped up alongside of him, and, by degrees, brought him between me and the fire "Sir," said I, "as I am only a midshipman, I don't care so much about honour as you do; and, therefore, if it makes no difference to you, I'll take the liberty of getting under your lee." He laughed, and said, "I did not know you were here, for I meant you should have gone with the others: but, since you are out of your station, Mr Mildmay, I will make that use of you which you so ingeniously proposed to make of me. My life may be of some importance here; but yours very little, and another midshipman can be had from the ship only for asking: so just drop astern, if you please, and do duty as a breastwork for me!"

"Certainly, sir," said I, "by all means;" and I took my station accordingly.

"Now," said the captain, "if you are *'doubled up,'* I will take you on my shoulders!"

I expressed myself exceedingly obliged, not only for the honour he had conferred on me, but also for that which he intended; but hoped I should have no occasion to trouble him.

Whether the enemy took pity on my youth and *innocence,* or whether they purposely missed us, I cannot say: I only know—I was very happy when I found myself inside the castle with a whole skin, and should very readily have reconciled myself to any measure which would have restored me even to the comforts and conveniences of a man-of-war's cockpit. All human enjoyment is comparative, and nothing ever convinced me of it so much and so forcibly as what took place at this memorable siege.

Fortune, and the well known cowardice of the Spaniards, released me from this jeopardy; they surrendered the citadel, after which the castle was of no use, and we ran down to our boats as fast as we could; and notwithstanding the very assiduous fire of the watchful *tirailleurs* on the hill, we all got on board without accident.

There was one very singular feature in this affair. The Swiss mercenaries in the French and Spanish services, opposed to each other, behaved with the greatest bravery, and did their duty with unexceeded fidelity; but being posted so near, and coming so often in contact with each other, they would cry truce for a quarter of an hour, while they made inquiries after their mutual friends; often recognizing each other as fathers and sons, brothers and near relatives, fighting on opposite sides. They would laugh and joke with each other, declare the truce at an end, then load their muskets, and take aim, with the same indifference, as regarded the object, as if they had been perfect strangers; but, as I before observed, fighting is a trade.

From Rosas we proceeded to join the admiral off Toulon; and being informed that a battery of six brass guns, in the port of Silva, would be in possession of the French in a few hours, we ran in, and anchored within pistol-shot of it. We lashed blocks to our lower mast-heads, rove hawsers through them, sent the ends on shore, made them fast to the guns, and hove off three of them, one after another, by the capstan; and had the end of the hawser on shore, ready for the others, when our marine videttes were surprised by the French, driven in, and retreated to the beach with the loss of one man taken prisoner.

Not having sufficient force on shore to resist them, we re-embarked our party, and the French, taking up a position behind the rocks, commenced a heavy fire of musketry upon us. We answered it with the same; and now and then gave them a great gun; but they had the advantage of position, and wounded ten or eleven of our men from their elevated stations behind the rocks. At sunset this ceased, when a boat came off from the shore, pulled by one Spaniard; he brought a letter for the captain, from the officer commanding the French detachment. It presented the French captain's compliments to ours; regretted the little interruption he had given to our occupation, remarked that the weather was cold, and as he had been ordered off in a hurry, he had not had time to provide himself; and as there was always a proper feeling among *braves gens,* requested a few gallons of rum for himself and followers.

This request was answered with a *polite note,* and the spirits required. The British captain hoped the commandant and his party would make themselves comfortable, and have a *bon repos.* The captain, however, intended the Frenchman should pay for the spirits, though not in money and sent in the bill about one o'clock in the morning.

All at that hour was as still as death; the French guard had refreshed themselves, and were enjoying the full extent of our captain's benefaction, when he observed to us that it was a pity to lose the boat which was left on shore, as well as the other brass guns, and proposed making the attempt to bring off both. Five or six of us stripped, and lowering ourselves into the water, very gently swam ashore, in a breathless kind of silence, that would have done honour to a Pawnee Loup Indian. The water was very cold, and at first almost took away my respiration. We landed under the battery, and having first secured our boat without noise, we crept softly up to where the end of the hawsers lay by the side of the guns, to which we instantly made them fast. About a dozen French soldiers were lying near, keeping watch, fast asleep

We might easily have killed them all; but as we considered they were under the influence of our rum, we abhorred such a violation of hospitality. We helped ourselves, however, to most of the muskets that were near us, and very quietly getting into the boat, put off and rowed with two oars to the ship. The noise of the oars woke some of the soldiers, who, jumping up, fired at us with all the arms they had left; and I believe soon got a reinforcement, for they fired both quick and well; and, as it was starlight and we were naked, our bodies were easily seen, so that the shot came very thick about us.

"Diving," said I, "is not running away;" so over we all went, except two. I was down like a porpoise, never rising till my head touched the ship's copper. I swam round the stern, and was taken in on the side opposite the enemy. My captain, I daresay, would have disdained such a compromise; but though I was as proud as he was, I always thought, with Falstaff, that "discretion was the better part of valour," especially in a midshipman.

The men left in the boat got safe on board with her. The hands were all ready, and the moment our oars splashed in the water, they hove round cheerfully, and the guns came galloping down the rocks like young kangaroos. They were soon under water, and long before the Frenchmen could get a cut at the hawsers. They then fired at them with their muskets, in hopes of stranding the rope, but they failed in that also. We secured the guns on board, and before daylight got under weigh, and made sail for the fleet, which we joined shortly afterwards.

I here learned that my own ship had fought a gallant action with an enemy's frigate, had taken her opponent, but had suffered so much that she was ordered home for repairs, and had sailed for England from Gibraltar.

I had letters of introduction to the rear-admiral, who was second in command; and I thought, under these circumstances the best thing I could do would be to "clean myself," as the phrase used to be in those days, and go on board and present them. I went accordingly, and saw the flag-captain, who took my letters in to the admiral, and brought out a verbal, and not a very civil message, saying, I might join the ship, if I pleased, until my own returned to the station. As it happened to suit my convenience, I *did* please; and the manner in which the favour was conferred disburdened my mind of any incumbrance of gratitude. The reception was not such as I might have expected: had the letters not been from people of distinction, and friends of the rear-admiral, I should much have preferred remaining in the frigate, whose captain also wished it, but that was not allowed.

To the flag-ship, therefore, I came, and why I was brought here, I never could discover, unless it was for the purpose of completing a menagerie, for I found between sixty and seventy midshipmen already assembled. They were mostly youngsters, followers of the rear-admiral, and had seen very little, if any, service, and I had seen a great deal for the time I had been afloat. Listening eagerly to my "yarns," the youthful ardour of these striplings kindled, and they longed to emulate my deeds. The consequence was numerous applications from the midshipmen to be allowed to join the frigates on the station; not one was contented in the flag-ship; and the captain having discovered that I was the tarantula which had bitten them, hated me accordingly, and not a jot more than I hated him.

The captain was a very large, ill-made, broad-shouldered man, with a lack-lustre eye, a pair of thick lips, and a very unmeaning countenance. He wore a large pair of epaulettes; he was irritable in his temper; and when roused, which was frequent, was always violent and overbearing. His voice was like thunder, and when he launched out on the poor midshipmen, they reminded me of the trembling bird which, when fascinated by the eye of the snake, loses its powers, and falls at once into the jaws of the monster. When much excited, he had a custom of shaking his shoulders up and down; and his epaulettes, on these occasions, flapped like the huge ears of a trotting elephant. At the most distant view of his person or sound of his voice, every midshipman, not obliged to remain, fled, like the land-crabs on a West India beach. He was incessantly taunting me, was sure to find some fault or other with me, and sneeringly called me "one of your frigate midshipmen."

Irritated by this unjust treatment, I one day answered that I was a frigate midshipman, and hoped I could do my duty as well as any line-of-battle midshipman, of my own standing, in the service. For this injudicious and rather impertinent remark, I was ordered aft on the quarter-deck, and the captain went in to the admiral, and asked permission to flog me; but the admiral refused, observing, that he did not admire the system of flogging young gentlemen: and, moreover, that in the present instance he saw no reason for it. So I escaped; but I led a sad life of it, and often did I pray for the return of my own ship.

Among other exercises of the fleet, we used always to reef topsails at sunset, and this was usually done by all the ships at the same moment, waiting the signal from the admiral to begin; in this exercise there was much foolish rivalry, and very serious accidents, as well as numerous punishments, took place, in consequence of one ship trying to excel another. On these occasions our captain would bellow and foam at the mouth like a mad bull, up and down the quarter-deck.

One fine evening the signal was made, the topsails lowered and the men laying out on the yards, when a poor fellow from the main-topsail yard fell, in his trying to lay out; and, striking his shoulder against the main channels, broke his arm. I saw he was disabled, and could not swim: and, perceiving him sinking, I darted overboard, and held him until a boat came and picked us up; as the water was smooth, and there was little wind, and the ship not going more than two miles an hour, I incurred little risk.

When I came on deck I found the captain fit for Bedlam, because the accident had delayed the topsails going to the mast-head quite as quick as the rest of the fleet. He threatened to flog the man for falling overboard, and ordered me off the quarter-deck. This was great injustice to both of us. Of all the characters I ever met with, holding so high a rank in the service, this man was the most unpleasant.

Shortly after, we were ordered to Minorca to refit; here, to my great joy, I found my own ship, and I "shook the dust off my feet," and quitted the flag with a light heart. During the time I had been on board, the admiral had never said, "How do ye do?" to me—nor did he say, "Good-bye," when I quitted. Indeed, I should have left the ship without ever having been honoured with his notice, if it had not happened, that a favourite pointer of his was a shipmate of mine. I recollect hearing of a man who boasted that the king had spoken to him; and when it was asked what he had said, replied, "He desired me to get out of his way."

My intercourse with the admiral was about as friendly and flattering. Pompey and I were on the poop. I presented him with a piece of hide to gnaw, by way of pastime. The admiral came on the poop, and seeing Pompey thus employed, asked who gave him that piece of hide? The yeoman of the signals said it was me. The admiral shook his long spy-glass at me, and said, "By G——, sir, if ever you give Pompey a bit of hide again, I will flog you."

This is all I have to say of the admiral, and all the admiral ever said to me.

CHAPTER VIII

Since laws were made for every degree,
I wonder we haven't better company on Tyburn tree.
"BEGGAR'S OPERA."

WHILE I was on board of this ship two poor men were executed for mutiny. The scene was far more solemn to me than anything I had ever beheld. Indeed it was the first thing of the kind I had ever been present at. When we hear of executions on shore, we are always prepared to read of some foul atrocious crime, some unprovoked and unmitigated offence against the laws of civilized society, which a just and merciful government cannot allow to pass unpunished. With us at sea there are many shades of difference; but that which the law of our service considers a serious offence is often no more than an ebullition of local and temporary feeling, which in some cases might be curbed, and in others totally suppressed by timely firmness and conciliation.

The ships had been a long time at sea, the enemy did not appear—and there was no chance either of bringing him to action, or of returning into port. Indeed nothing can be more dull and monotonous than a blockading cruise "in the team," as we call it; that is, the ships of the line stationed to watch an enemy. The frigates have, in this respect, every advantage; they are always employed on shore, often in action, and the more men they have killed, the happier are the survivors. Some melancholy ferment on board of the flag-ship I was in caused an open mutiny. Of course it was very soon quelled; and the ringleaders having been tried by a court-martial, two of them were condemned to be hanged at the yard-arm of their own ship, and were ordered for execution the following day but one.

Our courts-martial are always arrayed in the most pompous manner, and certainly are calculated to strike the mind with awe—even of a captain himself. A gun is fired at eight o'clock in the morning from the ship where it is to be held, and a union flag is displayed at the mizzen peak. If the weather be fine, the ship is arranged with the greatest nicety; her decks are as white as snow—her hammocks are stowed with care—her ropes are taut—her yards square—her guns run out—and a guard of marines, under the orders of a lieutenant, prepared to receive every member of the court with the honour due to his rank. Before nine o'clock they are all assembled; the officers in their undress uniform, unless an admiral is to be tried. The great cabin is prepared, with a long table covered with a green cloth. Pens, ink, paper, prayer-books, and the Articles of War, are laid round to every member. "Open the court," says the president.

The court is opened, and officers and men indiscriminately stand round. The prisoners are now brought in under the charge of the provost-marshal, a master-at-arms, with his sword drawn, and placed at the foot of the table, on the left hand of the judge-advocate. The court is sworn to do its duty impartially, and if there is any doubt, to let it go in favour of the prisoner. Having done this, the members sit down, covered if they please.

The judge-advocate is then sworn, and the order for the court-martial read. The prisoner is put on his trial; if he says anything to commit himself, the court stops him, and kindly observes, "We do not want your evidence against yourself; we want only to know what others can prove against you." The unfortunate man is offered any assistance he may require; and when the defence is over, the court is cleared; the doors are shut, and the minutes, which have been taken down by the judge-advocate, are carefully read over, the credibility of the witnesses weighed, and the president puts the question to the youngest member first, "Proved, or not proved?"

All having given their answer, if seven are in favour of proved, and six against, proved is recorded. The next question—if for mutiny or desertion, or other capital crime—"Flogging or death?" The votes are given in the same way; if the majority be for death, the judge-advocate writes the sentence, and it is signed by all the members, according to seniority, beginning with the president and ending with the judge-advocate. The court is now opened again, the prisoner brought in, and an awful and deep silence prevails. The members of the court all put their hats on, and are seated; every one else, except the provost-marshal is uncovered. As soon as the judge-advocate has read the sentence, the prisoners are delivered to the custody of the provost-marshal, by a warrant from the president, and he has charge of them till the time for the execution of the sentence.

About three o'clock in the afternoon, I received a message from one of the prisoners, saying, he wished much to speak with me. I followed the master-at-arms down to the screened cabin, in the gun-room, where the men were confined with their legs in irons. These irons consist of one long bar and a set of shackles. The shackles fit the small part of the leg, just above the ankle; and, having an eye on each end of them, they receive the leg. The end of the bar is then passed through, and secured with a padlock. I found the poor fellows sitting on a shot-box. Their little meal lay before them untouched; one of them cried bitterly; the other, a man of the name of Strange, possessed a great deal of equanimity, although evidently deeply affected. This man had been pretty well educated in youth, but having taken a wild and indolent turn, had got into mischief, and to save himself from a severe chastisement, had run away from his friends, and entered on board a man-of-war. In this situation he had found time, in the intervals of duty, to read and to think; he became, in time, sullen, and separated himself from the occasional merriment of his messmates; and it is not improbable that this moody temper had given rise to the mutinous acts for which he was to suffer.

This man now apologized for the liberty he had taken, and said he would not detain me long. "You see, sir," said he, "that my poor friend is quite overcome with the horror of his situation: nor do I wonder at it. He is very different from the hardened malefactors that are executed on shore: we are neither of us afraid to die; but such a death as this, Mr Mildmay— to be hung up like dogs, an example to the fleet, and a shame and reproach to our friends—this wrings our hearts! It is this consideration, and to save the feelings of my poor mother, that I have sent for you. I saw you jump overboard to save a poor fellow from drowning; so I thought you would not mind doing a good turn for another unfortunate sailor. I have made my will, and appointed you my executor; and with this power of attorney you will receive all my pay and prize-money, which I will thank you to give to my dear mother, whose address you will find written here. My motive for this is, that she may never learn the history of my death. You can tell her that I died for my country's good, which is very true, for I acknowledge the justice of my sentence, and own that a severe example is wanting. It is eleven years since I was in England; I have served faithfully the whole of that time, nor did I ever misbehave except in this one instance. I think if our good king knew my sad story, he would be merciful; but God's will be done! Yet, if I had a wish, it would be that the enemy's fleet would come out, and that I might die, as I have lived, defending my country. But, Mr Mildmay, I have one very important question to ask you—do you believe that there is such a thing as a future state?"

"Most surely," said I; "though we all live as if we believed there was no such thing. But why do you doubt it?"

"Because," said the poor fellow, "when I was an officer's servant, I was one day tending the table in the wardroom, and I heard the commander of a sloop of war, who was dining there with his son, say that it was all nonsense—that there was no future state, and the Bible was a heap of lies. I have never been happy since."

I told him that I was extremely sorry that any officer should have used such expressions at all, particularly before him; that I was incapable of restoring his mind to its proper state; but that I should recommend his immediately sending for the chaplain, who, I had no doubt, would give him all the comfort he could desire. He thanked me for this advice, and profited by it, as he assured me in his last moments.

"And now, sir," said he, "let me give *you* a piece of advice. When you are a captain, as I am very sure you will be, do not worry your men into mutiny by making what is called a smart ship. Cleanliness and good order are what seamen like; but niggling, polishing, scraping iron bars, and ring-bolts, and the like of that, a sailor dislikes more than a flogging at the gang-way. If, in reefing topsails, you happen to be a minute later than another ship, never mind it, so long as your sails are well reefed, and fit to stand blowing weather. Many a sail is split by bad reefing, and many a good sailor has lost his life by that foolish hurry which has done incredible harm in the navy. What can be more cruel or unjust than to flog the last man off the yard? seeing that he is necessarily the most active, and cannot get in without the imminent danger of breaking his neck; and, moreover, that one man *must* be last. Depend upon it, sir, 'that nothing is well done which is done in a hurry.' But I have kept you too long. God bless you, sir; remember my poor mother, and be sure you meet me on the forecastle to-morrow morning."

The fatal morning came. It was eight o'clock. The gun fired—the signal for punishment flew at our mast-head. The poor men gave a deep groan, exclaiming, "Lord have mercy upon us!—our earthly career and troubles are nearly over!" The master-at-arms came in, unlocked the padlock at the end of the bars, and, slipping off the shackles, desired the marine sentinels to conduct the prisoners to the quarter-deck.

Here was a scene of solemnity which I hardly dare attempt to describe. The day was clear and beautiful; the top-gallant yards were crossed on board of all the ships; the colours were flying; the crews were all dressed in white trousers and blue jackets, and hung in clusters, like bees, on the side of the rigging facing our ship: a guard of marines, under arms, was placed along each gangway, but on board of our ship they were on the quarter-deck. Two boats from each ship lay off upon their oars alongside of us, with a lieutenant's and a corporal's guard in each, with fixed bayonets. The hands were all turned up by the boatswain and his mates with a shrill whistle, and calling down each hatchway, "All hands attend punishment!"

You now heard the quick trampling of feet up the ladders, but not a word was spoken. The prisoners stood on the middle of the quarter-deck, while the captain read the sentence of the court-martial and the order from the commander-in-chief for the execution. The appropriate prayers and psalms having been read by the chaplain, with much feeling and devotion, the poor men were asked if they were ready; they both replied in the affirmative, but each requested to have a glass of wine, which was instantly brought. They drank it off, bowing most respectfully to the captain and officers.

The admiral did not appear, it not being etiquette; but the prisoners desired to be kindly and gratefully remembered to him; they then begged to shake hands with the captain and all the officers, which having done, they asked permission to address the ship's company. The captain ordered them all to come aft on the top and quarter-deck. The most profound silence reigned, and there was not an eye but had a tear in it.

William Strange, the man who had sent for me, then said, in a clear and audible tone of voice:—"Brother sailors, attend to the last words of a dying man. We are brought here at the instigation of some of you who are now standing in safety among the crowd: you have made fools of us, and we are become the victims to the just vengeance of the laws. Had you succeeded in the infamous design you contemplated, what would have been the consequences? Ruin, eternal ruin, to yourselves and to your families; a disgrace to your country, and the scorn of those foreigners to whom you proposed delivering up the ship. Thank God you did not succeed. Let our fate be a warning to you, and endeavour to show by your future acts your deep contrition for the past. Now, sir," turning to the captain, "we are ready."

This beautiful speech from the mouth of a common sailor must as much astonish the reader as it then did the captain and officers of the ship. But Strange, as I have shown, was no common man; he had had the advantage of education, and, like many of the ringleaders at the mutiny of the Nore, was led into the error of refusing to *obey,* from the conscious feeling that he was born to *command.*

The arms of the prisoners were then pinioned, and the chaplain led the way, reading the funeral service; the master-at-arms, with two marine sentinels, conducted them along the starboard gangway to the forecastle; here a stage was erected on either side, over the cathead, with steps to ascend to it; a tail block was attached to the boom-iron, at the outer extremity of each foreyard-arm, and through this a rope was rove, one end of which came down to the stage; the other was led along the yard into the catharpings, and thence down upon the main deck. A gun was primed and ready to fire, on the fore part of the ship, directly beneath the scaffold.

I attended poor Strange to the very last moment; he begged me to see that the halter, which was a piece of line, like a clothes' line, was properly made fast round his neck, for he had known men suffer dreadfully from the want of this precaution. A white cap was placed on the head of each man, and when both mounted the platform, the cap was drawn over their eyes. They shook hands with me, with their messmates, and with the chaplain, assuring him that they died happy, and confident in the hopes of redemption. They then stood still while the yard ropes were fixed to the halter by a toggle in the running noose of the latter; the other end of the yard-ropes were held by some twenty or thirty men on each side of the main deck, where two lieutenants of the ship attended.

All being ready, the captain waved a white handkerchief, the gun fired, and in an instant the poor fellows were seen swinging at either yard-arm. They had on blue jackets and white trousers, and were remarkably fine-looking young men. They did not appear to suffer any pain, and at the expiration of an hour, the bodies were lowered down, placed in coffins, and sent on shore for interment.

On my arrival in England, nine months after, I acquitted myself of my promise, and paid to the mother of William Strange upwards of fifty pounds, for pay and prize-money. I told the poor woman that her son had died a Christian, and had fallen for the good of his country; and having said this, I took a hasty leave, for fear she should ask questions.

That the execution of a man on board of a ship of war does not always produce a proper effect upon the minds of the younger boys, the following fact may serve to prove.

There were two little fellows on board the ship; one was the son of the carpenter, the other of the boatswain. They were both of them surprised and interested at the sight, but not proportionably shocked. The next day I was down in one of the wings, reading by the light of a purser's dip—*vulgo,* a farthing candle, when these two boys came sliding down the main hatchway by one of the cables. Whether they saw me, and thought I would not 'peach, or whether they supposed I was asleep, I cannot tell; but they took their seats on the cables, in the heart of the tier, and for some time appeared to be in earnest conversation. They had some articles folded up in a dirty check shirt and pocket-handkerchief; they looked up at the battens, to which the hammocks are suspended, and producing a long rope-yarn, tried to pass it over one of them; but unable to reach, one boy climbed on the back of the other, and effected two purposes, by reeving one end of the line, and bringing it down to the cables again. They next unrolled the shirt, and, to my surprise, took out the boatswain's kitten, about three months old; its fore paws were tied behind its back, its hind feet were tied together, and a fishing-lead attached to them; a piece of white rag was tied over its head as a cap.

It was now pretty evident what the fate of poor puss was likely to be, and why the lead was made fast to her feet. The rope-yarn was tied round her neck; they each shook one of her paws, and pretended to cry. One of the urchins held in his hand a fife, into which he poured as much flour as it would hold out of the handkerchief, the other held the end of the rope-yarn: every ceremony was gone through that they could think of.

"Are you ready ?" said the executioner, or he that held the line.

"All ready," replied the boy with the fife.

"Fire the gun!" said the hangman.

The boy applied one end of the fife to his mouth, blew out all the flour, and in this humble imitation of the smoke of a gun, poor puss was run up to the batten, where she hung till she was dead. I am ashamed to say I did not attempt to save the kitten's life, although I caused her foul murder to be revenged by the cat.

After the body had hung a certain time, they took it down and buried it in the shot-locker; this was an indictable offence, as the smell would have proved, so I lodged the information; the body was found, and as the facts were clear, the law took its course, to the great amusement of the bystanders, who saw the brats tied upon a gun, and well flogged.

The boatswain ate the kitten, first, he said, because he had "*larned*" to eat cats in Spain; secondly, because she had *not* died a natural death (I thought otherwise); and his last reason was more singular than either of the others: he had seen a picture in a church in Spain, of Peter's vision of the animals let down in the sheet, and there was a cat among them. Observing an alarm of scepticism in my eye, he thought proper to confirm his assertion with an oath.

"Might it not have been a rabbit?" said I.

"Rabbit, sir, d——n me, think I didn't know a cat from a rabbit? Why one has got short ears and long tail, and t'other has got *wicee wersee,* as we calls it."

A grand carnival masquerade was to be given at Minorca in honour of the English, and the place chosen for the exhibition was a church; all which was perfectly consistent with the Romish faith. I went in the character of a fool, and met many brother officers there. It was a comical sight to see the anomalous groups stared at by the pictures of the Virgin Mary and all the saints, whose shrines were lit up for the occasion with wax tapers. The admiral, rear-admiral, and most of the captains and officers of the fleet were present; the place was about a mile from the town.

Having hired a fool's dress, I mounted that very appropriate animal—a donkey, and set off amidst the shouts of a thousand dirty vagabonds. On my arrival, I began to show off in somersaults, leaps, and all kinds of practical jokes. The manner in which I supported the character drew a little crowd around me. I never spoke to an admiral or captain unless he addressed me first; and then I generally sold him a bargain. Being very well acquainted with the domestic economy of the ships on the station, a martinet asked me if I would enter for his ship. "No," said I, "you would give me three dozen for not lashing up my hammock properly." "Come with me," said another. "No," said I, "your bell-rope is too short—you cannot reach it to order another bottle of wine before all the officers have left your table." Another promised me kind treatment and plenty of wine. "No," said I, "in your ship I should be coals at Newcastle; besides, your coffee is too weak, your steward only puts one ounce into six cups."

These hits afforded a good deal of mirth among the crowd, and even the admiral himself honoured me with a smile. I bowed respectfully to his lordship, who merely said—"What do you want of me, fool?" "Oh, nothing at all, my lord," said I, "I have only a small favour to ask of you." "What is that?" said the admiral. "Only to make me a captain, my lord." "Oh, no," said the admiral, "we never make fools captains." "No!" said I, clapping my arms akimbo in a very impertinent manner, "then that, I suppose, is a new regulation. How long has the order in council been out?"

The good-humoured old chief laughed heartily at this piece of impertinence; but the captain whose ship I had so recently quitted was silly enough to be offended: he found me out, and went and complained of me to my captain the next day; but my captain only laughed at him, said he thought it an excellent joke, and invited me to dinner.

Our ship was ordered to Gibraltar, where we arrived soon after; and a packet coming in from England, I received letters from my father, announcing the death of my dearest mother. O how I then regretted all the sorrows I had ever caused her; how incessantly did busy memory haunt me with all my misdeeds, and recall to mind the last moment I had seen her! I never supposed I could have regretted her half so much. My father stated that in her last moments she had expressed the greatest solicitude for my welfare. She feared the career of life on which I had entered would not conduce to my eternal welfare, however much it might promise to my temporal advantage. Her dying injunctions to me were never to forget the moral and religious principles in which she had brought me up; and, with her last blessing, implored me to read my Bible, and take it as my guide through life.

My father's letter was both an affecting and forcible appeal; and never, in the whole course of my subsequent life, were my feelings so worked upon as they were on that occasion. I went to my hammock with an aching head and an almost broken heart. A retrospection of my life afforded me no comfort. The numerous acts of depravity or pride, of revenge or deceit, of which I had been guilty, rushed through my mind, as the tempest through the rigging, and called me to the most serious and melancholy reflections. It was some time before I could collect my thoughts and analyse my feelings; but when I recalled all my misdeeds—my departure from that path of virtue, so often and so clearly laid down by my affectionate parent—I was overwhelmed with grief, shame, and repentance. I considered how often I had been on the brink of eternity; and had I been cut off in my sins, what would have been my destiny? I started with horror at the dangers I had escaped, and looked forward with gloomy apprehension at those that still awaited me. I sought in vain, among all my actions since I left my mother's care, one single deed of virtue—one that sprang from a good motive. There was, it is true, an outward gloss and polish for the world to look at; but all was dark within: and I felt that a keener eye than that of mortality was searching my soul, where deception was worse than useless.

At twelve o'clock, before I had once closed my eyes, I was called to relieve the deck, having what is called the middle watch, *i.e.* from midnight till four in the morning. We had, the day before, buried a quarter-master, nick-named Quid, an old seaman who had destroyed himself by drinking— no very uncommon case in His Majesty's service. The corpse of a man who has destroyed his inside by intemperance is generally in a state of putridity immediately after death; and the decay, particularly in warm climates, is very rapid. A few hours after Quid's death, the body emitted certain effluvia de- noting the necessity of immediate interment. It was accordingly sewn up in a hammock; and as the ship lay in deep water, with a current sweeping round the bay, and the boats being at the same time all employed at the dockyard, the first lieutenant caused shot to be tied to the feet, and, having read the funeral service, launched the body overboard from the gangway, as the ship lay at anchor.

I was walking the deck, in no very happy state of mind, reflecting se- riously on parts of that Bible which for more than two years I had never looked into, when my thoughts were called to the summons which poor Quid had received, and the beauty of the funeral service which I had heard read over him—"I am the resurrection and the life." The moon, which had been obscured, suddenly burst from a cloud, and a cry of horror proceeded from the look-out man on the starboard gangway. I ran to inquire the cause, and found him in such a state of nervous agitation that he could only say,— "Quid—Quid!" and point with his finger into the water.

I looked over the side, and, to my amazement there was the body of Quid,

"All in dreary hammock shrouded,"

perfectly upright, and floating with the head and shoulders above water. A slight undulation of the waves gave it the appearance of nodding its head; while the rays of the moon enabled us to trace the remainder of the body underneath the surface. For a few moments, I felt a horror which I cannot describe, and contemplated the object in awful silence; while my blood ran cold, and I felt a sensation as if my hair was standing on end. I was com- pletely taken by surprise, and thought the body had risen up to warn me; but in a few seconds I regained my presence of mind, and I soon perceived the origin of this reappearance of the corpse. I ordered the cutter to be manned, and, in the meantime, went down to inform the first lieutenant of what had occurred. He laughed, and said, "I suppose the old boy finds salt water not quite so palatable as grog. Tie some more shot to his feet, and bring the old fellow to his moorings again. Tell him, the next time he trips his anchor, not to run on board of us. He had his regular allowance of prayer: I gave him the whole service, and I shall not give him any more." So saying, he went to sleep again.

This apparently singular circumstance is easily accounted for. Bodies decomposing from putridity, generate a quantity of gas, which swells them up to an enormous size, and renders them buoyant. The body of this man was thrown overboard just as decomposition was in progress: the shot made fast to the feet were sufficient to sink it at the time; but in a few hours after were not competent to keep it at the bottom, and it came up to the surface in that perpendicular position which I have described. The current in the bay being at the time either slack or irregular, it floated at the spot whence it had been launched into the water.

The cutter, being manned, was sent with more shot to attach to the body, and sink it. When they attempted to hold it with the boat-hook, it eluded the touch, turning round and round, or bobbing under the water, and coming up again, as if in sport: but accident saved them any further trouble; for the bowman, reproached by the boat's crew for not hooking the body, got angry, and darting the spike of the boat-hook into the abdomen, the pent-up gas escaped with a loud whiz, and the corpse instantly sank like a stone. Many jokes were passed on the occasion; but I was not in humour for joking on serious subjects: and before the watch was out I had made up my mind to go home, and to quit the service, as I found I had no chance of obeying my mother's dying injunctions if I remained where I was.

The next morning I stated my wishes to the captain, not of quitting the service, but of going home in consequence of family arrangements. This was about as necessary as that I should make a pilgrimage to Jerusalem. The captain had been told of the unpleasant news I had received, and having listened to all I had to say, he replied, that if I could make up my mind to remain with him it would be better for me.

"You are now," said he, "accustomed to my ways and do your work well; indeed, I have made honourable mention of you to the Admiralty in my public letter: you know your own business best" (here he was mistaken—he ought not to have parted with me for the reasons which I offered); "but my advice to you is to stay."

I thanked him—but being bent and determined on going home, he acceded to my request; gave me my discharge, and added a very handsome certificate of good conduct, far beyond the usually prescribed form; he also told me that if I chose to return to him he would keep a vacancy for me. I parted with the officers, my messmates, and the ship's company with regret. I had been more than three years with them; and my stormy commencement had settled down into a quiet and peaceful acknowledgment of my supremacy in the berth; my qualities were such as to make me a universal favourite and I was followed down the ship's side with the hearty good wishes of all. I was pulled in the cutter on board of a ship of the line, in which I was ordered to take my passage to England.

CHAPTER IX

How happy could I be with either,
Were t'other dear charmer away!

"BEGGAR'S OPERA."

HELL, they say, is paved with good intentions. If so, it has a much better pavement than it deserves; for the "trail of the serpent is over us all." Then why send to hell the greatest proof of our perfection before the fall, and of weakness subsequent to it? Honest and sincere professions of amendment must carry with them to the Throne of Grace a strong recommendation, even if we are again led astray by the allurements of sense and the snares of the world. At least, our tears of contrition and repentance, our sorrow for the past, and our firm resolves for the future, must have given "joy in heaven," and consequently cannot have been converted into pavement for the infernal regions.

Pleasure and pain, in youth, are, for the most part, transient impressions, whether they arise from possession or loss of worldly enjoyment, or from a sense of having done well or ill in our career. The excitement, though strong, is not durable; and thus it was with me. I had not been more than four days on board the ship of the line in which I took my passage to England, when I felt my spirits buoyant, and my levity almost amounting to delirium. The hours of reflection were at first shortened, and then dismissed entirely. The general mirth of my new shipmates at the thoughts of once more revisiting their dear native land—the anticipation of indulging in the sensual worship of Bacchus and Venus, the constant theme of discourse among the midshipmen; the loud and senseless applause bestowed on the coarsest ribaldry—these all had their share in destroying that religious frame of mind in which I had parted with my first captain, and seemed to awaken me to a sense of the folly I had been guilty of in quitting a ship, where I was not only at the head of my mess, but in a fair way for promotion. I considered that I had acted the part of a madman, and had again begun to renew my career of sin and of folly, a little, and but a little, sobered by the recent event.

We arrived in England after the usual passage from the Rock. I consented to pass two days at Portsmouth, with my new companions, to revisit our old haunts, and to commit those excesses which fools and knaves applauded and partook of, at my expense, leaving me full leisure to repent, after we separated. I, however, did muster resolution enough to pack my trunk; and, after an extravagant supper at the Fountain, retired to bed intoxicated, and the next morning, with an aching head, threw myself into the coach and drove off for London. A day of much hilarity is generally succeeded by one of depression. This is fair and natural; we draw too largely on our stock, and squander our enjoyment like our money, leaving us the next day with low spirits and a lower purse.

A stupid dejection succeeded the boisterous mirth of the overnight. I slumbered in a corner of the coach till about one o'clock, when we reached Godalming, where I alighted, took a slight refreshment, and resumed my seat. As we drove along, I had more leisure, and was in a fitter frame of mind to review my past conduct since I had quitted my ship at Gibraltar. My self-examination, as usual, produced no satisfactory results. I perceived that the example of bad company had swept away every trace of good resolution which I had made on the death of my mother. I saw, with grief, that I had no dependence on myself; I had forgotten all my good intentions, and the firm vows of amendment with which I had bound myself; and had yielded to the first temptation which came in my way.

In vain did I call up every black and threatening cloud of domestic sorrow, which was to meet me on my return home—the dreadful vacuum occasioned by my mother's death—the grief of my father—my brother and

my sisters in deep mourning, and the couch on which I had left the best of
parents, when I turned away my thoughtless head from her in the anguish
of her grief. I renewed my promise of amendment, and felt some secret
consolation in doing so.

When I arrived at my father's door, the servant who let me in, greeted
me with a loud and hearty welcome. I ran into the drawing-room, where I
found that my brother and sisters had a party of children to spend the
evening with them. They were dancing to the music of a piano, played on
by my aunt, while my father sat in his arm-chair, in high good-humour.

This was a very different scene from what I had expected. I was prepared for a sentimental and affecting meeting; and my feelings were all
worked up to their full bearing for the occasion. Judge, then, of the sudden
revulsion in my mind, when I found mirth and good-humour where I
expected tears and lamentations. It had escaped my recollection, that although the death of my mother was an event new to me, it had happened
six months before I had heard of it; and, consequently, with them grief
had given way to time. I was astonished at their apparent want of feeling;
while they gazed with surprise at the sight of me, and the symbols of woe
displayed in my equipment.

My father welcomed me with surprise; asked where my ship was, and
what had brought her home. The fact was, that in my sudden determination
to return to England, I had spared myself the trouble of writing to make
known my intentions; and, indeed, if I had written, I should have arrived as
soon as my letter, unless (which I ought to have done) I had written on my
arrival at Portsmouth, instead of throwing away my time in the very worst
species of dissipation. Unable, therefore, in the presence of many witnesses,
to give my father that explanation which he had a right to expect, I suffered
greatly for a time in his opinion. He very naturally supposed that some disgraceful conduct on my part was the cause of my sudden return. His brow
became clouded and his mind seemed occupied with deep reflection.

This behaviour of my father, together with the continued noisy mirth of
my brother and sisters, gave me considerable pain. I felt as if, in the sad
news of my mother's death, I had over-acted my part in the feeling I had
shown, and the sacrifice I had made in quitting my ship. On explaining to
my father, in private, the motives of my conduct, I was not successful. He
could not believe that my mother's death was the sole cause of my return

to England. I stood many firm and angry interrogations as to the possible good which could accrue to me by quitting my ship. I showed him the captain's handsome certificate, which only mortified him the more. In vain did I plead my excess of feeling. He replied with an argument that I feel to have been unanswerable—that I had quitted my ship when on the very pinnacle of favour, and in the road to fortune. "And what," said he, "is to become of the navy and the country, if every officer is to return home when he receives the news of the death of a relation?"

In proportion as my father's arguments carried conviction, they did away, at the same time, all the good impressions of my mother's dying injunction. If her death was a matter of so little importance, her last words were equally so; and from that moment I ceased to think of either. My father's treatment of me was now very different from what it had ever been during my mother's lifetime. My requests were harshly refused, and I was lectured more as a child than as a lad of *eighteen,* who had seen much of the world.

Coldness on his part was met by a spirit of resistance on mine. Pride came in to my assistance. A dispute arose one evening, at the finale of which I gave him to understand that if I could not live quietly under his roof I would quit it. He calmly recommended me to do so, little supposing that I should have taken his advice. I left the room, banging the door after me, packed up a few changes of linen, and took my departure, unperceived by any one, with my bundle on my shoulder, and about sixteen shillings in my pocket.

Here was a great mismanagement on the part of my father, and still greater on mine. He was anxious to get me afloat again, and I had no sort of objection to going; but his impatience and my pride spoiled all. Reflection soon came to me, but came too late. Night was fast approaching: I had no house over my head, and my exchequer was in no very flourishing condition.

I had walked six miles from my father's house, when I began to tire. It became dark, and I had no fixed plan. A gentleman's carriage came by; I took up a position in the rear of it, and had ridden four miles, when, as the carriage was slowly dragging up a hill, I was discovered by the parties inside; and the postilion, who had dismounted and been informed of it, saluted me with two or three smart cuts of his whip, intimating that I was of no use, but rather an incumbrance which could be dispensed with.

My readers know that I had long since adopted the motto of our northern neighbours, *Nemo me, &c.*; so waiting very quietly till the driver had mounted his horses, at the top of the hill, that he might be more at my mercy, I discharged a stone at his head which caused him to vacate his seat, and fall under his horse's belly. The animals, frightened at his fall, turned short round to the right, or they would have gone over him, and ran furiously down the hill. The post-boy, recovering his legs, followed his horses without bestowing a thought on the author of the mischief; and I made all the haste I could in the opposite direction, perfectly indifferent as to the fate of the parties inside of the carriage, for I still smarted with the blows I had received.

"Fools and unkind," muttered I, looking back, as they disappeared at the bottom of the hill, with frightful velocity, "you are rightly served. I was a trespasser, 'tis true, but a civil request would have had all the effect you required—that of inducing me to get down; but a whip to me—" And with my blood still boiling at the recollection, I hastily pursued my journey.

In a few minutes I reached the little town of ———, the lights of which were visible at the time the horses had turned down the hill and run away. Entering the first inn I came to, I found the large room below occupied by a set of strolling players, who had just returned from a successful performance of "Romeo and Juliet;" and, from the excitement among them, it was easy to perceive that that success had been fully equal to their expectations. The were fourteen in number, seated round a table, not indifferently covered with the good things of this life; they were clad in theatrical costume, which, with the rapid circulation of the bottle, gave the whole scene an air of romantic freedom, calculated to interest the mind of a thoughtless half-pay midshipman.

Being hungry after my walk, I determined to join the party at supper, which, being a *table d'hôte* was easily effected. One of the actresses, a sweet little, well-proportioned creature, with large black eyes, was receiving, with apparent indifference, the compliments of the better sort of bumpkins and young farmers of the neighbourhood. In her momentary and occasional smiles, she discovered a beautiful set of small, white teeth; but when she resumed her pensive attitude, I was sensible of an enchanting air of melancholy, which deeply interested me in favour of this poor girl, who was evidently in a lower situation in life than that for which she had been educated. The person who sat nearest to her vacated his seat as soon as he found his attentions were thrown away. I instantly took possession of the place, and, observing the greatest respect, entered at once into conversation with her.

Whether she was pleased with my address and language, as being superior to what she was usually compelled to listen to, or whether she was flattered by my assiduous attention, I know not; but she gradually unbent, and became more animated; showing great natural talent and a highly cultivated mind; so that I was every moment more astonished to find her in such a situation.

Our conversation had lasted a considerable time; and I had just made a remark to which she had not replied, apparently struggling with concealed emotion, when we were interrupted by a carriage driving up to the door, and cries of "Help! help!" I instantly quitted the side of my new acquaintance, and flew to answer the signal of distress.

A gentleman in the carriage was supporting a young lady in his arms, to all appearance lifeless. With my assistance, she was speedily removed into the house, and conveyed to a bedroom. A surgeon was sent for, but none was to be had; the only practitioner of the town being at that moment gone to attend one of those cases which, according to Mr Malthus, are much too frequent for the good of the country. I discovered that the carriage had been overturned, and that the young lady had been insensible ever since.

There was no time to be lost; I knew that immediate bleeding was absolutely necessary. I had acquired thus much of surgical knowledge in the course of my professional duties. I stated my opinion to the gentleman; and although my practice had been very slight, offered my services to perform the operation. This offer was accepted with thanks by the grateful father, for such I found he was. With my sharp penknife I opened a vein in one of the whitest arms I ever beheld. After a few moments, chafing, the blood flowed more freely; the pulse indicated returning animation; a pair of large blue eyes opened suddenly upon me like a masked battery; and so alarmingly susceptible was I of the tender passion, that I quite forgot the little actress whom I had left at the supper-table, and who, a few minutes before, had occupied my whole thoughts and attention.

Having succeeded in restoring the fair patient to consciousness, I prescribed a warm bed, some tea, and careful watching. My orders were punctually obeyed; I then quitted the apartment of my patient, and began to ruminate over the hurried and singular events of the day.

I had scarcely had time to decide in my own mind on the respective merits of my two rival beauties when the surgeon arrived; and, being ushered into the sick-room declared that the patient had been treated with skill, and that in all probability she owed her life to my presence of mind. "But, give me leave to ask," said the doctor addressing the father, "how the accident happened?" The gentleman replied that a scoundrel having got up behind the carriage, had been flogged off by the postilion; and, in revenge, had thrown a stone, which knocked the driver off his horse: they took fright, turned round, and ran away down the hill towards their own stables; and after running five miles, upset the carriage against a post, "by which accident," said he, "my poor daughter was nearly killed."

"What a villain!" said the doctor.

"Villain, indeed," echoed I; and so I felt I was. I turned sick at the thought of what my ungoverned passion had done; and my regret was not a little increased by the charms of my lovely victim; but I soon recovered from the shock, particularly when I saw that no suspicion attached to me. I therefore received the praises of the father and the doctor with a becoming modest diffidence; and, with a hearty shake of the hand from the grateful parent, was wished a good night and retired to my bed.

As I stood before the looking-glass, laying my watch and exhausted purse on the dressing-table, and leisurely untying my cravat, I could not forbear a glance of approbation at what I thought a very handsome and a very impudent face: I soliloquised on the events of the day, and, as usual, found the summing-up very much against me. "This, then sir," said I, "is your road to repentance and reform. You insult your father; quit his house; get up, like a vagabond, behind a gentleman's carriage; are flogged off, break the ribs of an honest man, who has a wife and family to support out of his hard earnings—are the occasion of a carriage being overturned, and very nearly cause the death of an amiable girl! And all this mischief in the short space of six hours, not to say a word of your intentions towards the little actress, which I presume are none of the most honourable. Where is all this to end?"

"At the gallows," said I, in reply to myself,—"the more probably, too, as my finances have no means of improvement, except by a miracle or highway robbery. I am in love with two girls, and have only two clean shirts; consequently there is no proportion between the demand and the supply."

With this medley of reflections I fell asleep. I was awoke early by the swallows twittering at the windows; and the first question which was agitated in my brain was what account I should give of myself to the father of the young lady, when interrogated by him, as I most certainly should be. I had my choice between truth and falsehood: the latter (such is the force of habit), I think, carried it hollow; but I determined to leave that point to the spur of the moment, and act according to circumstances.

My meditations were interrupted by the chambermaid, who, tapping at my door, said she came to tell me "that the gentleman that *belonged* to the young lady that I was so kind to, was waiting breakfast for me."

The thought of sitting at table with the dear creature whose brains I had so nearly spilled upon the road the night before quite overcame me; and leaving the fabric of my history to chance or to inspiration, I darted from my bedroom to the parlour, where the stranger awaited me. He received me with great cordiality, again expressed his obligations, and informed me that his name was Somerville, of ———.

I had some faint recollection of having heard the name mentioned by my father, and was endeavouring to recall to mind on what occasion, when Mr Somerville interrupted me by saying, that he hoped he should have the pleasure of knowing the name of the young gentleman who had conferred such an obligation upon him. I answered that my name was Mildmay; for I had no time to tell a lie.

"I should be happy to think," said he, "that you were the son of my old friend and school-fellow, Mr Mildmay of ———; but that cannot well be," said he, "for he had only two sons—one at college, the other as brave a sailor as ever lived, and now in the Mediterranean: but perhaps you are some relation of his?"

He had just concluded this speech, and before I had time to reply to it, the door opened and Miss Somerville entered. We have all heard a great deal about "love a first sight;" but I contend that the man who would not at the very first glimpse of Emily Somerville, have fallen desperately in love with her, could have had neither heart nor soul. If I thought her lovely when she lay in a state of insensibility, what did I think of her when her form had assumed its wonted animation, and her cheeks their natural colour? To describe a perfect beauty never was my forte. I can only say, that Miss Somerville, as far as I am a judge, united in her person all the component parts of the finest specimen of her sex in England; and these were joined in such harmony by the skilful hand of Nature, that I was ready to kneel down and adore her.

As she extended her white hand to me, and thanked me for my kindness, I was so taken aback with the sudden appearance and address of this beautiful vision, that I knew not what to say. I stammered out something, but have no recollection whether it was French or English. I lost my presence of mind, and the blushes of conscious guilt on my face at that moment, might have been mistaken for those of unsophisticated innocence. That these external demonstrations are often confounded, and that such was the case on the present occasion, there can be no doubt. My embarrassment was ascribed to that modesty ever attendant on real worth.

It has been said that true merit blushes at being discovered; but I have lived to see merit that could not blush, and the wane of it that could, while the latter has marched off with all the honours due to the former. The blush that burned on my cheek, at that moment, would have gone far to have condemned a criminal at the Old Bailey; but in the countenance of a handsome young man was received as the unfailing marks of "a pure ingenuous soul."

I had been too long at school to be ashamed of wearing laurels I had never won; and, having often received a flogging which I did not deserve, I thought myself equally well entitled to any advantages which the chances of war might throw in my way; so having set my tender conscience at rest, I sat myself down between my new mistress and her father, and made a most delightful breakfast. Miss Somerville, although declared out of danger by the doctor, was still languid, but able to continue her journey; and as they had not many miles further to go, Mr Somerville proposed a delay of an hour or two.

Breakfast ended, he quitted the room to arrange for their departure, and I found myself *tête-à-tête* with the young lady. During this short absence, I found out that she was an only daughter, and that her mother was dead; she again introduced the subject of my family name, and I found also that before Mrs Somerville's death, my father had been on terms of great intimacy with Emily's parents. I had not replied to Mr Somerville's question. A similar one was now asked by his daughter; and so closely was I interrogated by her coral lips and searching blue eyes, that I could not tell a lie. It would have been a horrid aggravation of guilt, so I honestly owned that I was the son of her father's friend, Mr Mildmay.

"Good heaven!" said she, "why had you not told my father so?"

"Because I must have said a great deal more; besides," added I, making her my confidante. "I am the midshipman whom Mr Somerville supposes to be in the Mediterranean, and I ran away from my father's house last night."

Although I was as concise as possible in my story, I had not finished before Mr Somerville came in.

"Oh, papa," said his daughter, "this young gentleman is Frank Mildmay, after all."

I gave her a reproachful glance for having betrayed my secret; her father was astonished—she looked confused, and so did I.

Nothing now remained for me but an open and candid confession, taking especial care, however, to conceal the part I had acted in throwing the stone. Mr Somerville reproved me very sharply, which I thought was taking a great liberty, but he softened it down by adding, "If you knew how dear the interests of your family are to me, you would not be surprised at my assuming the tone of a parent." I looked at Emily, and pocketed the affront.

"And, Frank," pursued he, "when I tell you, that, although the distance between your father's property and mine has in some measure interrupted our long intimacy, I have been watching your career in the service with interest, you will, perhaps, take my advice, and return home. Do not let me have to regret that one to whom I am under such obligations should be too proud to acknowledge a fault. I admire a high spirit in a good cause: but towards a parent it can never be justified. It may be unpleasant to you; but I will prepare the way by writing to your father: and do you stay here till you hear from me. I should wish for the pleasure of your company at ——— Hall; but your father has prior claims; and I hardly need tell you, that once restored and reconciled to him, I expect as long a visit as you can afford to pay me. Think on what I have said; and, in the meantime, as I daresay your finances are not very flourishing"—(thinks I, you are a witch!)—"allow me to leave this ten-pound note in your hands." This part of his request was much more readily complied with than the other.

He left the room, as he said, to pay the bill; but I believe it was to give his fair daughter an opportunity of trying the effect of her eloquence on my proud spirit, which gave no great promise of concession. A few minutes with *her*, did more than both the fathers could have effected, the most powerful motive to submission being the certainty that I could not visit at her father's house until a reconciliation had taken place between me and mine. I therefore told her that, at her solicitation, I would submit to any liberal terms.

This being agreed to, her father observed that the carriage was at the door, shook hands with me, and led his lovely daughter away, whose last nod and parting look confirmed all my good resolutions.

Reader, whatever you may think of the trifling incidents of the last twenty-four hours, you will find that they involved consequences of vast importance to the writer of this memoir. Pride induced me to quit my father's house; revenge stimulated me to an act which brought the heroine of this story on the stage, for such will Emily Somerville prove to be. But, alas! by what fatal infatuation was Mr Somerville induced to leave me my own master at an inn, with ten pounds in my pocket, instead of taking me with him to his own residence, and keeping me till he had heard from my father? The wisest men often err in points which at first appear of trivial importance, but which prove in the sequel to have been fraught with evil.

Left to myself, I ruminated for some time on what had occurred; and the beautiful Emily Somerville having vanished from my sight, I recollected the little fascinating actress from whom I had so suddenly parted on the preceding night; still I must say, that I was so much occupied with the charms of her successor, that I sought the society of the youthful Melpomene more with a view to beguile the time, than from any serious prepossession.

I found her in the large room, where they were all assembled. She received me as a friend, and evinced a partiality which flattered my vanity. In three days, I received a letter from Mr Somerville, inclosing one from my father, whose only request was, that I would return home, and meet him as if nothing unpleasant had occurred. This I determined to do; but I had now been so long in the company of Eugenia (for that was the actress's name), that I could not very easily part with her. In fact, I was desperately in love, after my fashion; and though perhaps I could not with truth say the same of her, yet that she was partial to my company was evident. I had obtained from her the history of her life, which, in the following chapter, I shall give in her own words.

CHAPTER X

*She is virtuous, though bred behind the scenes: and,
whatever pleasure she may feel in seeing herself applauded on
the stage, she would much rather pass for a modest girl, than
for a good actress.*

GIL BLAS

"MY father," said Eugenia, "was at the head of this company of strolling players; my mother was a young lady of respectable family, at a boarding-school. She took a fancy to my father in the character of 'Rolla'; and, being of course deservedly forsaken by her friends became a prima donna. I was the only fruits of this connection, and the only solace of my mother in her affliction; for she bitterly repented the rash step she had taken.

"At five years old, my father proposed that I should take the character of Cupid, in the opera of Telemaque. To this my mother strongly objected, declaring that I never should go upon the stage; and this created a disunion which was daily embittered by my father's unkind treatment both of my mother and myself. I never left her side for fear of a kick, which I was sure to receive when I had not her protection. She employed all her spare time in my instruction, and, notwithstanding the folly she had been guilty of, she was fully competent to the task.

"When I was seven years old, a relation of my mother died, and bequeathed fifteen thousand pounds, to be equally divided between her and her two sisters, securing my mother's portion in such a manner as to prevent my father having any control over it. As soon as my mother obtained this information, she quitted my father, who was too prudent to spend either his time or his money in pursuit of her. Had he been aware of her sudden change of fortune, he might have acted differently.

"We arrived in London, took possession of the property, which was all in the funds; and then, fearing my father might gain information of her wealth, my mother set off for France, taking me with her. There I passed the happiest days of my life; my mother spared no pains, and went to considerable expense in my education. The best masters were provided for me in singing, dancing, and music; and so much did I profit by their instruction, that I was very soon considered a pretty specimen of my countrywomen, and much noticed accordingly.

"From France we went to Italy, where we remained two years, and where my vocal education was completed. My poor mother lived all this time on the principal of her fortune, concluding it would last for ever. At last she was taken ill of a fever, and died. This was about a year ago, when I was only sixteen. Delirious many days before her death, she could give me no instructions as to my future conduct, or where to apply for resources. I happened, however, to know her banker in London, and wrote to him immediately; in answer, he informed me that a balance of forty pounds was all that remained in his hands.

"I believe he cheated me, but I could not help it. My spirits were not depressed at this news; I sold all the furniture; paid the little debts to the tradespeople, and, with nine pounds in my pocket, took my place in the diligence, and set off for London, where I arrived without accident. I read in the newspaper, at the inn, that a provincial company was in want of a young actress for genteel comedy. My mother's original passion for the stage had never left her; and, during our stay in France, we often amused ourselves with *la petite comédie,* in which I always took a part.

"Without resources, I thought a precarious mode of obtaining a livelihood was better than a vicious one, and determined to try my fortune on the stage: so I ordered a hack, and drove to the office indicated. I felt a degree of comfort, when I discovered that my father was the advertising manager, although I was certain he would never recognise me. I was engaged by the agent, the bargain was approved of, and in a day or two after, was ordered to a country town, some miles from the metropolis.

"I arrived; my father did not know me, nor did I wish that he should, as I did not intend to remain long in the company. In short, I aspired to the London boards; but aware that I wanted practice, without which it would have been useless to have offered myself, I accepted this situation without delay, and applied with great assiduity to the study of my profession. My father, I found, had married again; and my joining the company added nothing to his domestic harmony, my stepmother becoming immoderately jealous of me; but I took good care to keep my own secret, and never exposed myself for one moment to any suspicion of my character, which hitherto, thank Heaven! has been pure, though I am exposed to a thousand temptations, and beset by the actors to become the wife of one, or the mistress of another.

"Among those who proposed the latter, was my honoured father, to whom, on that account, I was one day on the point of revealing the secret of my birth, as the only means of saving myself from his importunities. He was, at last, taken ill, and died, only three months ago, not before I had completed my engagements, and obtained an increased salary of one guinea and a half per week. It is my intention to quit the company at the expiration of my present term, which will take place in two months, for I am miserable here, although I am quite at a loss to know what will be my future destination."

In return for her confidence, I imparted as much of my history as I thought it necessary for her to know. I became deeply fascinated—I forgot Miss Somerville, and answered my father's letter respectfully and kindly. He informed me that he had procured my name to be entered on the books of the guard-ship, at Spithead: but, that I might gain time to loiter by the side of Eugenia, I begged his permission to join my ship without returning home, alleging as a reason, that delay would soften down any asperity of feeling occasioned by the late fracas. This in his answer he agreed to, enclosing a handsome remittance; and the same post brought a pressing invitation from Mr Somerville to come to ——— Hall.

My little actress informed me that the company would set out in two days for the neighbourhood of Portsmouth; and, as I found that they would be more than a fortnight in travelling, I determined to accept the invitation, and quit her for the present. I had been more than a week in her society. At parting, I professed my admiration and love. Silence and a starting tear were her only acknowledgment. I saw that she was not displeased; and I left her with joyful anticipations.

But what did I anticipate, as I rolled heedlessly along in the chaise to ——— Hall? Sensual gratification at the expense of a poor defenceless orphan, whose future life would be clouded with misery. I could see my wickedness, and moralise upon it; but the devil was triumphant within me, and I consoled myself with the vulgar adage, "Needs must when the devil drives." With this, I dismissed the subject to think of Emily, whose residence was now in sight.

I arrived at ——— Hall, was kindly received and welcomed by both father and daughter; but on this visit, I must not dwell. When I reflect on it, I hate myself and human nature! Could I be trusted? yet I inspired unbounded confidence. Was I not as vicious as one of my age could be? Yet I made them believe I was almost perfection. Did I deserve to be happy? Yet I was so, and more so than I had ever been before or ever have been since. I was like the serpent in Eden, though without his vile intentions. Beauty and virtue united to keep my passions in subjection. When they had nothing to feed on, they concealed themselves in the inmost recesses of my bosom.

Had I remained always with Emily, I should have been reclaimed; but when I quitted her, I lost all my good feelings and good resolutions, not, however, before the bright image of virtue had lighted up in my bosom a holy flame which has never been entirely extinguished. Occasionally dimmed, it has afterwards burnt up with renewed brightness; and, as a beacon-light, has often guided me through perils that might have overwhelmed me.

Compelled at last to quit this earthly paradise, I told her, at parting, that I loved her, adored her; and to prove that I was in earnest, and that she believed me, I obtained a lock of her hair. When I left ——— Hall, it was my intention to have joined my ship, as I had agreed with my father; but the temptation to follow up my success with the fair and unfortunate Eugenia was too strong to be resisted; at least I thought so, and therefore hardly made an effort to conquer it. True I did, *pro forma,* make my appearance on board the guard-ship, had my name entered on the books, that I might not lose my time of servitude, and that I might also deceive my father. All this being duly accomplished, I obtained leave of absence from my first lieutenant, an old acquaintance, who, in a ship crowded with supernumerary midshipmen, was but too happy in getting rid of me and my chest.

I hastened to the rendezvous, and found the company in full activity. Eugenia, when we parted, expressed a wish that our acquaintance might not be renewed. She feared for her own character as well as mine, and very sensibly and feelingly observed that my professional prospects might be blasted; but, having made up my mind, I had an answer for all her objections. I presented myself to the manager, and requested to be admitted into the company.

Having taken this step, Eugenia saw that my attachment was not to be overcome; that I was willing to make any sacrifice for her. I was accepted; my salary was fixed at one guinea per week, with seven shillings extra for playing the flute. I was indebted for my ready admission into this society to my voice: the manager wanted a first singer. My talent in this science was much admired. I signed my agreement the same evening for two months; and, being presented in due form to my brethren of the buskin, joined the supper-table, where there was more of abundance than of delicacies. I sat by Eugenia, whose decided preference for me excited the jealousy of my new associates. I measured them all with my eye, and calculated that, with fair play, I was the best man among them.

The play-bills announced the tragedy of "Romeo and Juliet." I was to be the hero, and four days were allowed me to prepare myself. The whole of that time was passed in the company of Eugenia, who, while she gave me unequivocal proofs of attachment, admitted of no freedom. The day of re-hearsal arrived, I was found perfect, and loudly applauded by the company. Six o'clock came, the curtain rose, and sixteen tallow candles displayed my person to an audience of about one hundred people.

No one who has not been in the situation can form any idea of the nervous feeling of a débutant on such an occasion. The troupe, with the exception of Eugenia, was of a description of persons whom I despise, and the audience mostly clodhoppers, who could scarcely read or write; yet I was abashed, and acquitted myself badly, until the balcony scene, when I became enlivened and invigorated by the presence and smiles of my mistress. In the art of love-making I was at home, particularly with the Juliet of that night. I entered at once into the spirit of the great dramatist, and the curtain dropped amidst thunders of applause. My name was announced for a repetition of the play, and I was dragged forward before the curtain, to thank the grocers, tallow-chandlers, cheese-mongers, and ploughmen for the great honour they had done me. Heavens! how I felt the degradation; but it was too late.

The natural result of this constant intercourse with Eugenia may easily be anticipated. I do not attempt to extenuate my fault—it was inexcusable, and has brought its punishment; but for poor, forlorn Eugenia I plead; her virtue fell before my importunity and my personal appearance. She fell a victim to those unhappy circumstances of which I basely took the advantage.

Two months I had lived with her, as man and wife; forgot my family, profession, and even Emily. I was now upon the ship's books; and though no one knew anything of me, my father was ignorant of my absence from the ship—everything was sacrificed to Eugenia. I acted with her, strolled the fields, and vowed volumes of stuff about constancy. When we played, we filled the house; and some of the more respectable townspeople offered to introduce us to the London boards, but this we both declined. We cared for nothing but the society of each other.

And now that time has cooled the youthful ardour that carried me away let me do justice to this unfortunate girl. She was the most natural, unaffected and gifted person I ever met with. Boundless wit, enchanting liveliness, a strong mind, and self-devotion towards me, the first, and, I firmly believe, the only object she ever loved; and her love for me ceased only with her life. Her faults, though not to be defended, may be palliated and deplored, because they were the defects of education. Her infant days were passed in scenes of domestic strife, profligacy, and penury; her maturer years, under the guidance of a weak mother, were employed in polishing, not strengthening, the edifice of her understanding, and the external ornaments only served to accelerate the fall of the fabric, and to increase the calamity.

Bred up in France, and almost in the fervour of the Revolution, she had imbibed some of its libertine opinions; among others, that marriage was a civil contract, and if entered into at all, might be broken at the pleasure of either party. This idea was strengthened and confirmed in her by the instances she had seen of matrimonial discord, particularly in her own family. When two people, who fancied they loved, had bound themselves by an indissoluble knot, they felt from that time the irksomeness of restraint, which they would never have felt if they had possessed the power of separation; and would have lived happily together if they had not been compelled to do it. "How long you, my dear Frank," said Eugenia to me one day, "may continue to love me, I know not; but the moment you cease to love me, it were better that we parted."

These were certainly the sentiments of an enthusiast; but Eugenia lived long enough to acknowledge her error, and to bewail its fatal effects on her peace of mind.

I was awoke from this dream of happiness by a curious incident. I thought it disastrous at the time, but am now convinced that it was fraught with good, since it brought me back to my profession, recalled me to a sense of duty, and showed me the full extent of my disgraceful situation. My father, it appears, was still ignorant of my absence from my ship, and had come down, without my knowledge, on a visit to a friend in the neighbourhood. Hearing of "the interesting young man" who had acquired so much credit in the character of Apollo, as well as of Romeo, he was persuaded to see the performance.

I was in the act of singing "Pray Goody" when my eyes suddenly met those of my papa, who was staring like the head of Gorgon; and though his gaze did not turn me to stone, it turned me sick. I was stupified, forgot my part, ran off, and left the manager and the music to make the best of it. My father, who could hardly believe his eyes, was convinced when he saw my confusion. I ran into the dressing-room, where, before I had time to divest myself of Apollo's crown and petticoat, I was accosted by my enraged parent, and it is quite impossible for me to describe (taking my costume into consideration) how very much like a fool I looked.

My father sternly demanded how long I had been thus honourably employed. This was a question which I had anticipated, and, therefore, very readily replied, "Only two or three days;" that I had left Portsmouth for what we called "a lark," and I thought it very amusing.

"Very amusing, indeed, sir," said my father; "and pray, may I venture to inquire, without the fear of having a lie told me, how long this 'lark,' as you call it, is to continue?"

"Oh, to-morrow," said I, "my leave expires, and then I must return to my ship."

"Allow me the honour of keeping your company," said my father; "and I shall beg your captain to impose some little restraint as to time and distance on your future excursions."

Then rising in his tone, he added, "I am ashamed of you, sir; the son of a gentleman is not likely to reap any advantage from the society of strolling vagabonds and prostitutes. I had reason to think, by your last letters from Portsmouth, that you were very differently employed."

To this very sensible and parental reproof I answered, with a demure and innocent countenance (for I soon regained my presence of mind) that I did not think there had been any harm in doing that which most of the of officers of the navy did at one time or another (an assertion, by-the-by, much too general); that we often got up plays on board of ship, and that I wanted to practise.

"Practise, then with your equals," said my father, "not in company with rogues and street-walkers."

I felt that the latter name was meant for Eugenia, and was very indignant; but fortunately kept all my anger within board, and, knowing I was "all in the wrong," allowed my father to fire away without returning a shot. He concluded his lecture by commanding me to call upon him the next morning, at ten o'clock, and left me to change my dress, and to regain my good humour. I need not add that I did not return to the stage that night, but left the manager to make his peace with the audience in any way he thought proper.

When I informed Eugenia of the evening's adventure, she was inconsolable: to comfort her, I offered to give up my family and my profession, and live with her. At these words, Eugenia suddenly recollected herself. "Frank," said she, "all that has happened is right. We are both wrong. I felt that I was too happy, and shut my eyes to the danger I dared not face. Your father is a man of sense; his object is to reclaim you from inevitable ruin. As for me, if he knew of our connection, he could only despise me. He sees his son living with strolling players; and it is his duty to cut the chain, no matter by what means. You have an honourable and distinguished career marked out for you; I will never be an obstacle to your father's just ambition or your prosperity. I did hope for a happier destiny; but love blinded my eyes: I am now undeceived. If your father cannot respect me, he shall at least admire the resolution of the unhappy Eugenia. I have tenderly loved you, my dearest Frank, and never have loved any other, nor ever shall, but part we must: Heaven only knows for how long a time. I am ready to make every sacrifice to your fame and character—the only proof I can give of my unbounded love for you."

I embraced her as she uttered these words; and we spent a great part of the night in making preparations for my departure, arrangements for our future correspondence, and, if possible, for our future meetings. I left her early on the following morning; and with a heavy, I had almost said, a broken heart, appeared before my father. He was, no doubt, aware of my attachment and the violence of my passions, and prudently endeavoured to soothe them. He received me affectionately, did not renew the subject of the preceding night, and we became very good friends.

In tearing myself away from Eugenia, I found the truth of the French adage, *"Ce n'est que la première pas qui coûte;"* my heart grew lighter as I increased my distance from her. My father, to detach my mind still more from the unfortunate subject, spoke much of family affairs, of my brother and sisters, and lastly named Mr Somerville and Emily: here he touched on the right chord. The remembrance of Emily revived the expiring embers of virtue, and the recollection of the pure and perfect mistress of ——— Hall, for a time, dismissed the unhappy Eugenia from my mind. I told my father that I would engage never to disgrace him or myself any more, if he would promise not to name my late folly to Mr Somerville or his daughter.

"That," said my father, "I promise most readily; and with the greater pleasure, since I see, in your request, the strongest proof of the sense of your error."

This conversation passed on our road to Portsmouth, where we had no sooner arrived than my father, who was acquainted with the port-admiral, left me at the "George," while he crossed the street to call on him. The result of this interview was that I should be sent out immediately in some sea-going ship with a "tight captain."

There was one of this description just about to sail for Basque Roads; and, at the admiral's particular request, I was received on board as a super-numerary, there being no vacancies in the ship. My father, who by this time was wide awake to all my wiles, saw me on board; and then flattering him-self that I was in safe custody, took his leave and returned to the shore. I very soon found that I was under an embargo, and was not on any account to be allowed leave of absence.

This was pretty nearly what I expected; but I had my own resources. I had now learned to laugh at trifles, and I cared little about this decided step which his prudence induced him to take.

CHAPTER XI

"Our boat has one sail,
And the helmsman is pale;
A bold pilot, I trow
Who should follow us now,"
Shouted he.
As he spoke bolts of death
Speck'd their path o'er the sea.
"And fear'st thou, and fear'st thou?
And see'st thou, and hear'st thou?
And drive we not free
O'er the terrible sea,
I and thou?"

SHELLEY

THE reader may think I was over fastidious when I inform him that I cannot describe the disgust I felt at the licentious impurity of manners which I found in the midshipmen's berth; for although my connection with Eugenia was not sanctioned by religion or morality, it was in other respects pure, disinterested, and, if I may use the expression, patriarchal, since it was unsullied by inconstancy, gross language, or drunkenness. Vicious I was, and I own it to my shame; but at least my vice was refined by Eugenia, who had no fault but one.

As soon as I had settled myself in my new abode, with all the comfort that circumstances would permit, I wrote a long letter to Eugenia, in which I gave an exact account of all that had passed since our separation; I begged her to come down to Portsmouth and see me; told her to go to the "Star and Garter," as the house nearest the waterside, and consequently where I should be the soonest out of sight after I had landed. Her answer informed me that she should be there on the following day.

The only difficulty now was to get on shore. No eloquence of mine, I was sure, would induce the first lieutenant to relax his Cerberus-like guard over me. I tried the experiment, however; begged very hard "to be allowed to go on shore to procure certain articles absolutely necessary to my comfort."

"No, no," said Mr Talbot, "I am too old a hand to be caught that way.

I have my orders, and I would not let my father go on shore, if the captain ordered me to keep him on board; and I tell you, in perfect good humour, that out of this ship you do not go, unless you swim on shore, and that I do not think you will attempt. Here," continued he, "to prove to you there is no ill-will on my part, here is the captain's note."

It was short, sweet, and complimentary, as it related to myself, and was as follows:—

"Keep that d——d young scamp, Mildmay, on board."

"Will you allow me, then," said I, folding up the note, and returning it to him without any comment, "will you allow me to go on shore under the charge of the sergeant of marines?"

"That," said he, "would be just as much an infringement of my orders as letting you go by yourself. You cannot go on shore, sir."

These last words he uttered in a very peremptory manner, and, quitting the deck, left me to my own reflections and my own resources.

Intercourse by letter between Eugenia and myself was perfectly easy; but that was not all I wanted. I had promised to meet her at nine o'clock in the evening. It was now sunset; the boats were all hoisted up; no shore boat was near, and there was no mode of conveyance but *à la nage,* which Mr Talbot himself had suggested only as proving its utter impracticability; but he did not know me half so well at the time as he did afterwards.

The ship lay two miles from the shore, the wind was from the south-west, and the tide moving to the eastward; so that, with wind and tide both in my favour, I calculated on fetching South Sea Castle. After dark I took my station in the fore-channels. It was the 20th of March, and very cold. I undressed myself, made all my clothes up into a very tight bundle, and fastened them on my hat, which retained its proper position; then, lowering myself very gently into the water, like another Leander I struck out to gain the arms of my Hero.

Before I had got twenty yards from the ship, I was perceived by the sentinel, who, naturally supposing I was a pressed man endeavouring to escape, hailed me to come back. Not being obeyed, the officer of the watch ordered him to fire at me. A ball whizzed over my head, and struck the water between my hands. A dozen more followed, all of them tolerably well directed; but I struck out, and the friendly shades of night, and increasing distance from the ship, soon protected me. A waterman, seeing the flashes and hearing the reports of the muskets, concluded that he might chance to pick up a fare. He pulled towards me, I hailed him, and he took me in, before I had got half a quarter of a mile from the ship.

"I doubt whether you would ever have fetched the shore on that tack, my lad," said the old man. "You left your ship two hours too soon: you would have met the ebb-tide running strong out of the harbour; and the first thing you would have made, if you could have kept up your head above water, would have been the Ower's."

While the old man was pulling and talking, I was shivering and dressing, and made no reply; but begged him to put me on shore on the first part of South Sea Beach he could land at, which he did. I gave him a guinea, and ran, without stopping, into the garrison, and down Point Street to the Star and Garter, where I was received by Eugenia, who, with great presence of mind, called me her "*dear, dear* husband!" in the hearing of the people of the house. My wet clothes attracted her notice. I told her what I had done to obtain an interview with her. She shuddered with horror!—my teeth chattered with cold. A good fire, a hot and not very weak glass of brandy-and-water, together with her tears, smiles, and caresses, soon restored me.—The reader will, no doubt, here recall to mind the less agreeable remedy applied to me when I ducked the usher, and one recommended also by myself in similar cases, as having experienced its good effects: how much more I deserved it on this occasion than the former one, need not be mentioned.

So sweet was this stolen interview, that I vowed I was ready to encounter the same danger on the succeeding night. Our conversation turned on our future prospects; and, as our time was short, we had much to say.

"Frank," said the poor girl, "before we meet again, I shall probably be a mother; and this hope alone alleviates the agony of separation. If I have not you, I shall, at least, be blest with your image. Heaven grant that it may be a boy, to follow the steps of his father, and not a girl, to be as wretched as her mother. You, my dear Frank, are going on distant and dangerous service—dangers increased tenfold by the natural ardour of your mind: we may never meet again, or if we do, the period will be far distant. I ever have been, and ever will be constant to you, till death; but I neither expect, nor will allow of the same declaration on your part. Other scenes, new faces, youthful passions will combine to drive me for a time from your thoughts, and when you shall have attained maturer years, and a rank in the navy equal to your merits and your connections, you will marry in your own sphere of society; all these things I have made up my mind to, as events that must take place. Your person I know I cannot have—but do not, do not discard me from your mind. I shall never be jealous as long as I know you are happy, and still love your unfortunate Eugenia. Your child shall be no burthen to you until it shall have attained an age at which it may be put out in the world: then, I know you will not desert it for the sake of its mother. Dear Frank, my heart is broken; but you are not to blame; and if you were, I would die imploring blessings on your head." Here she wept bitterly.

I tried every means in my power to comfort and encourage this fascinating and extraordinary girl; I forgot neither vows nor promises, which, at the time, I fully intended to perform. I promised her a speedy and I trusted a happy meeting.

"God's will be done," said she, "come what will. And now, my dearest Frank, farewell—never again endanger your life and character for me as you did last night. I have been blest in your society, and even with the prospect of misery before me, cannot regret the past."

I tenderly embraced her, jumped into a wherry, at Point, and desired the waterman to take me on board the *I*——, at Spithead. The first lieutenant was on deck when I came up the side.

"I presume it was you whom we fired at last night?" said he, smiling.

"It was, sir," said I; "absolute necessity compelled me to go on shore, or I should not have taken such an extraordinary mode of conveyance."

"Oh, with all my heart," said the officer; "had you told me you intended to have swum on shore, I should not have prevented you; I took you for one of the pressed men, and directed the marines to fire at you."

"The pressed men are extremely obliged to you," thought I.

"Did you not find it devilish cold?" continued the lieutenant, in a strain of good humour, which I encouraged by my manner of answering.

"Indeed I did, sir," said I.

"And the jollies fired tolerably well, did they?"

"They did, sir; would they had had a *better mark*."

"I understand you," said the lieutenant; "but as you have not served your time, the vacancy would be of no use to you. I must report the affair to the captain, though I do not think he will take any notice of it; he is too fond of enterprise himself to check it in others. Besides, a lady is always a justifiable object, but we hope soon to show you some higher game."

The captain came on board shortly after, and took no notice of my having been absent without leave; he made some remark as he glanced his eye at me, which I afterwards learned was in my favour. In a few days we sailed, and arrived in a few more in Basque Roads. The British fleet was at anchor outside the French ships moored in a line off the Isle d'Aix. The ship I belonged to had an active part in the work going on, and most of us saw more than we chose to speak of; but as much ill-blood was made on that occasion, and one or two very unpleasant courts-martial took place, I shall endeavour to confine myself to my own personal narrative, avoiding anything that may give offence to the parties concerned. Some days were passed in preparing the fire-ships; and on the night of the 11th April, 1809, everything being prepared for the attempt to destroy the enemy's squadron, we began the attack. A more daring one was never made; and if it partly failed of success, no fault could be imputed to those who conducted the enterprise: they did all that man could do.

The night was very dark, and it blew a strong breeze directly in upon the Isle d'Aix, and the enemy's fleet. Two of our frigates had been previously so placed as to serve as beacons to direct the course of the fire-ships. They each displayed a clear and brilliant light; the fire ships were directed to pass between these, after which, their course up to the boom which guarded the anchorage, was clear, and not easily to be mistaken.

I solicited, and obtained permission to go on board one of the explosion vessels that were to precede the fire-ships. They were filled with layers of shells and powder, heaped one upon another: the quantity on board of each vessel was enormous. Another officer, three seamen, and myself were all that were on board of her. We had a four-oared gig, a small narrow thing (nick-named by the sailors a "coffin"), to make our escape in.

Being quite prepared, we started. It was a fearful moment; the wind freshened, and whistled through our rigging, and the night was so dark, that we could not see our bowsprit. We had only our foresail set; but with a strong flood-tide and a fair wind, with plenty of it, we passed between the advanced frigates like an arrow. It seemed to me like entering the gates of hell. As we flew rapidly along, and our own ships disappeared in the intense darkness, I thought of Dante's inscription over the portals: — "You who enter here, leave hope behind."

Our orders were to lay the vessel on the boom which the French had moored to the outer anchors of their ships of the line. In a few minutes after passing the frigates we were close to it; our boat was towing astern, with three men in it—one to hold the rope ready to let go, one to steer, and one to bale the water out, which, from our rapid motion, would otherwise have swamped her. The officer who accompanied me steered the vessel, and I held the match in my hand. We came upon the boom with a horrid crash; he put the helm down, and hid her broadside to it. The force of the tide acting on the hull, and the wind upon the foresail, made her heel gunwale to, and it was with difficulty I could keep my legs; at this moment, the boat was very near being swamped alongside. They had shifted her astern, and there the tide had almost lifted her over the boom; by great exertion they got her clear, and lay upon their oars: the tide and the wind formed a bubbling short sea, which almost buried her. My companion then got into the boat, desiring me to light the port-fire, and follow.

If ever I felt the sensation of fear, it was after I had lighted this port-fire, which was connected with the train. Until I was fairly in the boat, and out of the reach of the explosion—which was inevitable, and might be instantaneous—the sensation was horrid. I was standing on a mine; any fault in the port-fire, which sometimes will happen, any trifling quantity of gunpowder lying in the interstices of the deck, would have exploded the whole in a moment: had my hand trembled, which I am proud to say it did not, the same might have occurred. Only one minute and a half of port-fire was allowed. I had therefore no time to lose. The moment I had lit it, I laid it down very gently, and then jumped into the gig, with a nimbleness suitable to the occasion. We were off in a moment: I pulled the stroke oar, and I never plied with more zeal in all my life: we were not two hundred yards from her when she exploded.

A more terrific and beautiful sight cannot be conceived. but we were not quite enough at our ease to enjoy it. The shells flew up in the air to a prodigious height, some bursting as they rose, and others as they descended. The shower fell about us, but we escaped without injury. We made but little progress against the wind and tide; and we had the pleasure to run the gauntlet among all the other fire-ships, which had been ignited, and bore down on us in flames fore and aft. Their rigging was hung with Congreve rockets; and as they took fire, they darted through the air in every direction with an astounding noise, looking like large fiery serpents.

We arrived safely on board, and reported ourselves to the captain, who was on the hammocks, watching the progress of the fire-ships. One of these had been lighted too soon; her helm had not been lashed, and she had broached to, close to our frigate. I had had quite enough of adventure for that night, but was fated to have a little more.

"Mr Mildmay," said the captain, "you seem to like the fun; jump into your gig again, take four fresh hands" (thinks I, a fresh midshipman would not be amiss), "get on board of that vessel, and put her head the right way."

I did not like this job at all; the vessel appeared to be in flames from the jib-boom to the topsail; and I own I preferred enjoying the honours I had already gained, to going after others so very precarious; however, I never made a difficulty, and this was no time for exceptions to my rule. I touched my hat, said, "Ay, ay, sir," sang out for four volunteers, and, in an instant, I had fifty. I selected four, and shoved off on my new expedition.

As I approached the vessel, I could not at first discover any part that was not tenanted by the flames, the heat of which, at the distance of twenty or thirty feet, was far from pleasant, even in that cold night. The weather quarter appeared to be clearest of flames, but they burst out with great fury from the cabin windows. I contrived, with great difficulty, to reach the deck, by climbing up that part which was not actually burning, and was followed by one of the sailors. The mainmast was on fire, and the flakes of burning canvas from the boom mainsail fell on us like a snow-storm; the end of the tiller was burnt to charcoal, but on the midship part of it I passed a rope, and, assisted by the sailor, moved the helm, and got her before the wind.

While I was thus employed, I could not help thinking of my type, Don Juan. I was nearly suffocated before I had completed my work. I shoved off again, and away she flew before the wind. "I don't go with you this time," said I; *"J'ai été,"* as the Frenchman said, when he was invited to an English foxhunt.

I was as black as a negro when I returned on board, and dying with thirst. "Very well done, Mildmay," said the captain; "did you find it warm?" I pointed to my mouth, for it was so parched that I could not speak, and ran to the water-cask, where I drank as much as would have floated a canoe. The first thing I said, as soon as I could speak, was "D—— that fire-ship, and the lubber that set her on fire."

The next morning the French squadron was seen in a very disastrous state; they had cut their cables, and run on shore in every direction, with the exception of the flag ships of the admiral and rear-admiral, which lay at their anchors, and could not move till high water; it was then first quarter flood, so that they had five good hours to remain. I refer my readers to the court-martial for a history of these events: they have also been commented on, with more or less severity, by contemporary writers. I shall only observe, that had the captains of His Majesty's ships been left to their own judgment, much more would have been attempted; but with what success I do not presume to say.

My captain, as soon as he could see his mark, weighed, ran in, and engaged the batteries, while he also directed his guns at the bottoms of the enemy's ships, as they lay on shore on their beam ends. Isle d'Aix gave us a warm reception. I was on the forecastle, the captain of which had his head taken clean off, by a cannon-ball; the captain of the ship coming forward at the same moment, only said, "Poor fellow! throw him overboard; there is no time for a coroner's inquest now." We were a considerable time engaging the batteries, and the vessels near them, without receiving any assistance from our ships.

While this was going on, a very curious instance of muscular action occurred: a lad of eighteen years of age was on the forecastle, when a shot cut away the whole of his bowels, which were scattered over another mid-shipman and myself, and nearly blinded us. He fell—and after lying a few seconds, sprang suddenly on his feet, stared us horribly in the face, and fell down dead. The spine had not been divided; but with that exception, the lower was separated from the upper part of the body.

Some of our vessels seeing us so warmly engaged, began to move up to our assistance. One of our ships of the line came into action in such gallant trim, that it was glorious to behold. She was a beautiful ship, in what we call "high kelter;" she seemed a living body, conscious of her own superior power over her opponents, whose shot she despised, as they fell thick and fast about her, while she deliberately took up an admirable position for battle. And having furled her sails, and squared her yards, as if she had been at Spithead, her men came down from aloft, went to their guns, and opened such a fire on the enemy's ships and batteries, as would have delighted the great Nelson himself, could he have been present. The results of this action are well known, and do not need repeating here; it was one of the winding-up scenes of the war. The French, slow to believe their naval inferiority, now submitted in silence. Our navy had done its work; and from that time, the brunt of the war fell on the army.

The advocates of fatalism or predestination might adduce a strong illustration of their doctrine as evinced in the death of the captain of one of the French ships destroyed. This officer had been taken out of his ship by one of the boats of our frigate; but, recollecting that he had left on board nautical instruments of great value, he requested our captain to go with him in the gig, and bring them away before the ship was burned. They did go, and the boat being very small, they sat very close side by side, on a piece of board not much more than two feet long, which, for want of proper seats, was laid across the stern of the boat. One of the French ships was burning at the time; her guns went off as fast as the fire reached them; and a chance shot took the board from under the two captains: the English captain was not hurt; but the splinters entered the body of the French captain, and killed him. Late in the evening, the other French line-of-battle ships that were ashore were set fire to, and a splendid illumination they made: we were close to them, and the splinters and fragments of wreck fell on board of us.

Among our killed, was a Dutch boatswain's mate: his wife was on board, and the stick which he was allowed to carry in virtue of his office, he very frequently applied to the shoulders of his helpmate, in requital for certain instances of infidelity; nor, with all my respect for the fair sex, can I deny that the punishment was generally deserved. When the cannon-ball had deprived her of her lawful protector and the guardian of her honour, she sat by the side of his mangled remains, making many unavailing efforts to weep; a tear from one eye coursed down her cheek, and was lost in her mouth; one from the other eye started at the same time, but for want of nourishment, halted on her cheekbone, where, collecting the smoke and gunpowder which surrounded us, it formed a little black peninsula and isthmus on her face, and gave to her heroic grief a truly mourning tear. This proof of conjugal affection she would not part with until the following day, when having seen the last sad rites paid to the body of her faithful Achilles, she washed her face, and resumed her smiles, nor was she ungrateful to the ship's company for their sympathy.

We were ordered up to Spithead with despatches, and long before we arrived, she had made the sergeant of marines the happiest of men, under a promise of marriage at Kingston church, before we sailed on our next cruise, which promise was most honourably performed.

A midshipman's vacancy having occurred on board the frigate, the captain offered it to me. I gladly accepted of it; and while he was in the humour, I asked him for a week's leave of absence; this he also granted, adding, at the same time, "No more French leave, if you please." I need not say that not an hour of this indulgence was intended either for my father or even the dear Emily. No, Eugenia, the beloved, in her interesting condition, claimed my undivided care. I flew to G——, found the troop; but she, alas! had left it a fortnight before, and had gone no one knew whither.

Distracted with this fatal news, I sunk into a chair almost senseless, when one of the actresses brought me a letter: I knew the hand, it was that of Eugenia. Rushing into an empty parlour, I broke the seal, and read as follows:—

Believe me, my dearest Mildmay, nothing but the most urgent necessity could induce me to cause you the affliction which I know you will feel on reading these lines. Circumstances have occurred since we parted, that not only render it necessary that I should quit you, but also that we should not meet again for some time. and that you should be kept in ignorance of my place of abode. Our separation, though long, will not, I trust, be eternal; but years may elapse before we meet again. The sacrifice is great to me; but your honour and prosperity demand it. I have the same ardent love towards you that I ever had; and for your sake, will love and cherish your child. I am supported in *this* my trial, by a hope of our being again united. God in heaven bless you, and prosper all your undertakings. Follow up your profession. I shall hear and have constant intelligence of all your motions, and I shall pray to heaven to spare your life amidst all the dangers that your courage will urge you to encounter. Farewell! and forget not her who never has you one moment from her thoughts.

EUGENIA

P.S.—You may at times be short of cash; I know you are very thoughtless in that respect. A letter to the subjoined address will

always be attended to, and enable you to command whatever may
be necessary for your comfort. Pride might induce you to reject this
offer; but remember it is Eugenia that offers: and if you love her as
she thinks you do, you will accept it from her.

Here was mystery and paradox in copious confusion. "Obliged by cir-
cumstances to leave me—to conceal the place of her retirement"—yet com-
manding not only pecuniary resources for herself, but offering me any sum
I might require! I retired to my bed; but sleep forsook me, nor did I want
it. I had too much to think of, and no clue to solve my doubts. I prayed to
Heaven for her welfare, vowed eternal constancy, and at length fell asleep.
The next morning I took leave of my quondam associates, and returned to
Portsmouth, neither wishing to see my father, my family, or even the sweet
Emily. It however occurred to me that the same agent who could advance
money could forward a letter; and a letter I wrote, expressing all I felt. No
answer was returned; but as the letter never came back, I was convinced it
was received, and occasionally sent others, the contents of which my readers will, no doubt, feel obliged to me for suppressing, love-letters being of
all things in the world the most stupid, except to the parties concerned.

As I was not to see my Eugenia, I was delighted to hear that we were
again to be sent on active service. The Scheldt expedition was preparing,
and our frigate was to be in the advance; but our gallant and favourite captain was not to go with us; an acting captain was appointed, and every
exertion was used to have the ship ready. The town in the meantime was
as crowded with soldiers as Spithead and the harbour was with transports.
Late in July, we sailed, having two gunboats in tow, which we were ordered
to man. I applied for, and obtained the command of one of them, quite
certain that I should see more service, and consequently have more amusement, than if I remained on board the frigate. We convoyed forty or fifty
transports, containing the cavalry, and brought them all safe to an anchor off
Cadsand.

The weather was fine, and the water smooth; not a moment was lost in
disembarking the troops and horses; and I do not recollect ever having seen,
either before or since, a more pleasing sight. The men were first sent on
shore with their saddles and bridles: the horses were then lowered into the
water in running slings, which were slipped clear off them in a moment; and

as soon as they found themselves free, they swam away for the shore, which they saluted with a loud neigh as soon as they landed. In the space of a quarter of a mile we had three or four hundred horses in the water, all swimming for the shore at the same time; while their anxious riders stood on the beach waiting their arrival. I never saw so novel or picturesque a sight.

I found the gun-boat service very hard. We were stationed off Batz, and obliged to be constantly on the alert; but when Flushing surrendered we had more leisure, and we employed it in procuring some articles for our table, to which we had been too long strangers. Our money had been expended in the purchase of champagne and claret, in which articles we were no economists, consequently few florins could be spared for the purchase of poultry and butcher meat; but then these articles were to be procured, by the same means which had given us the island of Walcheren, namely powder and shot. The country people were very churlish, and not at all inclined to barter; and as we had nothing to give in exchange, we avoided useless discussion. Turkeys, by us short-sighted mortals, were often mistaken for pheasants; cocks and hens, for partridges; tame ducks and geese for wild; in short, such was our hurry and confusion—leaping ditches, climbing dykes, and fording swamps—that Buffon himself would never have known the difference between a goose and a peacock. Our game-bags were as capacious as our consciences, and our aim as good as our appetites.

The peasants shut all their poultry up in their barns, and very liberally bestowed all their curses upon us. Thus all our supplies were cut off, and foraging became at least a source of difficulty, if not of danger. I went on shore with our party, put a bullet into my fowling-piece, and, as I thought, shot a deer; but on more minute inspection, it proved to be a four months' calf. This was an accident that might have happened to any man. The carcass was too heavy to carry home, so we cut it in halves, not fore and aft down the backbone, as your stupid butchers do, but made a short cut across the loins, a far more compendious and portable method than the other. We marched off with the hind legs, loins, and kidney, having first of all buried the head and shoulders in the field, determined to call and take it away the following night.

We were partly seen, and severely scrutinized in our action by a neighbouring gun-boat, whose crew were no doubt as hungry as ourselves;

they got hold of one of our men, who, like a fool, let the cat out of the bag when a pint of grog got into it. The fellow hinted where the other half lay, and these *unprincipled rascals* went after it, fully resolved to appropriate it to themselves; but they were outwitted, as they deserved to be for their roguery. The farmer to whom the calf belonged had got a hint of what was done, and finding that we had buried one half of the calf, procured a party of soldiers ready to take possession of us when we should come to fetch it away; accordingly, the party who went from the other gun-boat after dark, having found out the spot, were very busy disinterring their prey, when they were surprised, taken prisoners, and marched away to the British camp, leaving the dead body behind.

We, quite unconscious of what was done, came soon after, found our veal, and marched off with it. The prisoners were in the meantime sent on board the flag ship, with the charge of robbery strongly preferred against them; indeed, *flagrante delicto* was proved. In vain they protested that they were not the slayers, but only went in search of what others had killed: the admiral, who was a kind-hearted man, said, that that was a very good story, but desired them "not to tell lies to old rogues," and ordered them all under arrest: at the same time giving directions for a most rigid scrutiny into the larder of the other gunboat, with a view, if possible, to discover the remains of the calf. This we had foreseen would happen, so we put it into one of the sailor's bags, and sank it with a lead-line in three fathoms water, where it lay till the inspection was over, when we dressed it, and made an excellent dinner, drinking success to His Majesty's arms by land and sea.

Whether I had been intemperate in food or libation I know not, but I was attacked with the Walcheren fever, and was sent home in a line-of-battle ship; and, perhaps, as Pangloss says, it was all for the best; for I knew I could not have left off my inveterate habits, and it would have been very inconvenient to me, and distressing to my friends, to have ended my brilliant career, and stopped these memoirs, at the beginning of the second and most interesting volume, by hanging the Author up, like a scarecrow, under the superintendence of the rascally provost-marshal, merely for catering on the land of a Walcheren farmer. Moreover, the Dutch were unworthy of liberty, as their actions proved, to begrudge a few fowls, or a fillet of veal, to the very men who came to rescue them from bondage;—and then their water, too, who ever drank such stuff? for my part, I never tasted it when I could get anything better. As to their nasty swamps and fogs, quite good enough for such croaking fellows as they are, what could induce an Englishman to live among them, except the pleasure of killing Frenchmen, or shooting game? Deprive us of these pursuits, which the surrender of Flushing effectually did, and Walcheren, with its ophthalmia and its agues, was no longer a place for a gentleman. Besides, I plainly saw that if there ever had been any intention of advancing to Antwerp, the time was now gone by; and as the French were laughing at us, and I never liked to be made a butt of, particularly by such chaps as these, I left the scene of our sorrows and disgraces without regret.

The farewell of Voltaire came into my mind. *"Adieu, Canaux, Canardes, et Canaille,"* which might be rendered into English thus:—"Good-bye, Dykes, Ducks, and Dutchmen." So I returned to my father's house to be nursed by my sister, and to astonish the neighbours with the history of our wonderful achievements.

CHAPTER XII

First came great Neptune, with his three-forkt mace,
That rules the seas, and makes them rise or fall:
His dewy locks did drop with brine apace
Under his diademe-imperiall:
And by his side his queene with coronall,
Fair Amphitrite.   .   .   .

.   .   .   .   .

These marched farre afore the other crew.

SPENSER

I REMAINED no longer at home than sufficed to restore my strength, after the serious attack of fever and ague which I had brought with me from Walcheren. Although my father received me kindly, he had not forgotten (at least I thought so) my former transgressions; a mutual distrust destroyed that intimacy which ought ever to exist between father and son. The thread was broken—it is vain to enquire how, and the consequence was, that the day of my departure to join a frigate on the North American station, was welcomed with joy by me, and seen unregretted by my father.

The ship I was about to join was commanded by a young nobleman, and as patricians were not so plentiful in the service at that time, as they have since become, I was considered fortunate in my appointment. I was ordered, with about thirty more supernumerary midshipmen, to take my passage in a ship of the line, going to Bermuda. The gun-room was given to us as our place of residence, the midshipmen belonging to the ship occupying the two snug berths in the cockpit.

Among so many young men of different habits and circumstances, all joining the ship at different periods, no combination could be made for forming a mess. The ship sailed soon after I got on board, and our party, during the voyage, was usually supplied from the purser's steward-room. I have thought it very wonderful, that a mess of eight or twelve seamen or marines will always make the allowance last from one week to another, and have something to spare; but with the same number of midshipmen the case is very different, and the larger the mess the more do their difficulties increase; they are never satisfied, never have enough, and if the purser will allow them, are always in debt for flour, beef, pork, and spirits. This is owing to their natural habits of carelessness; and our mess, for this reason, was particularly uncomfortable. The government was a democracy; but the caterer had at times been invested with dictatorial powers, which he either abused or was thought to abuse, and he was accordingly turned out, or resigned in disgust, at the end of two or three days.

Most of my messmates were young men, senior to me in the service, having passed their examinations, and were going to America for promotion: but when mustered on the quarter-deck, whether they appeared less manly or were, in fact, less expert in their duty, I know not; but certain it is, that the first lieutenant appointed me mate of a watch, and placed several of these aspirants under my orders: and so strong did we muster, that we stood in each other's way when on deck keeping our watch, seldom less than seventeen or eighteen in number.

In the gun-room we agreed very ill together, and one principal cause of this was our short allowance of food—daily skirmishes took place, and not unfrequently pitched battles; but I never took any other part in them than as a spectator, and the observations I made convinced me that I should have no great difficulty in mastering the whole of them.

The office of caterer was one of neither honour nor emolument, and it was voluntarily taken up, and peevishly laid down, on the first trifling provocation. With the ship's allowance, no being, less than an angel, could have given satisfaction. The division of beef and pork into as many parcels as there were claimants, always produced remonstrance, reproof, and blows. I was never quarrelsome, and took the part allotted to me quietly enough, until, they finding my disposition to submit, I found my portion daily decrease, and on the resignation of the thirteenth caterer, I volunteered my services, which were gladly accepted.

Aware of the danger and difficulty of my situation, I was prepared accordingly. On the first day that I shared the provisions, I took very good care of number one, and, as I had foreseen, was attacked by two or three for my lion-like division of the prey. Upon this, I made them a short speech, observing, that if they supposed I meant to take the trouble of catering for nothing, they were very much mistaken; that the small difference I made between their portions and mine, if equally divided among them, would not fill a hollow tooth, and that, after my own share, all others should be distributed with the most rigid impartiality, and scrupulous regard to justice.

This very reasonable speech did not satisfy them. I was challenged to decide the point *à la Cribb;* two candidates for the honour stepped out at once. I desired them to toss up; and having soon defeated the winner, I recommended him to return to his seat. The next man came forward, hoping to find an easy victory, after the fatigue of a recent battle; but he was mistaken, and retired with severe chastisement. The next day I took my seat, cleared for action—coat, waistcoat, and neckcloth off. I observed that I should proceed as I had done before, and was ready to hold a court of Oyer and Terminer; but no suitors appeared, and I held the office of caterer from that day till I quitted the ship, by the strongest of all possible claims—first, by election; and, secondly, by right of conquest.

We had not been many days at sea, before we discovered that our first lieutenant was a most abominable tyrant, a brutal fellow, a drunkard, and a glutton, with a long red nose, and a large belly, he frequently sent half-a-dozen grown-up midshipmen to the mast-head at a time. This man I determined to turn out of the ship, and mentioned my intention to my messmates, promising them success if they would only follow my advice. They quite laughed at the idea; but I was firm, and told them that it should come to pass, if they would but behave so ill as just to incur a slight

punishment or reprimand from "Nosey" every day; this they agreed to; and
not a day passed but they were either mast-headed, or put watch and watch.

They reported all to me, and asked my advice. "Complain to the captain," said I. They did, and were told that the first lieutenant had done his
duty. The same causes produced the same effects on each succeeding day;
and when the midshipmen complained, they had no redress. By my direction, they observed to the captain, "It is of no use complaining, sir; you
always take Mr Clewline's part." The captain, indeed, from a general sense
of propriety, gave his support to the ward-room officers, knowing that, nine
times in ten, midshipmen were in the wrong.

Things worked as I wished; the midshipmen persisted in behaving ill—
remonstrated, and declared that the first lieutenant did not tell the truth. For
a time, many of them lost the favour of the captain, but I encouraged them
to bear that, as well as the increased rancour of "Old Nosey." One day two
midshipmen, by previous agreement, began to fight on the lee gangway. In
those days, that was crime enough almost to have hanged them; they were
sent to the mast-head for three hours, and when they came down applied
to me for advice. "Go," said I, "and complain. If the first lieutenant says you
were fighting, tell the captain you were only showing how the first lieutenant pummelled the men last night when they were hoisting the topsails, and
the way he cut the marine's head, when he knocked him down the hatchway." All this was fairly done—the midshipmen received a reprimand, but
the captain began to think there might be some cause for these continued
complaints, which daily increased both in weight and number.

At last we were enabled to give the *coup de grâce.* A wretched boy in
the ship, whose dirty habits often brought him to the gun, was so hardened
that he laughed at all the stripes of the boatswain's cat inflicted on him by
the first lieutenant. "I will make him feel," said the enraged officer; so ordering a bowl of brine to be brought to him, he sprinkled it on the lacerated
flesh of the boy between every lash. This inhuman act, so unbecoming the
character of an officer and a gentleman, we all resented, and retiring to the
gun-room in a body, gave three deep and heavy groans in chorus. The effect
was dismal; it was heard in the ward-room, and the first lieutenant sent
down to desire we should be quiet; on which we immediately gave three
more, which sent him in a rage to the quarter-deck, where we were all
summoned, and the reason of the noise demanded. I had, till then, kept

myself in the background, content with being the *primum mobile*, without being seen. I was always strict to my duty, and never had been complained of; my coming forward, therefore, on this occasion, produced a fine stage effect, and carried great weight. I told the lieutenant we were groaning for the poor boy who had been pickled. This increased his rage, and he ordered me up to the mast-head. I refused to go until I had seen the captain, who at that moment made his appearance on deck. I immediately referred to him, related the whole story, not omitting to mention the repeated acts of tyranny which the lieutenant had perpetrated on us all. I saw in a moment that we had gained the day. The captain had given the most positive orders that no one should be punished without his express permission. This order the lieutenant had disobeyed, and that, added to his unpopular character, decided his fate. The captain walked into his cabin, and the next day signified to the first lieutenant, that he must quit the ship on her arrival in port, or be tried by a court-martial: this latter he knew he dared not stand.

I should have informed my reader that our orders were to see the East-India convoy as far as the tenth degree of north latitude, and then proceed to Bermuda. This was of itself a pleasant cruise, and gave us the chance of falling in either with an enemy or a recapture. Ships not intending to cross the line usually grant a saturnalia to the crew when they come to the tropic of Capricorn; it is thought to renovate their spirits, and to break the monotony of the cruise, or voyage, where time flows on in such a smooth, undeviating routine, that one day is not distinguishable from another. Our captain, a young man, and a perfect gentleman, never refused any indulgence to the men, compatible with discipline and the safety of the ship: and as the regular trade-wind blew, there was no danger of sudden squalls.— The ceremony of crossing the line, I am aware, has been often described— so has Italy and the Rhine; but there are varieties of ways of doing and relating these things; ours had its singularity, and ended, I am sorry to say, in a deep tragedy, which I shall remember "as long as memory holds her seat."

One beautiful morning, as soon as the people had breakfasted, they began to prepare, by stripping to their waists, and wearing nothing but a pair of duck trousers. The man at the mast-head called out that he saw something on the weather bow, which he thought was a boat; soon after, an unknown voice from the jib-boom hailed the ship; the officer of the watch answered; and the voice commanded him to heave to, as Neptune was coming on board. The ship was accordingly hove to with every formality, though going at the rate of seven miles an hour: the main-yard squared, the head and after-yards braced up.

As soon as the ship was hove to, a young man (one of the sailors) dressed in a smart suit of black, knee-breeches, and buckles, with his hair powdered, and with all the extra finery and mincing gait of an exquisite, came aft on the quarter-deck, and, with a most polished bow, took the liberty of introducing himself as *gentleman's gentleman* to Mr Neptune, who had been desired to precede his master and acquaint the commander of the vessel with his intended visit.

A sail had been extended across the forecastle by way of curtain, and from behind this, Neptune and his train, in full costume, shortly afterwards came forth.

The car of the god consisted of a gun-carriage: it was drawn by six black men, part of the ship's crew: they were tall muscular fellows, their heads were covered with sea-weed, and they wore a very small pair of cotton drawers: in other respects they were perfectly naked; their skins were spotted all over with red and white paint alternately; they had conch shells in their hands, with which they made a most horrible noise. Neptune was masked, as were many of his attendants, and none of the officers knew exactly by which of the men the god was represented; but he was a shrewd hand, and did his part very well. He wore a naval crown, made by the ship's armourer; in his right hand he held a trident, on the prongs of which there was a dolphin, which he had, he said, struck that morning; he wore a large wig, made of oakum, and a beard of the same materials, which flowed down to his waist; he was full powdered, and his naked body was bedaubed with paint.

The god was attended by a splendid court: his secretary of state, whose head was stuck full of the quills of the sea bird of these latitudes; his surgeon, with his lancet, pill-box, and his smelling-bottle; his barber, with a razor, whose blade was two feet long, cut off an iron hoop; and the barber's mate, who carried a small tub, as a shaving-box; the materials within I could not analyze, but my nose convinced me that no part of them came from Smith's, in Bond-street.

Amphitrite followed, on a similar carriage, drawn by six white men, whose costume was like the others. This goddess was personified by an athletic, ugly man, marked with the small-pox, dressed as a female, with a woman's night-cap on his head, ornamented with sprigs of sea-weed; she had a harpoon in her hand, on which was fixed an albicore; and in her lap lay one of the boys of the ship, dressed as a baby, with long clothes and a cap: he held in his hand a marlinspike, which was suspended round his neck with a rope yarn: this was to assist him in cutting his teeth, as the children on shore use a coral. His nurse attended him with a bucket full of burgoo, or hasty pudding with which she occasionally fed him out of the cook's iron ladle. Two or three stout men were habited as sea nymphs to attend on the goddess: they carried a looking-glass, some curry-combs, a birch-broom, and a pot of red paint by way of rouge.

As soon as the procession appeared on the forecastle, the captain attended by his steward, bearing a tray with a bottle of wine and some glasses, came out of his cabin, and the cars of the marine deities were drawn up on the quarter-deck. Neptune lowered his trident, and presented the dolphin to the captain, as Amphitrite did her albicore, in token of submission and homage to the representative of the King of Great Britain.

"I have come," said the god, "to welcome you into my dominions, and to present my wife and child." The captain bowed. "Allow me to ask after my brother and liege sovereign, the good old King George."

"He is not so well," said the captain, "as I and all his subjects could wish."

"More's the pity," replied Neptune; "and how is the Prince of Wales?"

"The Prince is well," said the captain, "and now governs as regent in the name of his royal father."

"And how does he get on with his wife?" said the inquisitive god.

"Bad enough," said the captain; "they agree together like a whale and a thrasher."

"Ah! I thought so," said the god of the sea. "His royal highness should take a leaf out of my book: never allow it to be doubtful who is commanding officer."

"And pray what might your majesty's specific be, to cure a bad wife?" said the captain.

"Three feet of the cross-jack brace every morning before breakfast, for a quarter of an hour, and half an hour on a Sunday."

"But why more on a Sunday than any other day?" said the captain.

"Why?" said Neptune, "why, because she'd been keeping Saturday night, to be sure; besides, she has less to do of a Sunday, and more time to think of her sins, and do penance."

"But you would not have a prince strike a lady, surely?"

"Wouldn't I? No to be sure, if she behave herself as *sich,* on no account; but if she gives tongue, and won't keep sober, I'd sarve her as I do Amphy— don't I, Amphy?" chucking the goddess under the chin. "We have no bad wives in the bottom of the sea: and so if you don't know how to keep 'em in order, send them to us."

"But your majesty's remedy is violent; we should have a rebellion in England, if the king was to beat his wife."

"Make the lords in waiting do it then," said the surly god; "and if they are too lazy, which I dare say they send for a boatswain's mate from the Royal Billy—he'd sarve her out, I warrant you; and, for half a gallon of rum, would teach the yeomen of the guard to dance the binnacle hornpipe into the bargain."

"His royal highness shall certainly hear your advice, Mr Neptune; but whether he will follow it or not is not for me to say. Would you please to drink his royal highness's good health?"

"With all my heart, sir; I was always loyal to my king, and ready to drink his health, and to fight for him."

The captain presented the god with a bumper of Madeira, and another to the goddess.

"Here's a good health and a long life to our gracious king and all the royal family. The roads are unkimmon dusty, and we hav'n't wet our lips since we left St Thomas on the line, this morning. But we have no time to lose, captain," said the sea god; "I see many new faces here, as requires washing and shaving; and if we add bleeding and physic, they will be all the better for it."

The captain nodded assent; and Neptune, striking the deck with the end of his trident, commanded attention, and thus addressed his court: "Heark ye, my Tritons, you are called here to shave, duck, and physic all as needs, but I command you to be gentle. I'll have no ill-usage; if we gets a bad name, we gets no more fees; and the first of you as disobeys my orders, I'll tie him to a ten-inch mortar, and sink him ten thousand fathoms deep in the ocean, where he shall feed on salt water and sea-weed for a hundred years:

begone to your work." Twelve constables, with thick sticks, immediately repaired to the hatchway, and sent down all who had not been initiated, guarding them strictly until they were called up one by one.

The cow-pen had been previously prepared for the bathing; it was lined with double canvas, and boarded, so that it held water, and contained about four butts, which was constantly renewed by the pump. Many of the officers purchased exemption from shaving and physic by a bottle of rum; but none could escape the sprinkling of salt water, which fell about in great profusion; even the captain received his share, but with great good-nature, and seemed to enjoy the sport. It was easy to perceive, on this occasion, who were favourites with the ship's company, by the degree of severity with which they were treated. The tyro was seated on the side of the cow-pen: he was asked the place of his nativity, and the moment he opened his mouth, the shaving-brush of the barber, which was a very large paint brush, was crammed in with all the filthy lather with which they covered his face and chin; this was roughly scraped off with the great razor. The doctor felt his pulse, and prescribed a pill, which was forced into his cheek; and the smell-ing-bottle, the cork of which was armed with short points of pins, was so forcibly applied to his nose as to bring blood; after this, he was thrown backwards into the bath, and allowed to scramble out the best way he could.

The master-at-arms, and ship's corporals, and purser's steward, were severely treated. The midshipmen looked out for the first lieutenant; but he kept so close under the wing of the captain, that for a long time we were unable to succeed. At length, some great uproar in the waist induced him to run down, when we all surrounded him, and plied him so effectually with buckets of water, that he was glad to run down the after-hatchway, and seek shelter in the gun-room; as he ran down, we threw the buckets after him, and he fell, like the Roman virgin, covered with the shields of the soldiers.

The purser had fortified himself in his cabin, and with his sword and pistols, rowed vengeance against all intruders; but the middies were not to be frightened with swords or pistols: so we had him out, and gave him a sound ducking, because he had refused to let us have more spirits than our allowance. He was paraded to the main deck in great form, his sword held over his head; his pistols, in a bucket of water, carried before him; and having been duly shaved, physicked, and soused into the cow-pen, he was allowed to return to his cabin, like a drowned rat.

The first lieutenant of marines was a great bore; he was always annoying us with his German flute. Having no ear of his own, he had no mercy on ours, so we handed him to the bath; and in addition to all the other luxuries of the day, made him drink half a pint of salt water, which we poured into his mouth, through his own flute, as a funnel. I now recollect that it was the cries of the poor marine which brought down the first lieutenant, who ordered us to desist, and we served him as hath been related.

Thus far all was hilarity and mirth; but the scene was very suddenly changed. One of the foretopmen, drawing water in the chains, fell overboard; the alarm was instantly given, and the ship hove to. I ran upon the poop, and, seeing that the man could not swim, jumped overboard to save him. The height from which I descended made me go very deep in the water, and when I arose I could perceive one of the man's hands. I swam towards him; but, O, God! what was my horror, when I found myself in the midst of his blood. I comprehended in a moment that a shark had taken him, and expected that every instant my own fate would be like his. I wonder I had not sunk with fear: I was nearly paralyzed. The ship, which had been going six or seven miles an hour, was at some distance, and I gave myself up for gone. I had scarcely the power of reflection, and was overwhelmed by the sudden, awful, and, as I thought certain approach of death in its most horrible shape. In a moment I recollected myself: and I believe the actions of five years crowded into my mind in as many minutes I prayed most fervently, and vowed amendment, if it should please God to spare me. My prayer was heard and I believe it was a special Providence that rescued me from the jaws of the fish. I was nearly a mile from the ship before I was picked up; and when the boat came alongside with me, three large sharks were under the stern. These had devoured the poor sailor, and, fortunately for me, had followed the ship for more prey, and thus left me to myself.

As I went up the side, I was received by the captain and officers in the most flattering manner; the captain thanked me in the presence of the ship's company for my praiseworthy exertions, and I was gazed on by all as an object of interest and admiration; but if others thought so of me, I thought not so of myself. I retired below to my berth with a loathing and contempt, a self-abasement, which I cannot describe. I felt myself unworthy of the mercy I had received. The disgraceful and vicious course of life I had led, burst upon me with horrible conviction. *"Cœlo tonantem credidimus Jovem regnare,"* says Horace; and it was only by the excitement of such peculiarly horrid situations, that the sense of a superintending power could be awakened within me, a hardened and incorrigible sinner.

I changed my clothes, and was glad when night came, that I might be left to myself; but oh, how infinitely more horrid did my situation appear! I shuddered when I thought of what I had gone through, and I made the most solemn promises of a new life. How transient were these feelings! How long did these good resolutions last? Just as long as no temptation came in the way; as long as there was no excitement to sin, no means of gratifying appetite. My good intentions were traced in the sand. I was very soon as thoughtless and as profane as ever, although frequently checked by the remembrance of my providential escape; and for years afterwards the thoughts of the shark taking me by the leg was accompanied by the acknowledgment that the devil would have me in like manner, if I did not amend.

If after this awakening circumstance, I could have had the good fortune to have met with sober-minded and religious people, I have no doubt but I might have had at this time much less to answer for; but that not being the case, the force of habit and example renewed its dominion over me, and I became nearly as bad as ever.

Our amusements in the gun-room were rough. One of them was to lie on the mess table, under the tiller, and to hold by the tiller ropes above, while we kicked at all who attempted to dislodge us, either by force or stratagem. Whoever had possession, had nine points of the law, and could easily oppose the whole. I one day held this envied position, and kept all at bay, when, unluckily, one of the passed midshipmen, who had got very drunk with the gunner, came in and made a furious attack on me. I gave him a kick on the face, that sent him with great violence on his back, among the plates and dishes, which had been removed from the dinner-table and placed between the guns. Enraged, as much at the laughter against him as at the blow he had received, he snatched up a carving fork, and, before any one was aware of his intention, stabbed me with it four times. I jumped up to punish him, but the moment I got on my legs was so stiff, that I fell back into the arms of my messmates.

The surgeon examined the wounds, which were serious; two of them nearly touched an artery. I was put to bed sick, and was three weeks confined to my berth. The midshipman who had committed this outrage, was very penitent when sober, and implored my pardon and forgiveness. Naturally good-natured, I freely forgave, because I was disarmed by submission. I never trampled on a prostrate foe. The surgeon reported me ill of a fever, which was true; for had the captain known the real fact, the midshipman, whose commission was signed, and in the ship, ready to be delivered to him on his arrival at Bermuda, would certainly have lost his promotion. My kindness to him, I believe, wounded him more than my resentment; he became exceedingly melancholy and thoughtful, gave up drinking, and was ever after greatly attached to me. I reckon this among the few good actions of my life, and own I have great pleasure in reflecting upon it.

We arrived at Bermuda soon after, having left the convoy in the latitude of ten degrees north. The supernumeraries were all discharged into their respective ships; and before we separated, we had the pleasure to see the first lieutenant take his passage in a ship bound to England. Most sincerely did we congratulate ourselves on the success of our intrigue.

CHAPTER XIII

Where the remote Bermudas ride,
In th' ocean's bosom.

ANDREW MARVELL

THERE is a peculiar kind of beauty among these islands, which we might really believe to be the abode of fairies. They consist of a cluster of rocks, formed by the zoophyte, or coral worm. The number of the islands is said to be equal to the days of the year. They are covered with a short green sward, dark cedar trees, and low white houses, which have a pretty and pleasing effect; the harbours are numerous, but shallow; and though there are many channels into them, there is but one for large ships into the principal anchorage.

Numerous caverns, whose roofs sparkle with the spars and stalactites formed by the dripping water, are found in every part of the islands. They contain springs of delicious coolness, to quench the thirst, or to bathe in. The sailors have a notion that these islands float, and that the crust which composes them is so thin as to be broken with little exertion. One man being confined in the guardhouse for having got drunk and misbehaved, stamped on the ground, and roared to the guard, "Let me cut, or, d——n your eyes, I'll knock a hole in your bottom, scuttle your island, and send you all to h—— together." Rocks and shoals abound in almost every direction, but chiefly on the north and west sides. They are, however, well known to the native pilots, and serve as a safeguard from nightly surprise or invasion.

Varieties of fish are found here, beautiful to the eye and delicious to the taste: of these, the best is the red grouper. When on a calm, clear day, you glide among these lovely islands, in your boat, you seem to be sailing over a submarine flower-garden, in which clumps of trees, shrubs, flowers, and gravel walks, are planted in wild, but regular confusion.

My chief employment was afloat, and according to my usual habit, I found no amusement unless it was attended with danger; and this propensity found ample gratification in the whale fishery, the season for which was just approaching. The ferocity of the fish in these southern latitudes appears to be increased, both from the heat of the climate and the care of their young, for which reason it would seem that the risk in taking them is greater than in the polar seas.

From what I am able to learn of the natural history of the whale, she brings forth her young seldom more than one at a time in the northern regions, after which, with the calf at her side, the mother seeks a more genial climate, to bring it to maturity. They generally reach Bermuda about the middle of March, where they remain but a few weeks, after which they visit the West India Islands, then bear away to the southward, and go round Cape Horn, returning to the polar seas by the Aleutian Islands and Behring's Straits, which they reach in the following summer; when the young whale, having acquired size and strength in the southern latitudes, is enabled to contend with his enemies in the north, and here also the dam meets the male again. From my own experience and the inquiries I have been enabled to make, I am tolerably certain that this is a correct statement of the migration of these animals, the females annually making the tour of the two great American continents, attended by their young.

The "maternal solicitude" of the whale makes her a dangerous adversary, and many serious accidents occur in the season for catching whales. On one occasion I had nearly paid with my life for the gratification of my curiosity. I went in a whale-boat rowed by coloured men, natives of the islands, who were very daring and expert in this pursuit. We saw a whale, with her calf, playing round the coral rocks; the attention which the dam showed to its young, the care she took to warn it of danger, was truly affecting. She led it away from the boats, swam round it, and sometimes she would embrace it with her fins, and roll over with it in the waves. We contrived to get the "'vantage ground" by going to seaward of her, and by that means drove her into shoal water among the rocks. At last we came so near the young one, that the harpooner poised his weapon, knowing that the calf once struck, the mother was our own, for she would never desert it. Aware of the danger and impending fate of its inexperienced offspring, she swam rapidly round it, in decreasing circles, evincing the utmost uneasiness and anxiety; but the parental admonitions were unheeded, and it met its fate.

The boat approached the side of the younger fish, and the harpooner buried his tremendous weapon deep in the ribs. The moment it felt the wound, the poor animal darted from us, taking out a hundred fathom of line; but a young fish is soon conquered when once well struck: such was the case in this instance; it was no sooner checked with the line than it turned on its back, and, displaying its white belly on the surface of the water, floated a lifeless corpse. The unhappy parent, with an instinct always more powerful than reason, never quitted the body.

We hauled in upon the line, and came close up to our quarry just as another boat had fixed a harpoon in the mother. The tail of the furious animal descended with irresistible force upon the very centre of our boat, cutting it in two, and killing two of the men; the survivors took to swimming for their lives in all directions. The whale went in pursuit of the third boat, but was checked by the line from the one that had struck her: she towed them at the rate of ten or eleven miles an hour: and had she had deep water, would have taken the boat down, or obliged them to cut away from her.

The two boats were so much employed that they could not come to our assistance for some time, and we were left to our own resources much longer than I thought agreeable. I was going to swim to the calf whale; but one of the men advised me not to do so, saying that the sharks would be as thick about him as the lawyers round Westminster Hall; and that I should certainly be snapped up if I went near: for my comfort he added, "These devils seldom touch a man if they can get anything else."

This might be very true; but I must confess I was very glad to see one of the boats come to our assistance, while the mother whale, encumbered with the heavy harpoon and line, and exhausted with the fountain of black blood which she threw up, drew near to her calf, and died by its side; evidently, in her last moments, more occupied with the preservation of her young than of herself.

As soon as she turned on her back, I had reason to thank the "Mudian" for his good advice; there were at least thirty or forty sharks assembled round the carcasses; and as we towed them in, they followed. When we had grounded them in the shallow water, close to the beach, the blubber was cut off; after which, the flesh was given to the black people, who assembled in crowds, and cut off with their knives large portions of the meat. The sharks as liberally helped themselves with their teeth; but it was very remarkable, that though the black men often came between them and the whale, they never attacked a man. This was a singular scene; the blacks with their white eyes and teeth, hallooing, laughing, screaming, and mixing with numerous sharks—the most ferocious monsters of the deep—yet preserving a sort of truce during the presence of a third object: it reminded me, comparing great things with small, of the partition of Poland.

I found that there was neither honour nor profit for me in this diversion, so I no more went a whale fishing, but took my passage to Halifax, in a schooner; one of those vessels built during the war, in imitation of the Virginia pilot boats; but, like most of our imitations, about as much resembling the original as a cow is like a hare, and bearing exactly the same proportion in point of velocity. And as if it had been determined that these vessels should in every respect disgrace the British flag, the command of them was conferred on officers whose conduct would not induce captains to allow them to serve under them, and who were therefore very unwisely sent into small vessels, where they became their own masters, and were many of them constantly drunk; such was the state of my commander from the time I sailed until we reached Halifax. The example of the lieutenant was followed by his mate, and three midshipmen; the crew, which consisted of twenty-five men, were kept sober by being confined to their allowance, and I had a hopeful prospect.

Fortunately, drinking was not among my vices. I could get "fresh," as we call it, when in good company and excited by wit and mirth; but I never went to the length of being drunk; and, as I advanced in years, pride and cunning made me still more guarded. I perceived the immense advantage which sobriety gave me over a drunkard, and I failed not to profit by it.

Keeping constantly on deck, almost night and day, I attended to the course of the vessel and the sail she carried, never taking the trouble to consult the lieutenant, who was generally senseless in his cabin. We made Sambro' Lighthouse (which is at the entrance of Halifax harbour) in the evening, and one of the midshipmen, who was more than half drunk, declared himself well acquainted with the place, and his offer to pilot the vessel in was accepted. As I had never been there before, I could be of no use; but being extremely doubtful of the skill of our pilot, I watched his proceedings with some anxiety.

In half an hour we found ourselves on shore on Cornwallis Island, as I afterwards learned, and the sea made a fair breach over us. This sobered the lieutenant and his officers; and as the tide fell, we found ourselves high and dry. The vessel fell over on her side, and I walked on shore, determined to trust myself no more with such a set of beasts. Boats came down from the dockyard at daylight, and took me and some others who had followed my example, together with our luggage, to the flag-ship. After two days, hard labour, the vessel was got off, and brought into the harbour. The admiral was informed of the whole transaction, and one of the captains advised him to try the lieutenant by a court-martial, or, at least, to turn him out of the vessel, and send him home. Unfortunately, he would not follow this advice, but sent him to sea again, with despatches. It was known that all hands were drunk on quitting the port; and the vessel ran upon a reef of rocks called the Sisters, where she sank, and every soul perished. Her mast-heads were seen just above water the next morning.

The frigate I was to join, came into harbour soon after I reached Halifax. This I was sorry for, as I found myself in very good quarters. I had letters of introduction to the best families. The place is proverbial for hospitality; and the society of the young ladies, who are both virtuous and lovely, tended in some degree to reform and polish the rough and libertine manners which I had contracted in my career. I had many sweethearts; but they were more like Emily than Eugenia. I was a great flirt among them, and would willingly have spent more time in their company; but my fate or fortune was to be accomplished, and I went on board the frigate, where I presented my introductory letters to the nobleman who commanded her. I expected to have seen an effeminate young man, much too refined to learn his business; but I was mistaken. Lord Edward was a sailor every inch of him: he knew a ship from stem to stern, understood the characters of seamen, and gained their confidence. He was, besides, a good mechanic—a carpenter, rope-maker, sail-maker, and cooper. He could hand, reef, and steer, knot and splice; but he was no orator: he read little, and spoke less. He was a man of no show. He was good-tempered, honest, and unsophisticated, with a large proportion of common sense. He was good-humoured and free with his officers; though, if offended he was violent, but soon calm again; nor could you ever perceive any assumption of consequence from his title of nobility. He was pleased with my expertness in practical seamanship; and before we left the harbour, I became a great favourite. This I took care to improve, as I liked him both for himself and his good qualities, independently of the advantages of being on good terms with the captain.

We were not allowed to remain long in this paradise of sailors, being ordered suddenly to Quebec. I ran round to say adieu to all my dear Arcadian friends. A tearful eye, a lock of hair, a hearty shake of a fair hand, were all the spoils with which I was loaded when I quitted the shore, and I cast many a longing, lingering look behind, as the ship glided out of the harbour; white handkerchiefs were waved from the beach, and many a silent prayer put up for our safe return from snowy bosoms and from aching hearts. I dispensed my usual quantum of vows of eternal love and fidelity before I left them, and my departure was marked in the calendar of Halifax as a black day, by at least seven or eight pairs of blue eyes.

We had not been long at sea before we spoke an Irish Guineaman from Belfast, loaded with emigrants for the United States: I think about seventeen families. These were contraband. Our captain had some twenty thousand acres on the island of St John's, or Prince Edward's, as it is now called, a grant to some of his ancestors, which had been bequeathed to him, and from which he had never received one shilling of rent, for the very best reason in the world, because there were no tenants to cultivate the soil. It occurred to our noble captain, that this was the very sort of cargo he wanted, and that these Irish people would make good clearers of his land, and improve his estate. He made the proposal to them, and as they saw no chance of getting to the United States, and provided they could procure nourishment for their families, it was a matter of indifference to them where they colonised, the proposal was accepted, and the captain obtained permission of the admiral to accompany them to the island, to see them housed and settled. Indeed, nothing could have been more advantageous for all parties; they increased the scanty population of our own colony, instead of adding to the number of our enemies. We sailed again from Halifax a few hours after we had obtained the sanction of the admiral, and, passing through the beautiful passage between Nova Scotia and the island of Cape Breton, known by the name of the Gut of Canso, we soon reached Prince Edward's Island.

We anchored in a small harbour near the estate, on which we found a man residing with his wife and family; this fellow called himself the steward, and from all I could see of him during our three weeks' stay, he appeared to me to be rascal enough for the stewardship of any noble man's estate in England. The captain landed, and took me as his aide-de-camp. A bed was prepared for his lordship in the steward's house, but he preferred sleeping on clean hay in the barn. This noble lord was a man whose thoughts seldom gave much labour to his tongue; he always preferred hearing others to talking himself; and whoever was his companion, he must always be at the expense of the conversation. Nor was it by the usual mode of simple narrative, that his mind was completely impressed with the image intended to be presented to him; he required three different versions, or paraphrases, of the same story or observation, and to these he had three different expletives or ejaculations. These were hum! eh! and ah! The first denoted attention; the second, part comprehension; and the third, assent and entire approval; to mark which more distinctly, the last syllable was drawn out to an immoderate length, and accompanied by a sort of half laugh.

I shall give one instance of our colloquial pastime. His lordship, after we had each taken up our quarters for the night, on the soft dry hay, thus began:

"I say,"—a pause.

"My lord?"

"What would they say in England, at our taking up such quarters?"

"I think, my lord, that as far as regards myself, they would say nothing; but as far as regards your lordship, they would say it was very indifferent accommodation for a nobleman."

"Hum!"

This I knew was the signal for a new version. "I was observing, my lord, that a person of your rank, taking up his quarters in a barn, would excite suspicion among your friends in England."

"Eh?" says his lordship.

That did not do—either your lordship's head or mine is very thick, thinks I. I'll try again, though dying to go to sleep. "I say, my lord, if the people in England knew what a good sailor you are, they would be surprised at nothing you did; but those who know nothing, would think it odd that you should be contented with such quarters."

"Ah!" said his lordship, triumphantly.

What further observations he was pleased to make that night I know not, for I fell fast asleep, and did not awake till the cocks and hens began to fly down from their roosts, and make a confounded clamour for their breakfasts, when his lordship jumped up, gave himself a good shake, and then gave me another of a different sort: it announced the purpose, however, of restoring me to that reason, of which the cackling of the poultry had only produced the incipient signs.

"Come, rouse out, you d—— lazy chap," said my captain. "Do you mean to sleep all day? we have got plenty to do."

"Ay, ay, my lord," said I. So up I jumped, and my toilet was completed in the same time, and by the same operation, as that of a Newfoundland dog, namely, a good shake.

A large party of the ship's company came on shore with the carpenter, bringing with them every implement useful in cutting down trees and building log-houses. Such was to be our occupation, in order to house these poor emigrants. Our men began to clear a patch of land, by cutting down a number of pine-trees, the almost exclusive natives of the wood, and, having selected a spot for the foundation, we placed four stems of trees in a parallelogram, having a deep notch in each end, mutually to fit and embrace each other. When the walls, by this repeated operation, were high enough, we laid on the rafters, and covered the roof with boughs of the fir, and the bark of the birch-tree, filling the interstices with moss and mud. By practice, I became a very expert engineer, and with the assistance of thirty or forty men, I could build a very good house in a day.

We next cleared, by burning and rooting up, as much land as would serve to sustain the little colony for the ensuing season; and having planted a crop of corn and potatoes, and given the settlers many articles useful in their new abode, we left them agreeably to our orders, and to my great joy returned to dear Halifax where I again was blessed with the sight of my innocent harem. I remember well that I received a severe rebuke from the captain for inattention to signals. One was addressed to us from the flag-ship; I was signal midshipman; but instead of directing my glass towards the old *Centurion,* it was levelled at a certain young Calypso, whose fair form I discovered wandering along the *"gazon fleuris:"* how long would I not have dwelt in this happy Arcadia, had not another Mentor pushed me off the rocks, and sent me once more to buffet the briny waves!

Contrary to the opinion of any rational being, the President of the United States was planning a war against England, and every ship in Halifax harbour was preparing to fight the Yankees. The squadron sailed in September. I bade adieu to the nymphs of Nova Scotia with more indifference than became me, or than the reception I had met with from them seemed to deserve; but I was the same selfish and ungrateful being as ever. I cared for no one but my own dear self, and as long as I was gratified, it mattered little to me how many broken hearts I left behind.

CHAPTER XIV

At once the winds arise,
The thunders roll, the forky lightning flies;
In vain the master issues out commands,
In vain the trembling sailors ply their hands:
The tempest unforeseen prevents their care,
And from the first, they labour in despair.

DRYDEN'S "FABLES"

HALIFAX is a charming, hospitable place: its name is associated with so many pleasing recollections, that it never fails to extort another glass from the bottle which, having been gagged, was going to pass the night in the cellaret. But only say "Halifax!" and it is like "Open sesame!"—out flies the cork, and down goes a bumper to the "health of all good lasses!"

I related, in the last chapter, an adventure with an Irish Guineaman, whose cargo my right honourable captain converted to the profitable uses of himself and his country. Another of these vessels had been fallen in with by one of our cruisers, and the commander of His Majesty's sloop, the *Humming Bird,* made a selection of some thirty or forty stout Hibernians to fill up his own complement, and hand over the surplus to the admiral.

Short-sighted mortals we all are, and captains of men-of-war are not exempted from this human imperfection! How much, also, drops between the cup and the lip! There chanced to be on board of the same trader two very pretty Irish girls of the better sort of *bourgeoisie;* they were going to join their friends at Philadelphia: the name of the one was Judy, and of the other Maria. No sooner were the poor Irishmen informed of their change of destination, than they set up a howl loud enough to make the scaly monsters of the deep seek their dark caverns. They rent the hearts of the poor tender-hearted girls; and when the thorough bass of the males was joined by the sopranos and trebles of the women and children, it would have made Orpheus himself turn round and gaze.

"Oh, Miss Judy! Oh, Miss Maria! would ye be so cruel as to see us poor craturs dragged away to a man-of-war, and not for to go and spake a word for us? A word to the captain wid your own pretty mouths, no doubt he would let us off."

The young ladies, though doubting the powers of their own fascinations, resolved to make the experiment; so, begging the lieutenant of the sloop to give them a passage on board, to speak with his captain, they added a small matter of finery to their dress, and skipped into the boat like a couple of mountain kids, caring neither for the exposure of legs nor the spray of the salt water, which, though it took the curls out of their hair, added a bloom to the cheeks which, perhaps, contributed in no small degree to the success of their project.

There is something in the sight of a petticoat at sea that never fails to put a man into a good humour, provided he be rightly constructed. When they got on board the *Humming Bird,* they were received by the captain, and handed down into the cabin, where some refreshments were immediately prepared for them, and every kind attention shown which their sex and beauty could demand. The captain was one of the best natured fellows that ever lived, with a pair of little sparkling black eyes that laughed in your face.

"And pray, young ladies," said he, "what may have procured me the honour of this visit?"

"It was to beg a favour of your honour," said Judy

"And his honour will grant it, too," said Maria; "for I like the look of him."

Flattered by this little shot of Maria's, the captain said that nothing ever gave him more pleasure than to oblige the ladies; and if the favour they intended to ask was not utterly incompatible with his duty, that he would grant it.

"Well then," said Maria, "will your honour give me back Pat Flannagan, that you have pressed just now?"

The captain shook his head.

"He's no sailor, your honour; but a poor bog-trotter: and he will never do you any good."

The captain again shook his head.

"Ask me anything else," said he, "and I will give it you."

"Well then," said Maria, "give us Felim O'Shaugnessy?"

The captain was equally inflexible.

"Come, come, your honour," said Judy, "we must not stand upon trifles nowadays. I'll give you a kiss, if you'll give me Pat Flannagan."

"And I another," said Maria, "for Felim."

The captain had one seated on each side of him; his head turned like a dog-vane in a gale of wind; he did not know which to begin with; the most ineffable good humour danced in his eyes, and the ladies saw at once that the day was their own. Such is the power of beauty, that this lord of the ocean was fain to strike to it. Judy laid a kiss on his right cheek; Maria matched it on his left; the captain was the happiest of mortals.

"Well, then," said he, "you have your wish; take your two men, for I am in a hurry to make sail."

"Is it sail ye are after making; and do ye mane to take all those pretty craturs away wid ye? No, faith! another kiss, and another man."

I am not going to relate how many kisses these lovely girls bestowed on this envied captain. If such are captain's perquisites, who would not be a captain? Suffice it to say, they released the whole of their countrymen, and returned on board in triumph. The story reached Halifax, where the good-humoured admiral only said he was sorry he was not a captain, and all the happy society made themselves very merry with it. The captain, who is as brave as he is good, was promoted soon after, entirely from his own intrinsic merit, but not for this action, in which candour and friendship must acknowledge he was defeated. The Lord-Chancellor used to say, he always laughed at the settlement of pin-money, as ladies were either kicked out of it or kissed out of it; but his lordship, in the whole course of his legal practice, never saw a captain of a man-of-war kissed out of forty men by two pretty Irish girls. After this, who would not shout, *"Erin go bragh!"*

Dashing with a fine breeze out of the harbour, I saw with joy the field of fortune open to me, holding out a fair promise of glory and riches. "Adieu!" said I, in my heart, "adieu, ye lovely Nova Scotians! learn in future to distinguish between false glitter and real worth. Me ye prized for a handsome person and a smooth tongue, while you foolishly rejected men of ten times my worth, because they wanted the outward blandishments."

We were ordered to Bermuda, and on our first quitting the port steered away to the southward with a fair wind at north-west. This breeze soon freshened into a gale at southeast, and blew with some violence, but after a while it died away to a perfect calm, leaving a heavy swell, in which the ship rolled incessantly. About eleven o'clock the sky began to blacken; and, before noon, had assumed an appearance of the most dismal and foreboding darkness; the sea-gulls screamed as they flew distractedly by, warning us to prepare for the approaching hurricane, whose symptoms could hardly be mistaken. The warning was not lost upon us, most of our sails were taken in, and we had, as we thought, so well secured everything, as to bid defiance to the storm. About noon it came with a sudden and terrific violence that astonished the oldest and most experienced seaman among us: the noise it made was horrible, and its ravages inconceivable.

The wind was from the north-west—the water as it blew on board, and all over us, was warm as milk; the murkiness and close smell of the air was in a short time dispelled; but such was the violence of the wind, that, on the moment of its striking the ship, she lay over on her side with her lee guns under water. Every article that could move was danced to leeward; the shot flew out of the lockers, and the greatest confusion and dismay prevailed below, while above deck things went still worse; the mizzenmast and the fore and main topmast went over the side; but such was the noise of the wind, that we could not hear them fall; nor did I, who was standing close to the mizzenmast at the moment, know it was gone, until I turned round and saw the stump of the mast snapped in two like a carrot. The noise of the wind "waxed louder and louder;" it was like one continued peal of thunder; and the enormous waves as they rose were instantly beheaded by its fury, and sent in foaming spray along the bosom of the deep; the storm stay-sails flew to atoms; the captain, officers, and men, stood aghast, looking at each other, and waiting the awful event in utter amazement.

The ship lay over on her larboard side so heavily as to force in the gun ports, and the nettings of the waist hammocks, and seemed as if settling bodily down; while large masses of water, by the force of the wind, were whirled up into the air; and others were pouring down the hatchways, which we had not had time to batten down, and before we had succeeded, the lower deck was half full, and the chests and hammocks were all floating about in dreadful disorder. The sheep, cow, pigs, and poultry, were all washed overboard out of the waist and drowned; no voice could be heard, and no orders were given; all discipline was suspended; every man was equal to his neighbour; captain and sweeper clung alike to the same rope for security.

The carpenter was for cutting away the masts, but the captain would not consent. A seaman crawled aft on the quarter-deck, and screaming into the ear of the captain, informed him that one of the anchors had broke a-drift, and was hanging by the cable under the bows. To have let it remain long in this situation, was certain destruction to the ship, and I was ordered forward to see it cut away; but so much had the gale and the sea increased in a few minutes, that a passage to the forecastle was not to be found: on the weather side, the wind and sea were so violent that no man could face them. I was blown against the boats, and with difficulty got back to the quarter-deck; and going over to leeward, I swam along the gangway under the lee of the boats, and delivered the orders, which with infinite difficulty at last were executed.

On the forecastle, I found the oldest and stoutest seamen holding on by the weather rigging, and crying like children: I was surprised at this, and felt proud to be above such weakness. While my superiors in age and experience were sinking under apprehension, I was aware of our danger; and saw very clearly, that if the frigate did not right very shortly, it would be all over with us; for in spite of our precautions, the water was increasing below. I swam back to the quarter-deck, where the captain, who was as brave a man as ever trod a plank stood at the wheel with three of the best seamen; but such were the rude shocks which the rudder received from the sea, that it was with the utmost difficulty they could prevent themselves being thrown over the ship's side. The lee quarter-deck guns were under water; but it was proposed to throw them overboard; and as it was a matter of life and death, we succeeded. Still she lay like a log, and would not right, and settled down in a very alarming manner. The violence of the hurricane was unabated, and the general feeling seemed to be, "To prayers!—to prayers!—all lost!"

The fore and mainmasts still stood, supporting the weight of rigging and wreck which hung to them, and which, like a powerful lever, pressed the labouring ship down on her side. To disengage this enormous top hamper, was to us an object more to be desired than expected. Yet the case was desperate, and a desperate effort was to be made, or in half an hour we should have been past praying for, except by a Roman Catholic priest. The danger of sending a man aloft was so imminent, that the captain would not order one on this service; but calling the ship's company on the quarter-deck, pointed to the impending wreck, and by signs and gestures, and hard bawling, convinced them that unless the ship was immediately eased of her burden, she must go down.

At this moment every wave seemed to make a deeper and more fatal impression on her. She descended rapidly in the hollows of the sea, and rose with dull and exhausted motion, as if she felt she could do no more. She was worn out in the contest, and about to surrender, like a noble and battered fortress, to the overwhelming power of her enemies. The men seemed stupified with the danger; and I have no doubt, could they have got at the spirits, would have made themselves drunk; and in that state, have met their inevitable fate. At every lurch, the mainmast appeared as if making the most violent efforts to disengage itself from the ship: the weather shrouds became like straight bars of iron, while the lee shrouds hung over in a semi-circle to leeward, or with the weather-roll, banged against the mast, and threatened instant destruction, each moment, from the convulsive jerks. We expected to see the mast fall, and with it the side of the ship to be beat in. No man could be found daring enough, at the captain's request, to venture aloft, and cut away the wreck of the main-top mast, and the main-yard, which was hanging up and down, with the weight of the top-mast and top-sail yard resting upon it. There was a dead and stupid pause, while the hurricane, if any thing, increased in violence.

I confess that I felt gratified at this acknowledgment of a danger which none dare face. I waited a few seconds, to see if a volunteer would step forward, resolved, if he did, that I would be his enemy for life, inasmuch as he would have robbed me of the gratification of my darling passion—unbounded pride. Dangers, in common with others, I had often faced, and been the first to encounter; but to dare that which a gallant and hardy crew of a frigate had declined, was a climax of superiority which I had never dreamed of attaining. Seizing a sharp tomahawk, I made signs to the captain that I would attempt to cut away the wreck, follow me who dared. I mounted the weather-rigging; five or six hardy seamen followed me; sailors will rarely refuse to follow where they find an officer to lead the way.

The jerks of the rigging had nearly thrown us overboard, or jammed us with the wreck. We were forced to embrace the shrouds with arms and legs; and anxiously, and with breathless apprehension for our lives, did the captain, officers, and crew, gaze on us as we mounted, and cheered us at every stroke of the tomahawk. The danger seemed passed when we reached the catharpens, where we had foot room. We divided our work, some took the lanyards of the topmast rigging, I, the slings of the main-yard. The lusty blows we dealt, were answered by corresponding crashes; and at length, down fell the tremendous wreck over the larboard gunwale. The ship felt instant relief; she righted, and we descended amidst the cheers, the applauses, the congratulations, and, I may add, the tears of gratitude, of most of our shipmates. The work now become lighter, the gale abated every moment, the wreck was gradually cleared away, and we forgot our cares.

This was the proudest moment of my life, and no earthly possession would I have taken in exchange for what I felt when I once more placed my foot on the quarter-deck. The approving smile of the captain—the hearty shake by the hand—the praises of the officers—the eager gaze of the ship's company, who looked on me with astonishment and obeyed me with alacrity, were something in my mind, when abstractedly considered, but nothing compared to the inward feeling of gratified ambition, a passion so intimately interwoven in my existence, that to have eradicated it, the whole fabric of my frame must have been demolished. I felt pride justified.

Hurricanes are rarely of long continuance; this was succeeded by a gale, which, though strong, was fine weather compared to what we had seen. We fell to work, rigged our jury-mast, and in a few days presented ourselves to the welcome gaze of the town of Halifax, which having felt the full force of the hurricane, expressed very considerable alarm for our safety. My arms and legs did not recover for some time from the effects of the bruises I had received in going aloft, and for some days I remained on board. When I recovered I went on shore, and was kindly and affectionately received by my numerous friends.

I had not been long at Halifax, before a sudden change took place in the behaviour of my captain towards me. The cause I could never exactly discover, though I had given myself some room for conjecture. I must confess, with sorrow, that notwithstanding his kindness to me on every occasion, and notwithstanding my high respect for him, as an officer and a gentleman, I had raised a laugh against him. But he was too good-humoured a man to be offended at such a harmless act of youthful levity; and five minutes were usually the limits of anger with this amiable man, on such occasions as I am about to relate.

The fact was this; my truly noble captain sported a remarkable wide pair of blue trousers. Whether he thought it sailor-like, or whether his tailor was afraid of putting his lordship to short allowance of cloth, for fear of phlogistic consequences, I know not; but broad as was the beam of his lordship, still broader and more ample in proportion were the folds of this essential part of his drapery, quite enough to have embraced twice the volume of human flesh contained within them, large as it undoubtedly was.

That "a stitch in time saves nine," is a wise saw; unhappily, like many others of the same thrifty kind, but little heeded in this our day. So it was with Lord Edward. A rent had, by some mischance been made in the central seam, and, on the morning of the hurricane, was still unmended. When the gale came, it sought a quarrel with any thing it could lay hold of, and the harmless trousers of Lord Edward became subject to its mighty and resistless devastation; the blustering Boreas entered by the seam aforesaid, and filled the trousers like the cheeks of a trumpeter. Yorkshire wool could not stand the inflated pressure—the dress split to ribbons, and soundly flagellated the very part it was intended to conceal. What could he do, "in sweet confusion lost and dubious *flutterings*"—the only defence left against the rude blast, was his shirt (for the weather was so warm that second garments were dispensed with), and this too being old, fled in tatters before the gale. In short, clap a sailor's jacket on the Gladiator in Hyde-park, and you have a fair view of Lord Edward in the hurricane.

The case was inconvenient enough; but as the ship was in distress, and we all expected to go to the bottom in half an hour, it was not worth while to quit the deck to replace the dress, which would have availed him nothing in the depths of the sea, particularly as we were not likely to meet with any ladies there; nor if there had been any, was it a matter of any moment whether we went to Davy's Locker with or without breeches; but when the danger was passed, the joke began to appear, and I was amusing a large company with the *tale* when his lordship came in. The titter of the ladies increased to a giggle, and then, by regular gradation, to a loud and uncontrollable laugh. He very soon discovered that he was the subject, and I the cause, and for a minute or two seemed sulky; but it soon went off, and I cannot think this was the reason of his change of sentiments; for, although it is high treason in a midshipman to look black at the captain's dog, much less to laugh at the captain under any circumstances, still I knew that my captain was too good a fellow to be offended with such a trifle. I rather suspect I was wished out of the ship by the first lieutenant and gun-room officers; and they were right, for where an inferior officer is popular with the men, discipline must suffer from it. I received a good-natured hint from Lord Edward, that another captain, in a larger frigate, would be happy to receive me. I understood him; we parted good friends, and I shall ever think of him with respect and gratitude.

My new captain was a very different sort of man, refined in his manner, a scholar and a gentleman. Kind and friendly with his officers, his library was at their disposal; the fore-cabin, where his books were usually kept, was open to all; it was the school-room of the young midshipmen, and the study of the old ones. He was an excellent draughtsman, and I profited not a little by his instructions; he loved the society of the ladies, so did I; but he being a married man was more select in his company, and more correct in his conduct than I could pretend to be.

We were ordered to Quebec, sailed through the beautiful Gut of Canso, and up the spacious and majestic St Lawrence, passing in sight of the Island of Anticosta. Nothing material occurred during the passage, save that a Scotch surgeon's-assistant, having adopted certain aristocratic notions, required a democratical lecture on heads, which was duly administered to him. He pretended that he was, by birth and education (at Edinburgh), entitled to be at the head of our mess. This I resisted, and soon taught the ambitious son of Esculapius that the science of defence was as important as the art of healing; and that if he was skilful in this latter, I would give him an opportunity of employing it on his own person: whereupon I implanted on his cinciput, occiput, os frontis, os nasi, and all other vulnerable parts of his body, certain concussions calculated to stupify and benumb the censorium, and to produce under each eye a quantity of black extravasated blood; while, at the same time, a copious stream of carmine fluid issued from either nostril. It was never my habit to bully or take any unfair advantage, so, having perceived a cessation of arms on his part, I put the usual interrogatives as to whether the party contending was satisfied; and being answered in the affirmative, I laid by my metacarpal bones until they might be farther wanted, either for reproof or correction.

We anchored off Cape Diamond, which divides the St Lawrence from the little river St Charles. The continuation of this cape, as it recedes, forms the Heights of Abraham, on which the immortal Wolfe defeated Montcalm, in the year 1759, when both the generals ended their glorious career on the field of battle. The city stands on the extremity of the cape, and has a very romantic appearance. The houses and churches are generally covered with tin, to prevent conflagration, to which this place was remarkably subject when the houses were covered with thatch or shingle. When the rays of the sun lay on the buildings, they had the appearance of being cased in silver.

One of our objects in going to Quebec was to procure men, of which the squadron was very deficient. Our seamen and marines were secretly and suddenly formed into press-gangs. The command of one of them was conferred on me. The officers and marines went on shore in disguise, having agreed on private signals and places of rendezvous; while the seamen on whom we could depend, acted as decoy ducks, pretending to belong to merchant vessels, of which their officer was the master, and inducing them to engage, for ten gallons of rum and three hundred dollars, to take the run home. Many were procured in this manner, and were not undeceived until they found themselves alongside of the frigate, when their oaths and execrations may be better conceived than described or repeated.

It may be proper to explain here that the vessels employed in the timber trade arrive in the month of June, as soon as the ice is clear of the river, and, if they do not sail by or before the end of October, are usually set fast in the ice, and forced to winter in the St Lawrence, losing their voyage, and lying seven or eight months idle. Aware of this, the sailors, as soon as they arrive, desert, and are secreted and fed by the crimps, who make their market of them in the fall of the year by selling them to the captains; procuring for the men an exorbitant sum for the voyage home, and for themselves a handsome *douceur* for their trouble, both from the captain and the sailor.

We were desired not to take men out of the merchant vessels, but to search for them in the houses of the crimps. This was to us a source of great amusement and singular adventure; for the ingenuity in concealing them was only equalled by the art and cunning exercised in the discovery of their abodes. Cellars and lofts were stale and out of use; we found more game in the interior of haystacks, church steeples, closets under fire-places where the fire was burning. Some we found headed up in sugar-hogsheads, and some concealed within bundles of hoop-staves. Sometimes we found seamen, dressed as gentlemen, drinking wine and talking with the greatest familiarity with people much above them in rank, who had used these means to conceal them. Our information led us to detect these excusable impositions.

I went into the country, about fifteen miles from Quebec, where I had heard of a crimp's preserve, and after a tedious search, discovered some good seamen on the rafters of an outhouse intended only to smoke and cure bacon; and as the fires were lighted, and the smoke ascending, it was difficult to conceive a human being could exist there: nor should we have discovered them if one of them had not coughed; on which he received the execrations of the others, and the whole party was instantly handed out. We immediately cut the strings of their trousers behind, to prevent their running away, (this ought never to be omitted), and, placing them and ourselves in the farmer's waggon, made him put his team to and drive us all to Quebec, the new-raised men joining with our own in all the jokes which flew thick about on the occasion of their discovery. It was astonishing to me how easily these fine fellows reconciled themselves to the thoughts of a man-of-war; perhaps the approaching row with the Yankees tended very much to preserve good humour. I became an enthusiast in man-hunting, although sober reflection has since convinced me of its cruelty, injustice, and inexpediency, tending to drive seamen from the country more than any measure the government could adopt; but I am not going to write a treatise on impressment. I cared not one farthing about the liberty of the subject, as long as I got my ship well manned for the impending conflict; and as I gratified my love of adventure, I was as thoughtless of the consequences as when I rode over a farmer's turnips in England, or broke through his hedges in pursuit of a fox.

A tradesman at Quebec had affronted me, by refusing to discount a bill which I had drawn on my father. I had no other means of paying him for the goods I had purchased of him, and was much disconcerted at his refusal, which he accompanied with an insult to myself and my cloth, never to be forgotten. Turning the paper over and over, he said, "a midshipman's bill is not worth a farthing, and I am too old a bird to be caught with such chaff."

Conscious that the bill was good, I vowed revenge. My search-warrant enabled me to go wherever I could get information of men being concealed—this was easily obtained from a brother mid (the poor man might as well have been in the hands of the holy brotherhood). My companion stated his firm conviction that sailors were concealed in the house; I applied to the captain, and received orders to proceed by all means in execution of my duty. The tradesman was a man of consequence in Quebec, being what is there called a large storekeeper, though we in England should have called him a shopkeeper. About one o'clock in the morning we hammered at his door with no gentle tap, demanding admittance in the name of our sovereign lord the king. We were refused, and forthwith broke open the door, and spread over his house like a nest of cockroaches. Cellars, garrets, maids' room, ladies' rooms, we entered, *sans ceremonie;* paid little regard to the Medicean costume of the fair occupants; broke some of the most indispensable articles of bedroom furniture; rattled the pots and pans about in the kitchen; and, finding the two sons of the master of the house, ordered them to dress and come with us, certain, we said, that they were sailors.

When the old tradesman saw me he began to smell a rat, and threatened me with severe punishment. I shewed him my search-warrant, and asked him if it was a *good bill.* After having inspected every part of the house, I departed, leaving the two young cubs half dead with fear. The next day, a complaint was lodged at the government-house; but investigation is a long word when a man-of-war is ordered on service. Despatches from Albany reached Quebec, stating that the President of the United States had declared war against England; in consequence of which, our captain took leave of the governor, and dropped down the river with all speed, so I never heard any more of my tradesman.

We arrived at Halifax full manned, and immediately received orders to proceed to sea, "to sink, burn, and destroy." We ran for Boston bay, when, on the morning we made the land, we discovered ten or twelve sail of merchant vessels. The first we boarded was a brig; one of our boats was lowered down; I got into her, and jumped on the deck of the Yankee, while the frigate continued in chase of the others. The master of the vessel sat on a hen-coop, and did not condescend to rise or offer me the least salute as I passed him; he was a short, thick, paunchy-looking fellow.

"You are an Englishman, I guess?"

"I guess I am," I said, imitating him with a nasal twang.

"I thought we shouldn't be long in our waters afore we met some of you old-country sarpents. No harm in what I've said, I hope?" added the master.

"Oh, no," said I, "not the least; it will make no difference in the long run. But where do you come from, and where are you bound?"

"Come from Smyrna, and bound to Boston, where I hope to be to-morrow morning, by the blessing of God, and a good conscience."

From this answer, I perceived that he was unacquainted with the war, and I therefore determined to play with him a little before I gave him the fatal news.

"And pray," said I, "what might your cargo consist of? you appear to be light."

"Not so light neither, I guess," said the man; "we have sweet oil, raisins, and what we calls notions."

"I have no notion," said I, "what they might be. Pray explain yourself."

"Why, you see, notions is what we call a little of all sorts like. Some likes one thing, you know, and some another: some likes sweet almonds, and some likes silk, and some likes opium, and some" (he added, with a cunning grin) "likes dollars."

"And are these the notions with which you are loaded?" said I.

"I guess they are," replied Jonathan.

"And what might your outward cargo have been?" said I.

"Salt fish, flour, and tobacco," was his answer.

"And is this all you have in return?" I asked. "I thought the Smyrna trade had been a very good one."

"Well, so it is," said the unwary Yankee. "Thirty thousand dollars in the cabin, besides the oil and the rest of the goods, an't no bad thing."

"I am very glad to hear of the dollars," said I.

"What odds does that make to you?" said the captain; "it won't be much on 'em as 'll come to your share."

"More than you may think," said I. "Have you heard the news as you came along?"

At the word "news," the poor man's face became the colour of one in the jaundice. "What news?" said he, in a state of trepidation that hardly admitted of utterance.

"Why, only that your president, Mr Madison, has thought fit to declare war against England."

"You're only a joking?" said the captain.

"I give you my word of honour I am serious," said I; "and your vessel is a prize to his Britannic majesty's ship, the ———."

The poor man fetched a sigh from the waistband of his trousers. "I am a ruined man," said he. "I only wish I'd known a little sooner of the war you talk about: I've got two nice little guns there forward; you shouldn't a had me so easily."

I smiled at his idea of resistance against a fast-sailing frigate of fifty guns; but left him in the full enjoyment of his conceit, and changing the subject, asked if he had any thing he could give us to drink, for the weather was very warm.

"No, I ha'n't," he replied, peevishly; "and if I had—"

"Come, come, my good fellow," said I, "you forget you are a prize; civility is a cheap article, and may bring you a quick return."

"That's true," said Jonathan, who was touched on the nicest point—self; "that's true, you are only a doing your duty. Here, boy, fetch up that ere demi John of Madeira, and for aught I know, the young officer might like a drop o'long cork; bring us some tumblers, and one o' they claret bottles out o' the starboard after locker."

The boy obeyed—and the articles quickly appeared. While this dialogue was going on, the frigate was in chase, firing guns, and bringing-to the different vessels as she passed them, dropping a boat on board of one, and making sail after another. We stood after her with all the sail we could conveniently carry.

"Pray," said the captain, "might I offer you a bit of something to eat? I guess you ha'n't dined yet, as it isn't quite meridian."

I thanked him, and accepted his offer: he ran down instantly to the cabin, as if to prepare for my reception; but I rather thought he wished to place some articles out of my sight, and this proved to be the case, for he stole a bag of dollars out of the cargo. In a short time, I was invited down. A leg of cured pork, and a roasted fowl, were very acceptable to a midshipman at any time, but particularly so to me; and, when accompanied by a few glasses of the Madeira, the barometer of my spirits rose in proportion to the depression of his.

"Come, captain," said I, filling a bumper of claret, "here's to a long and bloody war."

"D——n the dog that won't say amen to that," said the master; "but where do you mean to carry me to? I guess to Halifax. Sha'n't I have my clothes, and my own private *venter?*"

"All your private property," said I, "will be held sacred; but your vessel and cargo are ours."

"Well, well," said the man, "I know that; but if you behave well to me, you sha'n't find I'm ungrateful. Let me have my things, and I'll give you a bit o' news, as will be of sarvice to you."

He then told me, on my promising him his private venture, that we had not a moment to lose, for that a vessel, just visible on the horizon, was from Smyrna, richly laden; she was commanded by a townsman of his, and bound to the same place. I turned from him with contempt, and at the same moment made the signal to speak the frigate. On going on board, I told the captain what I had heard from the master of the prize, and the promise I had given. He approved of it; the proper number of men were instantly sent back to the brig, the prisoners taken out, and the frigate made sail in chase of the indicated vessel, which she captured that night at nine o'clock.

I would not willingly believe that such perfidy is common among the Americans. On parting with the master of my brig, a sharp dialogue took place between us.

"I guess I'll fit out a privateer, and take some o' your merchanters."

"Take care you are not taken yourself," said I, "and pass your time on board one of our prison ships; but, remember, whatever may happen, it's all your own fault. You have picked a German quarrel with us, to please Boney; and he will only spit in your face when you have done your best for him. Your wise president has declared war against the mother country."

"D——n the mother country," muttered the Yankee, "step-mother, I guess, you mean, tarnation seize her!!!"

We continued following the ship, and by night-time the frigate had secured eight prizes; one of them being a brig in ballast, the prisoners were put on board of her, my Yankee friend among the number, and turned adrift, to find their way home. We took care to give to all of them their private ventures and their clothes. I was in hopes of being allowed to go to Halifax with my prize; but the captain, knowing how I was likely to pass my time, kept me with him. We cruised two months, taking many privateers, some large and some small; some we burned, and some we scuttled.

One day we had one of these craft alongside, and having taken every thing out of her that was worth moving, we very imprudently set her on fire before she was clear of the ship's side; and as we were on a wind, it was some minutes before we could get her clear. In the meantime the fire began to blaze up in a very alarming manner under the mizzen chains, where, by the attraction of the two floating bodies, she seemed resolved to continue; but on our putting the helm up, and giving the vessel a sheer the contrary way, as soon as we were before the wind, she parted from us, to our great joy, and was soon in a volume of flame. Our reason for setting her on fire alongside was to save time, as we wanted to go in chase of another vessel, seen from the mast-head, and lowering a boat down to destroy this vessel would have detained us.

Before the end of the cruise, we chased a schooner, which ran on shore and bilged; we boarded her, brought away her crew and part of her cargo, which was very valuable. She was from Bordeaux, bound to Philadelphia. I was sent to examine her, and endeavour to bring away more of her cargo. The tide rising in her, we were compelled to rip up her decks, and discovered that she was laden with bales of silk, broad cloths, watches, clocks, laces, silk stockings, wine, brandy, bars of steel, olive-oil, &c., &c. I sent word of this to the captain; and the carpenter and plenty of assistants arriving, we rescued a great quantity of the goods from the deep or the Yankee boats, who would soon have been on board after we left her. We could perceive in the hold some cases, but they were at least four feet under water. It was confoundedly cold; but I thought there was something worth diving for, so down I went, and contrived to keep myself long enough under water to hook one end of a case, by which means we broke it out and got it up. It was excellent claret, and we were not withheld from drinking it by any scruples of conscience; for if I had not dived for it, it would never have come to the mouth of an Englishman. We discussed a three-dozen case among just so many of us, in a reasonable short time; and as it was October, we felt no ill effects from a frequent repetition of the dose.

I never felt colder, and diving requires much stimulant. From practice at this work, I could pick up pins and needles in a clear, sandy bottom; and, considering the density of the medium, could live like a beaver under water; but I required ample fees for my trouble. When we returned on board, we were very wet and cold, and the wine took no effect on us; but as soon as we thawed, like the horn of the great Munchausen, the secret escaped, for we were all tipsy. The captain inquired the cause of this the next day, and I very candidly told him the whole history. He was wise enough to laugh at it; some captains would have flogged every one of the men, and disgraced the officers.

On our return into port, I requested permission to go to England in order to pass my examination as lieutenant, having nearly completed my servitude as a midshipman. I was asked to remain out, and take my chance for promotion in the flag-ship; but more reasons than I chose to give, induced me to prefer an examination at a sea-port in England, and I obtained my discharge and came home. The reader will no doubt give me credit for having written some dozen of letters to Eugenia: youth, beauty, and transient possession had still preserved my attachment to her unabated. Emily I had heard of, and still loved with a purer flame. She was my sun; Eugenia my moon; and the fair favourites of the western hemisphere, so many twinkling stars of the first, second, and third magnitude. I loved them all more or less; but all their charms vanished, when the beauteous Emily shone in my breast with refulgent light.

I had received letters from my father, who wished me to come home, that he might present me to some of the great men of the nation, and secure my promotion to the highest ranks of the service. This advice was good, and, as it suited my views, I followed it. I parted with my captain on the best terms, took leave of all my messmates and the officers in the same friendly manner, and last, not least, went round to the ladies, kissing, hugging, crying, and swearing love and eternal attachment. Nothing, I declared, should keep me from Halifax, as soon as I had passed; nothing prevent my marrying one, as soon as I was a lieutenant; a second was to have the connubial knot tied when I was a commander; and a third, as soon as I was made a captain. Oh, how like was I to Don Galaor! Oh, how unlike the constant Amadis de Gaul! But, reader, you must take me as I was, not as I ought to have been.

After a passage of six weeks, I arrived at Plymouth, and had exactly completed my six years' servitude.

CHAPTER XV

Examine him closely, goodman Dry; spare him not.
Ask him impossible questions. Let us thwart him, let us
thwart him.

BEAUMONT AND FLETCHER

SOON after my arrival at Plymouth, notice was given by a general order, issued from the flag-ship, that a passing-day for the examination of midshipmen, as touching their qualifications for the rank of lieutenant, would be held on board the *Salvador del Mundo,* in Hamoaze. I lost no time in acquainting my father with this, and telling him that I felt quite prepared, and meant to offer myself. Accordingly, on the day appointed, your humble servant, with some fourteen or fifteen other youthful aspirants, assembled on board the flag-ship. Each was dressed out in our No.1 suits, in most exact and unquizzable uniform, with a large bundle of log-books under our arms. We were all huddled together in a small screened canvas cabin, like so many sheep ready for slaughter.

About eleven o'clock, the captains who were to be our Minos and our Rhadamanthus, made their appearance, and we all agreed that we did not much like the "cut of their jibs." At twelve o'clock the first name was called. The "desperate youth" tried to pluck up a little courage—he cleared his throat, pulled up his shirt collar, touched his neck-handkerchief, and seizing his cocked hat and journals, boldly followed the messenger into the captain's cabin, where three grave-looking gentlemen, in undress uniform, awaited him. They were seated at a round table; a clerk was at the elbow of the president; Moore's navigation, that wise redoubtable, lay before them; together with a nautical almanack, a slate and pencil, ink and paper. The trembling middy advanced to the table, and having most respectfully deposited his journals and certificates of sobriety and good conduct, was desired to sit down. The first questions were merely theoretical; and although in the gun-room, or in any other company, he would have acquitted himself with ease, he was so abashed and confounded, that he lost his head entirely, trembled at the first question, stared at the second, and having no answer to make to the third, was dismissed, with directions "to go to sea six months longer."

He returned to us with a most woe-begone countenance. I never saw a poor creature in greater mental torment. I felt for him the more, as I knew not how soon his case might be my own. Another was called, and soon returned with no better success; and the description he gave of the bullying conduct of the youngest passing captain was such as to damp the spirits, and enough to stultify minds so inexperienced as ours, and where so much depended on our success. This hint was, however, of great use to me. Theory, I found, was the rock on which they had split; and in this part of my profession, I knew my powers, and was resolved not to be bowled out by the young captain. But while I thus resolved, a third candidate was returned to us *re infecta;* and this was a young man on whose talents I could have relied: I began to doubt myself. When the fourth came out with a smiling face, and told us he had passed, I took a little breath; but even this comfort was snatched from me in a moment, by his saying that one of the passing captains was a friend of his father. Here then was solved an enigma; for this fellow, during the short time I was in his company, gave proof of being no better than a simpleton.

On my own name being called, I felt a flutter about the heart which I did not feel in action, or in the hurricane, or when, in a case more desperate than either, I jumped over-board at Spithead, to swim to my dear Eugenia. "Powers of Impudence, as well as Algebra," said I, "lend me your aid, or I am undone." In a moment the cabin door flew open, the sentinel closed it after me, and I found myself in the presence of this most awful triumvirate. I felt very like Daniel in the lions' den. I was desired to take a chair, and a short discussion ensued between the judges, which I neither heard nor wished to hear: but while it lasted, I had time to survey my antagonists from head to foot. I encouraged myself to think that I was equal to one of them; and if I could only neutralise him, I thought I should very easily floor the other two.

One of these officers had a face like a painted pumpkin; and his hand, as it lay on the table, looked more like the fin of a turtle; the nails were bitten so close off, that the very remains of them seemed to have retreated into the flesh, for fear of farther depredation, which the other hand was at the moment suffering. Thinks I to myself, "If ever I saw 'lodgings to let, unfurnished,' it is in that cocoa-nut, or pumpkin, or gourd of yours."

The next captain to him was a little, thin, lark, dried up, shrivelled fellow, with keen eyes, and a sharp nose. The midshipmen called him "Old Chili Vinegar," or, "Old Hot and Sour." He was what we term a martinet. He would keep a man two months on his black list, giving him a breech of a gun to polish and keep bright, never allowing him time to mend his clothes, or keep himself clean, while he was cleaning that which, for all the purposes of war, had better have been black. He seldom flogged a man; but he tormented him into sullen discontent, by what he called "keeping the devil out of his mind." This little night-mare, who looked like a dried eel-skin, I soon found was the leader of the band.

The third captain was a tall, well-looking, pompous man (he was the junior officer of the three), with a commanding and most unbending countenance: "He would not ope his mouth in way of smile, though Nestor swore the jest was laughable."

I had just time to finish my survey, and form a rough estimate of the qualities of my examiners, when I was put upon my trial by the president, who thus addressed me,

"You are perfect in the theory of navigation, I presume, Sir, or you would not come here?"

I replied, that I hoped I should be found so, if they would please to try me.

"Ready enough with his answer," said the tall captain; "I daresay this fellow is jaw-master-general in the cockpit.—Who did you serve your time with, Sir?"

I stated the different captains I had served with, particularly Lord Edward.

"Oh, ay, that's enough; you *must* be a smart fellow, if you have served with Lord Edward."

I understood the envious and sarcastic manner in which this was uttered, and prepared accordingly for an arduous campaign, quite sure that this man, who was no seaman, would have been too happy in turning back one of Lord Edward's midshipmen. Several problems were given to me, which I readily solved, and returned to them. They examined my logs and certificates with much seeming scrutiny, and then ventured a question in the higher branches of mathematics. This I also solved; but I found talent was not exactly what they wanted. The little skinny captain seemed rather disappointed that he could not find fault with me. A difficult problem in spherical trigonometry lay before them, carefully drawn out, and the result distinctly marked at the bottom; but this I was not, of course, permitted to see. I soon answered the question; they compared my work with that which had been prepared for them; and as they did not exactly agree, I was told that I was wrong. I was not disconcerted, and very deliberately looking over my work, I told them I could not discover any error, and was able to prove it by inspection, by Canon, by Gunter, or by figure.

"You think yourself a very clever fellow, I dare say," said the little fat captain.

"A second Euclid!" said the tall captain. "Pray, Sir, do you know the meaning of *'Pons Asinorum?'*"

"Bridge of Asses, Sir," said I, staring him full in the face, with a smile under the skin.

Now it was very clear to me that the little fat captain had never heard of the Asses Bridge before, and therefore supposed I was quizzing the tall captain, who, from having been what we used to term a "harbour-duty man" all his life, had heard of the *Pons Asinorum,* but did not know which of the problems of Euclid it was, nor how it was applicable to navigation. The fat captain, therefore burst into a horse laugh, saying, "I think he hits you hard; you had better let him alone: he will puzzle you presently."

Nettled at this observation of his brother officer, the tall captain was put upon his metal, and insisted that the question last proposed was not satisfactorily answered, and swore by G—— that he never would sign my certificate until I did it.

I persisted; the two works were compared: I was threatened to be turned back; when, lo, to the dismay of the party, the error was found in their own work. The fat captain, who was a well-meaning man, laughed heartily; the other two looked very silly and very angry.

"Enough of this, Sir," said the martinet: "now stand up, and let us see what you can do with a ship." A ship was supposed to be on the stocks; she was launched; I was appointed to her, and, as first lieutenant, ordered to prepare her for sea. I took her into dock, and saw her coppered; took her along the sheer-hulk, masted her; laid her to the ballast-wharf, took in and stowed her iron ballast and her tanks; moved off to a hulk or receiving ship, rigged her completely, bent her sails, took in guns, stores, and provisions; reported her ready for sea, and made the signal for a pilot; took her out of harbour, and was desired to conduct her into other harbours, pointing out the shoals and dangers of Portsmouth, Plymouth, Falmouth, the Downs, Yarmouth Roads, and even to Shetland.

But the little martinet and the tall captain had not forgiven me for being right in the problem, and my examination continued. They put my ship into every possible situation which the numerous casualties of a sea life present in such endless variety. I set and took in every sail, from a sky-sail to try-sail. I had my masts shot away, and I rigged jury-masts: I made sail on them, and was getting fairly into port, when the little martinet very cruelly threw my ship on her beam-ends on a dead lee-shore, a dark night, and blowing a hurricane, and told me to get her out of that scrape if I could. I replied that, if there was anchorage, I should anchor, and take my chance; but if there was no anchorage, neither he nor any one else could save the ship, without a change of wind, or the special interference of Providence. This did not satisfy old Chili Vinegar. I saw that I was persecuted, and that the end would be fatal to my hopes: I therefore became indifferent; was fatigued with the endless questions put to me; and, very fortunately for me, made a mistake, at least in the opinion of the tall captain. The question at that time was one which was much controverted in the service; namely, whether, on being taken flat aback, you should put your helm a turn or two alee, or keep it amidship? I preferred the latter mode; but the tall captain insisted on the former, and gave his reasons. Finding myself on debateable ground, I gave way, and thanked him for his advice, which I said I should certainly follow whenever the case occurred to me; not that I felt convinced then, and have since found that he was wrong; still my apparent tractability pleased his self-love, and he became my advocate. "He grinned horribly a ghastly smile," and, turning to the other captains, asked if they were satisfied.

This question, like the blow of the auctioneer's hammer, ends all discussion; for captains, on these occasions, never gainsay each other; I was told that my passing certificate would be signed. I made my best bow and my exit, reflecting, as I returned to the "sheep pen," that I had nearly lost my promotion by wounding their vanity, and had regained my ground by flattering it. Thus the world goes on; and from my earliest days, my mind was strengthened and confirmed in every vice by the pernicious example of my superiors.

I might have passed much more easily abroad. I remember, one fine day at sea, in the West Indies, a boat was lowered down, and sent with a young midshipman (whose time was not fairly served, and whose age and appearance indicated anything but nautical knowledge) to a ship then in company; in a quarter of an hour he returned, with his passing certificate. We were all astonished, and inquired what questions were put to him; he said, "None at all, except as to the health of my father and mother; and whether I would have port or white wine and water. On coming away," the brat added, "one of the captains desired I would, when I wrote home, give his best respects to Lord and Lady G. He had ordered a turkey to be picked and put in the boat for me, and wished me success."

This boy was soon afterwards made a post-captain; but fortunately for the service, died on his passage to England.

There was certainly some difference between this examination and mine; but when it was over, I rejoiced at the severity of my ordeal. My pride, my darling pride, was tickled at the triumph of my talents; and as I wiped away the perspiration from my forehead, I related my difficulties, my trials, and my success, with a degree of self-complacency that in any other person I should have called egregious vanity. One good effect resulted from my long examination, which continued an hour and a half—this was, that the captains passed all the other midshipmen with very few questions. They were tired of their employment; and thus it was only the poor unlucky devils that took off the fiery edge of their morning zeal, who suffered; and among "the plucked," it was known there were much cleverer fellows than many of those who had come off with flying colours.

There was one circumstance which amused me. When the captains came on deck, the little Chili Vinegar called me to him, and enquired whether I was any relation of Mr ———. I replied that he was my uncle.

"Bless my soul, Sir! why he is my most intimate friend. Why did you not tell me you were his nephew?"

I answered with an affected humility, very nearly allied to impertinence, that I could not see by his face that he knew my uncle; nor, indeed, had I known it, should I have thought it delicate to have mentioned it at such a time; as it might not only have implied a want of confidence in my own abilities, but also a suspicion that he might, by such a communication, have been induced to deviate from the rigid path of his duty, and might therefore have received it as a personal affront.

"All that is very fine, and very true," said the veteran; "but when you have an older head upon your shoulders, and have seen a little more of our service, you will learn to trust at least as much to friends as to merit; and rely on it, that if you could make yourself out cousin-german to the old tom-cat at the Admiralty, you would fare all the better for it. However, it's all over now, and there's an end of it; but make my compliments to your uncle, and tell him that you passed your examination in a manner highly creditable to you."

So saying, he touched his hat to the serjeant's guard, and slipped down the side into his gig. As he descended, I said to myself, "D——n your monkey face, you coffee-coloured little rascal—no thanks to you if I have passed. I suppose your father was breeches-mender to the first lord's butler, or else you shared your mother's milk with a lord in waiting, and that's the way you got the command of the ———."

Elated with the result of the day, I threw myself into the mail that evening, and reached my father's house in a short time after. My reception was kind and affectionate; but death had made sad havoc in my family during my late absence. My elder brother and two sisters had been successively called to join my poor mother in heaven, and all that remained now to comfort my father was a younger sister and myself. I must confess that my father received me with great emotion; his own heavy afflictions from the loss of his children, and the dangers I had undergone, as well as the authentic assurances he had received of my good conduct were more than sufficient to bury all my errors in oblivion; and he appeared, and I have no doubt really was, fonder and prouder of me than ever.

As to what my own feelings were on this occasion, I shall not attempt to disguise them. Sorry I certainly was for the death of my nearest relatives; but when the intelligence reached me, I was in the midst of the most active service. Death in all its forms had become familiar to me; and so little impression did the event make on my mind, that I did not interrupt the thread of my history to speak of it when it occurred. I take shame to myself for not feeling more; but I am quite sure, from this one instance in my life, that the feelings are blunted in proportion to the increase of misery around us; that the parent who, in a moment of peace and domestic tranquillity, would be agonized at the loss of one child, would view the death of ten with comparative indifference, when surrounded by war, pestilence, or famine.

My feelings, never very acute in this respect, were completely blunted by my course of life. Those fond recollections which, in a calm scene, would have wrung from me some tears to their memory, were now drowned or absorbed in the waste, the profligacy, and the dissipation of war; and shall I add, that I easily reconciled myself to a loss which was likely so much to increase my worldly gain. For my eldest brother, I own that, even from childhood, I had felt a jealousy and dislike, fostered, as I think, in some measure unwisely, and in part unavoidably, by the conduct of my parents. In all matters of choice or distinction, Tom was to have the preference, because he was the oldest: this I thought hard enough; but when Tom had new clothes at Midsummer and Christmas, and his old ones were converted to my use, I honestly own I wished the devil had Tom. As a point of economy, perhaps, this could not be avoided; but it engendered a hatred towards my brother which often made me, in my own little malignant mind, find excuses for the conduct of Cain.

Tom was, to be sure, what is called a good boy; *he* never soiled his clothes, as I did. I was always considered as a rantipole, for whom any thing was good enough. But when I saw my brother tricked out in new clothes, and his old duds covering me, like a scarecrow, I appeal to any honourable mind whether it was in human nature to feel otherwise than I did, with-out possessing an angelic disposition, to which I never pretended; and I fairly own that I did shed not one fiftieth part so many tears over Tom's grave, as I did over his dirty pantaloons, when forced to put them on.

As for my sisters, I knew little about them, and cared less: we met during the holidays, and separated, without regret, after a month's quarrelling. When I went to sea, I ceased to think about them, concluding there was no love lost; but when I found that death had for ever robbed me of two of them, I felt the irretrievable loss. I reproached myself with my coldness and neglect; and the affection I had denied to them, I heaped threefold on my remaining sister: even before I had ever seen her on my return, the tide of fraternal love flowed towards her with an uncontrollable violence. All that I ought to have felt towards the others, was concentrated in her, and displayed itself with a force which surprised even myself.

Perhaps the reader may be astonished that my first inquiry in London, when I had seen my father and my family, should not have been after poor Eugenia, whom I had left, and who also had quitted me, under such very peculiar and interesting circumstances. I cannot, however, claim much credit for having performed this duty. I did go, without loss of time, to her agent; and all that my most urgent entreaty could obtain from him was that she was well; that I still had credit at his house for any sum I chose to draw for in moderation; but that her place of abode must, till farther orders from her, remain a secret.

As my father did not want interest, and my claims were backed by good certificates, I received my commission as a lieutenant in his Majesty's navy about a fortnight after my arrival in London; but not being appointed to any ship, I resolved to enjoy the *"otium cum dig.,"* and endeavour to make myself some amends for the hard campaign I had so lately completed in North America. I felt the transport of being a something: at least, I could live independent of my father, let the worst come to the worst; and I shall ever think this step gave me more real pleasure than either of the two subsequent ones which I have lived to attain. No sooner, therefore, had I taken up my commission, than my thoughts turned on my Emily; and two days after the attainment of my rank, I mentioned to my father my intention of paying a visit to ———— Hall.

He was at the time in high good humour; we were sitting over our bottle of claret, after an excellent *tête-à-tête* dinner, during which I contributed very much to his amusement by the recital of some of my late adventures. He shuddered at my danger in the hurricane, and his good-humoured sides had well nigh cracked with laughter when I recounted my pranks at Quebec and Prince Edward's Island. When I spoke of Miss Somerville, my father said he had no doubt she would be happy to see me—that she was now grown a very beautiful girl, and was the toast of the county.

I received this information with an apparent cool indifference which I was far from feeling inwardly, for my heart beat at the intelligence. "Perhaps," said I, picking my teeth, and looking at my mouth in a little ivory *etui*—"perhaps she may be grown a fine girl: she bade fair to be so when I saw her; but fine girls are very plenty now-a-days, since the Vaccine has turned out the small-pox. Besides, the girls have now another chance of a good shape; they are allowed to take the air, instead of sitting all day, with their feet in the stocks and their dear sweet noses bent over a French grammar, under the rod of a French governess."

Why I took so much pains to conceal from the best of parents the real state of my heart, I know not, except that, from habit, deceit was to me more readily at hand than candour; certainly my attachment to this fair and virtuous creature could not cause me to blush, except at my own unworthiness of so much excellence. My father looked disappointed; I know not why; but I afterwards learned that the subject of our union had, since my brother's death, been discussed and agreed to between him and Mr Somerville; and that our marriage was only to be deferred until I should have attained the rank of captain, provided always that the parties were agreed.

"I thought," said my father, "that you were rather smitten in that quarter?"

"Me smitten, Sir?" said I, with a look of astonishment. "I have, it is true, a very high respect for Miss Somerville; but as for being in love with her, I trust no little attentions on my part have been so construed. I have paid her no more attention than I may have done to any pretty girl I meet with." (This was, indeed, true, too true.)

"Well, well," said my father, "it is a mistake on my part."

And here the conversation on that subject was dropped.

It appeared that after the little arrangement between Mr Somerville and my father, and when I had gone to join my ship in America, they had had some communication together, in which Mr Somerville disclosed, that having questioned his daughter, she had ingenuously confessed that I was not indifferent to her. She acknowledged, with crimson blushes, that I had requested and obtained a lock of her hair. This Mr Somerville told my father in confidence. He was not, therefore, at liberty to mention it to me; but it sufficiently accounts for his astonishment at my seeming indifference;

for the two worthy parents had naturally concluded that it was a match.

Confounded and bewildered by my asseveration, my father knew not whose veracity to impeach; but, charitably concluding there was some mistake, or that I was, as heretofore, a fickle, thoughtless being, considered himself bound in honour to communicate the substance of our conversation to Mr Somerville; and the latter no sooner received it, than he placed the letter in Emily's hands—a very comfortable kind of *avant-courier* for a lover, after an absence from his mistress of full three years.

I arrived at the hall, bursting with impatience to see the lovely girl, whose hold on my heart and affection was infinitely stronger than I had ever supposed. Darting from the chaise, I flew into the sitting-room, where she usually passed her morning. I was now in my twenty-second year; my figure was decidedly of a handsome cast; my face, what I knew most women admired. My personal advantages were heightened by the utmost attention to dress; the society of the fair Acadians had very much polished my manners, and I had no more of the professional roughness of the sea than what, like the crust on the port-wine, gave an agreeable flavour, my countenance was as open and as ingenuous as my heart was deceitful and desperately wicked.

Emily rose with much agitation, and in an instant was clasped in my arms: not that the movement was voluntary on her part; it was wholly on mine. She rather recoiled; but for an instant seemed to have forgotten the fatal communication which her father had made to her not two hours before. She allowed me—perhaps she could not prevent it—to press her to my heart. She soon, however, regained her presence of mind, and, gently disengaging herself, gave vent to her feelings in a violent flood of tears.

Not at the time recollecting the conversation with my father, much less suspecting that Emily had been made acquainted with it, I cannot but confess that this reception surprised me. My caresses were repulsed, as coming from one totally disqualified to take such freedom. She even addressed me as Mr Mildmay, instead of "Frank."

"What may all this mean, my dearest Emily," said I, "after so long an absence? What can I have done to make so great an alteration in your sentiments? Is this the reward of affection and constancy? Have I so long worn this dear emblem of your affection next my heart, in battle and in tempest, to be spurned from you like a cur on my return?"

I felt that I had a clear right to boast of constancy; nor were the flirtations of Halifax and Quebec at all incompatible with such a declaration. The fair sex will start at this proposition; but it is nevertheless true. Emily was to me what the Dutchman's best anchor was to him—he kept it at home, for fear of losing it. He used other anchors in different ports, that answered the purpose tolerably well; but this best bower he always intended to ride by in the Nieu deep, when he had escaped all the dangers and quicksands of foreign shores: such was Emily to me. I thought of her when in the very jaws of the shark; I thought of her when I mounted the rigging in the hurricane; I thought of her when bored and tormented to madness by the old passing captains; all, all I might gain in renown was for her. Why, then, traitor like, did I deny her? For no other reason that I can devise than that endless love of plot and deceit which had "grown with my growth."

Madame de Staël has pronounced love to be an episode in a man's life; and so far it is true. There are as many episodes in life as there are in novels and romances; but in neither case do they destroy the general plot of the history, although they may, for the time, distract or divert our attention. Here, then, is the distinction between passion and love. I felt a passion for Eugenia, love for Emily. And why? Because although it was through my own persuasions and entreaties that her scruples had been overcome; although it was through her affection for me which would not allow her to refuse me any demand, even to the sacrifice of herself, that Eugenia had fallen, still, in the eyes of society, she had fallen; and I did not offer up a pure and holy love to that which was not accounted pure. In this I gave way, ungratefully, to the heartless casuistry of the world. But Emily, enshrined in modesty, with every talent, equal, if not superior charms, defended by rank and connection, was a flower perpetually blooming on the stem of virtue, that it would have amounted to sacrilege to attempt to have plucked; and the attempt itself would have savoured of insanity, from the utter hopelessness of success. Every sentiment connected with her was pure, from mere selfishness. Not for worlds would I have injured her; because in destroying her peace of mind, my own would have fled for ever. When I contemplated our final union, I blushed for my own unworthiness; and looked forward to the day when, by repentance and amendment, I might be deemed worthy to lead her to the altar.

I had not time to pursue these reflections any farther. Emily heard my appeal, and rising from her seat in the most dignified manner, addressed me in the commanding language of conscious virtue and injured innocence.

"Sir," said she, "I trust I am too honest to deceive you, or any one; nor have I done that of which I need be ashamed. Whatever reasons I may have to repent of my misplaced confidence, I will make no secret of that which now compels me to change my opinion of you; you will find them amply detailed in this paper," at the same time putting into my hand a letter from my father to Mr Somerville.

In a moment the mystery was unravelled, and conviction flashed in my face like the priming of a musket. Guilty, and convicted on the clearest evidence, I had nothing left for it, but to throw myself on her mercy; but while I stood undecided, and unknowing what to do, Mr Somerville entered, and welcomed me with kind, but cool hospitality. Seeing Emily in tears, and my father's letter in her hand, he knew that an *éclaircissement* had taken place, or was in progress. In this situation, candour, and an honest confession that I felt a *mauvaise honte* in disclosing my passion to my father would undoubtedly have been my safest course; but my right trusty friend, the devil, stepped in to my assistance, and suggested deceit, or a continuation of that chain by which he had long since bound me, and not one link of which he took care should ever be broken; and fortunately for me, this plan answered, at the time, better than candour.

"I must acknowledge, sir," said I, "that appearances are against me. I can only trust to your patient hearing, while I state the real facts. Allow me first to say, that my father's observations are hardly warranted by the conversation which took place; and if you will please, in the first place, to consider that that very conversation originated in my expressing a wish and intention of coming down to see you, and to produce to your daughter the memento so carefully guarded during my long absence, you must perceive that there is an incongruity in my conduct, difficult to explain, but still, through all these mazes and windings, I trust that truth and constancy will be found at the bottom. You may probably laugh at the idea, but I really felt jealous of my father's praises so lavishly bestowed on Miss Somerville; and not supposing he was aware of my attachment, I began to fear he had pretensions of his own. He is a widower, healthy, and not old; and it appeared to me that he only wanted my admiration to justify his choice of a step-mother for myself and sister. Thus, between love for Miss Somerville, and respect for my father, I scarcely knew how to act. That I should for one moment have felt jealous of my father, I now acknowledge with shame: yet labouring under the erroneous supposition of his attachment to an object which had been the only one of my adoration, I could net make up my mind to a disclosure, which I feared would have renewed our differences, and produced the most insuperable bars to our future reconciliation. This thought burned in my brain, and urged the speed of the jaded post-horses. If you will examine the drivers, they will tell you, that the whole way from town, they have been stimulated by the rapping of a Spanish dollar on the glass of the chaise. I dreaded my father getting the start of me; and busy fancy painted him, to my heated imagination, kneeling at the feet of my beloved Emily. Condemn me not, therefore, too harshly; only allow me the same lenient judgment which you exercised when I first had the pleasure of making your acquaintance."

This last sentence delicately recalled the scene at the inn, and the circumstances of my first introduction. The defence was not bad; it wanted but one simple ingredient to have made it excellent—I mean truth; but the court being strongly biassed in favour of the prisoner, I was acquitted, and at the same time, "admonished to be more careful in future." The reconciliation produced a few more tears from my beloved Emily, who soon after slipped out of the room to recover her flurry.

When Mr Somerville and myself were left together, he explained to me the harmless plot which had been laid for the union between his daughter and myself. How true it is, that the falling out of lovers is the renewal of love! The fair, white hand extended to me, was kissed with the more rapture, as I had feared the losing of it for ever. None enjoy the pleasures of a secure port, but he who has been tempest tossed, and in danger of shipwreck.

The dinner and the evening were among the happiest I can remember. We sat but a short time over our wine, as I preferred following my mistress to the little drawing-room, where tea and coffee were prepared, and where the musical instruments were kept. Emily sang and played to me, and I sang and accompanied her; and I thought all the clocks and watches in the house were at least three hours too fast, when, as it struck twelve, the signal was made to retire.

I had no sooner laid my head on my pillow than I began to call myself to a severe account for my duplicity; for, somehow or other, I don't know how it is, conscience is a very difficult sort of gentleman to deal with. A tailor's bill you may avoid by crossing the channel; but the duns of conscience follow you to the antipodes, and will be satisfied. I ran over the events of the day; I reflected that I had been on the brink of losing my Emily by an act of needless and unjustifiable deceit and double-dealing. Sooner or later I was convinced that this part of my character would be made manifest, and that shame and punishment would overwhelm me in utter ruin. The success which had hitherto attended me was no set-off against the risk I ran of losing for ever this lovely girl, and the respect and esteem of her father. For her sake, therefore, I made a vow for ever to abandon this infernal system. I mention this more particularly as it was the first healthy symptom of amendment I had discovered, and one to which I long and tenaciously adhered, as far, at least, as my habits and pursuits in life would allow me. I forgot, at that time, that to be ingenuous it was necessary to be virtuous. There is no cause for concealment when we do not act wrong.

A letter from Mr Somerville to my father explained my conduct; and my father, in reply, said I certainly must have been mad. To this I assented, quoting Shakespeare—"the lunatic, the lover, and the poet, &c.!" So long as I was out of the scrape, I cared little about the impeachment of my rationality.

The days at the Hall flew, just like all the days of happy lovers, confoundedly fast. The more I saw of Emily, the firmer and faster did she rivet my chains. I was her slave: but what was best, I became a convert to virtue, because she was virtuous; and to possess her, I knew I must become as like her as my corrupt mind and unruly habits would permit. I viewed my past life with shame and contrition. When I attended this amiable, lovely creature to church on a Sunday, and saw her in the posture of devotion before her Maker, I thought her an angel, and I thought it heaven to be near her. All my thoughts and sentiments seemed changed and refined by her example and her company. The sparks of religion, so long buried in the ashes of worldly corruption and infidelity, began to revive. I recalled my beloved mother and the Bible to my recollection; and could I have been permitted to have remained longer with my "governess," I have no doubt that I should have regained both purity of mind and manner. I should have bidden adieu to vice and folly, because they could not have dwelt under the same roof with Emily; and I should have loved the Bible and religion, because they were beloved by her: but my untoward destiny led me a different way.

CHAPTER XVI

And oft his smooth and brilliant tongue
Would give the lie to his flushing cheek:
He was a coward to the strong:
He was a tyrant to the weak.

SHELLEY

MY father, as soon as he had obtained my promotion, asked for my being employed; and having had a promise from the Admiralty, that promise, unlike thousands of its predecessors and successors, was too rapidly fulfilled. I received a letter from my father, and a bouncing one from the Admiralty, by the same post, announcing officially my appointment to the D——— brig, of eighteen guns, at Portsmouth, whither I was directed to repair immediately, and take up my commission. In this transaction I soon after found there was an underplot, which I was too green to perceive at the time; but the wise heads of the two papas had agreed that a separation between the lovers was absolutely necessary, and that the longer it was delayed, the worse it would be for both of us: in short, that until I had attained my rank, nothing should be thought of in the way of matrimony.

As the reader is, no doubt, by this time pretty well versed in all the dialogue of parting lovers, I shall not intrude upon his or her patience with a repetition of that which has been much too often repeated, and is equally familiar to the prince and the ploughman. I should as soon think of describing the Devil's Punch Bowl, on the road to Portsmouth, where I arrived two days after my appointment.

I put up at Billett's, at the George, as a matter of course, because it was the resort of all the naval aristocracy, and directly opposite to the admiral's office. The first person for whom I made my kind inquiries was my captain elect; but he herded not with his brother epaulettes. He did not live at the George, nor did he mess at the Crown; he was not at the Fountain, nor the Parade Coffee-house; and the Blue Posts ignored him; but he was to be heard of at the Star and Garter, on the tip of Portsmouth Point. He did not even live there, but generally resided on board. This does not savour well; I never like your captains who live on board their ships in harbour; no ship can be comfortable, for no one can do as he pleases, which is the life and soul of a man-of-war, when in port.

To the Star and Garter I went, and asked for Captain G. I hoped I should not find him here; for this house had been, time out of mind, the rendezvous of warrant-officers, mates, and midshipmen. Here, however, he was; I sent up my card, and was admitted to his presence. He was seated in a small parlour, with a glass of brandy and water, or at least the remains of it, before him; his feet were on the fender, and several official documents which he had received that morning were lying on the table. He rose as I entered, and shewed me a short, square-built frame, with a strong projection of the sphere, or what the Spaniards call *bariga*. This rotundity of corporation was, however, supported by as fine a pair of Atlas legs as ever were worn by a Bath chairman. His face was rather inclined to be handsome; the features regular, a pleasant smile upon his lips, and a deep dimple in his chin. But his most remarkable feature was his eye; it was small, but piercing, and seemed to possess that long-sought *desideratum* of the perpetual motion, since it was utterly impossible to fix it for one moment on any object: and there was in it a lurking expression, which, though something of a physiognomist, I could not readily decipher.

"Mr Mildmay," said my skipper, "I am extremely happy to see you, and still more so that you have been appointed to my ship; will you be seated?"

As I obeyed, he turned round, and, rubbing his hands, as if he had just laid down his soap, he continued, "I always make it a rule, previous to an officer joining my ship, to learn something of his character from my brother captains; it is a precaution which I take, as I consider that one scabby sheep, &c. is strictly applicable to our service. I wish to have good officers and perfect gentlemen about me. There are, no doubt, many officers who can do their duty well, and with whom I should have no fault to find; but then there is a way of doing it—*a modus in rebus,* which a gentleman only can attain to; coarse manners, execrations, and abusive language render the men discontented, degrade the service, and are therefore very properly forbidden in the second article of war. Under such officers, the men always work unwillingly. I have taken the liberty to make some inquiries about you; and can only say, that all I have heard is to your advantage. I have no doubt we shall suit each other; and be assured it shall be my study to make you as comfortable as possible."

To this very sensible and polite address, I made a suitable reply. He then stated that he expected to sail in a few days; that the officer whom I was to supersede had not exactly suited his ideas, although he believed him to be a very worthy young man; and that, in consequence, he had applied and succeeded in obtaining for him another appointment; that it was necessary he should join his ship immediately; but, of course, he must first be superseded by me. "Therefore," said he, "you had better meet me on board the brig tomorrow morning at nine o'clock, when your commission shall be read; and after that I beg you will consider yourself your own master for a few days, as I presume you have some little arrangements to prepare for your cruise. I am aware," pursued he, smiling most benignantly, "that there are many little comforts which officers wish to attend to; such as fitting their cabins and looking to their mess, and a thousand other nameless things, which tend to pass the time and break up the monotony of a sea-life. Forty years have I trod the king's planks, man and boy, and not with any great success, as you may perceive, by the rank I now hold, and the life I am leading; for here I sit over a glass of humble grog, instead of joining my brother captains in their claret at the Crown; but I have two sisters to support, and I feel more satisfaction in doing my duty as a brother, than indulging my appetite; although I own I have no dislike to a glass of claret, when it does not come before me in a questionable shape: I mean when I have not got to pay for it, which I cannot afford. Now do not let me take up any more of your time. You have plenty of acquaintances that you wish to see, I have no doubt; and as for my yarns, they will do to pass away a watch, when we have nothing more attractive to divert us." So saying, he held out his hand, and shook mine most cordially. "To-morrow, at nine o'clock," he repeated; and I left him, much pleased with my interview.

I went back to my inn, thinking what a very fortunate fellow I was to have such an honest, straight-forward, bold, British hero of a captain, on my first appointment. I ordered my dinner at the George, and then strolled out to make my purchases, and give my orders for a few articles for sea service. I fell in with several old messmates; they congratulated me on my promotion, and declared I should give them a dinner to wet my commission, to which I readily consented. The day was named, and Mr Billett was ordered to provide accordingly.

Having dined *solus,* I amused myself in writing a long letter to my dear Emily; and with the assistance of a bottle of wine, succeeded in composing a tolerably warm and rapturous sort of a document, which I sealed, kissed, and sent to the post-office; after which, I built castles till bed time; but not one castle did I build, in which Emily was not the sole mistress. I went to bed, and slept soundly; and the next morning, by seven o'clock, I was arrayed in a spick-span new uniform, with an immensely large epaulette stuck on my right shoulder. Having breakfasted, I sallied out, and, in my own conceit, was as handsome a chap as ever buckled a sword belt. I skimmed with a light and vigorous foot down High-street.

"Boat, your honour?" said a dozen voices at once, as I reached New Sallyport, but I was resolved that Point-street should have a look at me, as well as High-street; so I kept a profound and mysterious silence, and let the watermen follow me to Point, just like so many sucking fish after a shark. I had two or three offers for volunteers to serve with me as I went along; but they were not of the right sex, so I did not take them.

"Boat to Spithead, your honour?" said a tough old waterman.

"Ay, you'll do," said I; so I jumped into his wherry, and we shoved off.

"What ship is your honour going to?" said the man.

"To the D—— brig."

"Oh, you are a-going to she, are you? To belong to her, mayhap?"

"Yes," I replied.

The waterman gave a sigh, feathered his oar, and never spoke another word till we came alongside. I did not regret his taciturnity, for I was always more amused with my own thoughts, than in conversing with illiterate people.

The brig was a most beautiful vessel. She mounted eighteen guns, and sat on the water like a duck. I perceived that the pendant was up for punishment, and this I thought rather an unusual sight at Spithead: I took it for granted that some aggravated offence, such as theft, or mutiny, had been committed. Seeing I was an officer, I was admitted alongside; so I paid the waterman, and sent him away. As I went up the side, I saw a poor fellow spread-eagled up to the grating, "according to the manners and customs of the natives," while the captain, officers, and ship's company stood round witnessing the athletic dexterity of a boatswain's mate, who, by the even, deep, and parallel marks of the cat on the white back and shoulders of the patient, seemed to be perfectly master of his business. All this did not surprise me: I was used to it; but after the address of my captain on the preceding day, I was very much surprised to hear language in direct violation of the second article of war.

Cursings and execrations poured out of his mouth with a volubility equal to any the most accomplished lady on the back of the Point.

"Boatswain's mate," roared the captain, "do your duty, or by G—— I will have *you* up, and give you four dozen yourself. One would think, d——n your b——d, that you were brushing flies off a sleeping Venus, instead of punishing a scoundrel, with a hide as thick as a buffalo's, and be d——d to him—do your duty, Sir, d——n your soul."

During this elegant address, the unhappy wretch had received four severe dozen, which the master-at-arms had counted aloud, and reported to the captain. "Another boatswain's mate," said he. The poor creature turned his head over his shoulders with an imploring look, but it was in vain. I watched the countenance of the captain, and the peculiar expression, which I could not decipher at my first interview, I now read most plainly: it was malignant cruelty, and delight in torturing his own species; he seemed to take a diabolical pleasure in the hateful operation which we were compelled to witness. The second boatswain's mate commenced, with a fresh cat, and gave a lash across the back of the prisoner, that made *me* start.

"One," said the master-at-arms, beginning to count.

"One!" roared the captain; "do you call that one? not a quarter of a one. That fellow is only fit for flyflapper at a pork shop! I'll disrate you, by G——d, you d——d Molly Mop; is that the way you handle a cat; that's only wiping the dirt off his back. Where's the boatswain?"

"Here," said a stout, gigantic, left-handed fellow, stepping forward, with a huge blue uniform coat and a plain anchor button, holding his hat in his left hand, and stroking his hair down his forehead with his right. I surveyed this man, as he turned himself about, and concluded, that the tailor who worked for him had been threatened with a specimen of his art, if he stinted him in cloth; for the skirts of his coat were ample, terminating in an inclined plane, the corners in front being much lower than the middle of the robe behind; the buttons on the hips were nearly pistol shot asunder.

"Give this man a dozen, Sir," said Captain G——; "and if you favour him, I'll put you under arrest, and stop your liquor."

This last part of the threat had more effect with Mr Pipes than the first. He began to peel, as the boxers call it; off came his capacious coat; a red waistcoat—full-sized for a Smithfield ox—was next deposited; then he untied a black silk handkerchief, and showed a throat, covered like that of a goat, with long brown hairs, thick as pack-thread. He next rolled up his shirt-sleeves above his elbow, and showed an arm and a back very like the Farnese Hercules, which, no doubt, all my readers have seen at the foot of the staircase at Somerset-house, when they have been to the exhibition.

This hopeful commentator on articles of war, seized his cat: the handle was two feet long, one inch and three quarters thick, and covered with red baize. The tails of this terrific weapon were three feet long, nine in number, and each of them about the size of that line which covers the springs of a travelling carriage. Mr Pipes, whose scientific display in this part of his art, had no doubt procured for him the warrant of a boatswain, in virtue of which he now stood as the vindicator of the laws of his country, handled his cat like an adept, looked at it from top to bottom, cleared all the tails, by the insertion of his delicate fingers, and combing them out, stretched out his left leg—for he was left-legged as well as left-handed—and measuring his distance with the accurate eye of an engineer, raised his cat high in air with his left hand, his right still holding the tips of the tails, as if to restrain their impatience; when, giving his arm and body a full swing, embracing three-fourths of the circle, he inflicted a tremendous stroke on the back of the unfortunate culprit. This specimen seemed to satisfy the amateur captain, who nodded approbation to the inquiring look of the amateur boatswain. The poor man lost his respiration from the force of the blow; and the tails of the cat coming from an opposite direction to the first four dozen, cut the flesh diamond-wise, bringing the blood at every blow.

I will not wound the feelings of my readers with a description of the poor wretch's situation. Even at this distance of time, I am shocked at it, and bitterly lament the painful necessity I have often been under of inflicting similar punishment; but I hope and trust I never did it without a cause, or in the wanton display of arbitrary power.

The last dozen being finished, the sum total was reported by the master-at-arms, "five dozen."

"Five dozen!" repeated Captain G——; "that will do—cast him off. And now, sir," said he, to the fainting wretch, "I hope this will be a warning to you, that the next time you wish to empty your beastly mouth, you will not spit on my quarter-deck."

"Heavens!" thought I, "is all this for spitting on the quarter-deck? and this, from the moralist of yesterday, who allowed neither oaths nor execrations, and has uttered more blasphemy in the last ten minutes, than I have heard for the last ten weeks?"

I had not yet caught the captain's eye—he was too intent on his amusement. As soon as the prisoner was cast loose, he commanded to pipe down, or in other words, to dismiss the people to their usual occupations, when I went up to him, and touched my hat.

"Oh! you are come, are you? Pipe, belay there—send every body aft on the quarter-deck."

My commission was then read: all hats off in respect to the sovereign, from whom the authority was derived. After this, I, being duly inaugurated, became the second lieutenant of the sloop; and the captain, without condescending to give me another word or look, ordered his gig to be manned, and was going on shore. I was not presented by him to any of the officers, which, in common courtesy, he ought to have done. This omission, however, was supplied by the first lieutenant, who invited me down into the gun-room, to introduce me to my new messmates. We left the tiger pacing up and down on his quarter-deck.

The first lieutenant was of the medium stature, a suitable height for a sloop of war, a spare figure of about forty years of age; he had but one eye, and that eye was as odd a one as the captain's. There was in it, however, unlike the captain's, an infinite deal of humour, and when he cocked it, as he constantly did, it almost spoke. I never saw three such eyes in two such heads. There was a lurking smile in the lieutenant's face, when I told him that the captain had desired me to come on board and read my commission, after which I might have two or three days to myself to prepare for sea.

"Well," said he, "you had better go and ask him now; but you will find him a rum one."

Accordingly, up I went to him. "Have you any objection to my going on shore, Sir?"

"Shore, Sir!" bellowed he; "and who the devil is to carry on the duty, if you go on shore? Shore, eh! I wish there was no shore, and then d——n the dog that couldn't swim! No, Sir; you have had shore enough. The service is going to h——l, Sir! A parcel of brats; with lieutenants, commissions before they should have been clear of the nursery! No, Sir: stay on board, or, d——n me, I'll break you, like an egg-shell, before you have taken the shine out of that fine new epaulette! No, no, by G——; no more cats here than catch mice. You stay on board, and do your duty: every man does his duty here; and let me see the —— that don't do it!"

I was in some measure prepared for this sublime harangue; but still there was sufficient room in my mind to admit of great astonishment at this sudden change of wind. I replied that he had promised me leave yesterday, and that, upon the strength of that promise, I had left all my things on shore, and that I was not in any way prepared to go to sea.

"I promised you leave, did I? Perhaps I did; but that was only to get you on board. I am up to your tricks, you d——d young chaps: when you get on shore, there is no getting you off again. No, no; no-catcheè no-habeè! You would not have made your appearance these three days, if I hadn't sugared the trap! Now I have got you, I'll keep you, d——n my eyes!"

I repeated my request to go on shore; but, without condescending to offer any farther reasons, he answered—

"I'd see you d——d first, Sir! And observe, I never admit of expostulation. Nothing affords me more pleasure than to oblige my officers in every thing reasonable; but I never permit reply."

Thought I to myself, "You certainly have escaped from hell, and I do not see how the infernal regions can do without you. You would have been one of the most ingenious tormentors of the damned. Domitian would have made you admiral, and your boatswain captain of the fleet!"

Having made this reflection, as I took a turn or two on deck, thinking what was best to be done, and knowing that "the king could do no wrong," the officer whom I had just superseded came up the hatchway, and, touching his hat very respectfully to the captain, asked whether he might go on shore.

"You may go to hell, and be d——d, Sir!" said the captain (who hated bad language); "you are not fit to carry guts to a bear!—you are not worth your salt; and the sooner you are off, the cleaner the ship will be! Don't stand staring at me, like a bull over a gate! Down, and pack up your traps, or I'll freshen your way!" raising his foot at the same time, as if he was going to kick him.

The young officer, who was a mild, gentlemanly, and courageous youth, did as he was bidden. I was perfectly astonished: I had been accustomed to sail with gentlemen. I had heard of martinets, and disciplinarians, and foul-mouthed captains; but this outdid all I ever could have conceived, and much more than I thought ever could have been submitted to by any correct officer. Roused to indignation, and determined not to be treated in this manner, I again walked up to him, and requested leave to go on shore.

"You have had your answer, Sir."

"Yes, I have, Sir," said I, "and in language that I never before heard on his Majesty's quarter-deck. I joined this ship as an officer and a gentleman, and as such I will be treated."

"Mutiny, by G——!" roared the captain. "Cock-a-hoop with your new commission, before the ink is dry!"

"As you please, Sir," I replied; "but I shall write a letter to the port-admiral, stating the circumstances and requesting leave of absence; and that letter I shall trouble you to forward."

"I'll be d——d if I do!" said he.

"Then, Sir," said I, "as you have refused to forward it, and in the presence of all the officers and ship's company, I shall forward it without troubling you."

This last shot of mine seemed to produce the same effect upon him that the last round does upon a beaten boxer; he did not come to time, but, muttering something, dived down the companion, and went into his cabin.

The first lieutenant now came up, and congratulated me on my victory. "You have puzzled and muzzled the bear completely," said he; "I have long wanted a coadjutor like yourself. Wilson, who is going to leave us, is the best creature that ever lived: but though brave as a lion before an enemy, he is cowed by this incarnate devil."

Our conversation was interrupted by a message from the captain, who desired to speak with me in his cabin. I went down; he received me with the benignant smile of our first acquaintance.

"Mr Mildmay," said he, "I always assume a little tartness with my officers when they first join" ("and when they quit you too," thought I), "not only to prove to them that I am, and will be the captain of my own ship, but also as an example to the men, who, when they see what the officers are forced to put up with, feel themselves more contented with their lot, and obey more readily; but, as I told you before, the comfort of my officers is my constant study—you are welcome to go ashore, and have twenty-four hours' leave to collect your necessaries."

To this harangue I made no reply; but, touching my hat, quitted the cabin. I felt so much contempt for the man that I was afraid to speak, lest I should commit myself.

The captain shortly after quitted the ship, telling the first lieutenant that I had permission to go on shore. I was now left at liberty to make acquaintance with my companions in misery—and nothing conduces to intimacy so much as community of suffering. My resistance to the brutality of our common taskmaster had pleased them; they told me what a tyrant and what a disgrace to the service he was, and how shameful it was that he should be entrusted with the command of so fine a vessel, or of any vessel at all, except it were a convict ship. The stories they told me of him were almost incredible, and nothing but the too well founded idea, that an officer trying his captain by a court-martial, had a black mark against him for ever after, and was never known to rise, could have saved this man from the punishment he so richly deserved: no officer, they said, had been more than three weeks in the ship, and they were all making interest to leave her.

In my report of what occurred in this vessel during the time I belonged to her, I must, in justice to the captains and commanders of his Majesty's navy observe, that the case was unique of its kind—such a character as Captain G—— was rarely met with in the navy then, and, for reasons which I shall give, will be still more rare in future. The first lieutenant told me that I had acted very judiciously in resisting at first his undue exertion of authority; that he was at once a tyrant, a bully, and a coward, and would be careful how he attacked me again. "But be on your guard," said he, "he will never forgive you; and, when he is most agreeable, there is the most mischief to be dreaded. He will lull you into security, and, whenever he can catch you tripping, he will try you by a court-martial. You had better go on shore, and settle all your business, and, if possible, be on board before your leave is out. It was only your threat of writing to the port-admiral that procured you leave of absence. You have nothing to thank him for: he would have kept you on board if he dared. I have never quitted the ship since I joined her;

and never has a day passed without a scene similar to what you have this morning witnessed. And yet," continued he, "if it were not for his cruelty to the men, he is the most amusing liar I ever heard. I am often more inclined to laugh than to be angry at him; he has a vein of wit and rich humour that runs through his composition, and never quits him. There is drollery even in his malice, and, if we cannot get clear of him, we must make the best of him."

I went on shore, collected all my clothes and the other articles of which I stood in need, and was on board my ship again the next morning before eight o'clock.

CHAPTER XVII

He will lie, Sir, with such volubility, that you would think
truth were a fool: drunkenness is his best virtue; for he will be
swine-drunk; and in his sleep he does little harm.

SHAKESPEARE

WHEN Captain G—— made his appearance, he seemed to be in the most amiable humour possible. As soon as he saw me, he said, "Ah, this is what I like; never break your leave even for five minutes. Now that I see I can trust you, you may go on shore again as soon as you please."

This speech might have done very well to any person before the mast; but as applied to an officer, I thought it rude and ungentlemanly.

The caterer had prepared lunch in the gun-room: it consisted of beef-steaks and broiled bullocks' kidneys, with fried onions; and their savoury smell rose in grateful steams up the skylight, and assailed the nostrils of the skipper. His facetious small-talk knew no bounds; he leaned over the frame, and, looking down, said—

"I say, something devilish good going on there below!"

The hint was taken, and the first lieutenant invited him down.

"I don't care if I do; I am rather peckish."

So saying, he was down the hatchway in the twinkling of one of his own funny eyes, as he feared the choice bits would be gone before he could get into action. We all followed him; and as he seated himself, he said—

"I trust, gentlemen, this is not the last time I shall sit in the gun-room, and that you will all consider my cabin as your own. I love to make my officers comfortable: nothing more delightful than a harmonious ship, where every man and boy is ready to go to h——l for his officers. That's what I call good fellowship—give and take—make proper allowances for one another's failings, and we shall be sorry when the time comes for us to part. I am afraid, however, that I shall not be long with you; for, though I doat upon the brig, the Duke of N—— and Lord George——, have given the first Lord a d——d *whigging* for not promoting me sooner; and, between ourselves, I don't wish to go farther. My post commission goes out with me to Barbadoes."

The first lieutenant cocked his eye; and quick as were the motions of that eye, the captain, with a twist of one of his own, caught a glimpse of it, before it could be returned to its bearing on the central object, the beef-steaks, kidneys, and onions. But it passed off without remark.

"A very capital steak this! I'll trouble you for some fat and a little gravy. We'll have some jollification when we get to sea; but we must get into blue water first: then we shall have less to do. Talking of broiling steaks, when I was in Egypt, we used to broil our beefsteaks on the rocks—no occasion for fire—thermometer at 200—hot as h——l! I have seen four thousand men at a time cooking for the whole army as much as twenty or thirty thousand pounds of steaks at a time, all hissing and frying at a time—just about noon, of course, you know—not a spark of fire! Some of the soldiers, who had been brought up as glass-blowers, at Leith, swore they never saw such heat. I used to go to leeward of them for a whiff, and think of old England! Ah, that's the country, after all, where a man may think and say what he pleases! But that sort of work did not last long, as you may suppose; their eyes were all fried out, d——n me, in three or four weeks! I had been ill in my bed, for I was attached to the 72nd regiment, seventeen hundred strong. I had a party of seamen with me; but the ophthalmia made such ravages, that the whole regiment, colonel and all, went stone blind—all, except one corporal! You may stare, gentlemen, but it's very true. Well, this corporal had a pre-cious time of it: he was obliged to lead out the whole regiment to water—he led the way, and two or three took hold of the skirts of his jacket, on each side; the skirts of these were seized again by as many more; and double the number to the last, and so all held on by one another, till they had all had

a drink at the well, and, as the devil would have it, there was but one well
among us all—so this corporal used to water the regiment just as a groom
waters his horses; and all spreading out, you know, just like the tail of a
peacock."

"Of which the corporal was the rump," interrupted the doctor.

The captain looked grave.

"You found it warm in that country?" inquired the surgeon.

"Warm!" exclaimed the captain; "I'll tell you what, doctor, when you go
where you have sent many a patient, and where, for that very reason, you
certainly will go, I only hope, for your sake, and for that of your profession
in general, that you will not find it quite so hot as we found it in Egypt. What
do you think of nineteen of my men being killed by the concentrated rays
of light falling on the barrels of the sentinels' bright muskets, and setting fire
to the powder? I commanded a mortar battery at Acre, and I did the French
infernal mischief with the shells. I used to pitch in among them when they
had sat down to dinner: but how do you think the scoundrels weathered on
me at last? D——n me, they trained a parcel of poodle dogs to watch the
shells when they fell, and then to run and pull the fuses out with their teeth.
Did you ever hear of such d——d villains? By this means, they saved hun-
dreds of men, and only lost half a dozen dogs—fact, by G——; only ask Sir
Sydney Smith; he'll tell you the same, and a d——d sight more."

The volubility of his tongue was only equalled by the rapidity of his
invention and the powers of mastication; for, during the whole of this entertaining monodrame, his teeth were in constant motion, like the traversing
beam of a steam boat; and as he was our captain as well as our guest, he
certainly took the lion's share of the repast.

"But, I say, Soundings," said he, addressing himself familiarly to the
master, who had not been long in the vessel, "let us see what sort of
stuff you have stowed the fore-hold with. You know I am a water drinker;
give me only the pure limpid stream, and a child may lead me. I seldom
touch liquor when the water is good." So saying, he poured out a tumbler,
and held it to his nose. "Stinks like h——! I say, master, are you sure the
bungs are in your casks? The cats have been contributing to the fluid.
We must qualify this;" and having poured one-half of the water, which
by the by was very good, he supplied the vacancy with rum. Then tasting
it, he said, "Come, Miss Puss; this will rouse you out, at any rate."

A moment's pause, while he held the bumper before his eye, and then, down it went, producing no other emotion than a deep sigh. "By the by, that's well thought of—we'll have no cats in the ship (except those which the depravity of human nature unhappily compels the boatswain to use). Mr Skysail, you'll look to that. Throw them all overboard."

Taking his hat, he rose from the table, and mounting the ladder, "On second thought," said he, addressing Skysail again, "I won't throw the cats overboard; the sailors have a foolish superstition about that animal—its d——d unlucky. No; put them alive in a bread-bag, and send them on shore in the bum-boat."

Recollecting that my dinner party at the George was to take place this day, and remembering the captain's promise that I should go on shore whenever I pleased, I thought it only necessary to say I was going, merely passing the usual compliment to my superior. I therefore went to him, with a modest assurance, and told him of my engagement and my intention.

"Upon my honour, Sir," cried he, putting his arms a-kimbo, and staring me full in the face; "you have a tolerable sea-stock of modest assurance; no sooner come on board than you ask leave to go on shore again, and at the same time you have the impudence to tell me, knowing how much I abhor the vice, that you mean to wet your commission, and of course to get beastly drunk, and to make others as bad as yourself. No, Sir; I'd have you to know, that as captain of this ship, and as long as I have the honour to command her, I am *magister morum.*"

"That is precisely what I was coming to, Sir," said I, "when you interrupted me. Knowing how difficult it is to keep young men in order, without the presence of some one whom they respect, and can look up to as an example, I was going to request the honour of your company as my guest. Nothing, in my opinion, could so effectually repress any tendency to improper indulgence."

"There you speak like a child of my own bringing up," replied Captain G——: "I did not give you credit for so much good sense. I am far from throwing a wet blanket over any innocent mirth. Man is man after all—give him but the bare necessaries of life, and he is no more than a dog. A little mirth on such an occasion, is not only justifiable, but praiseworthy. The health of a good king, like ours, God bless him, should always be drank in good wine; and as you say the party is to be select, and the occasion the wetting of your commission, I shall have no objection to come and give away the bride; but, remember, no hard drinking—no indecorum—and I'll do my best, not only to keep the young bloods in order, but to add my humble powers to the hilarity of the evening."

I thanked him for his kind condescension. He then gave a few directions to Skysail, the first lieutenant, and, ordering his gig to be manned, offered me a passage on shore.

This was, indeed, a mark of favour never before conferred on any officer in the ship, and all hands spontaneously turned out to see the sight. The first lieutenant cocked his eye, which was more than saying, "This is too good to last long." However, into the boat we went, and pulled away for old Sally-port. The harbour-tide rolling out, we passed close to the buoy of the *Boyne*.

"Ah! well I remember that old ship; I was midshipman of her when she blew up. I was signal midshipman. I was in the act of making the signal of distress, when up I went. Damnation! I thought I never should have come down any more."

"Indeed, Sir," said I, "I thought there had been no one on board at the time."

"No one on board!" repeated the captain, with scorn on his upper lip, "who did you get that from?"

"I heard it from a captain I served with in America."

"Then you may tell your captain, with my compliments, that he knew nothing at all about it. No one on board! Why, d—— me, Sir, the poop was crowded like a sheep-fold, and all bellowing to me for help. I told them all to go to h——, and just at that moment away we all went, sure enough. I was picked up senseless. I was told somewhere in Stokes-bay, and carried to Haslar hospital, where I was given over for three months—never spoke. At last I got well; and the first thing I did, was to take a boat and go and dive down the fore-hold of my old ship, and swam aft to the bread-room."

"And what did you see, Sir?" said I.

"Oh, nothing, except lots of human skeletons, and whitings in abundance, swimming between their ribs. I brought up my old quadrant out of the starboard wing, where I was adjusting it when the alarm was given. I found it lying on the table just where I left it. I never shall forget what a d——d rap we hit the old Queen Charlotte, with our larboard broadside;

every gun went slap into her, double-shotted. D——n my eyes, I suppose we diddled at least a hundred men."

"Why, Sir," said I, "I always understood she only lost two men on that occasion."

"Who told you that?" said Captain G——, "your old captain?"

"Yes, Sir," said I, "he was a midshipman in her."

"He be d——," said my skipper; "to my certain knowledge, three launch loads of dead bodies were taken out of her, and carried to the hospital for interment."

As the boat touched the landing-place, this accomplished liar had time to take breath, and, in fact, I was afraid he would have exhausted his stock of lies before dinner, and kept nothing for the dessert. When we landed, he went to his old quarters, at the Star and Garter, and I to the George. I reminded him, at parting, that six o'clock was my hour.

"Never fear me," said he.

I collected my company previous to his arrival, and told my friends that it was my determination to make him drunk, and that they must assist me, which they promised to do. Having once placed him in that predicament, I was quite sure I should stop his future discourses in favour of temperance. My companions, perfectly aware of the sort of man they had to deal with, treated him on his entrance with the most flattering marks of respect. I introduced them all to him in the most formal manner, taking them to him, one by one, just as we are presented at court—to compare great things with small. His good-humour was at its highest spring-tide; the honour of drinking wine with him was separately and respectfully asked, and most condescendingly granted to every person at the table.

"Capital salmon this," said the captain; "where does Billett get it from? By the by, talking of that, did you ever hear of the pickled salmon in Scotland?"

We all replied in the affirmative.

"Oh, you don't take. D—— it, I don't mean dead pickled salmon; I mean live pickled salmon, swimming about in tanks, as merry as grigs, and as hungry as rats."

We all expressed our astonishment at this, and declared we never heard of it before.

"I thought not," said he, "for it has only lately been introduced into this country, by a particular friend of mine Dr Mac. I cannot just now remember his d——d jaw-breaking Scotch name; he was a great chemist and geologist, and all that sort of thing—a clever fellow I can tell you, though you may laugh. Well—this fellow, Sir, took nature by the heels and capsized her, as we say. I have a strong idea that he had sold himself to the devil. Well—what does he do, but he catches salmon and puts them into tanks, and every day added more and more salt till the water was as thick as gruel, and the fish could hardly wag their tails in it. Then he threw in whole pepper corns, half-a-dozen pounds at a time, till there was enough. Then he began to dilute with vinegar, until his pickle was complete. The fish did not half like it at first; but habit is every thing, and when he shewed me his tank, they were swimming about as merry as a shoal of dace; he fed them with fennel chopped small, and black-pepper corns. 'Come, doctor,' says I, 'I trust no man upon tick; if I don't taste, I won't believe my own eyes, though I *can* believe my *tongue.*'" (We looked at each other.) "'That you shall do in a minute,' says he; so he whipped one of them out with a landing net; and when I stuck my knife into him, the pickle ran out of his body, like wine out of a claret bottle, and I ate at least two pounds of the rascal, while he flapped his tail in my face. I never tasted such salmon as that. Worth your while to go to Scotland, if it's only for the sake of eating live pickled salmon. I'll give you a letter, any of you, to my friend. He'll be d——d glad to see you; and then you may convince yourselves. Take my word for it, if once you eat salmon that way, you will never eat it any other."

We all said we thought that very likely.

The champagne corks flew as fast and as loud as his shells at Acre; but we were particularly reserved, depending entirely on his tongue for our amusement; and, finding the breeze of conversation beginning to freshen, I artfully turned the subject to Egypt, by asking one of my friends to demolish a pyramid of jelly, which stood before him, and to send some of it to the captain.

This was enough: he began with Egypt, and went on increasing in the number and magnitude of his lies, in proportion as we applauded them. A short-hand writer ought to have been there, for no human memory could do justice to this modern Munchausen. "Talking of the water of the Nile," said he, "I remember, when I was first lieutenant of the *Bellerophon* I went into Minorca with only six tons of water, and in four hours we had three hundred and fifty tons on board, all stowed away. I made all hands work. The admiral himself was up to the neck in water, with the rest of them. 'D——n it, admiral,' says I, 'no skulking.' Well—we sailed the next day; and such a gale of wind I never saw in all my life—away went all our masts, and we had nearly been swamped with the weather-roll. One of the boats was blown off the booms, and went clean out of sight before it touched the water. You may laugh at that, but that was nothing to the *Swallow* sloop of war. She was in company with us; she wanted to scud for it, but, by Jupiter, she was blown two miles up the country—guns, men, and all; and the next morning they found her flying jib-boom had gone through the church-window, and slap into the cheek of the picture of the Virgin Mary. The natives all swore it was done on purpose by d——d heretics. The captain was forced to arm his men, and march them all down to the beach, giving the ship up to the people, who were so exasperated that they set her on fire, and never thought of the powder which was on board. All the priests were in their robes, singing some stuff or another, to purify the church; but that was so much time thrown away, for in one moment away went church, priests, pictures, and people, all to the devil together."

Here he indulged himself in some vile language and scurrilous abuse of religion and its ministers. All priests were hypocritical scoundrels. If he was to be of any religion at all, he said, he should prefer being a Roman Catholic, "because, then, you know," added he, "a man may sin as much as he likes, and rub off as he goes, for a few shillings. I got my commission by religion, d——n me. I found my old admiral was a psalm-singer; so says I, 'my old boy, I'll give you enough of that' so I made the boatswain stuff me a hassock, and this I carried with me every where, that I might save my trousers, and not hurt my knees; so then I turned to and prayed all day long, and kept the people awake, singing psalms all night. I knelt down and prayed on the quarter-deck, main deck, and lower deck. I preached to the men in the tiers, when they coiled the cables, and groaned loud and deep when I heard an oath. The thing took—the admiral said I was the right sort, and he made a commander out of the greatest atheist in the ship. No sooner did I get hold of the sheepskin, than to the devil I pitched hassock and bible."

How long he might have gone on with this farrago, it is difficult to say; but we were getting tired of him, so we passed the bottle till he left off narrative, and took to friendship.

"Now I say (hiccup), you Frank, you are a devilish good fellow; but that one-eyed son of a gun, I'll try him by a court-martial, the first time I catch him drunk; I'll hang him at the yard-arm, and you shall be my first lieutenant and *custos-rot-torum,* d——n me. Only you come and tell me the first time he is disguised in liquor, and I'll settle him, d——n his cock eye—a saucy, Polyphemus-looking *son of a*—(hiccup) a Whitechapel bird-catcher."

Here his recollection failed him; he began to talk to himself, and to confound me with the first lieutenant.

"I'll teach him to write to port-admirals for leave—son of a sea cook."

He was now drawing to the finale, and began to sing,

> *"The cook of the huffy got drunk,*
> *Fell down the fore-scuttle, and*
> *Broke his gin bottle."*

Here his head fell back, he tumbled off his chair, and lay motionless on the carpet.

Having previously determined not to let him be exposed in the streets in that state, I had provided a bed for him at the inn; and, ringing the bell, I ordered the waiter to carry him to it. Having seen him safely deposited, untied his neckcloth, took of his boots, and raised his head a little, we left him, and returned to the table, where we finished our evening in great comfort, but without any other instance of intoxication.

The next morning, I waited on him. He seemed much annoyed at seeing me, supposing I meant, by my presence, to rebuke him for his intemperance; but this was not my intention. I asked him how he felt; and I regretted that the hilarity of the evening had been interrupted in so unfortunate a manner.

"How do you mean, sir? Do you mean to insinuate that I was not sober?"

"By no means, Sir," said I; "but are you aware, that in the midst of your delightful and entertaining conversation, you tumbled off your chair in an epileptic fit?—are you subject to these?"

"Oh, yes, my dear fellow, indeed I am; but it is so long since I last had one, that I was in hopes they had left me. I have invalided for them four times, and just at the very periods when, if I could have remained out, my promotion was certain."

He then told me I might remain on shore that day, if I pleased. I gave him credit for his happy instinct in taking the hint of the fit; and as soon as I left him, he arose, went on board, and flogged two men for being drunk the night before.

I did not fail to report all that had passed to my messmates, and we sailed a few days afterwards for Barbadoes.

On the first Sunday of our being at sea, the captain dined in the gun-room with the officers. He soon launched out into his usual strain of lying and boasting, which always irritated our doctor, who was a sensible young Welshman. On these occasions, he never failed to raise a laugh at the captain's expense, by throwing in one or two words at the end of each anecdote; and this he did in so grave and modest a manner, that without a previous knowledge of him, anyone might have supposed he was serious. The captain renewed his story of the corps of poodles to extract the fuses from the shells. "I hoped," he said, "to see the institution of such a corps among ourselves; and if I were to be the colonel of it, I should soon have a star on my breast."

"That would be the Dog Star," said the doctor, with extreme gaiety.

"Thank you, Doctor," said the captain; "not bad; I owe you one."

We laughed; the doctor kept his countenance; and the captain looked very grave; but he continued his lies, and dragged in as usual the name of Sir Sydney Smith to support his assertions. "If you doubt me, only ask Sir Sydney Smith; he'll talk to you about Acre for thirty-six hours on a stretch, without taking breath; his cockswain at last got so tired of it, that he nick-named him 'Long Acre.'"

The poor doctor did not come off scot free; the next day, he discovered that the deck leaked over his cabin, and the water ran into his bed. He began, with a hammer and some nails, to fasten up a piece of painted canvas, by way of shelter. The captain heard the noise of the hammer, and finding it was the doctor, desired him to desist. The doctor replied, that he was only endeavouring to stop some leaks over his bed: the captain said they should not be stopped; for that a bed of *leeks* was a very good bed for a Welshman.

"There, Doctor; now we are quits: that's for your Dog Star. I suppose you think nobody can make a pun or a pill, in the ship, but yourself?"

"If my pills were no better than your puns," muttered the doctor, "we should all be in a bad way."

The captain then directed the carpenter not to allow any nails to the doctor, or the use of any of his tools; he even told the poor surgeon that he did not know how to make a pill, and that "he was as useless as the Navy Board." He accused him of ignorance in other parts of his profession; and, ordering all the sick men on deck, rope-ended them to increase their circulation, and put a little life into them.

Many a poor sick creature have I seen receive a most unmerciful beating. My wonder was that the men did not throw him overboard; and I do really believe that if it had not been for respect and love to the officers, they would have done so. No sooner had we got into blue water, as he called it— that is, out of soundings—than he began his pranks, which never ceased till we reached Carlisle Bay. Officers and men were all treated alike, and there was no redress, for no one among us dared to bring him to a court-martial. His constant maxim was—"Keep sailors at work and you keep the devil out of their minds—all hands all day-watch, and watch all night."

"No man," said Jacky (the name we gave him) "eats the bread of idleness on board of my ship: work keeps the scurvy out of their bones, the lazy rascals."

The officers and men, for the first three weeks, never had a watch below during the day. They were harassed and worn to death, and the most mutinous and discontented spirit prevailed throughout the ship. One of the best seamen said, in the captain's hearing, that, "since the ship had been at sea, he had only had three watches below."

"And if I had known it," said the captain, "you should not have had that;" and turning the hands up, he gave him four dozen.

Whenever he flogged the men, which he was constantly doing, he never failed to upbraid them with ingratitude, and the indulgences which they received from him.

"By G——d, there is no man-of-war in the service that has so much indulgence. All you have to do, is to keep the ship clean, square the yards; hoist in your provisions, eat them; hoist your grog in, drink it, and strike the empty casks over the side; but Heaven itself would not please such a set of d——d fat, lazy, discontented rascals."

His language to the officers was beyond any thing I ever could have supposed would have proceeded from the mouth of a human being. The master, one day, incurred his displeasure, and he very flippantly told the poor man to go to h——.

"I hope, Sir," said the master, "I have as good a chance of going to Heaven as yourself."

"You go to Heaven!" said the captain, "you go to Heaven! Let me catch you there, and I will come and kick you out."

This was, indeed, shewing how far he would have carried his tyranny if he could. But our feelings are relieved from any violent shock at this apparent blasphemy, when we recollect that the poor man was an atheist; and that his idea of Heaven was that of a little parlour at the Star and Garter, with a good fire, plenty of grog, and pipes of tobacco.

He kept no table, nor did he ever drink any wine, except when he dined with us; but got drunk every night, more or less, on the ship's spirits, in his own cabin. He was always most violent in the evening. Our only revenge was laughing at his monstrous lies on Sunday, when he dined with us. One night, his servant came and told the midshipman of the watch, that the captain was lying dead drunk on the deck, in his cabin. This was communicated to me, and I determined to make the best use of it. I ran down to the cabin, taking with me the midshipman of the watch, the quartermaster, and two other steady men; and having laid the water-drinker in his bed, I noted down the date, with all the particulars, together with the names of the witnesses, to be used as soon as we fell in with the admiral.

The next day, I think he had some suspicion of what I had done, and it had nearly been fatal to me. It was blowing a fresh trade wind, and the vessel rolling very deep, when he ordered the booms to be cast loose and re-stowed. This was nothing short of murder and madness: but in spite of every remonstrance, he persisted, and the consequences were terrible. The lashings were no sooner cast off, than a spare top-mast fell and killed one of the men. This was enough to have completed our mischief for the day; but the devil had not done with us yet. The booms were secured, and the men were ordered to rattle the rigging down, which, as the vessel continued to roll heavily, was still more dangerous and, if possible, more useless than the former operation. He was warned of it, but in vain; and the men had not been aloft more than ten minutes, when one of them fell overboard. Why I should again have put my life in jeopardy, particularly after the warning of

the last voyage, I know not. I was perhaps vain of what I could do in the
water. I knew my powers; and with the hope of saving this unfortunate
victim to the folly and cruelty of the captain, I plunged after him into the sea,
feeling at the same time, that I was almost committing an act of suicide. I
caught hold of him, and for a time supported him; and, had the commonest
diligence and seamanship been shewn, I should have saved him. But the
captain, it appeared, when he found I was overboard, was resolved to get
rid of me, in order to save himself: he made use of every difficulty to prevent
the boat coming to me. The poor man was exhausted: I kept myself disengaged from him, when swimming round him; supported him occasionally
whenever he was sinking; but, finding at last that he was irrecoverably
gone—for though I had a firm hold of him, he was going lower and lower—
and, looking up, perceiving I was so deep that the water was dark over my
head, I clapped my knees on his shoulders, and, giving myself a little impe-
tus from the resistance, rose to the surface. So much was I exhausted, that
I could not have floated half a minute more, when the boat came and picked
me up.

The delay in heaving the ship to, I attributed to the scene I had witnessed the night before; and in this, I was confirmed by the testimony of the
officers. Having lost two men by his unseamanlike conduct, he would have
added deliberate murder of a third, to save himself from the punishment
which he knew awaited him. He continued the same tyrannical conduct, and
I had resolved that the moment we fell in with the admiral to write for a
court-martial on this man, let the consequences be what they might: I
thought I should serve my country and the navy by ridding it of such a
monster.

Several of the officers were under arrest, and notwithstanding the heat
of their cabins in that warm climate, were kept constantly confined to them
with a sentinel at the door. In consequence of this cruel treatment, one of
the officers became deranged. We made Barbadoes, and running round
Needham's Point into Carlisle Bay, we saw to our mortification, that neither
the admiral nor any ship of war was there, consequently our captain was
commanding officer in the port. Upon this, he became remarkably amiable,
supposing if the evil day was put off, it would be dispensed with altogether;
he treated me with particular attention, hoped we should have some fun
ashore; as the admiral was not come in, we should wait for him; tired of

kicking about at sea, he should take all his *duds* with him, and bring himself to an anchor on shore, and not come afloat again till we saluted his flag.

Neither the first lieutenant nor myself believed one word of this; indeed, we always acted upon the exact reverse of what he said; and it was well we did so in this instance. After we had anchored, he went ashore, and in about an hour returned, and stated that the admiral was not expected till next month; that he should, therefore, go and take up his quarters at Jemmy Cavan's, and not trouble the ship any more until the admiral arrived; he then left us, taking his trunk and all his dirty linen, dirty enough it was.

Some of the officers unfortunately believed that we were to remain, and followed the captain's example by sending their linen on shore to be washed. Skysail was firm, and so was I; the lieutenant cocked his eye, and said, "Messmate, depend on it there is something in the wind. I have sent one shirt on shore to be washed; and when that comes off, I will send another; if I lose that it is no great matter."

That night, at ten o'clock, Captain Jacky came on board, bringing his trunk and dirty linen, turned the hands up, up anchor, and ran out of Carlisle Bay and went to sea, leaving most of the officers' linen on shore. This was one of his tricks. He had received his orders when he landed in the morning; they were waiting for him, and his coming on board for his things, was only a run to throw us off our guard, and I suppose compel us, by the loss of our clothes, to be as dirty in appearance as he was himself, "but he always liked to make his officers comfortable."

We arrived at Nassau, in New Providence, without any remarkable incident, although the service continued to be carried on in the same disagreeable manner as ever. I continued, however, to get leave to go on shore; and finding no prospect of bringing the captain to justice, determined to quit the ship, if possible. This was effected by accident, otherwise I should have been much puzzled to have got clear of her. I fell between the boat and the wharf as I landed, and by the sudden jerk ruptured a small blood-vessel in my chest; it was of no great importance in itself, but in that climate required care, and I made the most of it. They would have carried me on board again, but I begged to be taken to the hotel. The surgeon of the regiment doing duty there attended me, and I requested him to make my case as bad as possible. The captain came to see me—I appeared very ill—his compassion was like that of the Inquisitor of the Holy Office, who cures his victim in order to enable him to go through further torments. His time of sailing arrived, and I was reported to be too ill to be removed. Determined to have me, he prolonged his stay. I got better; the surgeon's report was more favourable; but I was still unwilling to go on board. The captain sent me an affectionate message, to say that if I did not come, he would send a file of marines to bring me: he even came himself and threatened me; when, finding there were no witnesses in the room, I plainly told him that if he persisted in having me on board, it would be to his own destruction, for that I was fully determined to bring him to a court-martial for drunkenness and unofficerlike conduct, the moment we joined the admiral. I told him of the state in which I had found him. I recapitulated his blasphemies, and his lubberly conduct in losing the two men; he stared and endeavoured to explain; I was peremptory, and he whined and gave in, seeing he was in my power.

"Well then, my dear fellow," said Jacky, "since you are so very ill—sorry as I shall be to lose you—I must consent to your staying behind. I shall find it difficult to replace you; but as the comfort and happiness of my officers is my first object on all occasions, I will prefer annoying myself to annoying you." So saying, he held out his hand to me, which I shook with a hearty good-will, sincerely hoping that we might never meet again, either in this world or the next.

He was afterwards brought to a court-martial, for repeated acts of drunkenness and cruelty, and was finally dismissed from the service.

In giving this detail of Captain G——'s peculiarities, let it not be imagined, that even at that period such characters were common in the service. I have already said, that he was unique. Impressment and the want of officers at the early part of the war, gave him an opportunity of becoming a lieutenant; he took the weak side of the admiral to obtain his next step, and obtained the command of a sloop, from repeated solicitation at the Admiralty, and by urging his claims of long servitude. The service had received serious injury by admitting men on the quarter-deck from before the mast; it occasioned there being two classes of officers in the navy—namely, those who had rank and connections, and those who had entered by the "hawse-holes," as they were described. The first were favoured when young, and did not acquire a competent knowledge of their duty; the second, with few exceptions, as they advanced in their grades, proved, from want of education, more and more unfit for their stations. These defects have now been remedied; and as all young men who enter the service must have a regular education, and consequently be the sons of gentlemen, a level has been produced, which to a certain degree precludes favouritism, and perfectly bars the entrance to such men as Captain G——.

After the battle of Trafalgar, when England and Europe were indebted for their safety to the British fleet, the navy became popular, and the aristocracy crowded into it. This forwarded still more the melioration of the service, and under the succeeding naval administration, silent, certain, and gradual improvements, both in men, officers, and ships, took place. Subsequently, the navy has been still more fortunate, in having an officer called to its councils, whose active and constant employment at sea, previous to the peace of Paris, had given him a thorough insight into its wants and abuses. Unconnected with party, and unawed by power, he has dared to do his duty; and it is highly to the credit of the first lord, who has so long presided at the board, that the suggestions of this officer have met with due consideration; I can therefore assure my reader, that as long as his advice is attended to, he need be afraid of meeting with no more Captain G——s.

CHAPTER XVIII

There she goes, brimful of anger and jealousy. Mercy on the poor man!

"JEALOUS WIFE"

The dreadful fish that hath deserved the name Of Death.

SPENSER

AS the brig moved out of the harbour of Nassau, I moved out of bed; and as she set her royals and made sail, I put on my hat and walked out. The officers of the regiment quartered there, kindly invited me to join their mess, and the colonel enhanced the value of the offer by assigning for me good apartments in the barracks. I was instantly removed to cleanly and comfortable lodgings. I soon regained my strength, and was able to sit at the table where I found thirty-five young officers, living for the day, careless of the morrow; and, beyond that never bestowing a thought. It is a singular fact,

that where life is most precarious, men are most indifferent about its preservation; and, where death is constantly before our eyes, as in this country,
eternity is seldom in our thoughts: but so it is; and the rule extends still
further in despotic countries. Where the union between the head and shoulders may be dissolved in a moment by the sword of a tyrant, life is not so
valued, and death loses its terrors; hence the apathy and indifference with
which men view their executioners in that state of society. It seems as if
existence, like estates, was valuable in proportion to the validity of the title-
deeds by which they are held.

To digress no more. Although I was far from being even commonly
virtuous, which is about tantamount to absolute wickedness, I was no longer
the thoughtless mortal I had ever been since I left school. The society of
Emily, and her image graven on my heart; the close confinement to the brig,
and the narrow escape from death in the second attempt to save the poor
sailor's life, had altogether contributed their share to a kind of temporary
reformation, if not to a disgust to the coarser descriptions of vice. The lecture
I had received from Emily on deceit, and the detestable conduct of my last
captain, had, as I thought, almost completed my reformation. Hitherto I felt
I had acted wrong, without having the power to act right. I forgot that I had
never made the experiment. The declaration of Captain G——'s atheism was
so far from converting me, that from that moment I thought more seriously
than ever of religion. So great was my contempt for his character, that I
knew whatever he said must be wrong, and, like the Spartan drunken slave,
he gave me the greatest horror of vice.

Such was my reasoning, and such my sentiments, previous to any relapse into sin or folly. I knew its heinousness. I transgressed and repented;
habit was all powerful in me; and the only firm support I could have looked
to for assistance was, unfortunately, very superficially attended to. Religion,
for any good purposes, was scarcely in my thoughts. My system was a sort
of Socratic heathen philosophy—a moral code, calculated to take a man
tolerably safe through a quiet world, but not to extricate him from a laby-
rinth of long-practised iniquity.

The thoughtless and vicious conduct of my companions became to me
a source of serious reflection. Far from following their example, I felt myself
some degrees better than they were; and in the pride of my heart thanked
God that I was not like these publicans. My pharisaical arrogance concealed

from me the mortifying fact that I was much worse, and with very slight hopes of amendment. Humility had not yet entered my mind; but it was the only basis on which any religious improvement could be created—the only chance of being saved. I rather became refined in vice, without quitting it. Gross and sensual gratification, so easily obtained in the West Indies, was disgusting to me; yet I scrupled not to attempt the seduction of innocence, rather more gratified in the pursuit than in the enjoyment, which soon palled, and drove me after other objects.

I had, however, little occasion to exert my tact in this art in the Bahama Islands, where, as in all the other islands of the West Indies, there is a class of women, born of white fathers and mustee or mulatto women, nearly approaching in complexion to the European; many of them are brunettes, with long black hair, very pretty, good eyes, and often elegant figures. These ladies are too proud of the European blood in their veins to form an alliance with any male who has a suspicion of black in his genealogical table; consequently they seldom are married unless from interested motives, when, having acquired large property by will, they are sought in wedlock by the white settlers.

So circumstanced, these girls prefer an intercourse with the object of their choice to a legal marriage with a person of inferior birth; and, having once made their selection, an act of infidelity is of rare occurrence among them. Their affection and constancy will stand the test of time and of long separation; generous to prodigality, but jealous, and irritable in their jealousy, even to the use of the dagger and poison.

One of these young ladies found sufficient allurement in my personal charms to surrender at discretion, and we lived in that sort of familiar intercourse which, in the West Indies, is looked upon as a matter of necessity between the parties, and of indifference by every one else. I lived on in this Epicurean style for some months; until, most unfortunately, my *chere amie* found a rival in the daughter of an officer, high in rank, on the island. Smitten with my person, this fair one had not the prudence to conceal her partiality: my vanity was too much flattered not to take advantage of her sentiments in my favour; and, as usual, flirtation and philandering occupied most of my mornings, and sometimes my evenings, in the company of this fair American.

Scandal is a goddess who reigns paramount, not only in Great Britain, but also in all his Majesty's plantations; and her votaries very soon selected me as the target of their archery. My pretty Carlotta became jealous; she taxed me with inconstancy. I denied the charge; and as a proof of my innocence, she obtained from me a promise that I should go no more to the house of her rival; but this promise I took very good care to evade, and to break. For a whole fortnight, my domestic peace was interrupted either by tears, or by the most voluble and outrageous solos, for I never replied after the first day.

A little female slave, one morning, made me a signal to follow her to a retired part of the garden. I had shewn this poor little creature some acts of kindness, for which she amply repaid me. Sometimes I had obtained for her a holiday—sometimes saved her a whipping, and at others had given her a trifle of money; she therefore became exceedingly attached to me, and as she saw her mistress's anger daily increase, she knew what it would probably end in, and watched my safety like a little guardian sylph.

"No drinkee coffee, Massa," said she, "Missy putty obeah stuff in."

As soon as she had said this, she disappeared, and I went into the house, where I found Carlotta preparing the breakfast; she had an old woman with her, who seemed to be doing something which she was not very willing I should see. I sat down carelessly, humming a tune, with my face to a mirror, and my back to Carlotta, so that I was able to watch her motions without her perceiving it. She was standing near the fireplace, the coffee was by her, on the table, and the old woman crouched in the chimney corner, with her bleared eyes fixed on the embers. Carlotta seemed in doubt; she pressed her hands forcibly on her forehead; took up the coffeepot to pour me out a cup, then sat it down again; the old woman muttered something in their language; Carlotta stamped with her little foot, and poured out the coffee. She brought it to me—trembled as she placed it before me—seemed unwilling to let go her hold, and her hand still grasped the cup, as if she would take it away again. The old woman growled and muttered something, in which I could only hear the name of her rival mentioned. This was enough: the eyes of Carlotta lighted up like a flame; she quitted her hold of the salver, retreated to the fireplace, sat herself down, covered her face, and left me, as she supposed, to make my last earthly repast.

"Carlotta," said I, with a sudden and vehement exclamation. She started up, and the blood rushed to her face and neck, in a profusion of blushes, which are perfectly visible through the skins of these mulattos. "Carlotta," I repeated, "I had a dream last night, and who do you think came to me? It was Obeah!" (She started at the name.) "He told me not to drink coffee this morning, but to make the old woman drink it." At these words the beldam sprang up. "Come here, you old hag," said I. She approached trembling, for she saw that escape from me was impossible, and that her guilt was detected. I seized a sharp knife, and taking her by her few remaining grey and woolly hairs, said, "Obeah's work must be done: I do not order it, but he commands it; drink that coffee instantly."

So powerful was the name of Obeah on the ear of the hag, that she dreaded it more than my brandished knife. She never thought of imploring mercy, for she supposed it was useless after the discovery, and that her hour was come; she therefore lifted the cup to her withered lip, and was just going to fulfil her destiny and to drink, when I dashed it out of her hand, and broke it in a thousand pieces on the floor, darting, at the same time, a fierce look at Carlotta, who threw herself at my feet, which she fervently kissed in an agony of conflicting passions.

"Kill me! kill me!" ejaculated she, "it was I that did it. Obeah is great—he has saved you. Kill me, and I shall die happy, now you are safe—do kill me!

I listened to these frantic exclamations with perfect calmness. When she was a little more composed, I desired her to rise. She obeyed, and looked the image of despair, for she thought I should immediately quit her for the arms of her more fortunate rival, and she considered my innocence as fully established by the appearance of the deity.

"Carlotta," said I, "what would you have done if you had succeeded in killing me?"

"I will shew you," said she; when, going to a closet, the took out another basin of coffee; and before I could dash it from her lips, as I had the former one from the black woman, the infatuated girl had swallowed a small portion of it.

"What else can I do?" said she; "my happiness is gone for ever."

"No, Carlotta," said I; "I do not wish for your death, though you have plotted mine. I have been faithful to you, and loved you, until you made this attempt."

"Will you forgive me before I die?" said she; "for die I must, now that

I know you will quit me!" Uttering these words, she threw herself on the floor with violence, and her head coming in contact with the broken fragments of the basin, she cut herself, and bled so copiously that she fainted. The old woman had fled, and I was left alone with her, for poor little Sophy was frightened, and had hidden herself.

I lifted Carlotta from the floor, and, placing her in a chair, I washed her face with cold water; and having staunched the blood, I laid her on her bed, when she began to breathe and to sob convulsively. I sat myself by her side; and as I contemplated her pale face and witnessed her grief; I fell into a train of melancholy retrospection on my numerous acts of vice and folly.

"How many warnings," said I, "how many lessons am I to receive before I shall reform? How narrowly have I escaped being sent to my account 'unanealed' and unprepared! What must have been my situation if I had at this moment been called into the presence of my offended Creator? This poor girl is pure and innocent, compared with me, taking into consideration the advantages of education on my side, and the want of it on hers. What has produced all this misery and the dreadful consequences which might have ensued, but my folly in trifling with the feelings of an innocent girl, and winning her affections merely to gratify my own vanity; at the same time that I have formed a connection with this unhappy creature, the breaking of which will never cause me one hour's regret, while it will leave her in misery, and will, in all probability, embitter all her future existence? What shall I do? Forgive, as I hope to be forgiven: the fault was more mine than hers."

I then knelt down and most fervently repeated the Lord's Prayer, adding some words of thanksgiving, for my undeserved escape from death. I rose up and kissed her cold, damp forehead; she was sensible of my kindness, and her poor head found relief in a flood of tears. Her eyes again gazed on me, sparkling with gratitude and love, after all she had gone through. I endeavoured to compose her; the loss of blood had produced the best effects; and, having succeeded in calming her conflicting passions, she fell into a sound sleep.

The reader who knows the West Indies, or knows human nature, will not be surprised that I should have continued this connection as long as I remained on the island. From the artless manner in which Carlotta had conducted her plot; from her gestures and her agitation, I was quite sure that she was a novice in this sort of crime, and that should she ever relapse into her paroxysm of jealousy, I should be able to detect any farther attempt on my life. Of this, however, I had no fears, having by degrees discontinued my visits to the young lady who had been the cause of our fracas; and I never afterwards, while on the island, gave Carlotta the slightest reason to suspect my constancy. I was much censured for my conduct to the young lady, as the attentions I had shewn her, and her marked preference for me, had driven away suitors who really were in earnest, and they never returned to her again.

In these islands, the naturalist would find a vast store to reward investigation; they abound with a variety of plants, birds, fish, shells, and minerals. It was here that Columbus made his first landing, but in which of the islands I am not exactly certain; though I am very sure he did not find them quite so agreeable as I did, for he very soon quitted them, and steered away for St Domingo.

It is not, perhaps, generally known, that New Providence was the island selected for his residence by Blackbeard, the famous pirate; the citadel that stands on the hill above the town of Nassau, is built on the site of the fortress which contained the treasure of that famous freebooter. A curious circumstance occurred during my stay on this island, and which, beyond all doubt, was connected with the adventures of those extraordinary people, known by the appellation of Buccaneers. Some workmen were digging near the foot of the hill under the fort, when they discovered some quicksilver, and on inspection, a very considerable quantity was found; it had evidently been a part of the plunder of the pirates, buried in casks or skins, and these having decayed, the liquid ore naturally escaped down the hill.

Though not indifferent to the pleasures of the table, I was far from resigning myself to the Circean life led by the generality of young military men in the Bahamas.

The education which I had received, and which placed me far above the common run of society in the colonies induced me to seek for a companion whose mind had received equal cultivation; and such a one I found in Charles ———, a young lieutenant in the ——— regiment, quartered at Nassau. Our intimacy became the closer, in proportion as we discovered the sottish habits and ignorance of those around us. We usually spent our mornings in reading the classic authors with which we were both familiar; we spouted our Latin verses; we fenced; and we amused ourselves, occa-

sionally, with a game of billiards, but never ventured our friendship on a
stake for money. When the heat of the day had passed off, we strolled out,
paid a few visits, or rambled over the island; keeping as much aloof from the
barracks as possible, where the manner of living was so very uncongenial
to our notions. The officers began their day about noon, when they sat
down to breakfast; after that, they separated to their different quarters, to
read the novels, with which the presses of England and France inundated
these islands, to the great deterioration of morals. These books, which they
read lounging on their backs, or laid beside them and fell asleep over, occupied the hottest part of the day; the remainder, till the hour of dinner
arrived, was consumed in visiting and gossiping or in riding to procure an
appetite for dinner. Till four in the morning, their time was wholly devoted
to smoking and drinking; their beds received them in a state of intoxication
more or less; parade, at nine o'clock, forced them out with a burning brain
and parched tongue; they rushed into the sea, and found some refreshment
in the cool water, which enabled them to stand upright in front of their men;
the formal duty over, they retired again to their beds, where they lay till
noon, and then to breakfast.

Such were their days; can it be wondered at that our islands are fatal to
the constitution of Europeans, when this is their manner of life in a climate
always disposed to take advantage of any excess? The men too readily followed the example of their officers, and died off in the same rapid manner;
one of the most regular employments of the morning was to dig graves for
the victims of the night. Four or five of these receptacles was thought a
moderate number. Such was the fatal apathy in which these officers existed,
that the approach, nay, even the certainty of death, gave them no apparent
concern, caused no preparation, excited no serious reflection. They followed
the corpse of a brother-officer to the grave in military procession. These
ceremonies were always conducted in the evening, and often have I seen
these thoughtless young men throwing stones at the lanthorns which were
carried before them to light them to the burying-ground.

I was always an early riser, and believe I owe much of my good health
to this custom. I used to delight in a lovely tropical morning, when, with a
cigar in my mouth, I walked into the market. What would Sir William Curtis,
or Sir Charles Flower have said, could they have seen, as I did, the numbers
of luxurious turtle lying on their backs, and displaying their rich calapee to

the epicurean purchaser? Well, indeed might the shade of Apicius* lament
that America and turtle were not discovered in his days. There were the
guanas, too, in abundance, with their mouths sewed up to prevent their
biting; these are excellent food, although bearing so near a resemblance to
the alligator, and its diminutive European representative, the harmless lizard.
Muscovy ducks, parrots, monkeys, pigeons, and fish. Pine apples abounded,
oranges, pomegranates, limes, Bavarias, plantains, love apples, Abbogada
pears (better known by the name of subaltern's butter), and many other
fruits, all piled in heaps, were to be had at a low price. Such was the stock
of a New Providence market.

Of the human species, buyers and vendors, there were black, brown
and fair; from the fairest skin, with light blue eyes, and flaxen hair, to the jet-
black "Day and Martin" of Ethiopia; from the loveliest form of Nature's
mould, to the disgusting squaw, whose flaccid mammæ hung like inverted
bottles to her girdle, or are extended over her shoulder to give nourishment
to the little imp perched on her back; and here the urchin sits the live long
day, while the mother performs all the drudgery of the field, the house, or
the market.

The confusion of Babel did not surpass the present gabble of a West
India market. The loud and everlasting chatter of the black women, old and
young (for black ladies can talk as well as white ones), the screams of children, parrots, and monkeys; black boys and girls, clad *à la Venus,* white
teeth, red lips, black skins, and elephant legs, formed altogether a scene well
worth looking at; and now, since the steamers have acquired so much velocity, I should think would not be an unpleasant lounge for the fastidious
ennuyé of France or England. The beauty and coolness of the morning, the
lovely sky, and the cheerfulness of the slaves, whom our morbid philanthro-
pists wish to render happy, by making discontented, would altogether amply repay the trouble and expense of a voyage, to those who have leisure
or money enough to enable them to visit the tropical islands.

The delightful, and, indeed, indispensable amusement of bathing, is
particularly dangerous in these countries. In the shallows you are liable to
be struck by the stingray, a species of skate, with a sharp barb about the
middle of its tail; and the effect of the wound is so serious, that I have

---

* *Lyttleton's "Dialogues of the Dead."*

known a person to be in a state of frenzy from it for nearly forty-eight hours. In deeper water, the sharks are not only numerous but ravenous; and I sometimes gratified their appetites, and my own love of excitement, by purchasing the carcass of a dead cow, or horse. This I towed off, and anchored with a thick rope and a large stone; then, from my boat, with a harpoon, I amused myself in striking these devils as they crowded round for their meal. My readers will, I fear, think I am much too fond of relating adventures among these marine undertakers; but the following incident will not be found without interest.

In company with Charles, one beautiful afternoon, rambling over the rocky cliffs at the back of the island, we came to a spot where the stillness, and the clear transparency of the water invited us to bathe. In was not deep. As we stood above, on the promontory, we could see the bottom in every part. Under the little headland, which formed the opposite side of the cove, there was a cavern, to which, as the shore was steep, there was no access but by swimming, and we resolved to explore it. We soon reached its mouth, and were enchanted with its romantic grandeur and wild beauty. It extended, we found, a long way back, and had several natural baths, into all of which we successively threw ourselves, each, as they receded farther from the mouth of the cavern, being colder than the last. The tide, it was evident, had free ingress, and renewed the water every twelve hours. Here we thoughtlessly amused ourselves for some time, quoting Acis and Galatea, Diana, and her nymphs, and every classic story applicable to the scene.

At length, the declining sun warned us that it was time to take our departure from the cave, when, at no great distance from us, we saw the back, or dorsal fin of a monstrous shark above the surface of the water, and his whole length visible beneath it. We looked at him and at each other with dismay, hoping that he would soon take his departure, and go in search of other prey; but the rogue swam to and fro, just like a frigate blockading an enemy's port, and we felt, I suppose, very much as we used to make the French and Dutch feel last war, at Brest and the Texel.

The sentinel paraded before us, about ten or fifteen yards in front of the cave, tack and tack, waiting only to serve one, if not both of us, as we should have served a shrimp or an oyster. We had no intention, however, in this, as in other instances, of "throwing ourselves on the mercy of the court." In vain did we look for relief from other quarters; the promontory above us was inaccessible; the tide was rising, and the sun touching the clear blue edge of the horizon.

I, being the leader, pretended to a little knowledge in ichthyology, and told my companion that fish could hear as well as see, and that therefore the less we said the better; and the sooner we retreated out of his sight, the sooner he would take himself off. This was our only chance, and that a poor one; for the flow of the water would soon have enabled him to enter the cave and help himself, as he seemed perfectly acquainted with the *locale,* and knew that we had no mode of retreat but by the way we came. We drew back, out of sight; and I don't know when I ever passed a more unpleasant quarter of an hour. A suit in Chancery, or even a spring lounge in Newgate, would have been almost luxury to what I felt when the shades of night began to darken the mouth of our cave, and this infernal monster continued to parade, like a water-bailiff, before its door. At last, not seeing the shark's fin above water, I made a sign to Charles that, *coûte qui coûte,* we must swim for it; for we had notice to quit, by the tide; and if we did not depart, should soon have an execution in the house. We had been careful not to utter a word; and, silently pressing each other by the hand, we slipped into the water; when, recommending ourselves to Providence, which, for my part, I seldom forgot when I was in imminent danger, we struck out manfully. I must own I never felt more assured of destruction, not even when I swam through the blood of the poor sailor; for then the sharks had something to occupy them, but here they had nothing else to do but to look after us. We had the benefit of their undivided attention.

My sensations were indescribably horrible. I may occasionally write or talk of the circumstance with levity, but whenever I recall it to mind, I tremble at the bare recollection of the dreadful fate that seemed inevitable. My companion was not so expert a swimmer as I was, so that I distanced him many feet, when I heard him utter a faint cry. I turned round, convinced that the shark had seized him, but it was not so; my having left him so far behind had increased his terror, and induced him to draw my attention. I returned to him, held him up, and encouraged him. Without this, he would certainly have sunk; he revived with my help, and we reached the sandy beach in safety, having eluded our enemy; who, when he neither saw or heard us, had, as I concluded he would, quitted the spot.

Once more on terra firma, we lay gasping for some minutes before we spoke. What my companion's thoughts were, I do not know; mine were replete with gratitude to God, and renewed vows of amendment; and I have every reason to think, that although Charles had not so much room for reform as myself, his feelings were perfectly in unison with my own. We never afterwards repeated this amusement, though we frequently talked of our escape, and laughed at our terrors; yet on these occasions our conversation always took a serious turn: and, upon the whole, I am convinced that this adventure did us both a vast deal of good.

I had now been six months in these islands, had perfectly recovered my health, and became anxious for active employment. The brilliant successes of our rear-admiral at Washington made me wish for a share of the honour and glory which my brethren in arms were acquiring on the coast of North America; but my wayward fate sent me in a very opposite direction.

CHAPTER XIX

MIRA. *How came we ashore?*
PRO. *By Providence divine.*

.   .   .   .   .   .

Sit still, and hear the last of our sea-sorrow.
Here in this island we arrived.

"TEMPEST"

A FRIGATE called at the island for turtle; and, having represented my case to the captain, he offered to take me on board, telling me at the same time that he was going much farther to the southward, to relieve another cruiser, who would then return to England, and the captain of her would, no doubt, give me a passage home. I accordingly made hasty preparations for my departure; took leave of all my kind friends at the barracks, for kind indeed they were to *me,* although thoughtless and foolish towards themselves. I bade adieu to the families on the island, in whose houses and at whose tables I had experienced the most liberal hospitality; and last, though not least, I took leave of poor Carlotta.

This was a difficult task to perform, but it was imperative. I told her that I was ordered on board by my captain, who, being a very different person from the last, I dare not disobey. I promised to return to her soon. I offered her money and presents, but she would accept of nothing but a small locket, to wear for my sake. I purchased the freedom of poor Sophy, the black girl, who had saved my life. The little creature wept bitterly at my coming away; but I could do no more for her. As for Carlotta, I learned afterwards that she went on board every ship that arrived, to gain intelligence of me, who seldom or ever gave her a thought.

We sailed; and, steering away to the south-east with moderate winds and fine weather, captured, at the end of that time, a large American ship, which had made a devious course from the French coast, in hopes of avoiding our cruisers; she was about four hundred tons, deeply laden, and bound to Laguira, with a valuable cargo. The captain sent for me, and told me that if I chose to take charge of her, as prize master, I might proceed to England direct. This plan exactly suited me, and I consented, only begging to have a boatswain's mate, named Thompson, to go along with me; he was an old shipmate, and had been one of my gig's crew when we had the affair in Basque Roads; he was a steady, resolute, quiet, sober, raw-boned Caledonian, from Aberdeen, and a man that I knew would stand by me in the hour of need. He was ordered to go with me, and the necessary supply of provisions and spirits were put on board. I received my orders, and took my leave of my new captain, who was both a good seaman and an excellent officer. When I got on board the prize, I found all the prisoners busy packing up their things, and they became exceedingly alert in placing them in the boat which was to convey them on board the frigate. Indeed they all crowded into her with an unusual degree of activity; but this did not particularly strike my attention at the time. My directions were to retain the captain and one man with me, in order to condemn the vessel in the Court of Admiralty.

Occupied with many objects at once, all important to me, as I was so soon to part company with the frigate, I did not recollect this part of my orders, and that I was detaining the boat, until the young midshipman who had charge of her asked me if he might return on board and take the prisoners. I then went on deck, and seeing the whole of them, with their chests and bags, seated very quietly in the boat, and ready to shove off, I desired the captain and one of the American seamen to come on board again, and to bring their clothes with them. I did not remark the unwillingness of the captain to obey this order, until told of it by the midshipman; his chest and goods were immediately handed in upon deck, and the signal from the frig-ate being repeated, with a light for the boat to return (for it was now dark), she shoved off hastily, and was soon out of sight.

"Stop the boat! for God's sake stop the boat!" cried the captain.

"Why should I stop the boat?" said I; "my orders are positive, and you must remain with me."

I then went below for a minute or two, and the captain followed me.

"As you value your life, sir," said he, "stop the boat."

"Why?" asked I, eagerly.

"Because, sir," said he, "the ship has been scuttled by the men, and will sink in a few hours: you cannot save her, for you cannot get at her leaks."

I now did indeed see the necessity of stopping the boat; but it was too late: she was out of sight. The lanthorn, the signal for her return, had been hauled down, a proof that she had got on board. I hoisted two lights at the mizzen peak, and ordered a musket to be fired; but, unfortunately, the car-tridges had either not been put in the boat which brought me, or they had been taken back in her. One of my lights went out; the other was not seen by the frigate. We hoisted another light, but it gained no notice: the ship had evidently made sail. I stood after her as fast as I could, in hopes of her seeing us that night, or taking us out the next morning, should we be afloat.

But my vessel, deeply laden, was already getting waterlogged, and would not sail on a wind more than four miles an hour. All hope in that quarter vanished. I then endeavoured to discover from the captain where the leaks were, that we might stop them; but he had been drinking so freely, that I could get nothing from him but Dutch courage and braggadocia. The poor black man, who had been left with the captain, was next consulted. All he knew was, that, when at Bordeaux, the captain had caused holes to be bored in the ship's bottom, that he might pull the plugs out whenever he liked, swearing, at the same time, that she never should enter a British port. He did not know where the leaks were situated, though it was evident to me that they were in the after and also in the fore parts of the ship, low down, and now deep under water, both inside as well as out. The black man added, that the captain had let the water in, and that was all he knew.

I again spoke to the captain, but he was too far gone to reason with: he had got drunk to die, because he was afraid to die sober—no unusual case with sailors.

"Don't tell me; d——n me, who is a-feard to die? I arn't. I swore she should never enter a British port, and I have kept my word."

He then began to use curses and execrations; and, at last, fell on the deck in a fit of drunken frenzy.

I now called my people all together, and having stated to them the peril of our situation, we agreed that a large boat, which lay on the booms, should be instantly hoisted out, and stowed with every thing necessary for a voyage. Our clothes, bread, salt meat, and water, were put into her, with my sextant and spy-glass. The liquor, which was in the cabin, I gave in charge to the midshipman who was sent with me; and, having completely stowed our boat, and prepared her with a good lug-sail, we made her fast with a couple of stout tow-ropes, and veered her astern, with four men in her, keeping on our course in the supposed track of the frigate till day-light.

That wished-for hour arrived, but no frigate was to be seen, even from the mast-head. The ship was getting deeper and deeper, and we prepared to take to the boat. I calculated the nearest part of South America to be seven hundred miles from us, and that we were more than twice that distance from Rio Janeiro. I did not, however, despond, for, under all circumstances, we were extremely well off: and I inspired the men with so much confidence, that they obeyed in everything, with the utmost alacrity and cheerfulness, except in one single point.

Finding the ship could not in all probability float more than an hour or two, I determined to quit her, and ordered the boat alongside. The men got into her, stepped the mast, hooked on the lug-sail, ready to hoist at my orders; and, without my bidding, had spread my boat cloak in the stern-sheets, and made a comfortable place for me to repose in. The master proceeded to get into the boat, but the men repulsed him with kicks, blows, and hisses, swearing most dreadfully that if he attempted to come in, they would throw him overboard. Although in some measure I participated in their angry feeling, yet I could not reconcile myself to leave a fellow-creature thus to perish, even in the pit which he had dug for others, and this too at a time when we needed every indulgence from the Almighty for ourselves, and every assistance from his hand to conduct us into a port,

"He deserves to die; it is all his own doings," said they; "come into the boat yourself, Sir, or we must shove off without you."

The poor captain—who, after sleeping four hours, had recovered his senses, and felt all the horror of his situation—wept, screamed, tore his hair, laid hold of my coat, from which only the strength of my men could disengage him. He clung to life with a passion of feeling which I never saw in a criminal condemned by the law; he fell on his knees before me, as he appealed to us all, collectively and separately; he reminded us of his wife and starving children at Baltimore, and he implored us to think of them and of our own.

I was melted to tears, I confess; but my men heard him with the most stoical unconcern. Two of them threw him over to the opposite side of the deck; and before he could recover from the violence of the fall, pushed me into the boat, and shoved off. The wretched man had by this time crawled over to the side we had just left; and throwing himself on his knees, again screamed out, "Oh, mercy, mercy, mercy!—For God's sake, have mercy, if you expect any!—Oh, God! my wife and babes!"

His prayers, I lament to say, had no effect on the exasperated seamen. He then fell into a fit of cursing and blasphemy, evidently bereft of his senses; and in this state he continued for some minutes, while we lay alongside, the bowman holding on with the boat-hook only. I was secretly determined not to leave him, although I foresaw a mutiny in the boat in consequence. At length, I gave the order to shove off. The unhappy captain, who, till that moment, might have entertained some faint hope from the lurking compassion which he perceived I felt for him, now resigned himself to despair of a more sullen and horrible aspect. He sat himself down on one of the hen-coops, and gazed on us with a ghastly eye. I cannot remember ever seeing a more shocking picture of human misery.

While I looked at him, the black man, Mungo, who belonged to the ship, sprang overboard from the boat, and swam back to the wreck. Seizing a rope which hung from the gangway, he ascended the side, and joined his master. We called to him to come back, or we should leave him behind.

"No, massa," replied the faithful creature; "me no want to lib: no takee Massa Green, no takee me! Mungo lib good many years wi massa cappen. Mungo die wi massa, and go back to Guinea!

I now thought we had given the captain a sufficient lesson for his treachery and murderous intentions. Had I, indeed, ever seriously intended to leave him, the conduct of poor Mungo would have awakened me to a sense of my duty. I ordered Thompson, who was steering the boat, to put the helm a-starboard, and lay her alongside again. No sooner was this command given, than three or four of the men jumped up in a menacing attitude, and swore that they would not go back for him; that he was the cause of all their sufferings; and that if I chose to share his fate, I might, but into the boat he should not come. One of them, more daring than the rest, attempted to take the tiller out of Thompson's hand; but the trusty seaman seized him by the collar, and in an instant threw him overboard. The other men were coming aft to avenge this treatment of their leader; but I drew my sword, and pointing it at the breast of the nearest mutineer, desired him, on pain of instant death, to return to his seat. He had heard my character, and knew that I was not to be trifled with.

A mutineer is easily subdued with common firmness. He obeyed, but was very sullen, and I heard many mutinous expressions among the men. One of them said that I was not their officer—that I did not belong to the frigate.

"That," I replied, "is a case of which I shall not allow you to be the judges. I hold in my pocket a commission from the King's Lord High Admiral, or the commissioners for executing that duty. Your captain, and mine also, holds a similar commission. Under this authority I act. Let me see the man that dares dispute it—I will hang him at the yard-arm of the wreck before she goes down; and, looking at the man whom Thompson had thrown overboard, and who still held by the gunwale of the boat, without daring to get in, I asked him if he would obey me or not? He replied that he would, and hoped I would forgive him. I said that my forgiveness would depend entirely on the conduct of himself and the others; that he must recollect that if our own ship, or any other man-of-war, picked us up, he was liable, with three or four more, to be hanged for mutiny; and that nothing but his and their future obedience could save them from that punishment, whenever we reached a port.

This harangue had a very tranquillising effect. The offenders all begged pardon, and assured me they would deserve my forgiveness by their future submission.

All this passed at some little distance from the wreck, but within hearing; and while it was going on, the wind, which had been fair when we put of, gradually died away, and blew faintly from the south-west, directly towards the sinking wreck. I took advantage of this circumstance to read them a lecture. When I had subdued them, and worked a little on their feelings,

I said I never knew any good come of cruelty: whenever a ship or a boat had left a man behind who might have been saved, that disaster or destruction had invariably attended those who had so cruelly acted; that I was quite sure we never should escape from this danger, if we did not show mercy to our fellow-creatures. "God," said I, "has shown mercy to us, in giving us this excellent boat, to save us in our imminent danger; and He seems to say to us now, 'Go back to the wreck, and rescue your fellow-sufferer.' The wind blows directly towards her, and is foul for the point in which we intend to steer; hasten, then," pursued I, "obey the Divine will; do your duty, and trust in God. I shall then be proud to command you, and have no doubt of bringing you safe into port."

This was the "pliant hour;" they sprang upon their oars, and pulled back to the wreck with alacrity. The poor captain, who had witnessed all that passed, watched the progress of his cause with deep anxiety. No sooner did the boat touch the ship, than he leaped into her, fell down on his knees, and thanked God aloud for his deliverance. He then fell on my neck, embraced me, kissed my cheek, and wept like a girl. The sailors, meanwhile, who never bear malice long, good-naturedly jumped up, and assisted him in getting his little articles into the boat; and as Mungo followed his master, shook hands with him all round, and swore he should be a black prince when he went back to Guinea. We also took in one or two more little articles of general use, which had been forgotten in our former hurry.

We now shoved off for the last time; and had not proceeded more than two hundred yards from the ship, when she gave a heavy lurch on one side, recovered it, and rolled as deep on the other; then, as if endued with life and instinct, gave a pitch, and went down, head foremost, into the fathomless deep. We had scarcely time to behold this awful scene, when the wind again sprang up fair, from its old quarter, the east.

"There," said I, "Heaven has declared itself in your favour already. You have got your fair wind again."

We thanked God for this; and having set our sail, I shaped my course for Cape St Thomas, and we went to our frugal dinner with cheerful and grateful hearts.

The weather was fine—the sea tolerably smooth—and as we had plenty of provisions and water, we did not suffer much, except from an apprehension of a change of wind, and the knowledge of our precarious situation. On the fifth day after leaving the wreck we discovered land at a great distance. I knew it to be the island of Trinidad and the rocks of Martin Vas. This island, which lies in latitude twenty degrees south, and longitude thirty degrees west, is not to be confounded with the island of the same name on the coast of Terra Firma, in the West Indies, and now a British colony.

On consulting Horseberg, which I had in the boat, I found that the island which we were now approaching was formerly inhabited by the Portuguese, but long since abandoned. I continued steering towards it during the night, until we heard the breakers roaring against the rocks, when I hove-to, to windward of the land, till daylight.

The morning presented to our view a precipitous and rugged iron-bound coast, with high and pointed rocks, frowning defiance over the unappeaseable and furious waves which broke incessantly at their feet, and recoiled to repeat the blow. Thus for ages had they been employed, and thus for ages will they continue, without making any impression visible to the eye of man. To land was impossible on the part of the coast now under our inspection, and we coasted along, in hopes of finding some haven into which we might haul our boat, and secure her. The island appeared to be about nine miles long, evidently of volcanic formation, an assemblage of rocky mountains towering several hundred feet above the level of the sea. It was barren, except at the summit of the hills, where some trees formed a coronet, at once beautiful and refreshing, but tantalising to look at, as they appeared utterly inaccessible; and even supposing I could have discovered a landing-place, I was in great doubt whether I should have availed myself of it, as the island appeared to produce nothing which could have added to our comfort, while delay would only have uselessly consumed our provisions. There did not appear to be a living creature on the island, and the danger of approaching to find a landing-place was most imminent.

This unpromising appearance induced me to propose that we should continue our course to Rio Janeiro. The men were of another opinion. They said they had been too long afloat, cooped up, and that they should prefer remaining on the island to risking their lives any longer, in so frail a boat, on the wide ocean. We were still debating, when we came to a small spot of sand, on which we discovered two wild hogs, which we conjectured had come down to feed on the shell fish; this decided them, and I consented to run to leeward of the island, and seek for a landing-place. We sounded the west end, following the remarks of Horseberg, and ran for the cove of the Nine-Pin Rock. As we opened it, a scene of grandeur presented itself, which we had never met with before, and which in its kind is probably unrivalled in nature. An enormous rock rose, nearly perpendicularly, out of the sea, to the height of nine hundred or one thousand feet. It was as narrow at the base as it was at the top, and was formed exactly in the shape of the nine-pin, from which it derives its name. The sides appeared smooth and even to the top, which was covered with verdure, and was so far above us that the sea birds, which in myriads screamed around it, were scarcely visible two-thirds of the way up. The sea beat violently against its base—the feathered tribe, in endless variety, had been for ages the undisturbed tenants of this natural monument; all its jutting points and little projections were covered with their white dung, and it seemed to me a wonderful effort of Nature, which had placed this mass in the position which it held, in spite of the utmost efforts of the winds and waves of the wide ocean.

Another curious phenomenon appeared at the other end of the cove. The lava had poured down into the sea, and formed a stratum; a second river of fused rock had poured again over the first, and had cooled so rapidly as to hang suspended, not having joined the former strata, but leaving a vacuum between for the water to fill up. The sea dashed violently between the two beds, and spouted magnificently through holes in the upper bed of lava to the height of sixty feet, resembling much the spouting of a whale, but with a noise and force infinitely greater. The sound indeed was tremendous, hollow, and awful. I could not help mentally adoring the works of the Creator, and my heart sunk within me at my own insignificance, folly, and wickedness.

As we were now running along the shore, looking for our landing-place, and just going to take in the sail, the American captain, who sat close to the man at the helm, seemed attentively watching something on the larboard bow of the boat. In an instant he exclaimed, "Put your helm, my good fellow, port-hard." These words he accompanied with a push of the helm so violent, as almost to throw the man overboard who sat on the larboard quarter. At the same moment, a heavy sea lifted the boat, and sent her many yards beyond, and to the right of a pointed rock, just flush or even with the water, which had escaped our notice, and which none suspected but the American captain (for these rocks do not show breakers every minute, if they did they would be easily avoided). On this we should most certainly have been dashed to pieces, had not the danger been seen and avoided by the sudden and skilful motion of the helm; one moment more, and one foot nearer, and we were gone.

"Merciful God!" said I, "to what fate am I reserved at last? How can I be sufficiently thankful for so much goodness?"

I thanked the American for his attention—told my men how much we were indebted to him, and how amply he had repaid our kindness in taking him off the wreck.

"Ah, lieutenant," said the poor man, "it is a small turn I've done you for the kindness you have shown to me."

The water was very deep, the rocks being steep; so, we lowered our sail, and getting our oars out, pulled in to look for a landing. At the farther end of the cove, we discovered the wreck of a vessel lying on the beach. She was broken in two, and appeared to be copper-bottomed. This increased the eagerness of the men to land; we rowed close to the shore, but found that the boat would be dashed to pieces if we attempted it. The midshipman proposed that one of us should swim on shore, and, by ascending a hill, discover a place to lay the boat in. This I agreed to; and the quarter-master immediately threw off his clothes. I made a lead-line fast to him under his arms, that we might pull him in if we found him exhausted. He went over the surf with great ease, until he came to the breakers on the beach, through which he could not force his way; for the moment he touched the ground with his foot, the recoil of the sea, and what is called by sailors the under-tow, carried him back again, and left him in the rear of the last wave.

Three times the brave fellow made the attempt, and with the same result. At last he sunk, and we pulled him in very nearly dead. We, however, restored him by care and attention, and he went again to his usual duty. The midshipman now proposed that he should try to swim through the surf without the line, for that alone had impeded the progress of the quarter-master; this was true, but I would not allow him to run the risk, and we pulled along shore, until we came to a rock on which the surf beat very high, and which we avoided in consequence. This rock we discovered to be detached from the main. and within it, to our great joy, we saw smooth water; we pulled in, and succeeded in landing without much difficulty, and having secured our boat to a grapnel, and left two trusty men in charge of her, I proceeded

with the rest to explore the cove; our attention was naturally first directed
to the wreck which we had passed in the boat, and, after a quarter of an
hour's scrambling over huge fragments of broken rocks, which had been
detached from the sides of the hill, and encumbered the beach, we arrived
at the spot.

The wreck proved to be a beautiful copper-bottomed schooner, of
about a hundred and eighty tons burthen. She had been dashed on shore
with great violence, and thrown many yards above the high-water mark. Her
masts and spars were lying in all directions on the beach, which was strewed
with her cargo. This consisted of a variety of toys and hardware, musical
instruments, violins, flutes, fifes, and bird-organs. Some few remains of
books, which I picked up, were French romances, with indelicate plates,
and still worse text. These proved the vessel to be French. At a short distance from the wreck, on a rising knoll, we found three or four huts, rudely
constructed out of the fragments; and, a little farther off, a succession of
graves, each surmounted with a cross. I examined the huts, which contained
some rude and simple relics of human tenancy: a few benches and tables,
composed of boards roughly hewn out and nailed together; bones of goats,
and of the wild hog, with the remains of burnt wood. But we could not
discover any traces of the name of the vessel or owner; nor were there any
names marked or cut on the boards, as might have been expected, to show
to whom the vessel belonged, and what had become of the survivors.

This studied concealment of all information led us to the most accurate
knowledge of her port of departure, her destination, and her object of trade.
Being on the southwest side of the island, with her head lying to the north-
east, she had, beyond all doubt, been running from Rio Janeiro towards the
coast of Africa, and got on shore in the night. That she was going to fetch
a cargo of slaves was equally clear, not only from the baubles with which
she was freighted, but also from the interior fitting of the vessel, and from
a number of hand and leg shackles which we found among the wreck, and
which we knew were only used for the purposes of confining and securing
the unhappy victims of this traffic.

We took up our quarters in the huts for the night, and the next morning
divided ourselves into three parties, to explore the island. I have before
observed that we had muskets, but no powder, and therefore stood little
chance of killing any of the goats or wild hogs, with which we found the

island abounded. One party sought the means of attaining the highest summit of the island; another went along the shore to the westward; while myself and two others went to the eastward. We crossed several ravines, with much difficulty, until we reached a long valley, which seemed to intersect the island.

Here a wonderful and most melancholy phenomenon arrested our attention. Thousands and thousands of trees covered the valley, each of them about thirty feet high; but every tree was dead, and extended its leafless boughs to another—a forest of desolation, as if nature had at some particular moment ceased to vegetate! There was no underwood or grass. On the lowest of the dead boughs, the gannets, and other sea birds, had built their nests in numbers unaccountable. Their tameness, as Cooper says, "was shocking to me." So unaccustomed did they seem to man, that the mothers, brooding over their young, only opened their beaks, in a menacing attitude at us, as we passed by them.

How to account satisfactorily for the simultaneous destruction of this vast forest of trees, was very difficult; there was no want of rich earth for nourishment of the roots. The most probable cause appeared to me, a sudden and continued eruption of sulphuric effluvia from the volcano; or else, by some unusually heavy gale of wind or hurricane, the trees had been drenched with salt water to their roots. One or the other of these causes must have produced the effect. The philosopher, or the geologist, must decide.

We had the consolation to know that we should at least experience no want of food—the nests of the birds affording us a plentiful supply of eggs, and young ones of every age; with these we returned loaded to the cove. The party that had gone to the westward, reported having seen some wild hogs, but were unable to secure any of them; and those who had attempted to ascend the mountain, returned much fatigued, and one of their number missing. They reported that they had gained the summit of the mountain, where they had discovered a large plain, skirted by a species of fern tree, from twelve to eighteen feet high—that on this plain they had seen a herd of goats, and among them, could distinguish one of enormous size which appeared to be their leader. He was as large as a pony; but all attempts to take one of them were utterly fruitless. The man who was missing had followed them farther than they had. They waited some time for his return; but as he did not come to them, they concluded he had taken some other route to the cove. I did not quite like this story, fearing some dreadful accident had befallen the poor fellow, for whom we kept a watch, and had a fire burning the whole night, which, like the former one, we passed in the huts. We had an abundant supply of fire-wood from the wreck, and a stream of clear water ran close by our little village.

The next morning, a party was sent in search of the man, and some were sent to fetch a supply of young gannets for our dinner. The latter brought back with them as many young birds as would suffice for two or three days; but of the three who went in quest of the missing man, only two returned. They reported that they could gain no tidings of him: that they had missed one of their own number, who had, no doubt, gone in pursuit of his shipmate.

This intelligence occasioned a great deal of anxiety, and many surmises. The most prevalent opinion seemed to be that there were wild beasts on the island, and that our poor friends had become a prey to them. I determined, the next morning, to go in search of them myself, taking one or two chosen men with me. I should have mentioned, that when we left the sinking vessel, we had taken out a poodle dog, that was on board—first, because I would not allow the poor animal to perish; and, secondly, because we might, if we had no better food, make a dinner of him. This was quite fair, as charity begins at home.

This faithful animal became much attached to me, from whom he invariably received his portion of food. He never quitted me, nor followed any one else; and he was my companion when I went on this excursion.

We reached the summit of the first mountain, whence we saw the goats browsing on the second, and meant to go there in pursuit of the objects of our anxious search. I was some yards in advance of my companions, and the dog a little distance before me, near the shelving part of a rock, terminating in a precipice. The shelf I had to cross was about six or seven feet wide, and ten or twelve long, with a very little inclined plane towards the precipice, so that I thought it perfectly safe. A small rill of water trickled down from the rock above it, and, losing itself among the moss and grass, fell over the precipice below, which indeed was of a frightful depth.

This causeway was to all appearance safe, compared with many which we had passed, and I was just going to step upon it, when my dog ran before me, jumped on the fatal pass—his feet slipped from under him—he fell, and disappeared over the precipice! I started back—I heard a heavy squelch and a howl; another fainter succeeded, and all was still. I advanced with the utmost caution to the edge of the precipice, where I discovered that the rill of water had nourished a short moss, close and smooth as velvet, and so slippery as not to admit of the lightest footstep; this accounted for the sudden disappearance, and, as I concluded, the inevitable death of my dog.

My first thoughts were those of gratitude for my miraculous escape; my second unwillingly glanced at the fate of my poor men, too probably lying lifeless at the foot of this mountain. I stated my fears to the two seamen who were with me, and who had just come up. The whole bore too much the appearance of truth to admit of a doubt. We descended the ruins by a circuitous and winding way; and, after an hour's difficult and dangerous walk, we reached the spot, where all our fears were too fully confirmed. There lay the two dead bodies of our companions, and that of my dog, all mangled in a shocking manner; both, it would appear, had attempted to cross the shelf in the same careless way which I was about to do, when Providence interposed the dog in my behalf.

This singular dispensation was not lost upon me; indeed, latterly, I had been in such perils, and seen such hair-breadth escapes, that I became quite an altered and reflecting character. I returned to my men at the cove, thoughtful and melancholy; I told them of what had happened; and, having a Prayer-book with me in my trunk, I proposed to them that I should read the evening prayers, and a thanksgiving for our deliverance.

In this, the American captain, whose name was Green, most heartily concurred. Indeed, ever since this poor man had been received into the boat, he had been a very different character to what I had at first supposed him; he constantly refused his allowance of spirits, giving it among the sailors; he was silent and meditative; I often found him in prayer, and on these occasions I never interrupted him. At other times, he studied how he might make himself most useful. He would patch and mend the people's clothes and shoes, or show them how to do it for themselves. Whenever any hard work was to be done, he was always the first to begin, and the last to leave off; and to such a degree did he carry his attention and kindness, that we all began to love him, and to treat him with great respect. He took charge of a watch when we were at sea, and never closed his eyes during his hour of duty.

Nor was this the effect of fear, or the dread of ill-usage among so many Englishmen, whom his errors had led into so much misfortune. He very soon had an opportunity of proving that his altered conduct was the effect of sorrow and repentance. The next morning I sent a party round by the sea-shore, with directions to walk up the valley and bury the bodies of our unfortunate companions. The two men who had accompanied me were of the number sent on this service; when they returned, I pointed out to them how disastrous our residence had been on this fatal island, and how much better it had been for us if we had continued our course to Rio Janeiro, which, being only two hundred and fifty or two hundred and sixty leagues distant, we should by that time nearly have reached: that we were now expending the most valuable part of our provisions, namely—our spirits and tobacco; while our boat, our only hope and resource, was not even in safety, since a gale of wind might destroy her. I therefore proposed to make imme-diate preparations for our departure, to which all unanimously agreed.

We divided the various occupations; some went to fetch a sea stock of young birds, which were killed and dressed to save our salt provisions; others filled all our water-casks. Captain Green superintended the rigging, sails, and oars of the boat, and saw that every thing was complete in that department. The spirits remaining were getting low, and Captain Green, the midshipman, and myself, agreed to drink none, but reserve it for pressing emergencies. In three days after beginning our preparations, and the sev-enth after our landing, we embarked, and after being nearly swamped by the surf, once more hoisted our sail on the wide waters of the Atlantic Ocean.

We were not destined, however, to encounter many dangers this time, or to reach the coast of South America: for we had not been many hours at sea, when a vessel hove in sight; she proved to be an American privateer brig, of fourteen guns and one hundred and thirty men, bound on a cruise off the Cape of Good Hope. As soon as she perceived us, she bore down, and in half an hour we were safe on board; when having bundled all our little stock of goods on her decks, the boat was cut adrift. My men were not well treated until they consented to enter for the privateer which, after much persuasion and threats, they all did, except Thompson, contrary to my stron-gest remonstrances, and urging every argument in my power to dissuade them from such a fatal step.

I remonstrated with the captain of the privateer, on what I deemed a violation of hospitality. "You found me," I said, "on the wide ocean, in a frail boat, which some huge wave might have overwhelmed in a moment, or some fish in sport, might have tossed in the air. You received me and my people with all the kindness and friendship which we could desire; but you mar it, by seducing the men from their allegiance to their lawful sovereign, inducing them to become rebels, and subjecting them to a capital punishment whenever they may (as they most probably will) fall into the hands of their own government."

The captain, who was an unpolished, but sensible, clearheaded Yankee, replied that he was sorry I should take any thing ill of him; that no affront was meant to me; that he had nothing whatever to do with my men, until they came voluntarily to him, and entered for his vessel; that he could not but admit, however, that they might have been persuaded to take this step by some of his own people. "And, now, Leftenant," said he, "let me ask you a question. Suppose you commanded a British vessel, and ten or twelve of my men, if I was unlucky enough to be taken by you, should volunteer for your ship, and say they were natives of Newcastle, would you refuse them? Besides, before we went to war with you, you made no ceremony of taking men out of our merchant-ships, and even out of our ships of war, whenever you had an opportunity. Now, pray, where is the difference between your conduct and ours?"

I replied, that it would not be very easy, nor, if it were, would it answer any good purpose, for us to discuss a question that had puzzled the wisest heads, both in his country and mine for the last twenty years; that my present business was a case of its own, and must be considered abstractedly; that the fortune of war had thrown me in his power, and that he made a bad use of the temporary advantage of his situation, by allowing my men, who, after all, were poor, ignorant creatures, to be seduced from their duty, to desert their flag, and commit high treason, by which their lives were forfeited, and their families rendered miserable; that whatever might have been the conduct of his government or mine, whatever line pursued by this or that captain, no precedent could make wrong right; and I left it to himself (seeing I had no other resource) to say, whether he was doing as he would be done by?

"As for that matter," said the captain, "we privateer's-men don't trouble our heads much about it; we always take care of Number One; and if your men choose to say they are natives of Boston, and will enter for my ship,

I must take them. Why," continued he, "there is your best man, Thompson; I'd lay a demijohn of old Jamaica rum that he is a true-blooded Yankee, and if he was to speak his mind, would sooner fight under the stripes than the Union."

"D——n the dog that says yon of Jock Thompson," replied the Caledonian, who stood by. "I never deserted my colours yet, and I don't think I ever shall. There is only one piece of advice I would wish to give to you and your officers, captain. I am a civil spoken man, and never injured any soul breathing, except in the way of fair fighting; but if either you, or any of your crew, offer to bribe me, or in any way to make me turn my back on my king and country, I'll lay him on his back as flat as a flounder, if I am able, and if I am not able, I'll try for it."

"That's well spoken," said the captain, "and I honour you for it. You may rely on it that I shall never tempt you, and if any of mine do it, they must take their chance."

Captain Green heard all this conversation; he took no part in it, but walked the deck in his usual pensive manner. When the captain of the privateer went below to work his reckoning, this unhappy man entered into conversation with me—he began by remarking—

"What a noble specimen of a British sailor you have with you."

"Yes," I replied, "he is one of the right sort—he comes from the land where the education of the poor contributes to the security of the rich; where a man is never thought the worse of for reading his Bible, and where the generality of the lower orders are brought up in the honest simplicity of primitive Christians."

"I guess," said Green, "that you have not many such in your navy."

"More than you would suppose," I replied; "and what will astonish you is, that though they are impressed, they seldom, if ever, desert; and yet they are retained on much lower wages than those they were taken from, or could obtain; but they have a high sense of moral and religious feeling, which keeps them to their duty.

"They must needs be discontented for all that," said Green.

"Not necessarily so," said I: "they derive many advantages from being in the navy, which they could not have in other employments. They have pensions for long services or wounds, are always taken care of in their old age, and their widows and children have much favour shown them, by the government, as well as by other public bodies and wealthy individuals. But we must finish this discussion another time," continued I, "for I perceive the dinner is going into the cabin."

I received from the captain of the privateer every mark of respect and kindness that his means would allow. Much of this I owed to Green, and the black man Mungo, both of whom had represented my conduct in saving the life of him who had endangered mine and that of all my party. Green's gratitude knew no bounds—he watched me night and day, as a mother would watch a darling child; he anticipated any want or wish I could have, and was never happy until it was gratified. The seamen on board the vessel were all equally kind and attentive to me, so highly did they appreciate the act of saving the life of their countryman, and exposing my own in quelling a mutiny.

We cruised to the southward of the Cape, and made one or two captures; but they were of little consequence. One of them, being a trader from Mozambique, was destroyed; the other, a slaver from Madagascar, the captain knew not what to do with. He therefore took out eight or ten of the stoutest male negroes, to assist in working his vessel, and then let the prize go.

CHAPTER XX

But who is this? What thing of sea
Comes this way sailing,
Like a stately ship
With all her bravery on, and tackle trim?

SAMSON AGONISTES

THE privateer was called the *True-Blooded Yankee*. She was first bound to the island of Tristan d'Acunha, where she expected to meet her consort, belonging to the same owners, and who had preceded her when their directions were to cruise between the Cape and Madagascar, for certain homeward bound extra Indiamen, one or two of which she hoped would reward all the trouble and expense of the outfit.

We reached the island without any material incident. I had observed, with concern, that the second mate, whose name was Peleg Oswald, was a sour, ferocious, quarrelsome man; and that although I was kindly treated by the captain, whose name was Peters, and by the chief mate, whose name was Methusalem Solomon, I never could conciliate the good will of Peleg Oswald.

Green, the captain, who came with me, was, from the time I saved his life, an altered man. He had been, as I was informed, a drunken profligate; but from the moment when I received him into my boat, his manners and habits seemed as completely changed as if he were a different being. He never drank more than was sufficient to quench his thirst—he never swore—he never used any offensive language. He read the Scriptures constantly, was regular in his morning and evening devotion, and on every occasion of quarrel or ill-will in the brig, which was perpetually occurring, Green was the umpire and the peacemaker. He saved the captain and chief mate a world of trouble; by this system, violent language became uncommon on board, punishment was very rare, and very mild. The men were happy, and did their duty with alacrity; and but for Peleg Oswald, all would have been harmony.

We made the island about the 15th of December, when the weather was such as the season of the year might induce us to expect, it being then summer. We hove off to the north or windward side of the island, about two miles from the shore; we dared not go nearer on that side, for fear of what are called the "Rollers"—a phenomenon, it would appear, of terrific magnitude, on that sequestered little spot. On this extraordinary operation of nature, many conjectures have been offered, but no good or satisfactory reason has ever been assigned to satisfy my mind; for the simple reason, that the same causes would produce the same effect on St Helena, Ascension, or any other island or promontory exposed to a wide expanse of water. I shall attempt to describe the scene that a succession of Rollers would present, supposing, what has indeed happened, that a vessel is caught on the coast when coming in.

The water will be perfectly smooth—not a breath of wind—when, suddenly, from the north, comes rolling a huge wave, with a glassy surface, never breaking till it meets the resistance of the land, when it dashes down with a noise and a resistless violence that no art or effort of man could elude. It is succeeded by others. No anchorage would hold if there were anchorage to be had; but this is not the case; the water is from ninety to one hundred fathoms deep, and consequently an anchor and cable could scarcely afford a momentary check to any ship when thus assailed; or, if it did, the sea would, by being resisted, divide, break on board, and swamp her. Such was the fate of the unfortunate ———, a British sloop of war; which, after landing the captain and six men, was caught in the rollers, driven on shore, and every creature on board perished, only the captain and his boat's crew escaping. This unfortunate little vessel was lost, not from want of skill or seamanship in the captain or crew, for a finer set of men never swam salt water; but from their ignorance of this peculiarity of the island, unknown in any other that I ever heard of, at least to such an alarming extent. Driven close in to the land before she could find soundings, at last she let go three anchors; but nothing could withstand the force of the "Rollers," which drove her in upon the beach, when she broke in two as soon as she landed, and all hands perished in sight of the affected captain and his boat's crew, who buried the bodies of their unfortunate shipmates as soon as the sea had delivered them up.

There is another remarkable peculiarity in this island: its shores, to a very considerable extent out to sea, are surrounded with the plant, called *fucus maximus,* mentioned by Captain Cook; it grows to the depth of sixty fathoms, or one hundred and eighty feet, and reaches in one long stem to the surface, when it continues to run along to the enormous length of three or four hundred feet, with short alternate branches at every foot of its length. Thus, in the stormy ocean, grows a plant, higher and of greater length than any vegetable production of the surface of the earth, not excepting the banyan tree, which, as its branches touch the ground, takes fresh root, and may be said to form a separate tree. These marine plants resist the most powerful attacks of the mightiest elements combined; the winds and the waves in vain combine their force against them; uniting their foliage on the bosom of the waters, they laugh at the hurricane and defy its power. The leaves are alternate, and when the wind ruffles the water, they flap over, one after the other, with a mournful sound, doubly mournful to us from the sad association of ideas, and the loneliness of the island. The branches or tendrils of these plants are so strong and buoyant, when several of them happen to unite, that a boat cannot pass through them; I tried with my feet what pressure they would bear, and I was convinced that, with a pair of snow shoes, a man might walk over them.

Captain Peters kindly invited me to go on shore with him. We landed
with much difficulty, and proceeded to the cottage of a man who had been
left there from choice; he resided with his family: and, in imitation of another
great personage on an island to the northward of him, styled himself
"Emperor." A detachment of British soldiers had been sent from the Cape of
Good Hope to take possession of this spot: but after a time they were with-
drawn.

His present Imperial Majesty had, at the time of my visit, a black consort, and many snuff-coloured princes and princesses. He was in other respects a perfect Robinson Crusoe; he had a few head of cattle, and some
pigs; these latter have greatly multiplied on the island. Domestic fowls were
numerous, and he had a large piece of ground planted with potatoes, the
only place south of the Equator which produces them in their native perfection; the land is rich and susceptible of great improvement; and the soil is
intersected with numerous running springs over its surface. But it was impossible to look on this lonely spot without recalling to mind the beautiful
lines of Cowper—

"O Solitude, where are the charms
That sages have seen in thy face?"

Yet in this wild place, alarms and even rebellion had found their way,
the Emperor had but one subject, and this Caliban had ventured, in direct
violation of an imperial mandate, to kill a fowl for his dinner.

"Rebellion," said the enraged emperor, " is the son of witchcraft, and I
am determined to make an example of the offender."

I became the mediator between these two belligerents. I represented to
his imperial majesty, that, as far as the matter of example went, the severity
would lose its effect; for his children were as yet too young to be corrupted;
and, moreover, as his majesty was so well versed in scripture, he must know
that it was his duty to forgive. "Besides," I said, "her majesty the queen has
a strong arm, and can always assist in repelling or chastising any future act
of aggression or disobedience." I suspect that the moral code of his majesty
was not unlike my own: it yielded to the necessities of the time. He must
have found it particularly inconvenient not to be on speaking terms with his
prime minister and arch chancellor, whom he had banished to the opposite

side of the island on pain of death. The sentence was originally for six months; but on my intercession the delinquent was pardoned and restored to favour. I felt much self-complacency when I reflected on this successful instance of my mediatorial power, which had perhaps smothered a civil war in its birth.

The emperor informed me that an American whaler was lying at the east side of the island, filling with the oil of the walrus, or sea-horse; that she had been there at an anchor six weeks, and was nearly full. I asked to be shown the spot where the ——— was wrecked; he took me to her sad remains. She lay broken in pieces on the rocks; and, not far from her, was a mound of earth, on which was placed a painted piece of board by way of a tombstone. The fate of the vessel, together with the number of sufferers, were marked in rude but concise characters. I do not exactly remember the words, but in substance it stated, that underneath lay the remains of one hundred as fine fellows as ever walked on a plank, and that they had died, like British seamen, doing their duty to the last. This was a melancholy sight, especially to a sailor, who knew not how soon the same fate awaited him.

We rafted off several casks of water during that day, and on the following we completed our water, and then ran to the east end of the island to anchor near, and wait for our consort the whaler, the captain of which had come in his boat to visit us: I conversed with him, and was struck with one remark which he made.

"You Englishmen go to work in a queerish kind of way," said he; "you send a parcel of soldiers to live on an island where none but sailors can be of use. You listen to all that those red coats tell you; they never thrive when placed out of musket-shot from a gin-shop, and because *they* don't like it, you evacuate the island. A soldier likes his own comfort, although very apt to destroy that of other folks; and it a'n't very likely he would go and make a good report of an island that had neither women nor rum, and where he was no better than a prisoner. Now, if brother Jonathan had taken this island, I guess he would a' made it pay for its keep; he would have had two or three crews of whalers, with their wives and families, and all their little comforts about them, with a party of good farmers to till the land, and an officer to command the whole. The island can provide itself, as you may perceive, and all would have gone on well. It is just as easy to 'fish' the island from the shore as it is in vessel, and indeed much easier. Only land your boilers and casks, and a couple of dozen of good whaleboats, and this island would produce a revenue that would repay with profit all the money laid out upon it, for the sea-horses have no other place to go to, either to shed their coats in the autumn, or bring forth their young in the spring. The fishing and other duties would be a source of amusement to the sailors, who, if they chose, might return home occasionally in the vessels that came to take away the full casks of oil and land the empty ones."

The captain of the whaler returned to his ship, but, I suppose, forgot to give our captain very particular directions about the anchorage. We ran down to the east end of the island, and were just going to bring up, when, supposing himself too near the whaler, Peters chose to run a little further. I should have observed, that as we rounded the north-east point, the breeze freshed, and the squalls came heavy out of the gullies and deep ravines. We therefore shortened sail, and, passing very near the whaler, they hailed us; but it blew so fresh that we did not hear what they said; and, having increased our distance from the whaler to what was judged proper, let go the anchor.

Ninety fathoms of cable ran out in a crack, before she turned head to-wind; and, to our mortification, we found we had passed the bank upon which the whaler had brought up, and must have dropped our anchor into a well, for we had nineteen fathoms water under the bows, and only seven fathoms under the stern. The moon showed her face, just at this moment, and we had the further satisfaction of perceiving, that we were within fifty yards of a reef of rocks which lay astern of us, with their dirty, black heads above water.

We were very much surprised to find, notwithstanding the depth of water, that, during the lulls, we rode with a slack cable; but about two o'clock in the morning the cable parted, being cut by the foul ground. All sail was made immediately, but the rocks astern were so close to us, that you might have thrown a biscuit on them, and we thought the cruise of the *True-Blooded Yankee* was at an end; but it proved otherwise, for the same cause which produced the slack cable preserved the vessel. The *fucus maximus* we found had interposed between us and destruction; we had let go our anchor in this sub-marine forest, and had perched, as it were, on the tops of the trees; and, so thick were the leaves and branches, that they held us from driving, and prevented our going on shore when the cable had parted. We dragged slowly through the plants, and were very glad to see ourselves once more clear of this miserable spot.

> *"Better dwell in the midst of alarms,*
> *Than reign in this horrible place."*

But I sincerely wish all manner of success to this little empire, though I hope my evil stars will never take me to it again. We shaped our course for the Cape of Good Hope, for Captain Peters would not run further risk in waiting for the consort privateer.

Poor Thompson, notwithstanding all my exertions in his favour, was exposed to much ill-treatment on board the vessel, on account of his firm and unshaken loyalty. He seldom complained to me, but sometimes vindicated himself by a gentle hint from one of his ample fists on the nose or eye of the offender, and here the matter usually ended, for his character was so simple and inoffensive, that all the best men in the vessel loved him. One night, a man fell overboard—the weather was fine, and the brig had but little way; they were lowering down the jolly-boat from the stern, when one of the hooks by which she hung by the stern, broke, and four men were precipitated with violence into the water. Two of them could not swim, and all screamed loudly for help as soon as they came up from their dive. Thompson, seeing this, darted from the stern like a Newfoundland dog, swam to the weakest, supported him to the rudder chains, and, leaving him, went to another, bringing him to the stern of the vessel, and making a rope fast under his arms. In this way he succeeded in saving the whole of these poor fellows. Two of the five would certainly have sank but for his timely assistance, for they were some time before another boat could be got ready; and the other three owned that they much doubted whether they could have reached the vessel without help.

This conduct of Thompson was much applauded by all on board, and some asked him why he ventured his life for people who had used him so ill: he answered, that his mother and his Bible taught him to do all the good he could: and as God had given him a strong arm, he hoped he should always use it for the benefit of his brother in need.

It might have been supposed that an act like this would have prevented the recurrence of any further insult; but the more the Americans perceived

Thompson's value, the more eager were they to have him as their own. The second mate, whom I have already described as a rough and brutal fellow, one day proposed to him to belong to their vessel, certain, he added, that he would make his fortune by the capture of two, if not three, extra Indiamen, which they had information of on their passage.

Thompson looked the man fully in the face, and said, "Did ye no hear what I told the captain the ither day?"

"Yes," said the man, "I knew that, but that's what we call in our country 'all my eye.'"

"But they do not call it so in my country," said the Caledonian, at the same time planting his fist so full and plump in the left eye of the mate, that he fell like the *"humi bos,"* covering a very large part of the deck with his huge carcase.

The man got up, found his face bleeding plentifully, and his eye closed; but instead of resenting the insult himself, went off and complained to the captain. Many of the Americans, either from hatred or jealousy, went along with him, and clamorously demanded that the Englishman should be punished for striking an officer. When the story, however, came to be fairly explained, the captain said he was bound to confess that the second mate was the aggressor, inasmuch as he had acknowledged that he knew the penalty of the transgression before he committed the act; that he (the captain) had told Thompson, when he made the declaration, that he thought him perfectly right, and, consequently, he was bound to protect him by every law of hospitality as well as gratitude, after his services in saving the lives of their countrymen.

This did not satisfy the crew; they were clamorous for punishment, and a mutiny was actually headed by the second mate. There was, however, a large party on board who were in no humour to see an Englishman treated with such indignity. Of what country they were may readily be conjectured. The dispute ran high; and I began to think that serious consequences might ensue for it had continued from the serving of grog at twelve o'clock till near two; when casting my eyes over the larboard quarter, I perceived a sail, and told the captain of it; he instantly hailed the look-out-man at the mast head; but the look-out-man had been so much interested with what was going on upon deck, that he had come down into the main top to listen.

"Don't you see that sail on the larboard quarter?" said the captain.

"Yes, Sir," said the man.

"And why did you not report her?"

The man could make no reply to this question, for a very obvious reason.

"Come down here," said the captain; "let him be released, Solomon; we will show you a little Yankee discipline."

But before we proceed to the investigation of the crime, or the infliction of punishment, we must turn our eyes to the great object which rose clearer and clearer every five minutes above the horizon. The privateer was at this time under top sails, and top-gallant-sails, jib, and fore-sail, running to the north-east, with a fine breeze and smooth water.

"Leftenant," said the captain, "what do you think of her?"

"I think," said I, "that she is an extra Indiaman, and if you mean to speak her, you had better put your head towards her under an easy sail; by which means you will be so near by sunset, that if she runs from you, you will be able, with your superior sailing, to keep sight of her all night."

"I guess you are not far wrong in that," said the captain.

"I guess he is directly in the face of the truth," said the chief mate, who had just returned from the main top, where he had spent the last quarter of an hour in the most intense and absorbed attention to the cut of the stranger's sails. "If e'er I saw wood and canvas put together before in the shape of a ship, that there is one of John Bull's bellowing calves of the ocean, and not less than a forty-four gunner."

"What say you to that, leftenant?" said the captain.

"Oh, as to that," said the mate, "it isn't very likely that he's going to tell us the truth."

"Because you would not have done it yourself in the same situation," said I.

"Just so," said the mate.

And in fact, I must own that I had no particular wish to cruise for some months in this vessel, and go back for water at Tristan d'Acunha I therefore did not use my very best optical skill when I gave my opinion; but as I saw the stranger was nearing us very fast, although we were steering the same way, I made my mind up that I should very soon be out of this vessel, and on my way to England, where all my happiness and prospects were centred.

The chief mate took one more look—the captain followed his example;

they then looked at each other, and pronounced their cruise at an end.

"We are done, sir," said the mate; "and all owing to that d——d English renegado that you would enter on the books as one of the ship's company. But let's have him aft, and give him his discharge regularly."

"First of all," said the captain, "suppose we try what is to be done with our heels. They used to be good, and I never saw the brass-bottomed sarpent that could come anear us yet. Send the royal yards up—clear away the studding-sails—keep her with the wind just two points abaft the beam, that's her favourite position; and I think we may give the slip to that old-country devil in the course of the night."

I said nothing, but looked very attentively to all that was doing. The vessel was well manned, certainly, and all sail was set upon her in a very expeditious manner.

"Heave the log," said the captain.

They did so; and she was going, by their measurement, nine and six.

"What do you think your ship is doing?" said the captain to me.

"I think," said I, "she is going about eleven knots; and, as she is six miles astern of you, that she will be within gunshot in less than four hours."

"Part of that time shall be spent in paying our debts for this favour," said the captain. "Mr Solomon, let them seize that *no-nation* rascal up to the main rigging, and hand up two of your most hungry cats. Where is Dick Twist, he that was boatswain's mate of the *Statira;* and that red-haired fellow, you know, that swam away from the Maidstone in the *Rappahanock?*"

"You mean carroty Sam, I guess—pass the word for Sam Gall."

The two operators soon appeared, each armed with the instruments of his office; and I must say that, in malignity of construction, they were equal to any thing used on similar occasions even by Captain G——. The culprit was now brought forward, and to my surprise it was the very man whom Thompson, when in the boat, had thrown overboard for mutiny. I cannot say that I felt sorry for the cause or the effect that was likely to be produced by the disputes of the day.

"Seize him up," said the captain; "you were sent to the mast-head in your regular turn of duty; and you have neglected that duty, by which means we are likely to be taken: so, before my authority ceases, I will show you a Yankee trick."

"I am an Englishman," said the man, "and appeal to my officer for protection."

The captain looked at me.

"If I am the officer you appeal to," said I, "I do not acknowledge you; you threw off your allegiance when you thought it suited your purpose, and you now wish to resume it to screen yourself from a punishment which you richly deserve. I shall certainly not interfere in your favour."

"I was born," roared the cockney, "in Earl Street, Seven Dials—my mother keeps a tripe-shop—I am a true born Briton, and you have no right to flog me."

"You was a Yankee sailor from New London yesterday, and you are a tripe-seller, from Old London to-day. I think I am right in calling you a no-nation rascal, but we will talk about the right another time," said the captain; "meanwhile, Dick Twist, do you begin."

Twist obeyed his orders with skill and accuracy; and having given the prisoner three dozen, that would not have disgraced the leger-de-main of my friend the Farnese Hercules in the brig, Sam Gall was desired to take his turn. Sam acquitted himself *á merveille* with the like number; and the prisoner, after a due proportion of bellowing, was cast loose. I could not help reflecting how very justly this captain had got his vessel into jeopardy by first allowing a man to be seduced from his allegiance, and then placing confidence in him.

"Let us now take a look at the chase," said the captain; "zounds, she draws up with us. I can see her bowsprit-cap when she lifts; and half an hour ago I only saw her fore-yard. Cut away the jolly-boat from the stern, Solomon."

The chief mate took a small axe, and, with a steady blow at the end of each davit, divided the falls, and the boat fell into the sea.

"Throw these here two aftermost guns overboard," said the captain; "I guess we are too deep abaft, and they would not be of much use to us in the way of defence, for this is a wapper that's after us."

The guns in a few minutes were sent to their last rest; and for the next half-hour the enemy gained less upon them. It was now about half-past three P.M.; the courage of the Yankees revived; and the second mate reminded the captain that his black eye had not been reckoned for at the main rigging.

"Nor shall it be," said the captain, "while I command the *True-Blooded Yankee;* what is, is right; no man shall be punished for fair defence after warning. Thompson, come and stand aft."

The man was in the act of obeying this order, when he was seized on by some six or eight of the most turbulent, who began to tear off his jacket.

"Avast there, shipmates!" said Twist and Gall, both in a breath. "We don't mind touching up such a chap as this here tripeman; but not the scratch of a pin does Thompson get in this vessel. He is one of us; he is a seamen every inch of him, and you must flog us, and some fifty more, if once you begin; for d——n my eyes if we don't heave the log with the second mate, and then lay-to till the frigate comes along side."

The mutineers stood aghast for a few seconds; but the second mate, jumping on a gun, called out,

"Who's of our side? Are we going to be bullied by these d——d Britishers?"

"You are," said I, "if doing an act of justice is bullying. You are in great danger, and I warn you of it. I perceive the force of those whom you pretend to call Americans; and though I am the last man in the world to sanction an act of treachery by heaving the ship to, yet I caution you to beware how you provoke the bull-dog, who has only broke his master's chain 'for a lark,' and is ready to return to him. I am your guest, and therefore your faithful friend; use your utmost endeavours to escape from your enemy. I know what she is, for I know her well; and, if I am not much mistaken, you have scarcely more time, with all your exertions, than to pack up your things; for be assured, you will not pass twelve hours more under your own flag."

This address had a tranquillising effect. The captain, Captain Green, and Solomon, walked aft; and, to their great dismay, saw distinctly the water line of the pursuing frigate.

"What can be done?" said the captain; "she has gained on us in this manner, while the people were all aft settling that infernal dispute. Throw two more of the after guns overboard."

This order was obeyed with the same celerity as the former, but not with the same success. The captain now began to perceive, what was pretty obvious to me before, namely, that by dropping the boat from the extreme end of the vessel, where it hung like the pea on the steelyard, he did good; the lightening her also of the two aftermost guns, hanging over the dead wood of the vessel, were in like manner serviceable. But here he should have stopped; the effect of throwing the next two guns overboard was pernicious. The vessel fell by the head; her stern was out of the water; she steered wild, yawed, and decreased in her rate of sailing in a surprising manner.

"Cut away the bower anchors," said the captain.

The stoppers were cut, and the anchors dropped; the brig immediately recovered herself from her oppression, as it were, and resumed her former velocity; but the enemy had by this time made fearful approaches. The only hope of the captain and his crew was in the darkness; and as this darkness came on, my spirits decreased, for I greatly feared that we should have escaped. The sun had sunk some time below the horizon; the cloud of sail coming up a-stern of us began to be indistinct, and at last disappeared altogether in a black squall: we saw no more of her for nearly two hours.

I walked the deck with Green and the captain. The latter seemed in great perturbation; he had hoped to make his fortune, and retire from the toils and cares of a sea-life in some snug corner of the Western settlements, where he might cultivate a little farm, and lead the life of an honest man; "for *this* life," said he, "I am free to confess, is, after all, little better than highway robbery."

Whether the moral essay of the captain was the effect of his present danger, I will not pretend to say. I only know, that if the reader will turn back to some parts of my history, he will find me very often in a similar mood, on similar occasions.

The two captains and the chief mate now retired, after leaving me meditating by myself over the larboard gunwale, just before the main rigging. The consultation seemed to be of great moment; and, as I afterwards learned, was to decide what course they should steer, seeing that they evidently lost sight of their pursuer. I felt all my hopes of release vanish as I looked at them, and had made up my mind to go to New York.

At this moment, a man came behind me, as if to get a pull at the topgallant sheets; and while he hung down upon it with a kind of "yeo-ho," he whispered in my ear—"You may have the command of the brig if you like. We are fifty Englishmen—we will heave her to and hoist a light, if you will only say the word, and promise us our free pardon."

I pretended at first not to hear, but, turning round, I saw Mr Twist.

"Hold, villain!" said I; "do you think to redeem one act of treachery by another? and do you dare to insult the honour of a naval officer with a proposal so infamous? Go to your station instantly, and think yourself fortunate that I do not denounce you to the captain, who has a perfect right to throw you overboard—a fate which your chain of crimes fully deserves."

The man skulked away, and I went off to the captain, to whom I related the circumstance, desiring him to be on his guard against treachery.

"Your conduct, Sir," said the captain, "is what I should have expected from a British naval officer; and since you have behaved so honourably, I will freely tell you that my intention is to shorten sail to the topsails and foresail, and haul dead on a wind into that dark squall to the southward."

"As you please," said I; "you cannot expect that I should advise, nor would you believe me if I said I wished you success; but rely on it I will resist, by every means in my power, any unfair means to dispossess you of your command."

"I thank you, Sir," said the captain, mournfully; and, without losing any more time in useless words, "Shorten sail there," continued he, with a low but firm voice; "take in the lower and topmost studding-sail—hands aloft—in top-gallant studding-sails, and roll up the top-gallant sails."

All this appeared to be done with surprising speed, even to me who had been accustomed to very well conducted ships of war. One mistake, however, was made; the lower studding-sail, instead of being hauled in on deck, was let to fall overboard, and towed some time under the larboard bow before it was reported to the officers.

"Haul in the larboard braces—brace sharp up—port the helm, and bring her to the wind, quarter-master."

"Port, it is, Sir," said the man at the helm, and the vessel was close hauled upon the starboard tack; but she did not seem to move very fast, although she had a square mainsail, boom mainsail, and jib.

"I think we have done them at last," said the captain; "what do you think, leftenant?" giving me a hearty but very friendly slap on the back. "Come, what say you; shall we take a cool bottle of London particular after the fatigues of the day?"

"Wait a little," said I, "wait a little."

"What are you looking at there to windward?" said the captain, who perceived that my eye was fixed on a particular point.

Before I had time to answer, Thompson came up to me and said, "there is the ship, Sir," pointing to the very spot on which I was gazing. The captain heard this; and, as fear is ever quick-sighted, he instantly caught the object.

"Running is of no use now," said he; "we have tried her off the wind, our best going; she beats us at that; and on a wind; I don't think so much of her; but still, with this smooth water and fine breeze, she ought to move better. Solomon, there is something wrong, give a look all round."

Solomon went forward on the starboard side, but saw nothing. As he looked over the gangway and bow, coming round on the lee side of the forecastle, he saw some canvas hanging on one of the night-heads—"What have we here?" said he. No one answered. He looked over the fore chains, and found the whole lower studding-sail towing in the water.

"No wonder she don't move," said the mate; "here is enough to stop the Constitution herself. Who took in this here lower studding-sail?—But, never mind, we'll settle that tomorrow. Come over here, you forecastle men."

Some of the Americans came over to him, but not with very great alacrity. The sail could not be pulled in, as the vessel had too much way; and while they were ineffectually employed about it, the flash of a gun was seen to windward; and as the report reached our ears, the shot whistled over our heads, and darted like lightning through the boom mainsail.

"Hurra for old England," said Thompson; "the fellow that fired that shot shall drink my allowance of grog to-morrow."

"Hold your tongue, you d——d English rascal," said the second mate, "or I'll stop your grog for ever."

"I don't think you will," said the North Briton, "and if you take a friend's advice, you won't try." Thompson was standing on the little round-house or poop; the indignant mate jumped up, and collared him. Thompson disengaged him in the twinkling of an eye, and with one blow of his right hand in the pit of the man's stomach, sent him reeling over to leeward. He fell—caught at the boom-sheet—missed it, and tumbled into the sea, from whence he rose no more.

All was now confusion. "A man overboard!"—another shot from the frigate—another and another in quick succession. The fate of the man was forgotten in the general panic. One shot cut the aftermost main-shroud; another went through the boat on the booms. The frigate was evidently very near us. The men all rushed down to seize their bags and chests; the captain took me by the hand, and said "Sir, I surrender myself to you, and give you leave now to act as you think proper."

"Thompson," said I, "let go the main-sheet, and the main-brace." Running forward myself, I let go the main-tack, and bowlines; the main-yard came square of itself. Thompson got a lantern, which he held up on the starboard quarter.

The frigate passed close under the stern, shewing a beautiful pale side, with a fine tier of guns; and, hailing us, desired to know what vessel it was.

I replied, that it was the *True-Blooded Yankee* of Boston—that she had hove-to and surrendered.

CHAPTER XXI

"It is not," says Blake, "the business of a seaman to mind state affairs, but to hinder foreigners from fooling us."
DR JOHNSON'S "LIFE OF BLAKE"

THE FRIGATE came to the wind close under our lee, and a boat from her was alongside in a very few minutes. The officer who came to take possession, leaped up the side, and was on the deck in a moment. I received him, told him in few words what the vessel was, introducing the captain and Green, both of whom I recommended to his particular notice and attention for the kindness they had shown to me, I then requested he would walk down into the cabin, leaving a midshipman whom he brought with him in charge of the deck, and who, in the meanwhile, he directed to haul the mainsail up, and make the vessel snug. The prisoners were desired to pack up their things, and be ready to quit in one hour.

When lights were brought in the cabin, the lieutenant and myself instantly recognised each other.

"Bless my soul, Frank," said he, "what brought you here?"

"That," said I, "is rather a longer story than could be conveniently told before to-morrow; but may I ask what ship has taken the Yankee? I conclude it is the *R——*; and what rank does friend Talbot hold in her?"

"The frigate," said he, "is the *R——*, as you conjectured. We are on the

Cape station. I am first of her, and sent out here on promotion for the affair of Basque Roads."

"Hard, indeed," said I, "that you should have waited so long for what you so nobly earned; but come, we have much to do. Let us look to the prisoners, and if you will return on board, taking with you the captain, mate, and a few of the hands, whom I will select, as the most troublesome, and the most careless, I will do all I can to have the prize ready for making sail by day-light, when, if Captain T—— will give me leave, I will wait on him."

This was agreed to. The people whom I pointed out, were put into the boat, four of whose crew came aboard the brig to assist me. We soon arranged every thing, so as to be ready for whatever might be required. A boat returned with a fresh supply of hands, taking back about twenty more prisoners; and the midshipman, who brought them, delivered also a civil message from the captain, to say, he was glad to have the prize in such good hands, and would expect me to breakfast with him at eight o'clock; in the meantime, he desired, that as soon as I was ready to make sail, I should signify the same by showing two lights at the same height in the main rigging, and that we should then keep on a wind to the northward under a plain sail.

This was completed by four A.M., when we made the signal, and kept on the weather quarter of the frigate. I took a couple of hours' sleep, was called at six, dressed myself, and prepared to go on board at half past seven. I heard her drum and fife beat to quarters, the sweetest music next to the heavenly voice of Emily, I had ever heard. The tears rolled down my cheeks with gratitude to God, for once more placing me under the protection of my beloved flag. The frigate hove-to; soon after, the gig was lowered down, and came to fetch me; a clean white cloak was spread in the stern sheets: the men were dressed in white frocks and trousers, as clean as hands could make them, with neat straw hats, and canvas shoes. I was seated in the boat without delay, and my heart beat with rapture when the boatswain's mate at the gangway piped the side for me.

I was received by the captain and officers with all the kindness and affection which we lavish on each other on such occasions. The captain asked me a thousand questions, and the lieutenants and midshipmen all crowded round me to hear my answers. The ship's company were also curious to know our history, and I requested the captain would send the gig back for Thompson, who would assist me in gratifying the general curiosity. This was done, and the brave, honest fellow came on board. The first question he asked was, "Who fired the first shot at the prize?"

"It was Mr Spears, the first lieutenant of marines," said one of the men.

"Then Mr Spears must have my allowance of grog for the day," said Thompson; "for I said it last night, and I never go from my word."

"That I am ready to swear to," said Captain Peters, of the privateer: "I have known men of good resolutions, and you are one of them; and I have known men of bad resolutions, and he was one of them whom you sent last night to his long account; and it was fortunate for you that you did; for as sure as you now stand here, that man would have compassed your death, either by dagger, by water, or by poison. I never knew or heard of the man who had struck or injured Peleg Oswald with impunity. He was a Kentucky man, of the Ohio, where he had 'squatted' as we say; but he shot two men with his rifle, because they had declined exchanging some land with him. He had gouged the eye out of a third, for some trifling difference of opinion. These acts obliged him to quit the country; for, not only were the officers of justice in pursuit of him, but the man who had lost one eye kept a sharp look out with the other, and Peleg would certainly have had a rifle ball in his ear if he had not fled eastward, and taken again to the sea, to which he was originally brought up. I did not know all his history till long after he and I became shipmates. He would have been tried for his life; but having made some prize money, he contrived to buy off his prosecutors. I should have unshipped him next cruise, if it had pleased God I had got safe back."

While Peters was giving this little history of his departed mate, the captain's breakfast was announced, and the two American captains were invited to partake of it. As we went down the ladder under the half-deck, Peters and Green could not help casting an eye of admiration at the clean and clear deck, the style of the guns, and perfect union of the useful and ornamental, so inimitably blended as they are sometimes found in our ships of war. There was nothing in the captain's repast beyond cleanliness, plenty, hearty welcome, and cheerfulness.

The conversation turned on the nature, quality, and number of men in the privateer. "They are all seamen," said Peters, "except the ten black fellows."

"Some of them, I suspect, are English," said I.

"It is not for me to peach," said the wary American. "It is difficult always to know whether a man who has been much in both countries is a native of Boston in Lincolnshire, or Boston in Massachusetts; and perhaps they don't always know themselves. We never ask questions when a seaman ships for us."

"You have an abundance of our seamen, both in your marine and merchant service," said our captain.

"Yes," said Green; "and we are never likely to want them, while you impress for us."

"We impress for you?" said Captain T——, "how do you prove that?"

"Your impressment," said the American, "fills our ships. Your seamen will not stand it; and for every two men you take by force, rely on it, we get one of them as a volunteer."

Peters dissented violently from this proposition, and appeared angry with Green for making the assertion.

"I see no reason to doubt it," said Green; "I know how our fighting ships, as well as our traders, are manned. I will take my oath that more than two-thirds have run from the British navy, because they were impressed. You yourself have said so in my hearing, Peters—look at your crew."

Peters could stand conviction no longer; he burst into the most violent rage with Green; said that what ought never to have been owned to a British officer, he had let out, that it was true that America looked upon our system of impressment as the sheet-anchor of her navy; but he was sorry the important secret should ever have escaped from an American.

"For my part," resumed Green, "I feel so deeply indebted to this gallant young Englishman for his kindness to me, that I am for ever the friend of himself and his country, and have sworn never to carry arms against Great Britain, unless to repel an invasion of my own country."

Breakfast ended, we all went on deck, the ship and her prize were lying to; the hands were turned up; all the boats hoisted out; the prisoners and their luggage taken out of the prize, and, as the crew of the privateer came on board, they were all drawn up on the quarter-deck, and many of them known and proved to be Englishmen. When taxed and reproached for their infamous conduct, they said it was owing to them that the privateer had been taken, for that they had left the lower studding-sail purposely hanging over the night-head, and towing in the water, by which the way of the vessel had been impeded.

Captain Peters, who heard this confession, was astonished; and the captain of the frigate observed to him, that such conduct was exactly that which might be expected from any traitor to his country. Then, turning to the prisoners, he said, "the infamy of your first crime could scarcely have been increased; but your treachery to the new government, under which you had placed yourselves, renders you unworthy of the name of men; nor have you even the miserable merit you claim of having contributed to the capture, since we never lost sight of the chase from the first moment we saw her, and from the instant she hauled her wind, we knew she was ours."

The men hung down their heads, and when dismissed to go below, none of the crew of the frigate would receive them into their messes; but the real Americans were kindly treated.

We shaped our course for Simon's Bay, where we arrived in one week after the capture.

The admiral on the station refused to try the prisoners by a court-martial; he said it was rather a state question, and should send them all to England, where the lords of the admiralty might dispose of them as they thought proper.

The *True-Blooded Yankee* was libelled in the vice admiralty court at Cape Town, condemned as a lawful prize, and purchased into the service; and, being a very fine vessel of her class, the admiral was pleased to say, that as I had been so singularly unfortunate, he would give me the command of her as a lieutenant, and send me to England with some despatches, which had been waiting an opportunity.

This was an arrangement far more advantageous to me than I could have expected; but what rendered it still more agreeable was, that my friend Talbot, who was the first to shake me by the hand on board the prize, begged a passage home with me, he having, by the last packet, received his commander's commission. The admiral, at my request, also gave Captains Peters and Green permission to go home with me. Mungo, the black man, and Thompson, the quarter-master, with the midshipman who had been with me in the boat, were also of the party. My crew was none of the very best, as might be supposed; but I was not in a state to make difficulties; and, with half-a-dozen of the new Negroes, taken out of the trader, I made up such a ship's company as I thought would enable me to run to Spithead.

We laid in a good stock of provisions at the Cape. The Americans begged to be allowed to pay their part; but this I positively refused, declaring myself too happy in having them as my guests. I purchased all Captain Peters's wine and stock, giving him the full value for it. Mungo was appointed steward, for I had taken a great fancy to him; and my friend Talbot having brought all his things on board, and the admiral having given my final orders, I sailed from Simon's Bay for England.

There is usually but little of incident in a run home of this sort. I was not directed to stop at St Helena, and had no inclination to loiter on my way. I carried sail night and day to the very utmost. Talbot and myself became inseparable friends, and our cabin mess was one of perfect harmony. We avoided all national reflections, and abstained as much as possible from politics. I made a confidant of Talbot in my love affair with Emily. Of poor Eugenia, I had long before told him a great deal.

One day at dinner we happened to talk of swimming. "I think," said Talbot, "that my friend Frank is as good a hand at that as any of us. Do you remember when you swam away from the frigate at Spithead, to pay a visit to your friend, Mrs Melpomene, at Point?"

"I do," said I, "and also how generously you showered the musket-balls about my ears for the same."

"Your escape from either drowning or shooting on that occasion, among many others," said the commander, "makes me augur something more serious of your future destiny."

"That may be," said I; "but I dispute the legality of your act, in trying to kill me before you knew who I was, or what I was about. I might have been mad, for what you knew; or I might have belonged to some other ship; but, in any event, had you killed me, and had my body been found, a coroner's inquest would have gone very hard with you, and a jury still worse."

"I should have laughed at them," said Talbot.

"You might have found it no laughing matter," said I

"How?" replied Talbot, "what are sentinels placed for, and loaded with ball?"

"To defend the ship," said I; "to give warning of approaching danger;

to prevent men going out of the ship without leave; but never to take away the life of a man unless in defence of their own, or when the safety of the king's ship demands it."

"I deny your conclusion," said Talbot; "the articles of war denounce death to all deserters."

"True," said I, "they do, and also to many other crimes; but those crimes must first of all be proved before a court-martial. Now you cannot prove that I was deserting, and if you could, you had not the power to inflict death on me unless I was going towards the enemy. I own I was disobeying your orders, but even that would not have subjected me to more than a slight punishment, while your arbitrary act would have deprived the king, as I flatter myself, of a loyal, and not a useless subject; and if my body had not been found, no good could have accrued to the service from the severity of example. On the contrary, many would have supposed I had escaped, and been encouraged to make the same attempt."

"I am very sorry now," said Talbot, "that I did not lower down a boat to send after you; however, it has been a comfort to me since to reflect that the marines missed you."

This ended the subject: we walked the deck a little, talked of sweethearts, shaped the course for the night to make Fayal, which we were not far from, and then returned to our beds.

Falling into a sound sleep, it was natural that the conversation of the evening should have dwelt on my mind, and a strange mixture of disjointed thoughts, a compound of reason and insanity, haunted me till the morning. Trinidad and Emily, the Nine-Pin Rock, and the mysterious Eugenia, with her supposed son; the sinking wreck, and the broken schooner, all appeared separately or together.

> *"When nature rests,*
> *Oft, in her absence, mimic fancy wakes."*

I thought I saw Emily standing on the pinnacle of the Nine-Pin Rock, just as Lord Nelson is represented on the monument in Dublin, or Bonaparte in that of the Place Vendome; but with a grace as far superior to either, as the Nine-Pin Rock is in majesty and natural grandeur to those works of human art.

Emily, I thought, was clad in complete mourning, but looking radiant in health and loveliness, although with a melancholy countenance. The dear image of my mistress seemed to say, "I shall never come down from this pinnacle without your assistance." "Then," thinks I, "you will never come down at all." Then I thought Eugenia was queen of Trinidad, and that it was she who had placed Emily out of my reach on the rock; and I was entreating her to let Emily come down, when Thompson tapped at my cabin door, and told me that it was daylight, and that they could see the island of Fayal in the northeast, distant about seven leagues.

I dressed myself, and went on deck, saw the land, and a strange sail steering to the westward. The confounded dream still running in my head—like Adam, I "liked it not," and yet I thought myself a fool for not dismissing such idle stuff; still it would not go away. The Americans came on deck soon after; and seeing the ship steering to the westward, asked if I meant to speak her. I replied in the affirmative. We had then as much sail as we could carry; and as she had no wish to avoid us, but kept on her course, we were soon alongside of her. She proved to be a cartel, bound to New York with American prisoners.

In case of meeting with any vessel bound to the United States, the admiral had given me permission to send my prisoners home without carrying them to England. I had not mentioned this either to Peters or Green, for fear of producing disappointment; but when I found I could dispose of them so comfortably, I acquainted them with my intention. Their joy and gratitude were beyond all description; they thanked me a thousand times, as they did my friend Talbot for our kindness to them.

"Leftenant," said Peters, "I am not much accustomed to the company of you Englishmen; and if I have always thought you a set of tyrants and bullies, it arn't my fault. I believed what I was told; but now I have seen for myself, and I find the devil is never so black as he is painted." I bowed to the Yankee compliment. "Howsoever," he continued, "I should like to have a sprinkling of shot between us on fair terms. Do you bring this here brig to our waters; I hope to get another just like her, and as I know you are a d——d good fellow, and would as soon have a dust as sit down to dinner, I should like to try to get the command of the *True-Blooded Yankee* again."

"If you man your next brig, as you manned the last, with all your best hands Englishmen," said I, "I fear I should find it no easy matter to defend myself."

"That's as it may be," said the captain; "no man fights better than he with a halter round his neck: and remember what neighbour Green has said, for he has 'let the cat out of the bag:' we should have no Englishmen in our service, if they had not been pressed into yours."

I could make no return to this salute, because, like the gunner at Landguard Fort, I had no powder, and, in fact, I felt the rebuke.

Green stood by, but never opened his lips until the captain had finished; then holding out his hand to me, with his eyes full of tears, and his voice almost choked, "Farewell, my excellent friend," said he; "I shall never forget you; you found me a villain, and, by the blessing of God, you have made me an honest man. Never, never, shall I forget the day when, at the risk of your own life, you came to save one so unworthy of your protection; but God bless you! and if ever the fortune of war should send you a prisoner to my country, here is my address—what is mine is yours, and so you shall find."

The man who had mutinied in the boat, and afterwards entered on board the privateer, who was sent home with me to take his trial, held out his hand to Captain Green, as he passed him, to wish him good-by, but he turned away, saying, "A traitor to his country is a traitor to his God. I forgive you for the injury you intended to do me, and the more so, as I feel I brought it on myself; but I cannot degrade myself by offering you the hand of fellowship."

So saying, he followed Captain Peters into the boat. I accompanied them to the cartel, where, having satisfied myself that they had every comfort, I left them. Green was so overcome that he could not speak, and poor Mungo could only say, "Good-by, massa leptenant, me tinkee you berry good man."

I returned to my own vessel, and made sail for England: once more we greeted the white cliffs of Albion, so dear to every true English bosom. No one but he who has been an exile from its beloved shores can fully appreciate the thrill of joy on such an occasion. We ran through the Needles, and I anchored at Spithead, after an absence of fourteen months. I waited on the admiral, showed him my orders, and reported the prisoners, whom he desired me to discharge into the flag ship; "and now," said he, "after your extraordinary escape, I will give you leave to run up to town and see your family, to whom you are no doubt an object of great interest."

Here a short digression is necessary.

CHAPTER XXII

Such was my brother too,
So went he suited to his watery tomb:
If spirits can assume both form and suit,
You come to fright us.

"TWELFTH NIGHT"

SOON after the frigate which had taken me off from New Providence had parted company with the American prize that I was sent on board of, the crew of the former, it appeared, had been boasting among the American prisoners of the prize-money they should receive.

"Not you," said the Yankees; "you will never see your prize any more, nor any one that went in her."

These words were repeated to the captain of the frigate, when he questioned the mate and the crew, and the whole nefarious transaction came out. They said the ship was sinking when they left her, and that was the reason they had hurried into the boat. The mate said it was impossible to get at the leaks, which were in the fore peak, and under the cabin deck in the run; that he wondered Captain Green had not made it known, but he supposed he must have been drunk: "the ship," continued the mate, "must have gone down in twelve hours after we left her."

This was reported to the Admiralty by my captain, and my poor father was formally acquainted with the fatal story. Five months had elapsed since I was last heard of, and all hopes of my safety had vanished: this was the reason that when I knocked at the door, I found the servant in mourning: he was one who had been hired since my departure, and did not know me. Of course he expressed no surprise at seeing me.

"Good Heavens!" said I, "who is dead?"

"My master's only son, Sir," said the man, "Mr Frank, drowned at sea."

"Oh! is that all?" said I, "I am glad it's no worse."

The man concluded that I was an unfeeling brute, and stared stupidly at me as I brushed by him and ran up stairs to the drawing-room. I ought to have been more guarded; but, as usual, I followed the impulse of my feelings. I opened the door, when I saw my sister sitting at a table in deep mourning, with another young lady whose back was turned towards me. My sister screamed as soon as she saw me. The other lady turned round, and I beheld my Emily, my dear, dear Emily: she too was in deep mourning. My sister, after screaming, fell on the floor in a swoon. Emily instantly followed her example, and there they both lay, like two petrified queens in Westminster Abbey. It was a beautiful sight, "pretty, though a plague."

I was confoundedly frightened myself, and thought I had done a very foolish thing; but as I had no time to lose, I rang the bell furiously, and seeing some jars with fresh flowers in them, I caught them up and poured plentiful libations over the faces and necks of the young ladies; but Emily came in for much the largest share, which proves that I had neither lost my presence of mind nor my love for her.

My sister's maid, Higgins, was the first to answer the drawing-room bell, which, from its violent ringing, announced some serious event. She came bouncing into the room like a *recouchée* shot. She was an old acquaintance of mine; I had often kissed her when a boy, and she had just as often boxed my ears. I used to give her a ribbon to tie up her jaw with, telling her at the same time that she had too much of it. This Abigail, like a true lady's maid, seeing me, whom she thought a ghost, standing bolt upright, and the two ladies stretched out, as she supposed, dead, gave a loud and most interesting scream, ran out of the room for her life, nearly knocking down the footman, whom she met coming in.

This fellow, who was a country lout, the son of one of my father's tenants, only popped his head into the door, and saw the ladies lying on the carpet; he had probably formed no very good opinion of me from the manner in which I had received the news of my own demise, and seemed very much inclined to act the part of a mandarin, that is, nod his head and stand still.

"Desire some of the women to come here immediately," said I; "some one that can be of use; tell them to bring salts, eau de cologne, any thing. Fly, blockhead, goose, what do you stand staring at?"

The fellow looked at me, and then at the supposed corpses, which he must have thought I had murdered; and, either thunderstruck, or doubting whether he had any right to obey me, kept his head inside the door and his body outside, as if he had been in the pillory. I saw that he required some explanation, and cried out, "I am Mr Frank; will you obey me, or shall

I throw this jar at your head?" brandishing one of the china vases.

Had I been inclined to have thrown it, I should have missed him, for the fellow was off like a wounded porpoise. Down he ran to my father in the library; "Oh, Sir—good news—bad news—good news—"

"What news, fool?" said my father, rising hastily from his chair.

"Oh, Sir, I don't know, Sir; but I believe, Sir, Mr Frank is alive again, and both the ladies is dead."

My poor father, whose health and constitution had not recovered the shock of my supposed death, tremblingly leaned over his table, on which he rested his two hands, and desired the man to repeat what he had said. This the fellow did, half crying, and my father, easily comprehending the state of things, came upstairs. I would have flown into his arms, but mine were occupied in supporting my sweet Emily, while my poor sister lay senseless on the other side of me; for Clara's lover was not at hand, and she still lay in abeyance.

By this time "the hands were turned up," every body was on the alert, and every living creature in the house, not excepting the dog, had assembled in the drawing-room. The maids that had known me cried and sobbed most piteously, and the new comer kept them company from sympathy. The coachman, and footman, and groom, all blubbered and stared; and one brought water, and one a basin, and the looby of a footman something else, which I must not name; but in his hurry he had snatched up the first utensil that he thought might be of use; I approved of his zeal, but nodded to him to retire. Unluckily for him, the housemaid perceived the mistake which his absence of thought had led him into; and, snatching the mysterious vessel with her left hand, she hid it under her apron, while with her right she gave the poor fellow such a slap on the cheek, as to bring to my mind the tail of the whale descending on the boat at Bermuda. "You great fool," said she, "nobody wants that."

"There is matrimony in that slap," said I; and the event proved I was right—they were *asked* in church the Sunday following.

The industrious application of salts, cold water, and burnt rags, together with chafing of temples, opening of collars, and loosening the stay-laces of the young ladies, produced the happiest effects. Every hand, and every tongue was in motion; and with all these remedies, the eyes of the enchanting Emily opened, and beamed upon me, spreading joy and gladness over the face of creation, like the sun rising out of the bosom of the Atlantic, to cheer the inhabitants of the Antilles after a frightful hurricane. In half an hour, all was right; "the guns were secured—we beat the retreat;" the servants retired. I became the centre of the picture. Emily held my right, my father my left; dear Clara hung round my neck. Questions were put and answered as fast as sobs and tears would admit of their being heard. The interlude was filled up with the sweetest kisses from the rosiest of lips; and I was in this half hour rewarded for all I had suffered since I had sailed from England in the diabolical brig for Barbadoes.

It was, I own, exceedingly wrong to have taken the house, as it were, by storm, when I knew they were in mourning for me; but I forgot that other people did not require the same stimulus as myself. I begged pardon; was kissed again and again, and forgiven. Oh, it was worth while to offend to be forgiven by such lips, and eyes, and dimples. But I am afraid this thought is borrowed from some prose or poetry; if so, the reader must forgive me, and so must the author, who may have it again, now I have done with it, for I shall never use it any more.

My narrative was given with as much modesty and brevity as time and circumstances would admit. The coachman was despatched on one of the best carriage-horses express to Mr Somerville, and the mail coach was loaded with letters to all the friends and connections of the family.

This ended, each retired to dress for dinner. What a change had one hour wrought in this house of mourning, now suddenly turned into a house of joy! Alas! how often is the picture reversed in human life! The ladies soon reappeared in spotless white; emblems of their pure minds. My father had put off his sables, and the servants came in their usual liveries, which were very splendid.

Dinner being announced, my father handed off Emily; I followed with my sister. Emily, looking over her shoulder, said, "Don't be jealous, Frank."

My father laughed, and I vowed revenge for this little satirical hit.

"You know the forfeit," said I, "and you shall pay it."

"I am happy to say that I am both able and willing," said she, and we sat down to dinner, but not before my father had given thanks in a manner more than usually solemn and emphatic. This essential act of devotion, so often neglected, brought tears into the eyes of all. Emily sank into her chair, covered her face with her pocket-handkerchief, and relieved herself with tears. Clara did the same. My father shook me by the hand, and said, "Frank, this is a very different kind of repast to what we had yesterday. How little did we know of the happiness that was in store for us!"

The young ladies dried their eyes, but had lost their appetites: in vain did Emily endeavour to manage the tail of a small smelt. I filled a glass of wine to each. "Come," said I, "in sea phrase, spirits are always more easily stowed away than dry provisions; let us drink each other's health, and then we shall get on better."

They took my advice, and it answered the purpose. Our repast was cheerful, but tempered and corrected by a feeling of past sorrow, and a deep sense of great mercies from Heaven.

> *"If Heaven were every day like this,*
> *Then 'twere indeed a Heaven of bliss."*

Reader, I know you have long thought me a vain man—a profligate, unprincipled Don Juan, ready to pray when in danger, and to sin when out of it: but as I have always told you the truth, even when my honour and character were at stake, I expect you will believe me now, when I say a word in my own favour. That I felt gratitude to God for my deliverance and safe return, I do most solemnly aver; my heart was ready to burst with the escape of this feeling, which I suppressed from a false sense of shame, though I never was given much to the melting mood; moreover, I was too proud to show what I thought a weakness, before the great he-fellows of footmen. Had we been in private, I could have fallen down on my knees before that God whom I had so often offended; who had rescued me twice from the jaws of the shark; who had lifted me from the depth of the sea when darkness covered me; who had saved me from the poison and the wreck, and guided me clear of the rock at Trinidad; and who had sent the dog to save me from a horrible death.

These were only a small part of the mercies I had received; but they were the most recent, and consequently had left the deepest impression on my memory. I would have given one of Emily's approving smiles, much as I valued them, to have been relieved from my oppressed feelings by a hearty flood of tears, and by a solemn act of devotion and thanksgiving; but I felt all this, and that feeling, I hope, was accounted to me for righteousness. For the first time in my life, the love of God was mixed up with a pure and earthly love for Emily, and affection for my family.

The ladies sat with us some time after the cloth was removed, unable to drag themselves away, while I related my "hair-breadth escapes." When I spoke of the incident of trying to save the poor man who fell overboard from the brig—of my holding him by the collar, and being dragged down with him until the sea became dark over my head— Emily could bear it no longer; she jumped up, and falling on her knees, hid her lovely face in my sister's lap, passionately exclaiming, "Oh, do not, do not, my dear Frank, tell me any more—I cannot bear it—indeed, I cannot bear it."

We all gathered round her, and supported her to the drawing-room, where we diverted ourselves with lighter and gayer anecdotes. Emily tried a tune on the pianoforte, and attempted a song; but it would not do: she could not sing a gay one, and a melancholy one overpowered her. At twelve o'clock, we all retired to our apartments, and before I slept I spent some minutes in devotion, with vows of amendment which I fully intended to keep.

The next morning, Mr Somerville joined us at breakfast. This was another trial of feeling for poor Emily, who threw herself into her father's arms, and sobbed aloud. Mr Somerville shook me most cordially by the hand with both of his, and eagerly demanded the history of my extraordinary adventures, of which I gave him a small abridgment. I had taken the opportunity of an hour's *tête-à-tête* with Emily, which Clara had considerately given us before breakfast, to speak of our anticipated union; and finding there were no other obstacles than those which are usually raised by "maiden pride and bashful coyness," so natural, so becoming, and so lovely in the sex, I determined to speak to the grey-beards on the subject.

To this Emily at last consented, on my reminding her of my late narrow escapes. As soon, therefore, as the ladies had retired from the dinner table, I asked my father to fill a bumper to their health; and, having swallowed mine in all the fervency of the most unbounded love, I popped the question to them both. Mr Somerville and my father looked at each other, when the former said—

"You seem to be in a great hurry, Frank."

"Not greater, Sir," said I, "than the object deserves." He bowed, and my father began—

"I cannot say," observed the good old gentleman, "that I much approve of matrimony before you are a commander. At least, till then, you are not your own master."

"Oh, if I am to wait for that, Sir," said I, "I may wait long enough; no man is ever his own master in our service, or in England. The captain is commanded by the admiral, the admiral by the Admiralty, the Admiralty by the Privy Council, the Privy Council by the Parliament, the Parliament by the people, and the people by printers and their devils."

"I admire your logical chain of causes and effects," said my father; "but we must, after all, go to the *lace manufactory* at Charing-cross, to see if we cannot have your shoulders fitted with a pair of epaulettes. When we can see you command your own sloop of war, I shall be most happy, as I am sure my good friend Somerville will be also, to see you command his daughter, the finest and the best girl in the county of ———."

No arguments could induce the two old gentlemen to bate one inch from these *sine quâ non*. It was agreed that application should be made to the Admiralty forthwith for my promotion; and when that desirable step was obtained, that then Emily should have the disposal of me for the honeymoon.

All this was a very pretty story for them on the score of prudence, but it did not suit the views of an ardent lover of one-and-twenty; for though I knew my father's influence was very great at the Admiralty, I also knew that an excellent regulation had recently been promulgated, which prevented any lieutenant being promoted to the rank of commander until he had served two years at sea from the date of his first commission; nor could any commander, in like manner, be promoted before he had served one year in that capacity. All this was no doubt very good for the service, but I had not yet attained sufficient *amor patriæ* to prefer the public to myself; and I fairly wished the regulation, the makers of it, in the cavern at New Providence, just about the time of high water.

I put it to the ladies whether this was not a case of real distress, after all my hardships and my constancy, to be put off with such an excuse? The answer from the Admiralty was so far favourable, that I was assured I should be promoted as soon as my time was served, of which I then wanted two months. I was appointed to a ship fitting at Woolwich, and before she could be ready for sea, my time would be completed, and I was to have my commission as a commander. This was not the way to ensure her speedy equipment, as far as I was concerned; but there was no help for it; and as the ship was at Woolwich, and the residence of my fair one at no great distance, I endeavoured to pass my time, during the interval, between the duties of love and war; between obedience to my captain, and obedience to my mistress; and by great good fortune, I contrived to please both, for my captain gave himself no trouble about the ship or her equipment.

Before I proceeded to join, I made one more effort to break through the inflexibility of my father. I said I had undergone the labours of Hercules; and that if I went again on foreign service, I might meet with some young lady who would send me out of the world with a cup of poison, or by some fatal spell break the magical chain which now bound me to Emily. This poetical imagery had no more effect on them, than my prose composition. I then appealed to Emily herself. "Surely," said I, "your heart is not as hard as those of our inflexible parents? surely you will be my advocate on this occasion? Bend but one look of disapprobation on my father with those heavenly blue eyes of yours, and, on my life, he will strike his flag."

But the gipsy replied, with a smile (instigated, no doubt, from head-quarters), that she did not like the idea of her name appearing in the *Morning Post* as the bride of a lieutenant. "What's a lieutenant, now-a-days?" said she; "nobody. I remember when I was on a visit at Fareham, I used to go to Portsmouth to see the dock-yard and the ships, and there was your great friend the tall admiral, Sir Hurricane Humbug, I think you call him, driving the poor lieutenants about like so many sheep before a dog; there was one always at his heels, like a running footman; and there was another that appeared to me to be chained, like a mastiff, to the door of the admiral's office, except when the admiral and family walked out, and then he brought up the rear with the governess. No, Frank, I shall not surrender at discretion, with all my charms, to any thing less than a captain, with a pair of gold epaulettes."

"Very well," replied I, looking into the pier glass, with tolerable self-complacency; "if you choose to pin your happiness on the promises of a first lord of the Admiralty, and a pair of epaulettes, I can say no more. There is no accounting for female taste; some ladies prefer gold lace and wrinkles, to youth and beauty—I am sorry for them, that's all."

"Frank," said Emily, "you must acknowledge that you are vain enough to be an admiral at least."

"The admirals are much obliged to you for the compliment," said I. "I trust I should not disgrace the flag, come when it will; but to tell you the truth, my dear Emily, I cannot say I look forward to that elevation, with any degree of satisfaction. Three stars on each shoulder, and three rows of gold lace round the cuff, are no compensation, in my eyes, for grey hairs, thin legs, a broken back, a church-yard cough, and to be laughed at or pitied by all the pretty girls in the country into the bargain."

"I am sorry for you, my hero," said the young lady; "but you must submit."

"Well then, if I must, I must," said I; "but give me a kiss in the meantime."

I asked for one, and took a hundred, and should have taken a hundred more, but the confounded butler came in, and brought me a letter on service, which was neither more nor less than an order to join my ship forthwith; *sic transit,* &c.

Pocketing my disappointment with as much *sang froid* as I could muster, I continued to beguile the time and to solace myself for my past sufferings, by as much enjoyment as could be compressed into the small space of leisure time allotted to me. Fortunately, the first lieutenant of the frigate was what we used to call "a hard officer;" he never went on shore, because he had few friends and less money. He drew for his pay on the day it became due, and it lasted till the next day of payment; and as I found he doated on a Spanish cigar, and a *correct* glass of cognac grog—for he never drank to excess—I presented him with a box of the former, and a dozen of the latter, to enable him to bear my nightly absence with Christian composure.

As soon as the day's work was ended, the good-natured lieutenant used to say, "Come, Mr Mildmay, I know what it is to be in love; I was once in love myself, though it is a good many years ago, and I am sure I shall get into the good graces of your Polly (for so he called Emily) if I send you to her arms. There is the jolly for you: send the boat off as soon as you have landed, and be with us at nine to-morrow morning, to meet the midshipman and the working party in the dock-yard."

All this was perfectly agreeable to me. I generally got to Mr Somerville's temporary residence on Blackheath by the time the dressing-bell rang, and never failed to meet a pleasant party at dinner. My father and dear Clara were guests in the house as well as myself. By Mr Somerville's kind permission, I introduced Talbot, who, being a perfect gentleman in his

manners, a man of sound sense, good education, and high aristocratic connections, I was proud to call my friend. I presented him particularly to my
sister, and took an opportunity of whispering in Emily's ear, where I knew
it would not long remain, that he possessed the indispensable qualification
of two epaulettes. "Therefore," said I, "pray do not trust yourself too near him,
for fear you should be taken by surprise, like the *True-Blooded Yankee.*"

Talbot knowing that Emily was bespoken, paid her no more than the
common attentions which courtesy demands; but to Clara his demeanour
was very different: and her natural attractions were much enhanced in his
eyes, by the friendship which we had entertained for each other ever since
the memorable affair of swimming away from the ship at Spithead; from that
time he used jocularly to call me "Leander."

But before I proceed any further with this part of my history, I must beg
leave to detain the reader one minute only, while I attempt to make a sketch
of my dear little sister Clara. She was rather fair, with a fine, small, oval, well-
proportioned face, sparkling black and speaking eyes, good teeth, pretty red
lips, very dark hair, and plenty of it, hanging over her face and neck in curls
of every size; her arms and bust were such as Phidias and Praxiteles might
have copied; her waist was slender; her hands and feet small and beautiful.
I used often to think it was a great pity that such a love as she was should
not be matched with some equally good specimen of our sex; and I had
long fixed on my friend Talbot as the person best adapted to command this
pretty little, tight, fast-sailing, well-rigged smack.

Unluckily, Clara, with all her charms, had one fault, and that, in my
eyes, was a very serious one. Clara did not love a sailor. The soldiers she
doated on. But Clara's predilections were not easily overcome, and that
which had once taken root grew up and flourished. She fancied sailors were
not well bred; that they thought too much of themselves or their ships; and,
in short, that they were as rough and unpolished as they were conceited.

With such obstinate and long-rooted prejudices against all of our profession, it proved no small share of merit in Talbot to overcome them. But
as Clara's love for the army was more general than particular, Talbot had a
vacant theatre to fight in. He began by handing her to dinner, and with
modest assurance seated himself by her side. But so well was he aware of
her failing, that he never once alluded to our unfortunate element; on the

contrary, he led her away with every variety of topic which he found best suited to her taste: so that she was at last compelled to acknowledge that he might be one exception to her rule, and I took the liberty of hoping that I might be another.

One day at dinner Talbot called me "Leander," which instantly attracted the notice of the ladies, and an explanation was demanded; but for a time it was evaded, and the subject changed. Emily, however, joining together certain imperfect reports which had reached her ears, through the kindness of "some friends of the family," began to suspect a rival, and the next morning examined me so closely on the subject, that fearing a disclosure from other quarters, I was compelled to make a confession.

I told her the whole history of my acquaintance with Eugenia, of my last interview, and of her mysterious departure. I did not even omit the circumstance of her offering me money; but I concealed the probability of her being a mother. I assured her that it was full four years and a half since we had met; and that as she knew of my engagement, it was unlikely we should ever meet again. "At any rate," I said, "I shall never seek her; and if accident should throw me in her way, I trust I shall behave like a man of honour."

I did not think it necessary to inform her of the musket-shots fired at me by order of Talbot, as that might have injured him in the estimation of both Emily and Clara. When I had concluded my narrative, Emily sighed and looked very grave. I asked her if she had forgiven me.

"Conditionally," said she, "as you said to the mutineers."

CHAPTER XXIII

In all states of Europe, there are a set of men who assume
from their infancy a pre-eminence independent of their moral
character. The attention paid to them from the moment of their
birth, gives them the idea that they are formed for command,
and they soon learn to consider themselves a distinct species:
and, being secure of a certain rank and station, take no pains to
makes themselves worthy of it.

RAYNAL

IT is now time to make my reader acquainted with my new ship and new captain. The first was a frigate of the largest class, built on purpose to cope with the large double-banked frigates of the Yankees. She carried thirty long twenty-four pounders on her main deck, and the same number of forty-two pound carronades on her quarter-gangways and forecastle.

I had been a week on board, doing duty during the day and flirting on shore, at Mr Somerville's, at Blackheath, during the evening. I had seen no captain yet, and the first lieutenant had gone on shore one morning to stretch his legs. I was commanding officer; the people were all at their dinner; it was a drizzling soft rain, and I was walking the quarter-deck by myself, when a shore-boat came alongside with a person in plain clothes. I paid him no attention, supposing him to be a wine merchant, or a slop-seller, come to ask permission to serve the ship. The stranger looked at the dirty man-ropes, which the side-boys held off to him, and inquired if there was not a clean pair? The lad replied in the negative; and the stranger perceiving there was no remedy, took hold of the dirty ropes and ascended the side.

Reaching the quarter-deck, he come up to me, and showing a pair of sulphur-coloured gloves, bedaubed with tar and dirt, angrily observed, "By G——, Sir, I have spoiled a new pair of gloves."

"I always take my gloves off when I come up the side," said I.

"But I choose to keep mine on," said the stranger. "And why could not I have had a pair of clean ropes?"

"Because," said I, "my orders are only to give them when the side is piped."

"And why was not the side piped for me, Sir?"

"Because, Sir, we never pipe the side until we know who it is for."

"As sure as I shall sit in the House of Peers, I will report you to your captain for this," said he.

"We only pipe the side for officers in uniform," said I; "and I am yet to learn by what right you demand that honour."

"I am, Sir," said he (showing his card), ". . . ., &c. Do you know me now?"

"Yes, Sir," said I, "as a gentleman; but until I see you in a captain's uniform, I cannot give you the honours you demand:" as I said this, I touched my hat respectfully.

"Then, Sir," said he, "as sure as I shall sit in the House of Peers, I shall let you know more of this:" and having asked whether the captain was on board, and received an answer in the negative, he turned round and went down the side into his boat, without giving me an opportunity of supplying him with a pair of clean ropes. He pulled away for the shore, and I never heard any thing more of the dirty ropes and soiled gloves.

This officer, I afterwards learned, was in the habit of interlarding his discourse with this darling object of his ambition; but as he is now a member of the Upper House, it is to be supposed he has exchanged the affidavit for some other. While he commanded a ship, he used to say, "As sure as I shall sit in the House of Peers, I will flog you, my man;" and when this denunciation had passed his lips, the punishment was never remitted. With us, the reverse of this became our bye-word; lieutenants, midshipmen, sailors and marines, asserted their claim to veracity by saying, "As sure as I shall *not* sit in the House of Peers."

This was the noble lord, who when in the command of one of his Majesty's ships in China, employed a native of that country to take his portrait. The resemblance not having been flattering, the artist was sharply rebuked by his patron. The poor man replied, "Ai awe, master, how can handsome face make if handsome face no have got?" This story has, like many other good stories, been pirated, and applied to other cases; but I claim it as the legitimate property of the navy, and can vouch for its origin as I have related.

My messmates dropped in one after another until our number was completed; and at length a note, in an envelope addressed to the first lieutenant "on service," and marked on the lower left hand corner with the name of the noble writer, announced that our captain would make his appearance on the following day. We were of course prepared to receive him in our full uniforms with our cocked hats and swords, with the marine guard under arms. He came alongside at half-past twelve o'clock, when the men were at dinner, an unusual hour to select, as it is not the custom ever to disturb them at their meals if it can be avoided. He appeared in a sort of undress frock coat, fall down collar, anchor buttons, no epaulettes, and a lancer's cap, with a broad gold band.

This was not correct, but as he was a lord, he claimed privilege, and on this rock of privilege we found afterwards that he always perched himself on every occasion. We were all presented to him; and to each he condescended to give a nod. His questions were all confined to the first lieutenant, and all related to his own comforts. "Where is my steward to lie? where is my valet to sleep? where is my cow-pen? and where are my sheep to be?" We discovered when he had been one hour in our company, that his noble self was the god of his idolatry. As for the details of the ship and her crew, masts, rigging, stowage, provisions, the water she would carry, and how much she drew, they were subjects on which he never fatigued his mind.

One hour having expired since he had come on board, he ordered his boat, and returned to the shore, and we saw no more of him until we arrived at Spithead, when his lordship came on board, accompanied by a person whom we soon discovered was a half-pay purser in the navy: a man who, by dint of the grossest flattery and numerous little attentions, had so completely ingratiated himself with his patron, that he had become as necessary an appendage to the travelling equipage, as the portmanteau or the valet-de-chambre. This despicable toady was his lordship's double; he was a living type of the Gnatho of Terence; and I never saw him without remembering the passage that ends *"si negat id quoque nego."* Black was white, and white was black with toady, if his lordship pleased; he messed in the cabin, did much mischief in the ship, and only escaped kicking, because he was too contemptible to be kicked.

My fair readers are no doubt anxious to know how I parted with Emily, and truly I am not unwilling to oblige them, though it is, indeed, a tender subject. As soon as we received our orders to proceed to Spithead, Mr Somerville, who had kept his house at Blackheath while the ship was fitting, in hopes that my promotion might have taken place before she was ready, now prepared to quit the place. To the renewed application of my father, the answer was that I must go abroad for my promotion. This at once decided him to break up his summer quarters, very wisely foreseeing that unless he did so, my services would be lost to my ship; and if he and Emily did not leave me behind at Woolwich, I should probably be left behind by my captain: he therefore announced his intended departure within twenty-four hours.

Emily was very sorry, and so was I. I kindly reproached her with her cruelty; but she replied with a degree of firmness and good sense, which I could not but admire, that she had but one counsellor, and that was her father, and that until she was married, she never intended to have any other;

that by his advice she had delayed the union: and as we were neither of us very old people, "I trust in God," said she, "we may meet again." I admired her heroism, gave her one kiss, handed her into her carriage, and we shook hands. I need not say I saw a tear or two in her eyes. Mr Somerville saw the shower coming on, pulled up the glass, gave me a friendly nod, and the carriage drove off. The last I saw of Emily, at that time, was her right hand, which carried her handkerchief to her eyes.

After the dear inmates were gone, I turned from the door of the house in disgust, and ran direct to my boat, like a dog with a tin-kettle. When I got on board, I hated the sight of every body, and the smell of every thing; pitch, paint, bilge-water, tar and rum, entering into horrible combination, had conspired against me: and I was as sick and as miserable as the most love-sick seaman can conceive. I have before observed that we had arrived at Spithead, and as I have nothing new to say of that place, I shall proceed to sea.

We sailed for the North American station, the pleasantest I could go to when away from Emily. Our passage was tedious, and we were put on short allowance of water. Those only who have known it will understand it. All felt it but the captain; who, claiming privilege, took a dozen gallons every day to bathe his feet in, and that water, when done with, was greedily sought for by the men. There was some murmuring about it, which came to the captain's ears, who only observed, with an apathy peculiar to Almack's,

"Well, you know, if a man has no privilege, what's the use of being a captain?"

"Very true, my lord," said the toad-eater, with a low bow.

I will now give a short description of his lordship. He was a smart, dapper, well made man, with a handsome, but not an intellectual countenance; cleanly and particular in his person; and, assisted by the puffs of Toady, had a very good opinion of himself; proud of his aristocratic birth, and still more vain of his personal appearance. His knowledge on most points was superficial—high life, and anecdotes connected with it, were the usual topics of his discourse; at his own table he generally engrossed all the conversation: and while his guests drank his wine, "they laughed with counterfeited glee," &c. His reading was comprised in two volumes octavo, being the Memoirs of the Count de Grammont, which amusing and aristocratical work was never out of his hand. He had been many years at sea; but strange to say, knew nothing, literally nothing, of his profession. Seamanship, navigation, and every thing connected with the service, he was perfectly ignorant of. I had heard him spoken of as a good officer, before he joined us; and I must, in justice to him, say that he was naturally good tempered, and I believe as brave a man as ever drew a sword.

He seldom made any professional remark, being aware of his deficiency, and never ventured beyond his depth intentionally. When he came on the quarter-deck, he usually looked at the weather main-brace, and if it was not as taut as a bar, would order it to be made so. Here he could not easily commit himself; but it became a bye-word with us when we laughed at him below. He had a curious way of forgetting, or pretending to forget, the names of men and things, I presume, because they were so much beneath him; and in their stead, substituted the elegant phrases of "What's-his-name," "What-do-ye-call-'em," and "thingumbob."

One day he came on deck, and actually gave me the following very intelligible order. "Mr, What's-his-name, have the goodness to—what-do-ye-call-'em,—the,—the thingumbob."

"Ay, ay, my lord," said I. "Afterguard! haul taut the weather main-brace." This was exactly what he meant.

He was very particular and captious when not properly addressed. When an order is given by a commanding officer, it is not unusual to say, "Very good, Sir;" implying that you perfectly understand, and are going cheerfully to obey it. I had adopted this answer, and gave it to his lordship when I received an order from him, saying "Very good, my lord."

"Mr Mildmay," said his lordship, "I don't suppose you mean anything like disrespect, but I will thank you not to make that answer again: it is for *me* to say 'very good,' and not you. You seem to approve of my order, and I don't like it; I beg you will not do it again, you know."

"Very good, my lord," said I, so inveterate is habit. "I beg your lordship's pardon, I mean very well."

"I don't much like that young man," said his lordship to his toady, who followed him up and down the quarter-deck, like "the bob-tail cur," looking his master in the face. I did not hear the answer, but of course it was an echo.

The first time we reefed topsails at sea, the captain was on deck; he said nothing, but merely looked on. The second time, we found he had caught

all the words of the first lieutenant, and repeated them in a loud and pompous voice, without knowing whether they were applicable to the case or not.
The third time he fancied he was able to go alone, and down he fell—he
made a sad mistake indeed. "Hoist away the fore-topsail," said the first lieutenant. "Hoist away the fore-topsail," said the captain. The men were stamp-
ing aft, and the topsail yards travelling up to the mast-head very fast, when
they were stopped by a sudden check with the fore-topsail haul-yards.

"What's the matter?" said the first lieutenant, calling to me, who was at
my station on the forecastle.

"Something foul of the topsail-tie," I replied.

"What's the matter forward?" said the captain.

"Topsail-tie is foul, my lord," answered the first lieutenant.

"D——n the topsail-tie! cut it away. Out knife there, aloft! I *will* have the
topsail hoisted; cut away the topsail-tie."

For the information of my land readers, I should observe that the topsail-tie was the very rope which was at that moment suspending the yard
aloft. The cutting it would have disabled the ship until it could have been
repaired; and had the order been obeyed, the topsail-yard itself, would, in
all probability, have been sprung or broke in two on the cap.

We arrived at Halifax without falling in with an enemy; and as soon as
the ship was secured, I went on shore to visit all my dear Dulcineas, every
one of whom I persuaded, that on her account alone I had used my utmost
interest to be sent out on the station. Fortunately for them and for me, I was
not long permitted to trifle away my time. We were ordered to cruise on the
coast of North America. It was winter and very cold; we encountered many
severe gales of wind, during which time we suffered much from the frequent
and sudden snowstorms, north-east gales, and sharp frosts, which rendered
our running-rigging almost unmanageable, and obliged us to pour boiling
water into the sheaves of the blocks to thaw them, and allow the ropes to
traverse; nor did the cold permit the captain to honour us with his presence
on deck more than once in the twenty-four hours.

We anchored off a part of the coast, which was not in a state of defence,
and the people being unprotected by their own government, considered
themselves as neutrals, and supplied us with as much fish, poultry, and vegetables, as we required. While we lay here, the captain and officers frequently went on shore for a short time without molestation. One night, after

the captain had returned, a snow-storm and a gale of wind came on. The captain's gig, which ought to have been hoisted up, was not; she broke her painter, and went adrift, and had been gone some time before she was missed. The next morning, on making inquiry, it was found that the boat had drifted on shore a few miles from where we lay; and that having been taken possession of by the Americans, they had removed her to a hostile part of the coast, twenty-two miles off. The captain was very much annoyed at the loss of his boat, which he considered as his own private property, although built on board by the king's men, and with the king's plank and nails.

"As my private property," said his lordship, "it ought to be given up, you know."

I did not tell him that I had seen the sawyers cutting an anchor-stock into the plank of which it was built, and that the said plank had been put down to other services in the expense-book. This, however, was no business of mine; nor had I any idea that the loss of this little boat would so nearly produce my final catastrophe; so it was, however, and very serious results took place in consequence of this accident.

"They *must* respect private property, you know," said the captain to the first lieutenant.

"Yes," answered the lieutenant; "but they do not know that it is private property."

"Very true: then I will send and tell them so;" and down he went to his dinner.

The yawl was ordered to be got ready, and hoisted out at daylight, and I had notice given me that I was to go away in her. About nine o'clock the next morning, I was sent for into the cabin; his lordship was still in bed, and the green silk curtains were drawn close round his cot.

"Mr Thingamy," said his lordship, "you will take the what's-his-name, you know."

"Yes, my lord," said I.

"And you will go to that town, and ask for my thingumbob."

"For your gig, my lord?" said I.

"Yes, that's all."

"But, my lord, suppose they won't give it to me?"

"Then take it."

"Suppose the gig is not there, my lord, and if there, suppose they refuse to give it up?"

"Then take every vessel out of the harbour."

"Very well, my lord. Am I to put the gun in the boat? Or to take muskets only?"

"Oh, no, no arms—take a flag of truce—No. 8 (white flag) will do."

"Suppose they will not accept the flag of truce, my lord?"

"Oh, but they will: they always respect a flag of truce, you know."

"I beg your lordship's pardon, but I think a few muskets in the boat would be of service."

"No, no, no,—no arms. You will be fighting about nothing. You have your orders, Sir."

"Yes," thinks I, "I have. If I succeed, I am a robber; if I fail, I am liable to be hanged on the first tree."

I left the cabin, and went to the first lieutenant. I told him what my orders were. This officer was, as I before observed, a man who had no friends, and was therefore entirely dependent on the captain for his promotion, and was afraid to act contrary to his lordship's orders, however absurd. I told him, that whatever might be the captain's orders, I would not go without arms.

"The orders of his lordship must be obeyed," said the lieutenant.

"Why," said I, irritated at his folly, "you are as clever a fellow as the skipper."

This he considered so great an affront, that he ran down to his cabin, saying, "You shall hear from me again for this, Sir."

I concluded that he meant to try me by a court-martial, to which I had certainly laid myself open by this unguarded expression; but I went on the quarter-deck, and, during his absence, got as many muskets into the boat as I wanted, with a proper proportion of ammunition. This was hardly completed, before the lieutenant came up again, and put a letter into my hands: which was no more than the very comfortable intelligence, that, on my return from the expedition on which I was then going, he should expect satisfaction for the affront I had offered him. I was glad, however, to find it was no worse. I laughed at his threat; and, as the very head and front of my offending was only having compared him to the captain, he could not show any resentment openly, for fear of displeasing his patron. In short, to be offended at it, was to offer the greatest possible affront to the man he looked up to for promotion, and thus destroy all his golden prospects.

As I put this well-timed challenge into my pocket, I walked down the side, got into my boat, and put off. It wanted but one hour of sunset when I reached the part where this infernal gig was supposed to be, and the sky gave strong indications of an approaching gale. Indeed, I do not believe another captain in the navy could have been found who, at such a season of the year, would have risked a boat so far from the ship on an enemy's coast and a lee-shore, for such a worthless object.

My crew consisted of twenty men and a midshipman. When we arrived off the mouth of the harbour, we perceived four vessels lying at anchor, and pulled directly in. We had, however, no opportunity of trying our flag of truce, for as soon as we came within range of musket-shot, a volley from two hundred concealed militiamen struck down four of my men. There was then nothing left for it but to board, and bring out the vessels. Two of them were aground, and we set them on fire, it being dead low water (thanks to the delay in the morning): in doing this, we had more men wounded. I then took possession of the other two vessels, and giving one of them in charge of the midshipman, who was quite a lad, I desired him to weigh his anchor. I gave him the boat, with all the men except four, which I kept with me. The poor fellow probably lost more men, for he cut his cable, and got out before me. I weighed my anchor, but had one of my men killed by a musket ball in doing it. I stood out after the midshipman. We had gained an offing of four miles, when a violent gale and snow-storm came on. The sails belonging to the vessel all blew to rags immediately, being very old. I had no resource, except to anchor, which I did on a bank, in five fathom water. The other vessel lost all her sails, and, having no anchor, as I then conjectured, and afterwards learned, drifted on shore, and was dashed to pieces, the people being either frozen to death, wounded, or taken prisoners.

The next morning I could see the vessel lying on shore a wreck, covered with ice. A dismal prospect to me, as at that time I knew not what had become of the men. My own situation was even less enviable; the vessel was frail, and deeply laden with salt: a cargo, which, if it by any means gets wet, is worse than water, since it cannot be pumped out, and becomes as heavy as lead; nothing could, in that event, have kept the vessel afloat, and we had no boat in case of such an accident. I had three men with me, besides the dead body, in the cabin, and a pantry as clear as an empty house: not an article of any description to eat. I was four miles from the shore, in a heavy gale of wind, the pleasure of which was enhanced by snow, and the bitterest cold I ever experienced. We proceeded to examine the vessel, and found that there was on board a quantity of sails and canvas, that did not fit, but had been bought with an intention of making up for this vessel, and not before she wanted them; there was also an abundance of palms, needles, and twine; but to eat, there was nothing except salt, and to drink, nothing but one cask of fresh water. We kindled a fire in the cabin, and made ourselves as warm as we could, taking a view on deck now and then, to see if she drove, or if the gale abated. She pitched heavily, taking in whole seas over the forecastle, and the water froze on the deck. The next morning we found we had drifted a mile nearer to the shore, and the gale continued with unabated violence. The other vessel lay a wreck, with her masts gone, and as it were *in terrorem,* staring us in the face.

We felt the most pinching hunger; we had no fuel after the second day, except what we pulled down from the bulkheads of the cabin. We amused ourselves below, making a suit of sails for the vessel, and drinking hot water to repel the cold. But this work could not have lasted long; the weather became more intensely cold, and twice did we set the prize on fire, in our liberality with the stove to keep ourselves warm. The ice formed on the surface of the water in our kettle, till it was dissolved by the heat from the bottom. The second night passed like the first; and we found, in the morning, that we had drifted within two miles of the shore. We completed our little sails this day, and with great difficulty contrived to bend them.

The men were now exhausted with cold and hunger, and proposed that we should cut our cable and run on shore; but I begged them to wait till the next morning, as these gales seldom lasted long. This they agreed to: and we again huddled together to keep ourselves warm, the outside man pulling the dead man close to him by way of a blanket. The gale this night moderated, and towards the morning the weather was fine, although the wind was against us, and to beat her up to the ship was impossible. From the continued freezing of the water, the bob-stays and the rigging were coated with ice five or six inches thick, and the forecastle was covered with two feet of clear ice, showing the ropes coiled underneath it.

There was no more to be done: so, desiring the men to cut the cable,

I made up my mind to run the vessel on shore, and give myself up. We hoisted the fore-sail, and I stood in with the intention of surrendering myself and people at a large town which I knew was situated about twelve miles farther on the coast. To have given myself up at the place where the vessels had been captured, I did not think would have been prudent.

When we made sail on the third morning, we had drifted within half a mile of the shore, and very near the place we had left. Field pieces had been brought down to us. They had the range, but they could not reach us. I continued to make more sail, and to creep along shore, until I came within a few cables' length of the pier, where men, women, and children were assembled to see us land; when suddenly a snow-storm came on; the wind shifted, and blew with such violence, that I could neither see the port, nor turn the vessel to windward into it; and as I knew I could not hold my own, and that the wind was fair for our ship, then distant about forty miles, we agreed to up helm and scud for her.

This was well executed. About eleven at night we hailed her, and asked for a boat. They had seen us approaching, and a boat instantly came, taking us all on board the frigate, and leaving some fresh hands in charge of the prize.

I was mad with hunger and cold, and with difficulty did we get up the side, so exhausted and feeble were the whole of us. I was ordered down into the cabin, for it was too cold for the captain to show his face on deck. I found his lordship sitting before a good fire, with his toes in the grate; a decanter of Madeira stood on the table, with a wine glass, and most fortunately, though not intended for my use, a large rummer. This I seized with one hand and the decanter with the other; and, filling a bumper, swallowed it in a moment, without even drinking his lordship's good health. He stared, and I believe thought me mad. I certainly do own that my dress and appearance perfectly corresponded with my actions. I had not been washed, shaved, or "cleaned," since I had left the ship, three days before. My beard was grown, my cheeks hollow, my eyes sunk, and for my stomach, I leave that to those fortunate Frenchmen who escaped from the Russian campaign, who only can appreciate my sufferings. My whole haggard frame was enveloped in a huge blue flushing coat, frosted, like a plum-cake, with ice and snow.

As soon as I could speak, I said, "I beg pardon, my lord, but I have had nothing to eat or drink since I left the ship."

"Oh, *then* you are very welcome," said his lordship; "I never expected to see you again."

"Then why the devil did you send me?" thought I to myself.

During this short dialogue, I had neither been offered a chair nor any refreshment, of which I stood so much in need; and if I had been able, should have been kept standing while I related my adventures. I was about to commence, when the wine got into my head; and to support myself, I leaned, or rather staggered, on the back of a chair.

"Never mind now," said the captain, apparently moved from his listless apathy by my situation; "go and make yourself comfortable, and I will hear it all to-morrow."

This was the only kind thing he had ever done for me; and it came so *apropos,* that I felt grateful to him for it, thanked him, and went below to the gun-room, where, notwithstanding all I had heard and read of the dangers of repletion after long abstinence, I ate voraciously, and drank proportionably, ever and anon telling my astonished messmates, who were looking on, what a narrow escape the dead body had of being dissected and broiled. This, from the specimen of my performance, they had no difficulty in believing. I recommended the three men who had been with me to the care of the surgeon; and, with his permission, presented each of them with a pint of hot brandy and water, well sweetened, by way of a night cap. Having taken these precautions, and satisfied the cravings of nature on my own part, as well as the cravings of curiosity on that of my messmates, I went to bed, and slept soundly till the next day at noon.

Thus ended this anomalous and fatal expedition: an ambassador sent with the sacred emblem of peace, to commit an act of hostility under its protection. To have been taken under such circumstances, would have subjected us to be hung like dogs on the first tree; to have gone unarmed, would have been an act of insanity, and I therefore took upon me to disobey an unjust and absurd order. This, however, must not be pleaded as an example to juniors, but a warning to seniors how they give orders without duly weighing the consequences: the safest plan is always to obey. Thus did his Majesty's service lose eighteen fine fellows, under much severe suffering, for a boat, "the *private* property" of the captain, not worth twenty pounds.

The next day, as soon as I was dressed, the first lieutenant sent to speak to me. I then recollected the little affair of the challenge. "A delightful after-piece," thought I, "to the tragedy, to be shot by the first lieutenant only for calling him as clever a fellow as the captain." The lieutenant, however, had no such barbarous intentions; he had seen and acknowledged the truth of my observation, and, being a well meaning north-countryman, he offered me his hand, which I took with pleasure, having had quite enough of stimulus for that time.

CHAPTER XXIV

BELL. *You have an opportunity now, Madam, to revenge yourself upon him for affronting your squirrel.*
BELIN. *O, the filthy, rude beast.*
ARAM. *'Tis a lasting quarrel.*

"OLD BACHELOR"

WE sailed the next day, and after one month more of unsuccessful cruising, arrived safe at Halifax, where I was informed that an old friend of my father's, Sir Hurricane Humbug, of whom some mention has already been made in this work, had just arrived. He was not in an official character, but had come out to look after his own property. It is absolutely necessary that I should here, with more than usual formality, introduce the reader to an intimate acquaintance with the character of Sir Hurricane.

Sir Hurricane had risen in life by his own ingenuity, and the patronage of a rich man in the South of England: he was of an ardent disposition, and was an admirable justice of peace, when the *argumentum baculinum* was required, for which reason he had been sent to reduce two or three refractory establishments to order and obedience; and, by his firmness and good humour, succeeded. His tact was a little knowledge of everything (not like Solomon's, from the hyssop to the cedar), but from the boiler of a potato to the boiler of a steam-boat, and from catching a sprat to catching a whale; he could fatten pigs and poultry, and had a peculiar way of improving the size, though not the breed of the latter; in short, he was "jack of all trades and master of none."

I shall not go any farther back with his memoirs than the day he chose to teach an old woman how to make mutton-broth. He had, in the course of an honest discharge of his duty, at a certain very dirty sea-port town, incurred the displeasure of the lower orders generally: he nevertheless would omit no opportunity of doing good, and giving advice to the poor, gratis. One day he saw a woman emptying the contents of a boiling kettle out of her door into the street. He approached, and saw a leg of mutton at the bottom, and the unthrifty housewife throwing away the liquor in which it had been boiled.

"Good woman," said the economical baronet, "do you know what you are doing? A handful of meat, a couple of carrots, and a couple of turnips, cut up into dice, and thrown into that liquor, with a little parsley, would make excellent mutton-broth for your family."

The old woman looked up, and saw the ogre of the dockyard; and either by losing her presence of mind, or by a most malignant slip of the hand, she contrived to pour a part of the boiling water into the shoes of Sir Hurricane. The baronet jumped, roared, hopped, stamped, kicked off his shoes, and ran home, d——ning the old woman, and himself too, for having tried to teach her how to make mutton-broth. As he ran off, the ungrateful hag screamed after him, "Sarves you right; teach you to mind your own business."

The next day, in his magisterial capacity, he commanded the attendance of "the dealer in slops." "Well, Madam, what have you got to say for yourself for scalding one of his Majesty's Justices of the Peace? don't you know that I have the power to commit you to Maidstone gaol for the assault?"

"I beg your honour's pardon, humbly," said the woman; "I did not know it was your honour, or I am sure I wouldn't a done it; besides, I own to your honour, I had a drop too much."

The good-natured baronet dismissed her with a little suitable advice, which no doubt the good woman treated as she did that relative to the mutton-broth.

My acquaintance with Sir Hurricane had commenced at Plymouth, when he kicked my ship to sea in a gale of wind, for fear we should ground on our beef bones. I never forgave him for that. My father had shown him great civility, and had introduced me to him. When at Halifax, we resided in the same house with a mutual friend, who had always received me as his own son. He had a son of my own age, with whom I had long been on terms of warm friendship, and Ned and I confederated against Sir Hurricane. Having paid a few visits *en passant,* as I landed at the King's Wharf, shook hands with a few pretty girls, and received their congratulations on my safe return, I went to the house of my friend, and, without ceremony, walked into the drawing-room.

"Do you know, Sir," said the footman, "that Sir Hurricane is in his room? but he is very busy," added the man, with a smile.

"Busy or not," said I, "I am sure he will see me," so in I walked.

Sir Hurricane was employed on something, but I could not distinctly make out what. He had a boot between his knees and the calves of his legs, which he pressed together, and as he turned his head round, I perceived that he held a knife between his teeth.

"Leave the door open, messmate," said he, without taking the least notice of me. Then rising, he drew a large, black, tom cat, by the tail, out of the boot, and flinging it away from him to a great distance, which distance was rapidly increased by the voluntary exertion of the cat, which ran away as if it had been mad, "There," said he, "and be d——d to you, you have given me more trouble than a whole Kentucky farm-yard; but I shall not lose my sleep any more, by your d——d caterwauling."

All this was pronounced as if he had not seen me—in fact, it was a soliloquy, for the cat did not stay to hear it. "Ah!" said he, holding out his hand to me, "how do you do? I know your face, but d——n me if I have not forgot your name."

"My name, Sir," said I, "is Mildmay."

"Ah, Mildmay, my noble, how do you do? how did you leave your father? I knew him very well—used to give devilish good feeds—many a plate I've dirtied at his table—don't care how soon I put my legs under it again;—take care, mind which way you put your helm—you will be aboard of my chickabiddies—don't run athwart hawse."

I found, on looking down, that I had a string round my leg, which fastened a chicken to the table, and saw many more of these little creatures attached to the chairs in the room; but for what purpose they were thus domesticated I could not discover.

"Are these pet chickens of yours, Sir Hurricane?" said I.

"No," said the admiral, "but I mean them to be pet capons, by and by, when they come to table. I finished a dozen and a half this morning, besides that d——d old tom cat."

The mystery was now explained, and I afterwards found out (every man having his hobby) that the idiosyncrasy of this officer's disposition had led him to the practice of neutralising the males of any species of bird or beast, in order to render them more palatable at the table.

"Well, sir," he continued, "how do you like your new ship—how do you like your old captain?—good fellow, isn't he?—d——n his eyes—countryman of mine—I knew him when his father hadn't as much money as would jingle on a tombstone. That fellow owes every thing to me. I introduced him to the duke of ——, and he got on by that interest; but, I say, what do you think of the Halifax girls?—nice! a'n't they?"

I expressed my admiration of them.

"Ay, ay, they'll do, won't they?—we'll have some fine fun—give the girls a party at George's Island—hay-making—green gowns—ha, ha, ha. I say, your captain shall give us a party at Turtle Cove. We are going to give the old commissioner a feed at the Rockingham—blow the roof of his skull off with champagne—do you dine at Birch Cove to-day? No, I suppose you are engaged to Miss Maria, or Miss Susan, or Miss Isabella—ha, sad dog, sad dog—done a great deal of mischief," surveying me from head to foot.

I took the liberty of returning him, the same compliment; he was a tall raw-boned man, with strongly marked features, and a smile on his countenance that no modest woman could endure. In his person he gave me the idea of a discharged life-guardsman; but from his face you might have supposed that he had sat for one of Rubens' Satyrs. He was one of those people with whom you become immediately acquainted; and before I had been an hour in his company, I laughed very heartily at his jokes—not very delicate, I own, and for which he lost a considerable portion of my respect; but he was a source of constant amusement to me, living as we did in the same house.

I was just going out of the room when he stopped me—"I say, how should you like to be introduced to some devilish nice Yankee girls, relations of mine, from Philadelphia? and I should be obliged to you to show them attention; very pretty girls, I can tell you, and will have good fortunes—you may go farther and fare worse. The old dad is as rich as a Jew—got the gout in both legs—can't hold out much longer—nice pickings at his money bags, while the devil is picking his bones."

There was no withstanding such inducements, and I agreed that he should present me the next day.

Our dialogue was interrupted by the master of the house and his son, who gave me a hearty welcome; the father had been a widower for some years, and his only son Ned resided with him, and was intended to succeed to his business as a merchant. We adjourned to dress for dinner; our bed-rooms were contiguous, and we began to talk of Sir Hurricane.

"He is a strange mixture," said Ned. "I love him for his good temper; but I owe him a grudge for making mischief between me and Maria; besides, he talks balderdash before the ladies, and annoys them very much."

"I owe him a grudge too," said I, "for sending me to sea in a gale of wind."

"We shall both be quits with him before long," said Ned; "but let us now go and meet him at dinner. To-morrow I will set the housekeeper at him for his cruelty to her cat; and if I am not much mistaken, she will pay him off for it."

Dinner passed off extremely well. The admiral was in high spirits; and as it was a bachelor's party, he earned his wine. The next morning we met at breakfast. When that was over, the master of the house retired to his office, or pretended to do so. I was going out to walk, but Ned said I had better stay a few minutes; he had something to say to me; in fact, he had prepared a treat without my knowing it.

"How did you sleep last night, Sir Hurricane?" said the artful Ned.

"Why, pretty well; considering," said the admiral, "I was not tormented by that old tom cat. D——n me, Sir, that fellow was like the Grand Signior, and he kept his seraglio in the garret, over my bed-room, instead of being at his post in the kitchen, killing the rats that are running about like coach-horses."

"Sir Hurricane," said I, "it's always unlucky to sailors, if they meddle with cats. You will have a gale of wind, in some shape or another, before long."

These words were hardly uttered, when, as if by preconcerted arrange-ment, the door opened, and in sailed Mrs Jellybag, the housekeeper, an elderly woman, somewhere in the latitude of fifty-five or sixty years. With a low courtesy and contemptuous toss of her head, she addressed Sir Hurri-cane Humbug.

"Pray, Sir Hurricane, what have you been doing to my cat?"

The admiral, who prided himself in putting any one who applied to him on what he called the wrong scent, endeavoured to play off Mrs Jellybag in the same manner.

"What have I done to your cat, my dear Mrs Jellybag? Why, my dear Madam" (said he, assuming an air of surprise), "what *should* I do to your cat?"

"You *should* have left him alone, Mr Admiral; that cat was my property; if my master permits you to ill-treat the poultry, that's his concern; but that cat was mine, Sir Hurricane—mine, every inch of him. The animal has been ill-treated, and sits moping in the corner of the fire-place, as if he was dying; he'll never be the cat he was again."

"I don't think he ever will, my dear Mrs Housekeeper," answered the admiral, drily.

The lady's wrath now began to kindle. The admiral's cool replies were like water sprinkled upon a strong flame, increasing its force, instead of checking it.

"Don't dear *me,* Sir Hurricane. I am not one of *your dears—your dears* are all in Dutchtown—more shame for you, an old man like you."

"Old man!" cried Sir Hurricane, losing his placidity a little.

"Yes, old man; look at your hair—as grey as a goose's."

"Why, as for my hair, that proves nothing, Mrs Jellybag, for though there may be snow on the mountains, there is still heat in the valleys. What d'ye think of my metaphor?"

"I am no more a *metafore* than yourself, Sir Hurricane; but I'll tell you what, you are a *cock-and-hen* admiral, a dog-in-the-manger barrownight, who was jealous of my poor tom cat, because—, I won't say what. Yes, Sir Hurricane, all hours of the day you are leering at every young woman that passes, out of our windows—and an old man too; you ought to be ashamed of yourself—and then you go to church of a Sunday, and cry, 'Good Lord, deliver us.'"

The housekeeper now advanced so close to the admiral, that her nose nearly touched his, her arms akimbo, and every preparation for boarding. The admiral, fearing she might not confine herself to vocality, but begin to beat time with her fists, thought it right to take up a position; he therefore very dexterously took two steps in the rear, and mounted on a sofa; his left was defended by an upright piano, his right by the breakfast-table, with all the tea-things on it; his rear was against the wall, and his front depended on himself in person. From this commanding eminence he now looked down on the housekeeper, whose nose could reach no higher than the seals of her adversary's watch; and in proportion as the baronet felt his security, so rose his choler. Having been for many years Proctor at the great universities of Point-street and Blue-town, as well as member of Barbican and North Corner, he was perfectly qualified, in point of classical dialect, to maintain the honour of his profession. Nor was the lady by any means deficient. Although she had not taken her degree, her tongue from constant use had acquired a fluency which nature only concedes to practice.

It will not be expected, nor would it be proper, that I should repeat all that passed in this concluding scene, in which the housekeeper gave us good reason to suppose that she was not quite so ignorant of the nature of the transaction as she would have had us believe.

The battle having raged for half an hour with great fury, both parties desisted, for want of breath, and consequently of ammunition. This produced a gradual cessation of firing, and by degrees the ships separated—the admiral, like Lord Howe on the first of June, preserving his position, though very much mauled; and the housekeeper, like the Montague, *running down* to join her associates. A few random shots were exchanged as they parted, and at every second or third step on the stairs, Mrs Margaret brought to, and fired, until both were quite out of range; a distant rumbling noise was heard, and the admiral concluded, by muttering that she might go—, somewhere, but the word died between his teeth.

"There, admiral," said I, "did not I tell you that you would have a squall?"

"Squall! yes—d——m my blood," wiping his face; "how the spray flew from the old beldam! She's fairly wetted my trousers, by God. Who'd ever thought that such a purring old b——h could have shown such a set of claws!—War to the knife! By heavens, I'll make her remember this."

Notwithstanding the admiral's threat, hostilities ceased from that day. The cock-and-hen admiral found it convenient to show a white feather; interest stood in the way, and barred him from taking his revenge. Mrs Jellybag was a faithful servant, and our host neither liked that she should be interfered with, or that his house should become an arena for such conflicts; and the admiral, who was peculiarly tenacious of undrawing the strings of his purse, found it convenient to make the first advances. The affair was, therefore, amicably arranged—the tom cat was, in consideration of his sufferings, created a baronet, and was ever afterwards dignified by the title of

Sir H. Humbug; who certainly was the most eligible person to select for god-father, as he had taken the most effectual means of weaning him from "the pomps and vanities of this wicked world."

It was now about one o'clock, for this dispute had ran away with the best part of the morning, when Sir Hurricane said, "Come, youngster, don't forget your engagements—you know I have got to introduce you to my pretty cousins—you must mind your P's and Q's with the uncle, for he is a sensible old fellow—has read a great deal, and thinks America the first and greatest country in the world."

We accordingly proceeded to the residence of the fair strangers, whom the admiral assured me had come to Halifax from mere curiosity, under the protection of their uncle and aunt. We knocked at the door, and the admiral inquired if Mrs M'Flinn was at home; we were answered in the affirmative. The servant asked our names. "Vice Admiral Sir Hurricane Humbug," said I, "and Mr Mildmay."

The drawing-room door was thrown open, and the man gave our names with great propriety. In we walked; a tall, grave-looking, elderly lady received us, standing bolt upright in the middle of the room; the young ladies were seated at their work.

"My dear Mrs M'Flinn," said the admiral, "how do you do? I am delighted to see you and your fair nieces looking so lovely this morning." —The lady bowed to this compliment—a courtesy she was not quite up to —"Allow me to introduce my gallant young friend, Mildmay—young ladies, take care of your hearts—he is a great rogue, I assure you, though he smiles so sweet upon you."

Mrs M'Flinn bowed again to me, hoped I was very well, and inquired "how long I had been in these parts."

I replied that I had just returned from a cruise, but that I was no stranger in Halifax.

"Come, officer," said the admiral, taking me by the arm, "I see you are bashful—I must make you acquainted with my pretty cousins. This, Sir, is Miss M'Flinn—her christian name is Deliverance. She is a young lady whose beauty is her least recommendation."

"A very equivocal compliment," thought I.

"This, Sir, is Miss Jemima; this is Miss Temperance; and this is Miss Deborah. Now that you know them all by name, and they know you, I hope you will contrive to make yourself both useful and agreeable."

"A very pretty sinecure," thinks I to myself, "just as if I had not my hands full already." However, as I never wanted small talk for pretty faces, I began with Jemima. They were all pretty, but she was a love—yet there was an awkwardness about them that convinced me they were not of the *bon ton* of Philadelphia. The answers to all my questions were quick, pert, and given with an air of assumed consequence; at the same time I observed a mode of expression which, though English, was not well-bred English.

"Did you come through the United States," said I, "into the British territory, or did you come by water?"

"Oh, by water," screamed all the girls at once, "and *liked* to have been eaten up with the nasty roaches."

I did not exactly know what was meant by "roaches," but it was explained to me soon after. I inquired whether they had seen a British man-of-war, and whether they would like to accompany me on board of that which I belonged to? They all screamed out at same moment—

"No, we never have seen one, and should like to see it of all things. When will you take us?"

"To-morrow," said I, "if the day should prove fine."

Here the admiral, who had been making by-play with the old chaperon, turned round, and said:

"Well, Mr Frank, I see you are getting on pretty well without my assistance."

"Oh, we all like him very much," said Temperance; "and he says he will take us on board his ship."

"Softly, my dear," said the aunt: "we must not think of giving the gentleman the trouble, until we are better acquainted."

"I am sure, aunt," said Deborah, "we are very well acquainted."

"Then," said the aunt, seeing she was in the minority, "suppose you and Sir Hurricane come and breakfast with us to-morrow morning at eleven o'clock, after which, we shall all be very much at your service."

Here the admiral looked at me with one of his impudent leers, and burst into a loud laugh; but I commanded my countenance very well, and rebuked him by a steady and reserved look.

"I shall have great pleasure," said I, to the lady, "in obeying your orders from eleven to-morrow morning, till the hour of dinner, when I am engaged."

So saying, we both bowed, wished them a good morning, and left the room. The door closed upon us, and I heard them all exclaim—"What a charming young man!"

I went on board, and told the first lieutenant what I had done; he, very good-naturedly, said he would do his best, though the ship was not in order for showing, and would have a boat ready for us at the dock-yard stairs at one o'clock the next day.

I went to breakfast at the appointed hour. The admiral did not appear, but the ladies were all in readiness, and I was introduced to their uncle— a plain, civil-spoken man, with a strong nasal twang. The repast was very good; and as I had a great deal of work before me, I made hay while the sun shone. When the rage of hunger had been a little appeased, I made use of the first belle to inquire if a lady whom I once had the honour of knowing, was any relation of theirs, as she bore the same name, and came, like them, from Philadelphia.

"Oh, dear, yes, indeed, she is a relation," said all the ladies together; "we have not seen her this seven years, when did you see her last?"

I replied that we had not met for some time; but that the last time I had heard of her, she was seen by a friend of mine at Turin on the Po. The last syllable was no sooner out of my mouth, than tea, coffee, and chocolate was out of theirs, all spirting different ways, just like so many young grampuses. They jumped up from the table and ran away to their rooms, convulsed with laughter, leaving me alone with their uncle. I was all amazement, and I own felt a little annoyed.

I asked if I had made any serious lapsus, or said any thing very ridiculous or indelicate; if I had, I said I should never forgive myself.

"Sir," said Mr M'Flinn, "I am very sure you meant nothing indelicate; but the refined society of Philadelphia, in which these young ladies have been educated, attaches very different meanings to certain words, to what you do in the old country. The back settlements, for instance, so called by our ancestors, we call the western settlements, and we apply the same term, by analogy, to the human figure and dress. This is a mere little explanation, which you will take as it is meant. It cannot be expected that *'foreigners'* should understand the niceties of our language."

I begged pardon for my ignorance; and assured him I would be more cautious in future. "But pray tell me," said I, "what there was in my last observation which could have caused so much mirth at my expense?"

"Why, Sir," said Mr M'Flinn, "you run me hard there; but since you force me to explain myself, I must say that you used a word exclusively confined to bed-chambers."

"But surely, Sir," said I, "you will allow that the name of a celebrated river, renowned in the most ancient of our histories, is not to be changed from such a refined notion of false delicacy?"

"There you are wrong," said Mr M'Flinn. "The French, who are our in-structors in every thing, teach us how to name all these things; and I think you will allow that they understand true politeness."

I bowed to this dictum, only observing, that there was a point in our language where delicacy became indelicate; that I thought the noble river had a priority of claim over a contemptible vessel; and, reverting to the former part of his discourse, I said that we in England were not ashamed to call things by their proper names; and that we considered it a great mark of ill-breeding to go round about for a substitute to a common word, the vulgar import of which a well bred and modest woman ought never to have known.

The old gentleman felt a little abashed at this rebuke, and, to relieve him, I changed the subject, hoping that the ladies would forgive me for this once, and return to their breakfasts.

"Why, as for that matter," said the gentleman, "the Philadelphia ladies have very delicate appetites, and I dare say they have had enough."

Finding I was not likely to gain ground on that tack, I steered my own course, and finished my breakfast, comforting myself that much execution had been done by the ladies on the commissariat department, before the "Po" had made its appearance.

By the time I had finished, the ladies had composed themselves; and the pretty Jemima had recovered the saint-like gravity of her lovely mouth. Decked in shawls and bonnets, they expressed much impatience to be gone.

We walked to the dock-yard, where a boat with a midshipman attended, and in a few minutes conveyed us alongside of my ship. A painted cask, shaped like a chair, with a whip from the main yard-arm, was let down into the boat; and I carefully packed the fair creatures, two at a time, and sent them up. There was a good deal of giggling, and screaming, and loud laughing, which rather annoyed me; for as they were not my friends, I had no wish that my messmates should think they belonged to that set in Halifax in which I was so kindly received.

At length, all were safely landed on the quarter-deck, without the exposure of an ancle, which they all seemed to dread. Whether their ancles were not quite so small as Mr M'Flinn wished me to suppose their appetites were, I cannot say.

"La! aunt," said Deborah, "when I looked up in the air, and saw you and Deliverance dangling over our heads, I thought if the rope was to break, what a 'squash' you would have come on us: I am sure you would have *paunched us.*"

Determined to have the Philadelphia version of this elegant phrase, I inquired what it meant, and was informed, that in their country when any one had his bowels *squeezed* out, they called it *"paunching."*

"Well," thought I, "after this, you might swallow the Po without spoiling your breakfasts." The band struck up "Yankee Doodle," the ladies were in ecstacy, and began to caper round the quarter-deck.

"La! Jemima," said Deborah, "what have you done to the western side of your gown? it is all over white."

This was soon brushed off, but the expression was never forgotten in the ship, and always ludicrously applied.

Having shown them the ship and all its wonders, I was glad to conduct them back to the shore. When I met the admiral, I told him I had done the honours, and hoped the next time he had any female relatives, he would keep his engagements, and attend to them himself.

"Why, now, who do you think they are?" said the admiral.

"Think!" said I, "why, who should they be but your Yankee cousins?"

"Why, was you such a d——d flat as to believe what I said, eh? Why, their father keeps a shop of all sorts at Philadelphia, and they were going to New York, on a visit to some of their relatives, when the ship they were in was taken and brought in here."

"Then," said I, "these are not the *bon ton* of Philadelphia?"

"Just as much as Nancy Dennis is the *bon ton* of Halifax," said the admiral; "though the uncle, as I told you, is a sensible fellow in his way."

"Very well," said I; "you have caught me for once; but remember, I pay you for it."

And I was not long in his debt. Had he not given me this explanation, I should have received a very false impression of the ladies of Philadelphia, and have done them an injustice for which I should never have forgiven myself.

The time of our sailing drew near. This was always a melancholy time in Halifax; but my last act on shore was one which created some mirth, and enlivened the gloom of my departure. My friend Ned and myself had not yet had an opportunity of paying off Sir Hurricane Humbug for telling tales to Maria, and for his false introduction to myself. One morning we both came out of our rooms at the same moment, and were proceeding to the breakfast parlour, when we spied the admiral performing some experiment. Unfortunately for him, he was seated in such a manner, just clear of a pent-house, as to be visible from our position; and at the same time, the collar of his coat would exactly intersect the segment of a circle described by any fluid, projected by us over this low roof, which would thus act as a conductor into the very pole of his neck.

The housemaid (these housemaids are always the cause or the instruments of mischief, either by design or neglect), had left standing near the window a pail nearly filled with dirty water, from the wash-hand basins, &c. Ned and I looked at each other, then at the pail, then at the admiral. Ned thought of his Maria: I of my false introduction. Without saying a word, we both laid our hands on the pail, and in an instant, souse went all the contents over the admiral.

"I say, what's this?" he roared out. "Oh, you d——d rascals!"

He knew it could only be us. We laughed so immoderately, that we had not the power to move or to speak; while the poor admiral was spitting, sputtering, and coughing, enough to bring his heart up.

"Infernal villains! No respect for a flag-officer? I'll serve you out for this."

The tears rolled down our cheeks; but not with grief. As soon as the admiral had sufficiently recovered himself to go in pursuit, we thought it time to make sail. We knew we were discovered; and as the matter could not be made worse, we resolved to tell him what it was for. Ned began.

"How do you do, admiral? you have taken a shower-bath this morning."

He looked up, with his teeth clenched—"Oh, it's you, is it? Yes, I thought it could be no one else. Yes, I have had a shower-bath, and be d——d to you; and that sea-devil of a friend of yours. Pretty pass the service has come to, when officers of my rank are treated in this way. I'll make you both envy the tom-cat."

"Beware the housekeeper, admiral," said Ned. "Maria has made it up with me, admiral, and she sends her love to you."

"D——n Maria."

"Oh, very well, I'll tell her so," said Ned.

"Admiral," said I, "do you remember when you sent the ——— to sea in a gale of wind, when I was midshipman of her? Well, I got just as wet that night as you are now. Pray, admiral, have you any commands to the Misses M'Flinn?"

"I'll tell you when I catch hold of you," said Sir Hurricane, as he moved up stairs to his room, dripping like Pope's Lodona, only not smelling so sweet.

Hearing a noise, the housekeeper came up, and all the family assembled to condole with the humid admiral, but each enjoying the joke as much as ourselves. We however paid rather dearly for it. The admiral swore that neither of us should eat or drink in the house for three days; and Ned's father, though ready to burst with laughter, was forced in common decency to say that he thought the admiral perfectly right after so gross a violation of hospitality.

I went and dined on board my ship, Ned went to a coffee-house; but on the third morning after the shower, I popped my head into the breakfast parlour, and said,

"Admiral, I have a good story to tell you, if you will let me come in."

"I'd see you d——d first, you young scum of a fish pond. Be off, or I'll shy the ham at your head."

"No, but indeed, my dear Admiral, it is such a nice story; it is one just to your fancy."

"Well then, stand there and tell it, but don't come in, for if you do—"

I stood at the door and told him the story.

"Well, now," said he, "that is a good story, and I will forgive you for it." So with a hearty laugh at my ingenuity, he promised to forgive us both, and I ran and fetched Ned to breakfast.

This was the safest mode we could have adopted to get into favour, for the admiral was a powerful, gigantic fellow, that could have given us some very awkward squeezes. The peace was very honourably kept, and the next day the ship sailed.

CHAPTER XXV

They turned into a long and wide street, in which not a
single living figure appeared to break the perspective. Solitude is
never so overpowering as when it exists among the works of man.
In old woods, or on the tops of mountains, it is graceful and
benignant, for it is at home; but where thick dwellings are,
it wears a ghost-like aspect.

INESILLA

WE were ordered to look out for the American squadron that had done so much mischief to our trade; and directed our course, for this purpose, to the coast of Africa. We had been out about ten days, when a vessel was seen from the mast-head. We were at that time within about one hundred and eighty leagues of the Cape de Verd Islands. We set all sail in chase, and soon made her out to be a large frigate, who seemed to have no objection to the meeting, but evidently tried her rate of sailing with us occasionally: her behaviour left us no doubt that she was an American frigate, and we cleared for action.

The captain, I believe, had never been in a sea fight, or if he had, he had entirely forgotten all he had learned; for which reason, in order to re-fresh his memory, he laid upon the capstan-head, the famous epitome of John Hamilton Moore, now obsolete, but held at that time to be one of the most luminous authors who had ever treated on maritime affairs. John, who certainly gives a great deal of advice on every subject, has, amongst other valuable directions, told us how to bring a ship into action, according to the best and most approved methods, and how to take your enemy afterwards, if you can. But the said John must have thought red hot shot could be heated by a process somewhat similar to that by which he heated his own nose, or he must entirely have forgotten "the manners and customs in such cases used at sea," for he recommends, as a prelude or first course to the entertainment, a good dose of red hot shot, served up the moment the guests are assembled; but does not tell us where the said dishes are to be cooked. No doubt whatever that a broadside composed of such ingredients, would be a great desideratum in favour of a victory, especially if the enemy should happen to have none of his own to give in return.

So thought his lordship, who walking up to the first lieutenant, said, "Mr Thingamay, don't you think red hot what-do-ye-call-ums should be given in the first broadside to that thingumbob?"

"Red hot shot, do you mean, my lord?"

"Yes," said his lordship; "don't you think they would settle his hash?"

"Where the devil are we to get them, my lord?" said the first lieutenant, who was not the same that wanted to fight me for saying he was as clever a fellow as the captain: that man had been unshipped by the machinations of Toady.

"Very true," said his lordship.

We now approached the stranger very fast, when, to our great mortification, she proved to be an English frigate; she made the private signal, it was answered; showed her number, we showed ours, and her captain being junior officer came on board, to pay his respects and show his order. He was three weeks from England, brought news of a peace with France, and, among other treats, a navy list, which, next to a bottle of London porter, is the greatest luxury to a sea officer in a foreign climate.

Greedily did we all run over this interesting little book, and among the names of the new made commanders, I was overjoyed to find my own; the last on the list to be sure, but that I cared not for. I received the congratulations of my messmates; we parted company with the stranger, and steered for the island of St Jago, our captain intending to complete his water in Port Praya Bay, previous to a long cruise after the American squadron.

We found here a slave vessel in charge of a naval officer, bound to England; and I thought this a good opportunity to quit, not being over anxious to serve as a lieutenant when I knew I was a commander. I was also particularly anxious to return to England for many reasons, the hand of my dear Emily standing at the head of them. I therefore requested the captain's permission to quit the ship; and as he wished to give an acting order to one of his own followers, he consented. I took my leave of all my messmates, and of my captain, who, though an unfeeling coxcomb and no sailor, certainly had some good points about him; in fact, his lordship was a gentleman; and had his ship fallen in with an enemy, she would have been well fought, as he had good officers, was sufficiently aware of his own incapability, would take advice, and as a man of undaunted bravery, was not to be surpassed in the service.

On the third day after our arrival, the frigate sailed. I went on board the slaver, which had no slaves on board except four to assist in working the vessel; she was in a filthy state, and there was no inn on shore, and of course no remedy. Port Praya is the only good anchorage in the island; the old town of St Jago was deserted, in consequence of there being only an open roadstead before it, very unsafe for vessels to lie in. The town of Port Praya is a miserable assemblage of mud huts; the governor's house, and one more, are better built, but they are not so comfortable as a cottage in England. There were not ten Portuguese on the island, and above ten thousand blacks, all originally slaves; and yet every thing was peaceable, although fresh arrivals of slaves came every day.

It was easy to distinguish the different races: the Yatoffes are tall men, not very stoutly built; most of them are soldiers. I have seen ten of them standing together, the lowest not less than six feet two or three inches. The Foulahs, from the Ashantee country, are another race, they are powerful and muscular, ill-featured, badly disposed, and treacherous. The Mandingoes are a smaller race than the others, but they are well disposed and tractable.

The island of slaves is kept in subjection by slaves only, who are enrolled as soldiers, miserably equipped; a cap and a jacket was all they owed to art, nature provided the rest of their uniform. The governor's orderly alone sported a pair of trousers, and these were on permanent duty, being transferred from one to the other as their turn for that service came on.

I paid my respects to the governor, who, although a Portuguese, chose to follow the fashion of the island, and was as black as most of his subjects. After a few French compliments, I took my leave. I was curious to see the old town of St Jago, which had been abandoned; and after a hot walk of two hours over uncultivated ground, covered with fine goats, which are the staple of the island, I reached the desolate spot.

It was melancholy to behold: it seemed as if the human race were extinct. The town was built on a wide ravine running down to the sea; the houses were of stone, and handsome; the streets regular and paved, which proves that it had formerly been a place of some importance; but it is surprising that a spot so barren as this island generally is should ever have had any mercantile prosperity. Whatever it did enjoy, I should conceive must have been anterior to the Portuguese having sailed round the Cape of Good

Hope; and the solidity and even elegance of construction among the buildings justifies the supposition.

The walls were massive, and remained entire; the churches were numerous, but the roofs of them and the dwelling-houses had mostly fallen in. Trees had grown to a considerable height in the midst of the streets, piercing through the pavements and raising the stones on each side; and the convent gardens were a mere wilderness. The cocoa-nut tree had thrust its head through many a roof, and its long stems through the tops of the houses; the banana luxuriated out of the windows. The only inhabitants of a town capable of containing ten thousand inhabitants, were a few friars who resided in a miserable ruin which had once been a beautiful convent. They were the first negro friars I had ever seen; their cowls were as black as their faces, and their hair grey and woolly. I concluded they had adopted this mode of life as being the laziest; but I could not discover by what means they could gain a livelihood, for there were none to give them anything in charity.

The appearance of these poor men added infinitely to the necromantic character of the whole melancholy scene. There was a beauty, a loveliness, in these venerable ruins, which delighted me. There was a solemn silence in the town, but there was a small, still voice, that said to me: "London may one day be the same—and Paris; and you and your children's children will all have lived and had their loves and adventures; but who will the wretched man be, that shall sit on the summit of Primrose Hill, and look down upon the desolation of the mighty city, as I, from this little eminence, behold the once flourishing town of St Jago?"

The goats were browsing on the side of the hill, and the little kids frisking by their dams. "These," thought I, "perhaps are the only food and nourishment of these poor friars." I walked to Port Praya, and returned to my floating prison, the slave ship. The officer who was conducting her home, as a prize, was not a pleasant man; I did not like him: and nothing passed between us but common civility. He was an old master's mate, who had probably served his time thrice over; but having no merit of his own, and no friends to cause that defect to be overlooked, he had never obtained promotion: he therefore naturally looked on a young commander with envy. He had only given me a passage home, from motives which he could not resist; first, because he was forced to obey the orders of my late captain; and, secondly, because my purse would supply the cabin with the necessary stock of refreshments, in the shape of fruit, poultry, and vegetables, which are to be procured at Port Praya; he was therefore under the necessity of enduring my company.

The vessel, I found, was not to sail on the following day, as he intended. I therefore took my gun, at daybreak, and wandered with a guide up the valleys, in search of the pintados, or Guinea fowl, with which the island abounds; but they were so shy that I never could get a shot at them; and I returned over the hills, which my guide assured me was the shortest way. Tired with my walk, I was not sorry to arrive at a sheltered valley, where the palmetto and the plantain offer a friendly shade from the burning sun. The guide, with wonderful agility, mounted the cocoa-nut tree, and threw down half a dozen nuts. They were green, and their milk I thought the most refreshing and delicious draught I had ever taken.

The vesper bells at Port Praya were now summoning the poor black friars to their devotion; and a stir and bustle appeared among the little black boys and girls, of whose presence I was till then ignorant. They ran from the coverts, and assembled near the front of the only cottage visible to my eye. A tall elderly negro man came out, and took his seat on a mound of turf a few feet from the cottage; he was followed by a lad, about twenty years of age, who bore in his hand a formidable cowskin. For the information of my readers, I must observe that a cowskin is a large whip, made like a riding whip, out of the hide of the hippopotamus, or sea-cow, and is proverbial for the severity of punishment it is capable of inflicting. After the executioner came, with slow and measured steps, the poor little culprits, five boys and three girls, who, with most rueful faces, ranged themselves, rank and file, before the old man.

I soon perceived that the hands were turned up for punishment; but the nature of the offence I had yet to learn: nor did I know whether any order had been given to strip. With the boys this would have been supererogatory, as they were quite naked. The female children had on cotton chemises, which they slowly and reluctantly rolled up, until they had gathered them close under their armpits.

The old man then ordered the eldest boy to begin his Pater Noster; and simultaneously the whipper-in elevated his cowskin by way of encouragement. The poor boy watched it, out of the corner of his eye, and then began "Pattery nobstur, qui, qui, qui—(here he received a most severe lash from the cowskin bearer)—is in silly," roared the boy, as if the continuation had been expelled from his mouth by the application of external force in an opposite direction—"sancty fisheter nom tum, adveny regnum tum, fi notun tas, ta, ti, tu, terror," roared the poor fellow, as he saw the lash descending on his defenceless back—

"Terror indeed," thought I.

"Pannum nossum quotditty hamminum da nobs holyday, e missy nobs debitty nossa si cut nos demittimissibus debetenibas nossimus e, ne, nos hem-duckam in, in, in temptationemum, sed lillibery nos a ma—ma—" Here a heavy lash brought the very Oh! that was "caret" to complete the sentence.

My readers are not to suppose that the rest of the class acquitted themselves with as much ability as their leader, who, compared to them, was perfectly erudite; the others received a lash for every word, or nearly so. The boys were first disposed of, in order, I suppose, that they might have the full benefit of the applicant's muscles; while the poor girls had the additional pleasure of witnessing the castigation until their turn came; and that they were aware of what awaited them was evident, from their previous arrangement and disposition of dress, at the commencement of the entertainment. The girls accordingly came up one after another to say their Ave Maria, as more consonant to their sex; but I could scarcely contain my rage when the rascally cowskin was applied to them, or my laughter when, smarting under its lash, they exclaimed, "Benedicta Mulieribus," applying their little hands with immoderate pressure to the afflicted part.

I could have found in my heart to have wrested the whip out of the hands of the young negro, and applied it with all my might to him, and his old villain of a master, and father of these poor children, as I soon found he was. My patience was almost gone when the second girl received a lash for her "Plena Gratia." She screamed, and danced, and lifted up her poor legs in agony, rubbing herself on her *"west"* side, as the Philadelphia ladies call it, with as much assiduity as if it had been one of those cases in which friction is prescribed by the faculty.

But the climax was yet to come. A grand stage effect was to be produced before the falling of the curtain. The youngest girl was so defective in her lesson, that not one word of it could be extracted from her, even by the cowskin; nothing but piercing shrieks, enough to make my heart bleed, could the poor victim utter. Irritated at the child's want of capacity to repeat by rote what she could not understand, the old man darted from his seat, and struck her senseless to the ground.

I could bear no more. My first impulse was to wrest the cowskin from the negro's hand, and revenge the poor bleeding child as she lay motionless on the ground; but a moment's reflection convinced me that such a step would only have brought down a double weight of punishment on the victims when I was gone; so, catching up my hat, I turned away with disgust, and walked slowly towards the town and bay of Port Praya, reflecting as I went along what pleasant ideas the poor creatures must entertain of religion, when the name of God and of the cowskin were invariably associated in their minds. I began to parody one of Watts's hymns—

> *"Lord! how delightful 'tis to see*
> *A whole assembly worship thee."*

The indignation I felt against this barbarous and ignorant negro was not unmingled with some painful recollections of my own younger days, when, in a christian and protestant country, the bible and prayer-book had been made objects of terror to my mind; tasks, greater than my capacity could compass, and floggings in proportion were not calculated to forward the cause of religious instruction in the mind of an obstinate boy.

Reaching the water-side, I embarked on board of my slaver; and the next day sailed for England. We had a favourable passage until we reached the chops of the channel, when a gale of wind from the north-east caught us, and drove us down so far to the southward that the prize master found himself under the necessity of putting into Bordeaux to refit, and to replenish his water.

I was not sorry for this, as I was tired of the company of this officer, who was both illiterate and ill-natured, neither a sailor nor a gentleman. Like many others in the service, who are most loud in their complaints for want of promotion, I considered that even in his present rank he was what we called a *king's hard bargain*—that is, not worth his salt; and promoting men of his stamp would only have been picking the pocket of the country. As soon, therefore, as we had anchored in the Gironde, off the city of Bordeaux, and had been visited by the proper authorities, I quitted the vessel and her captain, and went on shore.

Taking up my abode at the Hotel d'Angleterre, my first care was to order a good dinner; and having despatched that, and a bottle of Vin de Beaune (which, by the by, I strongly recommend to all travellers, if they can get it, for I am no bad judge), I asked my *valet de place* how I was to dispose of myself for the remainder of the evening?

"*Mais, monsieur,*" said he, "*il faut aller au spectacle.*"

"*Allons,*" said I, and in a few minutes I was seated in the stage-box of the handsomest theatre in the world.

What strange events—what unexpected meetings and sudden separations are sailors liable to—what sudden transitions from grief to joy, from joy to grief, from want to affluence, from affluence to want! All this the history of my life, for the last six months, will fully illustrate.

CHAPTER XXVI

You will proceed in pleasure and in pride,
Beloved, and loving many; all is o'er
For me on earth, except some years to hide
My shame and sorrow deep in my heart's core.

"DON JUAN"

I PAID little attention to the performance; for the moment I came to the house, my eyes were rivetted on an object from which I found it impossible to remove them. "It is," said I, "and yet it cannot be; and yet why should it not?" A young lady sat in one of the boxes; she was elegantly attired, and seemed to occupy the united attentions of many Frenchmen, who eagerly caught her smiles.

"Either that is Eugenia," thought I, "or I have fallen asleep in the ruins of St Jago, and am dreaming of her. That is Eugenia, or I am not Frank. It is her, or it is her ghost." Still I had not that moral certainty of the identity, as to enable me to go at once to her, and address her. Indeed, had I been certain, all things considered, the situation we were in would have rendered such a step highly improper.

"If that be Eugenia," thought I, again, "she has improved both in manner and person. She has a becoming *embonpoint,* and an air *de bon societé* which, when we parted she had not."

The more intensely I gazed, the more convinced was I that I was right; the immovable devotion of my eyes attracted the attention of a French officer, who sat near me.

"*C'est une jolie femme, n'est-ce pas, monsieur?*"

"*Vraiment,*" said I. "Do you know her name?"

"*Elle s'appelle Madame de Rosenberg.*"

"Then I am wrong, after all," said I to myself. "Has she a husband, Sir?"

"*Pardonnez-moi, elle est veuve, mais elle a un petit garçon de cinq ans, beau comme un ange.*"

"That is her," said I again, reviving. "Is she a Frenchwoman?"

"*Du tout, Monsieur, elle est une de vos compatriottes; c'est un fort joli exemplaire.*"

She had only been three months at Bordeaux, and had refused many very good offers in marriage. Such was the information I obtained from my obliging neighbour; and I was now convinced that Madame de Rosenberg could be no other than Eugenia. Every endeavour to catch her eye proved abortive. My only hope was to follow the carriage.

When the play was over, I waited with an impatience like that of a spirited hunter who hears the hounds. At last, the infernal squalling of the vocalists ceased, but not before I had devoutly wished that all the wax candles in the house were down their throats and burning there. I saw one of the gentlemen in the box placing the shawl over her shoulders, with the most careful attention, while the bystanders seemed ready to tear him in pieces, from envy. I hurried to the door, and saw her handed into her carriage, which drove off at a great pace. I ran after it, jumped up behind, and took my station by the side of the footman.

"*Descendez donc, Monsieur,*" said the man.

"I'll be d——d if I do," said I.

"*Comment donc?*" said the man.

"*Tais-toi bête,*" said I, "*ou je te brulerai la cervelle.*"

"*Vous f——e,*" said the man, who behaved very well, and instantly began to remove me, *vi et armis;* but I planted a stomacher in his fifth button, which I knew would put him *hors de combat* for a few minutes, and by that time, at the rate the carriage was driving, my purpose would have been answered. The fellow lost his breath—could not hold on or speak—so tumbled off and lay in the middle of the road.

As he fell on dry ground and was not an English sailor, I did not jump after him, but left him to his own ease, and we saw no more of him, for we were going ten knots, while he lay becalmed without a breath of wind. This was one of the most successful acts of usurpation recorded in modern history. It has its parallels, I know; but I cannot now stop to comment on them, or on my own folly and precipitation. I was as firmly fixed behind the carriage, as Bonaparte was on the throne of France after the battle of Eylau.

We stopped at a large *porte cochère,* being the entrance to a very grand house, with lamps at the door, within a spacious court yard; we drove in and drew up. I was down in a moment, opened the carriage door, and let down the steps. The lady descended, laid her hand on my arm without perceiving that she had changed her footman, and tripped lightly up the stairs. I followed her into a handsome saloon, where another servant in livery had placed lights on the table. She turned round, saw me, and fainted in my arms.

It was, indeed, Eugenia, herself; and with all due respect to my dear Emily, I borrowed a thousand kisses while she lay in a state of torpor, in a fauteuil to which I carried her. It was some few minutes before she opened her eyes; the man-servant, who had brought the lights, very properly never quitted the room, but was perfectly respectful in his manner, rightly conceiving that I had some authority for my proceedings.

"My dearest Frank," said Eugenia, "what an unexpected meeting! What, in the name of fortune, could have brought you here?"

"That," said I, "is a story too long, Eugenia, for a moment so interesting as this. I also might ask you the same question; but it is now one o'clock in the morning and, therefore, too late to begin with inquiry. This one question, however, I must ask—are you a mother?"

"I am," said Eugenia, "of the most lovely boy that ever blessed the eyes of a parent; he is now in perfect health and fast asleep—come to-morrow, at ten o'clock, and you shall see him."

"To-morrow," said I, with surprise, "to-morrow, Eugenia? Why am I to quit your house?"

"That also you shall know, to-morrow," said she; "but now you must do as you are desired. To-morrow, I will be at home to no one but you.

Knowing Eugenia as I did, it was sufficient that she had decided. There was no appeal; so, kissing her again, I wished her a good night, quitted her,

and retired to my hotel. What a night of tumult did I pass! I was tossed from
Emily to Eugenia, like a shuttlecock between two battledores. The latter
never looked so lovely; and to the natural loveliness of her person, was
added a grace and a polish, which gave a lustre to her charms, which almost
served Emily as I had served the footman. I never once closed my eyes
during the night—dressed early the next morning, walked about, looked at
Chateau Trompette and the Roman ruins—thought the hour of ten would
never strike, and when it did, I struck the same moment at her door.

The man who opened it to me was the same whom I had treated so ill
the night before; the moment he saw me, he put himself into an attitude at
once of attack, defence, remonstrance, and revenge, all connected with the
affair of the preceding evening.

"Ah, ah, vous voilà donc! ce n'était pas bienfait, Monsieur."

"Oui," said I, "très nettement fait, et voilà encore," slipping a Napoleon
into his hand.

"Ca s'arrange très-joliment, Monsieur," said the man, grinning from ear
to ear, and bowing to the ground.

"C'est Madame, que vous voulez donc?"

"Oui," said I.

He led, I followed; he opened the door of a breakfast parlour—"tenez,
Madame, voici le Monsieur que m'a renversé hier au soi."

Eugenia was seated on a sofa, with her boy by her side, the loveliest
little fellow I had ever beheld. His face was one often described, but rarely
seen; it was shaded with dark curling ringlets, his mouth, eyes, and complexion had much of his mother, and, vanity whispered me, much more of
myself. I took a seat on the sofa, and with the boy on my knee, and Eugenia
by my side, held her hand, while she narrated the events of her life since the
time of our separation.

"A few days," said she, "after your departure for the Flushing expedition, I read in the public prints, that 'if the nearest relation of my mother
would call at ———, in London, they would hear of something to their
advantage.' I wrote to the agent, from whom I learned, after proving my
identity, that the two sisters of my mother, who, you may remember, had
like sums left them by the will of their relative, had continued to live in a
state of single blessedness; that, about four years previous, one of them had
died, leaving every thing to the other, and that the other had died only two

months before, bequeathing all her property to my mother, or her next heir; or, in default of that, to some distant relation. I, therefore, immediately came into a fortune of ten thousand pounds, with interest; and I was further informed that a great-uncle of mine was still living, without heirs, and was most anxious that my mother or her heirs should be discovered. An invitation was therefore sent to me to go down to him, and to make his house my future residence.

"At that time, the effects of my indiscretion were but too apparent, and rendered, as I thought, deception justifiable. I put on widow's weeds, and gave out that my husband was a young officer, who had fallen a victim to the fatal Walcheren fever; that our marriage had been clandestine, and unknown to any of his friends: such was my story and appearance before the agent, who believed me. The same fabrication was put upon my grand-uncle, with equal success. I was received into his house with parental affection; and in that house I gave birth to the dear child you now hold in your arms—to your child, my Frank—to the only child I shall ever have. Yes, dear Eugenio," continued she, pressing her rosy lips on the broad white neck of the child, "you shall be my only care, my solace, my comfort, and my joy. Heaven, in its mercy, sent the cherub to console its wretched mother in the double pangs of guilt and separation from all she loved; and Heaven shall be repaid, by my return to its slighted, its insulted laws. I feel that my sin is forgiven; for I have besought forgiveness night and day, with bitter tears, and Heaven has heard my prayer. 'Go, and sin no more,' was said to me; and upon these terms I have received forgiveness.

"You will no doubt ask, why did I not let you know all this? and why I so carefully secreted myself from you? My reasons were founded on the known impetuosity of your character. You, my beloved, who could brave death, and all the military consequences of desertion from a ship lying at Spithead, were not likely to listen to the suggestions of prudence when Eugenia was to be found; and, having once given out that I was a widow, I resolved to preserve the consistency of my character for my own sake— for your sake, and for the sake of this blessed child, the only drop that has sweetened my cup of affliction. Had you by any means discovered my place of abode, the peace of my uncle's house, and the prospects of my child had been for ever blasted.

"Now then say, Frank, have I, or have I not, acted the part of a Roman mother? My grand-uncle having declared his intention of making me heir to his property, for his sake, and yours, and for my child, I have preserved the strict line of duty, from which God, in his infinite mercy, grant that I may never depart.

"I first resolved upon not seeing you until I could be more my own mistress; and when, at the death of my respected relative, I was not only released from any restraint on account of his feelings, but also became still more independent in my circumstances, you might be surprised that I did not immediately impart to you the change of fortune which would have enabled us to have enjoyed the comfort of unrestricted communication. But time, reflection, the conversation and society of my uncle and his select friends, the care of my infant, and the reading of many excellent books had wrought a great change in my sentiments. Having once tasted the pleasures of society among virtuous women, I vowed to Heaven that no future act of mine should ever drive me from it. The past could not be recalled; but the future was my own.

"I took the sacrament after a long and serious course of reading; and, having made my vows at the altar, with the help of God, they are unchangeable. Dramatic works, the pernicious study and poison of my youthful ardent mind, I have long since discarded; and I had resolved never to see you again, until after your marriage with Miss Somerville had been solemnised. Start not! By the simplest and easiest means I have known all your movements—your dangers, your escapes, your undaunted acts of bravery and self-devotion for the sake of others.

"'Shall I then,' said I to myself, 'blast the prospects of the man I love—the father of my boy? Shall I, to gratify the poor, pitiful ambition of becoming the wife of him, to whom I once was the mistress, sacrifice thus the hopes and fortune of himself and family, the reward of a virtuous maiden?' In all this I hope you will perceive a proper share of self-denial. Many, many floods of bitter tears of repentance and regret have I shed over my past conduct; and I trust, that what I have suffered and what I shall suffer, will be received as my atonement at the Throne of Grace. True, I once looked forward to the happy period of our union, when I might have offered myself to you, not as a portionless bride; but I was checked by one maddening, burning, inextinguishable thought. I could not be received into that society to which you were entitled. I felt that I loved you, Frank; loved you too well to betray you. The woman that had so little respect for herself, was unfit to be the wife of Francis Mildmay.

"Besides, how could I do my sweet boy the injustice to allow him to have brothers and sisters possessing legitimate advantages over him? I felt that our union never could be one of happiness, even if you consented to take me as your wife, of which I had my doubts; and when I discovered, through my emissaries, that you were on the point of marriage with Miss Somerville, I felt that it was all for the best; that I had no right to complain; the more so as it was I who (I blush to say it) had seduced you.

"But, Frank, if I cannot be your wife—and alas! I know too well that that is impossible—will you allow me to be your friend, your dear friend, as the mother of your child, or, if you please, as your sister? But there the sacred line is drawn; it is a compact between my God and myself. You know my firmness and decision; once maturely deliberated, my resolution formed, it is not, I think, in man to turn me. Do not, therefore, make the attempt; it will only end in your certain defeat and shame, and in my withdrawing from your sight for ever. You will not, I am sure, pay me so bad a compliment as to wish me to renew the follies of my youth. If you love me, respect me; promise, by the love you bear to Miss Somerville, and your affection for this poor boy, that you will do as I wish you. Your honour and peace of mind, as well as mine, demand it."

This severe rebuke, from a quarter, whence I least expected it, threw me back with shame and confusion. As if a mirror had been held up to me, I saw my own deformity. I saw that Eugenia was not only the guardian of her own honour, but of mine, and of the happiness of Miss Somerville, against whom I now stood convicted of foul deceit and shameful wrong. I acknowledged my fault, I assured Eugenia that I was bound to her, by every tie of honour, esteem, and love; and that her boy and mine should be our mutual care.

"Thank you, dearest," said she: "you have taken a heavy load from my mind: henceforth remember we are brother and sister. I shall now be able to enjoy the pleasure of your society; and now, as that point is settled, let me know what has occurred to you since we parted—the particulars I mean, for the outline I have had before."

I related to her everything which had happened to me, from the hour of our separation to the moment I saw her so unexpectedly in the theatre. She was alternately affected with terror, surprise, and laughter. She took a hearty crying spell over the motionless bodies of Clara and Emily, as they lay on the floor; but recovered from that, and went into hysterics of laughter, when I described the footman's mistake, and the slap on the face bestowed on him by the housemaid.

My mind was not naturally corrupt. It was only so at times, and from peculiar circumstances; but I was always generous, and easily recalled to a sense of my duty, when reminded of my fault. Not for an empire would I have persuaded Eugenia to break her vow. I loved and respected the mother of my child; the more when I reflected that she had been the means of preserving my fidelity to Emily. I rejoiced to think that my friendship for the one, and love for the other, were not incompatible. I wrote immediately to Emily, announcing my speedy return to England.

"Having the most perfect reliance on your honour, I shall now," said Eugenia, "accept of your escort to London, where my presence is required. Pierre shall accompany us—he is a faithful creature, though you used him so ill."

"That," said I, "is all made up, and Pierre will be heartily glad of another tumble for the same price."

All our arrangements were speedily made. The house was given up— a roomy travelling barouche received all our trunks; and, seated by the side of Eugenia, with the child between us, we crossed the Gironde, and took our way through Poictiers, Tours, and Orleans, to Paris; here we remained but a short time. Neither of us were pleased with the manners and habits of the French; but as they have been so fully described by the swarms of English travellers who have infested that country with their presence, and this with the fruits of their labours, I shall pass as quietly through France, as I hope to do through the Thames Tunnel, when it is completed, but not before.

Eugenia consulted me as to her future residence; and here I own I committed a great error, but, I declare to Heaven, without any criminal intention. I ventured to suggest that she should live in a very pretty village a few miles from ———— Hall, the residence of Mr Somerville, and where, after my marriage, it was intended that I should continue to reside with Emily. To this village, then, I directed her to go, assuring her that I should often ride over and visit her.

"Much as I should enjoy your company, Frank," said Eugenia, "this is a measure fraught with evil to all parties; nor is it fair dealing towards your future wife."

Unhappily for me, that turn for duplicity, which I had imbibed in early life, had not forsaken me, notwithstanding the warnings I had received, and the promises of amendment which I had made. Flattering myself that I intended no harm, I overruled all the scruples of the excellent Eugenia. She despatched a confidential person to the village; on the outskirts of which, he procured for her a commodious, and even elegant cottage ornée ready furnished. She went down with her child and Pierre to take possession; and I to my father's house, where my appearance was hailed as a signal for a grand jubilee.

Clara I found had entirely changed her unfavourable opinion of sea officers, induced thereto by the engaging manners of my friend Talbot, on whom I was delighted to learn she was about to bestow her very pretty little white hand at the altar. This was a great triumph to the navy, for I always told Clara, laughingly, that I never would forgive her if she quitted the service; and as I entertained the highest respect for Talbot, I considered the prospects of my sister were very bright and flattering, and that she had made a choice very likely to secure her happiness. "Rule Britannia," said I to Clara; "Blue for ever!"

The next morning I started for Mr Somerville's, where I was of course received with open arms; and the party, a few days after, having been increased by the arrival of my father with Clara and Talbot, I was as happy as a human being could be. Six weeks was the period assigned by my fair one as the very shortest in which she could get rigged, bend new sails, and prepare for the long and sometimes tedious voyage of matrimony. I remonstrated at the unconscionable delay.

"Long as it may appear," she said, "it is much less time than you took to fit out your fine frigate for North America."

"That frigate was not got ready even then by any hurry of mine," said I; "and if ever I come to be first lord of the Admiralty, I shall have a bright eye on the young lieutenants and their sweethearts at Blackheath, particularly when a ship is fitting in a hurry at Woolwich."

Much of this kind of sparring went on, to the great amusement of all parties; meanwhile, the ladies employed themselves in running up milliner's bills, and their papas employed themselves in discharging them. My father was particularly liberal to Emily in the articles of plate and jewellery, and Mr Somerville equally kind to Clara. Emily received a trinket box, so beautifully fitted and so well filled, that it required a cheque of no trifling magnitude to cry quits with the jeweller; indeed my father's kindness was so great, that I was forced to beg he would set some bounds to his liberality.

I was so busy and so happy, that I had let three weeks pass over my head without seeing Eugenia. I dreamed of her at last, and thought she upbraided me; and the next day, full of my dream, as soon as breakfast was over, I recommended the young ladies to the care of Talbot, and, mounting my horse, rode over to see Eugenia. She received me kindly, but she had suffered in her health, and was much out of spirits. I inquired the reason, and she burst into tears. "I shall be better, Frank," said she, "when all is over, but I must suffer now; and I suffer the more acutely from a conviction that I am only paying the penalty of my own crime. Perhaps," continued she, "had I never departed from virtue, I might at this moment have held in your heart the envied place of Miss Somerville; but as the righteous decrees of Providence having provided punishment to tread fast in the footsteps of guilt, I am now expiating my faults, and I have a presentiment that although the struggle is bitter, it will soon be over. God's will be done; and may you, my dear Frank, have many, many happy years in the society of one you are bound to love before the unhappy Eugenia."

Here she sank on a sofa, and again wept bitterly.

"I feel," said she, "now, but it is too late—I feel that I have acted wrongly in quitting Bordeaux. There I was loved and respected; and if not happy, at least I was composed. Too much dependence on my resolution, and the vanity of supposing myself superior in magnanimity to the rest of my sex, induced me to trust myself in your society. Dearly, alas! have I paid for it. My only chance of victory over myself was flight from you, after I had given the irrevocable sentence; by not doing so, the poison has again found its way to my heart. I feel that I love you; that I cannot have you; and that death, very shortly, must terminate my intolerable sufferings."

This affecting address pierced me to the soul; and now the consequences of my guilt and duplicity rushed upon me like a torrent through a bursting flood-gate. I would have resigned Emily, I would have fled with Eugenia to some distant country, and buried our sorrows in each other's bosoms; and, in a state of irrepressible emotion, I proposed this step to her.

"What do I hear, my beloved?" said she (starting up with horror from the couch on which she was sitting, with her face between her knees), "what! is it you that would resign home, friends, character, the possession of a virtuous woman, all, for the polluted smiles of an—"

"Hold! hold! my Eugenia," said I; "do not, I beseech you, shock my ears with an epithet which you do not deserve! Mine, mine, is all the guilt; forget me, and you will still be happy."

She looked at me, then at her sweet boy, who was playing on the carpet—but she made no answer; and then a flood of tears succeeded.

It was, indeed, a case of singular calamity for a beautiful young creature to be placed in. She was only in her three-and-twentieth year—and, lovely as she was, nature had scarcely had time to finish the picture. The regrets which subdued my mind on that fatal morning may only be conceived by those who, like me, have led a licentious life—have, for a time, buried all moral and religious feeling, and have been suddenly called to a full sense of their guilt, and the misery they have entailed on the innocent. I sat down and groaned. I cannot say I wept, for I could not weep; but my forehead burned, and my heart was full of bitterness.

While I thus meditated, Eugenia sat with her hand on her forehead, in a musing attitude. Had she been reverting to her former studies, and thrown herself into the finest conceivable posture of the tragic muse, her appearance would not have been half so beautiful and affecting. I thought she was praying, and I think so still. The tears ran in silence down her face; I kissed them off, and almost forgot Emily.

"I am better now, Frank," said the poor, sorrowful woman; "do not come again until after the wedding. When will it take place?" she inquired, with a trembling and a faltering voice.

My heart almost burst within me, as I told her, for I felt as if I was signing a warrant for her execution. I took her in my arms, and, tenderly embracing her, endeavoured to divert her thoughts from the mournful fate that too evidently hung over her; she became tranquil, and I proposed taking a stroll in the adjoining park. I thought the fresh air would revive her.

She agreed to this; and, going to her room, returned in a few minutes. To her natural beauty was added on that fatal day a morning dress, which more than any other became her; it was white, richly trimmed, and fashionably made up by a celebrated French milliner. Her bonnet was white muslin, trimmed with light blue ribbons, and a sash of the same colour confined her slender waist. The little Eugenio ran before us, now at my side, and now at his mother's. We rambled about for some time, the burthen of our conversation being the future plans and mode of education to be adopted for the child; this was a subject on which she always dwelt with peculiar pleasure.

Tired with our walk, we sat down under a clump of beech trees, near a grassy ascent, winding among the thick foliage, contrived by the opulent owner to extend and diversify the rides in his noble domain. Eugenio was playing around us, picking the wild flowers, and running up to me to inquire their names.

The boy was close by my side, when, startled at a noise, he turned round and exclaimed—

"Oh! look, mamma, look, papa, there is a lady and a gentleman a-riding."

I turned round, and saw Mr Somerville and Emily on horseback, within six paces of me; so still they stood, so mute, I could have fancied Emily a wax-work figure. They neither breathed nor moved; even their very horses seemed to be of bronze, or, perhaps the unfortunate situation in which I found myself made me think them so. They had come as unexpectedly on us as we had discovered them. The soft turf had received the impression of their horses' feet, and returned no sound; and if they snorted, we had either not attended to them in the warmth of our conversation, or we had never heard them.

I rose up hastily—coloured deeply—stammered, and was about to speak. Perhaps it was better that I did not; but I had no opportunity. Like apparitions they came, and like apparitions they vanished. The avenue from whence they had so silently issued, received them again, and they were gone before Eugenia was sensible of their presence.

CHAPTER XXVII

Fare thee well; and if for ever—
Still for ever fare thee well:
Even though unforgiving, never
'Gainst thee shall my heart rebel.

BYRON

I WAS so stunned with this contretemps, that I fell senseless to the ground; and it was long before the kind attentions and assiduity of Eugenia could restore me. When she had succeeded, my first act was one of base ingratitude, cruelty, and injustice: I spurned her from me, and upbraided her as the cause of my unfortunate situation. She only replied with tears. I quitted her and the child without bidding them adieu, little thinking I should never see them again. I ran to the inn, where I had left my horse, mounted, and rode back to ——— Hall.

Mr Somerville and his daughter had just arrived, and Emily was lifted off her horse, and obliged to be carried up to her room.

Clara and Talbot came to enquire what had happened. I could give no account of it; but earnestly requested to see Emily. The answer returned was that Miss Somerville declined seeing me. In the course of this day, which, in point of mental suffering, exceeded all I had ever endured in the utmost severity of professional hardship, an explanation had taken place between myself, my father, and Mr Somerville. I had done that by the impulse of dire necessity which I ought to have done at first of my own free will. I was caught at last in my own snare. "The trains of the devil are long," said I to myself, "but they are sure to blow up at last."

The consequence of the explanation was my final dismissal, and a return of all the presents which my father and myself had given to Emily. My conduct, though blamable, was not viewed in that heinous light, either by my father or Mr Somerville; and both of them did all that could be done to restore harmony. Clara and Talbot interposed their kind offices, but with no better success. The maiden pride of the inexorable Emily had been alarmed by a beautiful rival, with a young family, in the next village. The impression had taken hold of her spotless mind, and could not be removed. I was false, fickle, and deceitful, and was given to understand that Miss Somerville did not intend to quit her room until she was assured by her father that I was no longer a guest in the house.

Under these painful circumstances, our remaining any longer at the Hall was both useless and irksome—a source of misery to all.

My father ordered his horses the next morning, and I was carried back to London, more dead than alive. A burning fever raged in my blood; and the moment I reached my father's house, I was put to bed, and placed under the care of a physician, with nurses to watch me night and day. For three weeks I was in a state of delirium; and when I regained my senses, it was only to renew the anguish which had caused my disorder, and I felt any sentiment except gratitude for my recovery.

My dear Clara had never quitted me during my confinement. I had taken no medicine but from her hand. I asked her to give me some account of what had happened. She told me that Talbot was gone—that my father had seen Mr Somerville, who had informed him that Emily had received a long letter from Eugenia, narrating every circumstance, exculpating me, and ac-cusing herself. Emily had wept over it, but still remained firm in her reso-lution never to see me more—"And I am afraid, my dear brother," said Clara, "that her resolution will not be very easily altered. You know her character, and you should know something about our sex; but sailors, they say, go round the world without going into it. This is the only shadow of an excuse I can form for you, much as I love and esteem you. You have hurt Emily in the nicest point, that in which we are all the most susceptible of injury. You have wounded her pride, which our sex rarely, if ever, forgive. At the very moment she supposed you were devoted to her—that you were wrapped up in the anticipation of calling her your own, and counting the minutes with impatience until the happy day arrived; with all this persuasion on her mind, she comes upon you, as the traveller out of the wood suddenly comes upon the poisonous snake in his path, and cannot avoid it. She found you locked hand-in-hand with another, a fortnight before marriage, and with the fruits of unlawful love in your arms. What woman could forgive this? I would not, I assure you. If Tal——, I mean if any man were to serve me so, I would tear him from my heart, even if the dissolution of the whole frame was to be the certain consequence. I consider it a kindness to tell you, Frank, that you have no hope. Much as you have and will suffer, she, poor girl, will suffer more; and, although she will never accept you, she will not let your place be supplied by another, but sink, broken-hearted, into her grave. You, like all other men, will forget this; but what a warning ought it to be to you, that, sooner or later, guilt will be productive of misery! This you have fully proved: your licentious conduct with this woman has ruined her peace for ever, and Divine vengeance has dashed from your lips the cup which contained as much happiness as this world could afford: nor has the penalty fallen on you alone—the innocent, who had no share in the crime, are partakers in the punishment; we are all as miserable as yourself. But God's will be done," continued she, as she kissed my aching forehead, and her tears fell on my face.

How heavenly is the love of a sister towards a brother! Clara was now everything to me. Having said thus much to me on the subject of my fault (and it must be confessed that she had not been niggardly in the article of words), she never named the subject again, but sought by every means in her power to amuse and to comfort me. She listened to my exculpation; she admitted that our meeting at Bordeaux was as unpremeditated as it was unfortunate; she condemned the imprudence of our travelling together, and still more the choice of a residence for Eugenia and her son.

Clara's affectionate attention and kind efforts were unavailing. I told her so, and that all hopes of happiness for me in this world were gone for ever.

"My dear, dear brother," said the affectionate girl, "answer me one question. Did you ever pray?"

My answer will pretty well explain to the reader the sort of religion mine was:—

"Why, Clara," said I, "to tell you the truth, though I may not exactly pray, as you call it, yet words are nothing. I feel grateful to the Almighty for his favours when he bestows them on me; and I believe a grateful heart is all he requires."

"Then, brother, how do you feel when he afflicts you?"

"That I have nothing to thank him for," answered I.

"Then, my dear Frank, that is not religion."

"May be so," said I; "but I am in no humour to feel otherwise, at present, so pray drop the subject."

She burst into tears. "This," said she, "is worse than all. Shall we receive good from the hand of the Lord, and shall we not receive evil?"

But seeing that I was in that sullen and untameable state of mind, she did not venture to renew the subject.

As soon as I was able to quit my room, I had a long conversation with my father, who, though deeply concerned for my happiness, said he was quite certain that any attempt at reconciliation would he useless. He therefore proposed two plans, and I might adopt whichever was the most likely to divert my mind from my heavy affliction. The first was, to ask his friends at the Admiralty to give me the command of a sloop of war; the second, that I should go upon the continent, and, having passed a year there, return to England, when there was no knowing what change of sentiment time and absence might not produce in my favour. "For," said he, "there is one very remarkable difference in the heart of a man and of a woman. In the first, absence is very often a cure for love. In the other, it more frequently cements and consolidates it. In your absence, Emily will dwell on the bright parts of your character, and forget its blemishes. The experiment is worth making, and it is the only way which offers a chance of success."

I agreed to this. "But," said I, "as the war with France is now over, and that with America will be terminated no doubt very shortly, I have no wish to put you to the expense, or myself to the trouble, of fitting out a sloop of war in time of peace, to be a pleasure-yacht for great lords and ladies, and myself to be neither more or less than a *maître d'hotel:* and, after having spent your money and mine, and exhausted all my civilities, to receive no thanks, and hear that I am esteemed at Almack's only 'a tolerable sea brute enough.' A ship, therefore," continued I, "I will not have; and as I think the continent holds out some novelty at least, I will, with your consent, set off."

This point being settled, I told Clara of it. The poor girl's grief was immoderate. "My dearest brother, I shall lose you, and be left alone in the world. Your impetuous and unruly heart is not in a state to be trusted among the gay and frivolous French. You will be at sea without your compass—you have thrown religion overboard—and what is to guide you in the hour of trial?"

"Fear not, dear Clara," said I; "my own energies will always extricate me from the dangers you apprehend."

"Alas! it is these very energies which I dread," said Clara; "but I trust that all will be for the best. Accept," said she, "of this little book from poor brokenhearted Clara; and, if you love her, look at it sometimes."

I took the book, and embracing her affectionately, assured her, that for her sake I would read it.

When I had completed my arrangements for my foreign tour, I determined to take one last look at ———— Hall before I left England. I set off unknown to my family; and contrived to be near the boundaries of the park by dusk. I desired the post-boy to stop half a mile from the house, and to wait my return. I cleared the paling; and, avoiding the direct road, came up to the house. The room usually occupied by the family was on the ground floor, and I cautiously approached the window. Mr Somerville and Emily were both there. He was reading aloud; she sat at the table with a book before her: but her thoughts, it was evident, were not there; she had inserted her taper fingers into the ringlets of her hair, until the palms of her hand reached her forehead; then, bending her head towards the table, she leaned on her elbows, and seemed absorbed in the most melancholy reflections.

"This, too, is my work," said I; "this fair flower is blighted, and withering by the contagious touch of my baneful hand. Good Heaven! what a wretch am I! whoever loves me is rewarded by misery. And what have I gained by this wide waste and devastation, which my wickedness has spread around me? Happiness? no, no—that I have lost for ever. Would that my loss were all! would that comfort might visit the soul of this fair creature and another. But I dare not—I cannot pray; I am at enmity with God and man. Yet I will make an effort in favour of this victim of my baseness. O God," continued I, "if the prayers of an outcast like me can find acceptance, not for myself, but for her, I ask that peace which the world cannot give; shower down thy blessings upon her, alleviate her sorrows, and erase from her memory the existence of such a being as myself. Let not my hateful image hang as a blight upon her beauteous frame."

Emily resumed her book, when her father had ceased reading aloud; and I saw her wipe a tear from her cheek.

The excitement occasioned by this scene, added to my previous illness, from the effects of which I had not sufficiently recovered, caused a faintness; I sat down under the window, in hopes that it would pass off. It did not, however; for I fell, and lay on the turf in a state of insensibility, which must have lasted nearly half an hour. I afterwards learned from Clara, that Emily had opened the window, it being a French one, to walk out and recover herself. By the bright moon-light, she perceived me lying on the ground. Her first idea was, that I had committed suicide; and, with this impression, she shut the window, and tottering to the back part of the room, fainted. Her father ran to her assistance, and she fell into his arms. She was taken up to her room, and consigned to the care of her woman, who put her to bed; but she was unable to give any account of herself, or the cause of her disorder, until the following day.

For my own part, I gradually came to my senses, and with difficulty regained my chaise, the driver of which told me I had been gone about an hour. I drove off to town, wholly unaware that I had been observed by any one, much less by Emily. When she related to her father what she had seen, he either disbelieved or affected to disbelieve it, and treated it as the effects of a distempered mind, the phantoms of a disordered imagination; and she at length began to coincide with him.

I started for the continent a few days afterwards. Talbot, who had seen little of Clara since my rejection by Emily, and subsequent illness, offered my father to accompany me; and Clara was anxious that he should go, as she was determined not to listen to any thing he could say during my affliction; she could not, she said, be happy while I was miserable, and gave him no opportunity of conversing with her on the subject of their union.

We arrived at Paris; but so abstracted was I in thought, that I neither saw nor heard any thing. Every attention of Talbot was lost upon me. I continued in my sullen stupor, and forgot to read the little book which dear Clara had given, and which, for her sake, I had promised to read. I wrote to Eugenia on my arrival; and disburthened my mind in some measure, by acknowledging my shameful treatment of her. I implored her pardon; and, by return of post, received it. Her answer was affectionate and consoling; but she stated that her spirits, of course, were low, and her health but indifferent.

For many days my mind remained in a state of listless inanity; and Talbot applied, or suffered others to apply, the most pernicious stimulant that could be thought of to rouse me to action. Taking a quiet walk with him, we met some friends of his; and, at their request, we agreed to go to the saloons of the Palais Royal. This was a desperate remedy, and by a miracle only was I saved from utter and irretrievable ruin. How many of my countrymen have fallen victims to the arts practised in that horrible school of vice, I dare not say! Happy should I be to think that the infection had not reached our own shores, and found patrons among the great men of the land. They have, however, both felt the consequences, and been forewarned of the danger. *They* have no excuse: *mine* was, that I had been excluded from the society of those I loved. Always living by excitement, was it surprising that, when a gaming-table displayed its hoards before me, I should have fallen at once into the snare?

For the first time since my illness, I became interested, and laid down my money on those abhorred tables. My success was variable; but I congratulated myself that at length I had found a stimulus; and I anxiously awaited the return of the hour when the doors would again be opened, and the rooms lighted up for the reception of company. I won considerably; and night after night found me at the table—for avarice is insatiable; but my good luck left me: and then the same motive induced me to return, with the hope of winning back what I had lost.

Still fortune was unpropitious, and I lost very considerable sums. I became desperate; and drew largely on my father. He wrote to beg that I would be more moderate; as twice his income would not support such an expenditure. He wrote also to Talbot, who informed him in what manner the money had been expended; and that he had in vain endeavoured to divert me from the fatal practice. Finding that no limits were likely to be put to my folly, my father very properly refused to honour any more of my bills.

Maddened with this intimation, for which I secretly blamed Talbot, I drew upon Eugenia's banker bill after bill, until the sum amounted to more than what my father had paid. At length a letter came from Eugenia. It was but a few lines.

"I know too well, my dearest friend," said she, "what becomes of the money you have received. If you want it all, I cannot refuse you; but remember that you are throwing away the property of your child."

This letter did more to rouse me to a sense of my infamous conduct than the advice of Talbot, or the admonitions of my father. I felt I was acting like a scoundrel; and I resolved to leave off gaming. "One night more," said I, "and then, if I lose, there is an end of it; I go no more." Talbot attended me: he felt he was in some measure the cause of my being first initiated in this pernicious amusement: and he watched my motions with unceasing anxiety.

The game was *rouge et noir.* I threw a large sum on the red. I won, left the stake, doubled, and won again. The heap of gold had increased to a large size, and still remained to abide the chance of the card. Again, again, and again, it was doubled. Seven times had the red card been turned up; and seven times had my gold been doubled. Talbot, who stood behind me, implored and begged me earnestly to leave off.

"What may be the consequence of one card against you? Trust no more to fortune; be content with what you have got."

"That," muttered I, "Talbot, is of no use; I must have more."

Again came up the red, to the astonishment of the bystanders; and to their still greater astonishment, my gold, which had increased to an enormous heap, still remained on the table. Talbot again entreated me not to tempt fortune foolishly.

"Folly," said I, "Talbot, has already been committed; and one more card will do the business. It must be done."

The bankers knowing, after eight red cards had been turned up, how great the chance was of regaining all their losses by a double or quits, agreed to the ninth card. Talbot trembled like a leaf. The card was turned; it came up red, and the bank was broke.

Here all play ceased for that night. The losers, of course, vented their feelings in the most blasphemous execrations; while I quietly collected all my winnings, and returned home in a *fiacre,* with Talbot, who took the precaution of requesting the attendance of two *gens d'armes.* These were each rewarded with a Napoleon.

"Now, Talbot," said I, "I solemnly swear, as I hope to go to heaven, never to play again." And this promise I have most religiously kept. My good fortune was one instance in ten thousand, among those who have been ruined in that house. The next morning I refunded all I had drawn upon Eugenia, and all my father had supplied me with, and there still remained a considerable residue.

Determined not to continue in this vortex of dissipation any longer, where my resolution was hourly put to the test, Talbot and myself agreed to travel down to Brest, an arsenal we were both desirous of seeing.

CHAPTER XXVIII

PAL. *Thou art a traitor, Arcite, and a fellow*
False as thy title to her. Friendship, blood,
And all the ties between us, I disclaim.

ARC. *You are mad.*

PAL. *I must be,*
Till thou art worthy, Arcite, it concerns me!
And, in this madness if I hazard thee
And take thy life, I deal but truly.

ARC. *Fie, Sir!*

"TWO NOBLE KINSMEN"

WE quitted Paris two days after; and a journey of three days, through an
uninteresting country, brought us to the little town of Granville, on the sea-
coast, in the channel. We remained at this delightful place some days; and
our letters being regularly forwarded to us, brought us intelligence from
England. My father expressed his astonishment at my returning the money
drawn for; and trusted, unaccountable as the restitution appeared, that I was
not offended, and would consider him my banker, as far as his expenditure
and style of living would permit him to advance.

Eugenia, in her letters, reproached herself for having written to me; and
concluded that I had drawn so largely upon her, merely to prove her sincer-
ity. She assured me that her caution to me was not dictated by selfishness,
but from a consideration for the child.

Clara's letter informed me that every attempt, even to servility, had been
made, in order to induce Emily to alter her determination, but without success; and that a coolness had, in consequence, taken place, and almost an
entire interruption of the intimacy between the families. She also added, "I
am afraid that your friend is even worse than yourself; for I understand that
he is engaged to another woman, and has been so for years. Now, as I must
consider that the great tie of your intimacy is his supposed partiality to me,
and as I conceive you are under a false impression with respect to his sin-
cerity, I think it my duty to make you acquainted with all I know. It is
impossible that you can esteem the man who has trifled with the feelings of

your sister; and I sincerely hope that the next letter from you will inform me of your having separated."

How little did poor Clara think, when she wrote this letter, of the consequences likely to arise from it; that in thus venting her complaints, she was exploding a mine which was to produce results ten times more fatal than any thing which had yet befallen us?

I was at this period in a misanthropic state of mind, hating myself and every one about me. The company of Talbot had long been endured, not enjoyed; and I would gladly have availed myself of any plausible excuse for a separation. True, he was my friend, had proved himself so; but I was in no humour to acknowledge favours. Discarded by her I loved, I discarded every one else. Talbot was a log and a chain, and I thought I could not get rid of him too soon. This letter, therefore, gave me a fair opportunity of venting my spleen; but instead of a cool dismissal, as Clara requested, I determined to dismiss him or myself to another world.

Having finished reading my letter, I laid it down, and made no observation. Talbot, with his usual kind and benevolent countenance, inquired if I had any news? "Yes," I replied, "I have discovered that you are a villain!"

"That is news, indeed," said he; "and strange that the brother of Clara should have been the messenger to convey it; but this is language, Frank, which not even your unhappy state of mind can excuse. Retract your words."

"I repeat them," said I. "You have trifled with my sister, and are a villain." (Had this been true, it was no more than I had done myself; but my victims had no brothers to avenge their wrongs.)

"The name of Clara," replied Talbot, "calms me; believe me, Frank, you are mistaken. I love her, and have always had the most honourable intentions towards her."

"Yes," said I, with a sarcastic sneer, "at the time that you have been engaged to another woman for years. To one or the other you must acknowledge yourself a scoundrel: I do not, therefore, withdraw my appellation, but repeat it; and as you seem so very patient under injuries, I inform you that you must either meet me on the sands this evening, or consent to be stigmatised with another name still more revolting to the feelings of an Englishman."

"Enough, enough, Frank," said Talbot, with a face in which conscious innocence and manly fortitude were blended; "you have said more than I ever expected to have heard from you, and more than the customs of the world will allow me to put up with. What must be, must; but I still tell you, Frank, that you are wrong—that you are fatally deluded, and that you will bitterly repent the follies of this day. It is yourself with whom you are angry, and you are venting that anger on your friend."

The words were thrown away on me. I felt a secret malignant pleasure, which blindly impelled me forward, with the certainty of glutting my revenge, by either destroying or being destroyed. My sole preparation for this dreadful conflict was my pistols; no other did I think of, not even the chances of sending my friend and fellow-mortal, or going myself into the presence of an Almighty judge. My mind was absorbed in secret pleasure, at the idea of that acute misery which Emily would suffer if I fell by the hand of Talbot.

I repaired to the rendezvous, where I found Talbot waiting. He came up to me, and again said, "Frank, I call heaven to witness that you are mistaken. You are wrong. Suspend your opinion, at least, if you will not recall your words."

Totally possessed by the devil, and not to be convinced, till too late, I replied to his peaceful overture by the most insulting irony: "You were not afraid to fire at a poor boy in the water," said I, "though you do not like to stand a shot in return. Come, come, take your ground, be a man, stand up, don't be afraid."

"For myself," said Talbot, with a firm and placid resignation of countenance, "I have no fears; but for you, Frank, I have great cause of alarm:" so saying, he snatched up the loaded pistol which I threw down to him.

We had no seconds; nor was there any person in sight. It was a bright moonlight, and we walked to the water's edge, where the reflux of the tide had left the sand firm to the tread. Here we stood back to back. The usual distance was fourteen paces. Talbot refused to measure his, but stood perfectly still. I walked ten paces, and turned round, "Ready," said I in a low voice.

We both raised our arms; but Talbot, instantly dropping the muzzle of his pistol, said, "I cannot fire at the brother of Clara."

"I can at her insulter," answered I; and, taking deliberate aim, fired, and my ball entered his side. He bounded, gave a half turn round in the air, and fell on his face to the ground.

How sudden are the transitions of the human mind! how close does remorse follow the gratification of revenge! The veil dropped from my eyes;

I saw in an instant the false medium, the deceitful vision which had thus allured me into what the world calls "an affair of honour." "Honour," good heaven! had made me a murderer, and the voice of my brother's blood cried out for vengeance.

The manly and athletic form, which one minute before excited my most malignant hatred, when now prostrate and speechless, became an object of frantic affection. I ran to Talbot, and when it was too late perceived the mischief I had done. Murder, cruelty, injustice, and, above all, the most detestable ingratitude, flashed at once into my overcrowded imagination. I turned the body round, and tried to discover if there were any signs of life. A small stream of blood ran from his side, and, about two feet from him, was lost in the absorbing sand; while from the violence of his fall the sand had filled his mouth and nostrils. I cleaned them out; and, staunching the wound with my handkerchief, for the blood flowed copiously at every respiration, I sat on the sea-shore by his side, supporting him in my arms. I only exclaimed, "Would to God the shark, the poison, the sword of the enemy, or the precipice of Trinidad had destroyed me before this fatal hour."

Talbot opened his languid eyes, and fixed them on me with a glassy stare; but he did not speak. Suddenly, recollection seemed for a moment to return—he recognised me, and, O God, his look of kindness pierced my heart.

He made several efforts to speak, and at last said, in broken accents, and at long and painful intervals,

"Look at letter—writing-desk—read all—explain—God bless—" His head fell back, and he was dead.

Oh, how I envied him! Had he been ten thousand times more guilty than I had ever supposed him, it would have given no comfort to my mind. I had murdered him, and too late I acknowledged his innocence. I know not why, and can scarcely tell how I did it, but I took of my neckcloth, and bound it tightly round his waist, over the wound. The blood ceased to flow. I left the body, and returned to our lodging, in a state of mental prostration and misery, proportioned to the heat and excitement with which I had quitted it.

My first object was to read the letters which my poor friend had referred to. On my arrival, both our servants were up. My hands and clothes were dyed with blood, and they looked at me with astonishment. I ran hastily upstairs, to avoid them, and took the writing-desk, the key of which I knew hung to his watch-chain. Seizing the poker, I split it open, and took out the packet he mentioned. At this moment his servant entered the room.

"*Et mon maître, Monsieur, où est-il?*"

"I have murdered him," said I, "and you will find him in the sands, near the signal-post; and," continued I, "I am now robbing him!"

My appearance and actions seemed to prove the truth of my assertion. The man flew out of the room; but I was regardless of everything, and even wonder why I should have given my attention to the letters at all, especially as I had now convinced myself of Talbot's innocence. The packet, however, I did read; and it consisted of a series of letters between Talbot and his father, who had engaged him to a young lady of rank and fortune, without consulting him—*un mariage de convenance*—which Talbot had resisted in consequence of his attachment to Clara.

I have already stated that Talbot was of high aristocratic family; and this marriage being wished for by the parents of both parties, they had given it out as being finally settled to take place on the return of Talbot to England. In the last letter, the father had yielded to his entreaties in favour of Clara; only requesting him not to be precipitate in offering himself, as he wished to find some excuse for breaking off the match; and, above all, he fatally enjoined profound secrecy till the affair was arranged. Here, then, was everything explained. Indeed, before I had read these letters, my mind did not need this damning proof of his innocence and my guilt.

Just as I had finished reading, the *gens d'armes* entered my room, and, with the officers of justice, led me away to prison. I walked mechanically. I was conducted to a small building in the centre of a square. This was a *cachot*, with an iron-grated window on each of its four sides, but without glass. There was no bench, or table, or anything but the bare walls and the pavement. The wind blew sharply through. I had not even a great-coat; but I felt no cold or personal inconvenience, for my mind was too much occupied by superior misery. The door closed on me, and I heard the bolts turn. There was not an observation made on either part, and I was left to myself.

"Well," said I, "Fate has now done its worst, and Fortune will be weary at last of tormenting a wretch that she can sink no lower! Death has no terrors for me; and, after death!" But, even in my misery, I scarcely gave a thought to what might happen in futurity. It might occasionally have obtruded itself on my mind, but was quickly dismissed: I had adopted the atheistical creed of the French Revolution.

"Death is eternal sleep, and the sooner I go to sleep the better!" thought I. The only point that pressed itself on my mind was the dread of a public execution. This my pride revolted at; for pride had again returned, and resumed its empire, even in my *cachot*.

As the day dawned, the noise of the carts and country people coming into the square with their produce, roused me from my reverie, for I had not slept. The prison was surrounded by all ages and all classes, to get a sight of the English murderer; and the light and the air were stopped out of each window by human faces pressed against the bars. I was gazed at as a wild beast; and the children, as they sat on their mothers' shoulders to look at me, received a moral lesson and a warning at my expense.

As a tiger, in his cage, wearies the eye by incessantly walking and turning, so I paced my den; and if I could have reached one of the impertinent gazers, through the slanting aperture and three foot wall, I should have throttled him. "All these people," said I, "and thousands more, will witness my last moments on the scaffold!"

Stung with this dreadful thought, with rage I searched in my pockets for my penknife, to relieve me at once from my torments and apprehensions; and had I found it, I should certainly have committed suicide. Fortunately I had left it at home, or it would have been buried, in that moment of frenzy, in the carotid artery; for as well as others, I knew exactly where to find it.

The crowd at length began to disperse; the windows were left, except now and then an urchin of a boy showed his ragged head at the grille. Worn out with bodily fatigue and mental suffering, I was going to throw myself along upon the cold stones, when I saw the face of my own servant, who advanced in haste to the window of the prison, exclaiming with joy—

"*Courage, mon cher maître; Monsieur Talbot n'est pas mort.*"

"Not dead!" exclaimed I (falling unconsciously on my knees, and lifting up my clasped hands and haggard eyes to Heaven): "not dead! God be praised. At least there is a hope that I may escape the crime of murder."

Before I could say more, the mayor entered my *cachot:* with the officers of the police, and informed me that a *procès-verbal* had been held; that my friend had been able to give the clearest answers to all their questions; and that it appeared from the evidence of *Monsieur Talbot* himself, that it was an affair *d'honneur,* fairly decided; that the brace of pistols found in the water had confirmed his assertions; "And therefore, Monsieur," continued the mayor, "whether your friend lives or dies, *tout a été fait en règle, et vous êtes libre.*"

So saying, he bowed very politely, and pointed to the door; nor was I so ceremonious as to beg him to show me the way; out I ran, and flew to the apartment of Talbot, who had sent my servant to say how much he wished to see me. I found him in bed. As I entered, he held out his hand to me, which I covered with kisses, and bathed with my tears.

"Oh, Talbot!" said I, "can you forgive me?"

He squeezed my hand, and from exhaustion let it fall. The surgeon led me out of the room, saying, "All depends on his being kept quiet." I then learned that he owed his life to two circumstances—the first was, my having bound my neckcloth round the wound; the other was, that the duel took place below high-water mark. The tide was rising when I left him; and the cold waves, as they rippled against his body, had restored him to animation. In this state he was found by his servant, not many minutes before the flood would have covered him, for he had not strength to remove out of its way. I ascertained also that the ball had entered his liver, and had passed out without doing farther injury.

I now dressed myself, and devoutly thanking God for his miraculous preservation, took my seat by the bed-side of the patient, which I never quitted until his perfect recovery. When this was happily completed, I wrote to my father and to Clara, giving both an exact account of the whole transaction. Clara, undeceived, made no scruple of acknowledging her attachment. Talbot was requested by his father to return home. I accompanied him as far as Calais, where we parted; and in a few weeks after, I had the pleasure of hearing that my sister had become his wife.

Left to myself, I returned slowly, and much depressed in spirits, to Quillac's; where, ordering post-horses, I threw myself into my travelling carriage, into which my valet had, by my orders, previously placed my luggage.

"Where are you going to, Monsieur?" said the valet.

"Au diable!" said I.

"Mais les passeports?" said the man.

I felt that I had sufficient passports for the journey I had proposed; but correcting myself, said, "to Switzerland." It was the first name that came into my head; and I had heard that it was the resort of all my countrymen whose heads, hearts, lungs, or finances were disordered. But, during my journey, I neither saw nor heard any thing, consequently took no notes, which my readers will rejoice at, because they will be spared that inexhaustible supply to the trunk makers, "A Tour through France and Switzerland." I travelled night and day; for I could not sleep. The allegory of Io and the gad-fly, in the heathen mythology, must surely have been intended to represent the being, who, like myself, was tormented by a bad conscience. Like Io, I flew; and like her, was I pursued by the eternal gad-fly, wherever I went, and in vain did I try to escape it.

I passed the Great St Bernard on foot. This interested me as I approached it. The mountains below, and the Alps above, were one mass of snow and ice, and I looked down with contempt on the world below me. I took up my abode in the convent for some time; my ample contributions to the box in the chapel, made me a welcome sojourner beyond the limited period allowed to travellers, and I felt less and less inclined to quit the scene. My amusement was climbing the most frightful precipices, followed by the large and faithful dogs, and viewing nature in her wildest and most sublime attire. At other times, when bodily fatigue required rest, I sat down, with morbid melancholy, in the receptacle for the bodies of those unfortunate persons who had perished in the snow. There would I remain for hours, musing on their fate: the purity of the air admitted neither putrefaction, or even decay, for a very considerable time; and they lay, to all appearance, as if the breath had even then only quitted them, although, on touching those who had been there for years, they would often crumble into dust.

Roman Catholics, we know, are ever anxious to make converts. The prior asked me whether I was not a protestant? I replied, that I was of no religion; which answer was, I believe, much nearer to the truth than any other I could have given. The reply was far more favourable to the hopes of the monks, than if I had said I was a heretic or a moslem. They thought me much more likely to become a convert to *their* religion, since I had none of my own to oppose to it. The monks immediately arranged themselves in theological order, with the whole armour of faith, and laid constant siege to me on all sides; but I was not inclined to any religion, much less to the one I despised. I would sooner have turned Turk.

I received a letter from poor unhappy Eugenia—it was the last she ever wrote. It was to acquaint me with the death of her lovely boy, who, having wandered from the house, had fallen into a trout-stream, where he was found drowned some hours after. In her distracted state of mind, she could add no more than her blessing, and a firm conviction that we should never meet again in this world. Her letter concluded incoherently; and although I should have said, in the morning, that my mind had not room for another sorrow, yet the loss of this sweet boy, and the state of his wretched mother, found a place in my bosom for a time, to the total exclusion of all other cares. She requested me to hasten to her without delay, if I wished to see her before she died.

I took leave of the monks, and travelled with all speed to Paris, and thence to Calais. Reaching Quillac's hotel, I received a shock which, although I apprehended danger, I was not prepared for. It was a letter from Eugenia's agent, announcing her death. She had been seized with a brain fever, and had died at a small town in Norfolk, where she had removed soon after our last unhappy interview. The agent concluded his letter by saying, that Eugenia had bequeathed me all her property, which was very considerable, and that her last rational words to him were, that I was her first and her only love.

I was now callous to suffering. My feelings had been racked to insensibility. Like a ship in a hurricane, the last tremendous sea had swept everything from the decks—the vessel was a wreck, driving as the storm might chance to direct. In the midst of this devastation, I looked around me, and the only object which presented itself to my mind, as worthy of contemplation, was the tomb which contained the remains of Eugenia and her child. To that I resolved to repair.

CHAPTER XXIX

With sorrow and repentance true,
Father, I trembling come to you.

SONG

I ARRIVED at the town where poor Eugenia had breathed her last, and near to which was the cemetery in which her remains were deposited. I went to the inn, whence, after having dismissed my post-boy and ordered my luggage to be taken up to my room, I proceeded on foot towards the spot. I

was informed that the path lay between the church and the bishop's palace.
I soon reached it; and, inquiring for the sexton, who lived in a cottage hard
by, requested he would lead me to a certain grave, which I indicated by
tokens too easily known.

"Oh, you mean the sweet young lady, as died of grief for the loss of her
little boy. There it is," continued he, pointing with his finger; "the white
peacock is now sitting on the headstone of the grave, and the little boy is
buried beside it."

I approached, while the humble sexton kindly withdrew, that I might,
without witnesses, indulge that grief which he saw was the burthen of my
aching heart. The bird remained, but without dressing its plumage, without
the usual air of surprise and vigilance evinced by domestic fowls, when
disturbed in their haunts. This poor creature was moulting; its feathers were
rumpled and disordered; its tail ragged. There was no beauty in the animal,
which was probably only kept as a variety of the species; and it appeared
to me as if it had been placed there as a lesson to myself. In its modest attire,
in its melancholy and pensive attitude, it seemed, with its gaudy plumage,
to have dismissed the world and its vanities, while in mournful silence it
surveyed the crowded mementoes of eternity.

"This is my office, not thine," said I, apostrophising the bird, which,
alarmed at my near approach, quitted its position, and disappeared among
the surrounding tombs. I sat down, and fixing my eyes on the name which
the tablet bore, ran over, in a hurried manner, all that part of my career
which had been more immediately connected with the history of Eugenia.
I remembered her many virtues; her self-devotion for my honour and happiness; her concealing herself from me, that I might not blast my prospects
in life by continuing an intimacy which she saw would end in my ruin; her
firmness of character, her disinterested generosity, and the refinement of
attachment which made her prefer misery and solitude to her own gratification in the society of the man she loved. She had, alas! but one fault, and
that fault was loving me. I could not drive from my thoughts, that it was
through my unfortunate and illicit connection with her that I had lost all that
made life dear to me.

At this moment (and not once since the morning I awoke from it) my
singular dream recurred to my mind. The thoughts which never had once
during my eventful voyage from the Bahamas to the Cape, and thence to

England, presented themselves in my waking hours, must certainly have possessed my brain during sleep. Why else should it never have occurred to my rational mind that the connection with Eugenia would certainly endanger that intended with Emily? It was Eugenia that placed Emily in mourning, out of my reach, and, as it were, on the top of the Nine-Pin Rock.

Here, then, my dream was explained; and I now felt all the horrors of that reality which I thought at the time was no more than the effect of a disordered imagination. Yet I could not blame Eugenia; the poor girl had fallen a victim to that deplorable and sensual education which I had received in the cockpit of a man-of-war. I, I alone was the culprit. She was friendless, and without a parent to guide her youthful steps; she fell a victim to my ungoverned passions. Maddened with anguish of head and heart, I threw myself violently on the grave: I beat my miserable head against the tombstones; I called with frantic exclamation on the name of Eugenia; and at length sank on the turfs between the two graves, in a state of stupor and exhaustion, from which a copious flood of tears in some measure relieved me.

I was aroused by the sound of wheels and the trampling of horses; and, looking up, I perceived the bishop's carriage and four, with out-riders, pass by. The livery and colour of the carriage were certainly what is denominated quiet; but there was an appearance of state which indicated that the owner had not entirely "renounced the pomps and vanities of this wicked world," and my spleen was excited.

"Ay, sweep along," I bitterly muttered, "worthy type indeed of the apostles! I like the pride that apes humility. Is that the way yon teach your flock to 'leave all, and follow me'?" I started up suddenly, saying to myself, "I will seek this man in his palace, and see whether I shall be kindly received and consoled, or be repulsed by a menial."

The thought was sudden, and, being conceived almost in a state of frenzy, was instantly executed. "Let me try," said I, "whether a bishop can 'administer to the mind diseased' as well as a country curate?"

I moved on with rapidity to the palace, more in a fit of desperation than with a view of seeking peace of mind. I rang loudly and vehemently at the gate, and asked whether the bishop was at home. An elderly domestic, who seemed to regard me with astonishment, answered in the affirmative, and desired me to walk into an ante-room, while he announced me to his master.

I now began to recall my scattered senses, which had been wandering, and to perceive the absurdity of my conduct; I was therefore about to quit the palace, into which I had so rudely intruded, without waiting for my audience, when the servant opened the door and requested me to follow him.

By what inscrutable means are the designs of Providence brought about! While I thought I was blindly following the impulse of passion, I was, in fact, guided by unerring Wisdom. A prey to desperate and irritated feelings, I anticipated, with malignant pleasure, that I should detect hypocrisy—that one who ought to set an example, should be weighed by me, and found wanting; instead of which I stumbled on my own salvation! Where I expected to meet with pride and scorn, I met with humility and kindness. When I had looked around on the great circle bounded by the visible horizon, and could perceive no friendly port in which I might lay my shattered vessel, behold it was close at hand!

I followed the servant with a kind of stupid indifference, and was ushered into the presence of a benevolent-looking old man, between sixty and seventy years of age. His whole external appearance, as well as his white hairs, commanded respect amounting almost to admiration. I was not prepared to speak, which he perceived, and kindly began.

"As you are a stranger to me, I fear, from your care-worn countenance, that it is no common occurrence which has brought you here. Sit down: you seem in distress; and if it is in my power to afford you relief, you may be assured that I will do so."

There was in his manner and address an affectionate kindness which overcame me. I could neither speak nor look at him; but, laying my head on the table, and hiding my face with my hands, I wept bitterly. The good bishop allowed me reasonable time to recover myself, and, with extreme good breeding, mildly requested that, if it were possible, I would confide to him the cause of my affliction.

"Be not afraid or ashamed, my good lad," said he, "to tell me your sorrows. If we have temporal blessings, we do not forget that we are but the almoners of the Lord: we endeavour to follow his example; but, if I may judge from appearance, it is not pecuniary aid you have come to solicit."

"No, no," replied I; "it is not money that I want:" but, choked with excess of feeling, I could say no more.

"This is indeed a more important case than one of mere bodily want," said the good man. "*That* we might very soon supply; but there seems something in your condition which requires our more serious attention. I thank the Almighty for selecting me to this service; and, with his blessing, we shall not fail of success."

Then, going to the door, he called to a young lady, who I afterwards found was his daughter; and, holding the door ajar as he spoke, that I might not be seen in my distress, said, "Caroline, my dear, write to the duke, and beg him to excuse my dining with him today. Tell him that I am kept at home by business of importance; and give orders that I be not interrupted on any account."

He then turned the key in the door; and, drawing a chair close to mine, begged me, in the most persuasive manner, to tell him every thing without reserve, in order that he might apply such a remedy as the case seemed to demand.

I first asked for a glass of wine, which was instantly brought; he received it at the door, and gave it to me with his own hand.

Having drank it, I commenced the history of my life in a brief outline, and ultimately told him all; nearly as much in detail as I have related it to the reader. He listened to me with an intense and painful interest, questioning me as to my feelings on many important occasions; and having at length obtained from me an honest and candid confession, without any extenuation,

"My young friend," said he, "your life has been one of peculiar temptation and excess. Much to deplore, much to blame, and much to repent of; but the state of feeling which induced you to come to me, is a proof that you now only require that which, with God's help, I trust I shall be able to supply. It is now late, and we both of us require some refreshment. I will order in dinner, and you must send to the inn for your portmanteau."

Perceiving that I was about to answer, "I must take no denial," resumed he. "You have placed yourself under my care as your physician, and you must follow my prescriptions. My duty is as much more important, compared to the doctor's, as the soul is to the body."

Dinner being served, he dismissed the servants as soon as possible, and then asked me many questions relative to my family, all of which I answered without reserve. He once mentioned Miss Somerville; but I was so overcome, that he perceived my distress, and, filling me a glass of wine, changed the subject.

If I thought that any words of mine could do justice to the persuasive discourses of this worthy bishop, I would have benefited the world by making them public; but I could not do this; and I trust that none of my readers will have so much need of them as I had myself. I shall, therefore, briefly state, that I remained in the palace ten days, in the most perfect seclusion.

Every morning the good bishop dedicated two or three hours to my instruction and improvement; he put into my hands one or two books at a time, with marks in them, indicating the pages which I ought to consult. He would have introduced me to his family; but this I begged, for a time, to decline, being too much depressed and out of spirits; and he indulged me in my request of being allowed to continue in the apartments allotted to me.

On the seventh morning, he came to me, and after a short conversation, informed me that business would require his absence for two or three days, and that he would give me a task to employ me during the short time he should be gone. He then put into my hand a work on the sacrament. "This," said he, "I am sure you will read with particular attention, so that on my return I may invite you to the feast." I trembled as I opened the book. "Fear not, Mr Mildmay," said he; "I tell you, from what I see of your symptoms, that the cure will be complete."

Having said this, he gave me his blessing, and departed. He returned exactly at the end of three days, and after a short examination, said he would allow me to receive the sacrament, and that the holy ceremony should take place in his own room privately, well knowing how much affected I should be. He brought in the bread and wine; and having consecrated and partaken of them himself, agreeably to the forms prescribed, he made a short extempore prayer in my behalf.

When he had done this, he advanced towards me, and presented the bread. My blood curdled as I took it in my mouth; and when I had tasted the wine, the type of the blood of that Saviour, whose wounds I had so often opened afresh in my guilty career, and yet upon the merits of which I now relied for pardon, I felt a combined sensation of love, gratitude and joy—a lightness and buoyancy of spirits, as if I could have left the earth below me, disburthened of a weight that had, till then, crushed me to the ground. I felt that I had faith—that I was a new man—and that my sins were forgiven; and, dropping my head on the side of the table, I remained some minutes in grateful and fervent prayer.

The service being ended, I hastened to express my acknowledgments to my venerable friend.

"I am but the humble instrument, my dear young friend," said the bishop; "let us both give thanks to the almighty Searcher of hearts. Let us hope that the work is perfect—for then, you will be the occasion of 'joy in heaven.' And now," continued he, "let me ask you one question. Do you feel in that state of mind that you could bear any affliction which might befall you, without repining?"

"I trust, Sir," answered I, "that I could bear it, not only cheerfully, but thankfully; and I now acknowledge that it is good for me that I have been in trouble."

"Then all is right," said he; "and with such feelings I may venture to give you this letter, which I promised the writer to deliver with my own hand."

As soon as my eye caught the superscription, "Gracious Heaven!" exclaimed I; "it is from my Emily."

"Even so," said the bishop.

I tore it open. It contained only six lines, which were as follows:—

Our mutual kind friend, the bishop, has proved to me how proud and how foolish I have been. Forgive me, dear Frank, for I too have suffered much, and come as soon as possible to your ever affectionate

EMILY.

This, then, was the object of the venerable bishop's absence. Bending beneath age and infirmity, he had undertaken a journey of three hundred miles, in order to ensure the temporal as well as eternal welfare of a perfect stranger—to effect a reconciliation, without which he saw that my worldly happiness was incomplete. I was afterwards informed, that notwithstanding the weight of his character and holy office, he had found Emily more decided in her rejection than he had anticipated; and it was not until he had sharply rebuked her for her pride and unforgiving temper, that she could be brought to listen with patience to his arguments. But having at length convinced her that the tenure of her own hopes depended on her forgiveness of others, she relented, acknowledged the truth of his remarks, and her undiminished affection for me. While she made this confession, she was in the same position before the bishop, that I was when I received her letter—on my knees, and in tears.

He gave me his hand, raised me up, "And, now, my young friend," said he, "let me give you one caution. I hope and I trust that your repentance is sincere. If it be not, the guilt must rest on your head; but I trust in God that all is as it should be. I will not, therefore, detain you any longer: you must be impatient to be gone. Refreshment is prepared for you: my horses will take you the first stage. Have you funds sufficient to carry you through? for it is a long journey, as my old bones can testify."

I assured him that I was sufficiently provided; and, expressing my thanks for his kindness, wished that it was in my power to prove my gratitude. "Put me to the test, my lord," said I, "if you possibly can."

"Well, then," replied he, "I will: when the day for your union with Miss Somerville is fixed, allow me to have the pleasure of joining your hands, should it please God to spare me so long. I have removed the disease; but I must trust to somebody else to watch and prevent a relapse. And believe me, my dear friend, however well-inclined a man may be to keep in the straight path, he gains no little support from the guidance and example of a lovely and virtuous woman."

I promised readily all he asked; and having finished a slight lunch, again shook hands with the worthy prelate, jumped into my carriage, and drove off. I travelled all night; and the next day was in the society of those I loved, and who had ever loved me, in spite of all my perverseness and folly.

A few weeks after, Emily and I were united by the venerable bishop, who, with much emotion, gave us his benediction; and as the prayer of the righteous man availeth much, I felt that it was recorded in our favour in Heaven. Mr Somerville gave the bride away. My father, with Talbot and Clara, were present; and the whole of us, after all my strange vicissitudes, were deeply affected at this reconciliation and union.

THE END.

SQUARE SAILS

1 Mizzen-royal
2 Main-royal
3 Fore-royal
4 Mizzen-top gallant
5 Main-top gallant
6 Fore-top gallant
7 Mizzen-top
8 Main-top
9 Fore-top
10 Driver
11 Main-course
12 Fore-course

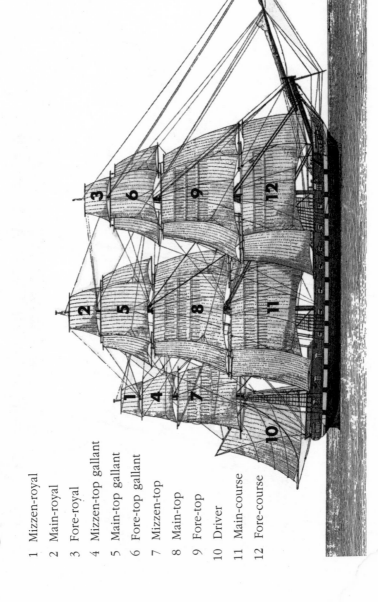

FORE-AND-AFT SAILS

1 Main-top-gallant-stay-sail
2 Mizzen-top-mast-stay-sail
3 Main-top-mast-stay-sail
4 Mizzen
5 Mizzen-stay-sail
6 Main-stay-sail
7 Fore-stay-sail
8 Fore-top-mast-stay-sail
9 Standing jib
10 Flying jib

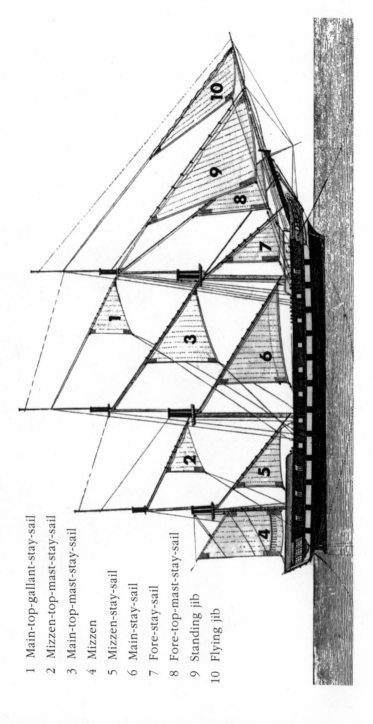

GLOSSARY

abaft (Also *aft*) Toward the rear of a ship.

athwart Across. Transversely.

battery An emplacement for artillery. Also, a number of pieces of artillery.

belay Secure a rope by giving it several cross-turns around each end of a cleat-pin, etc. Also used as a command meaning "stop!" or "enough!" or "disregard!"

boatswain (Also *bosun*) The naval petty officer who inspects the rigging, sails, anchors, cables, and ropes. He also hurries the men to their duties.

booms Long poles (spars) rigged from the ends of yards to extend sails.

boom-irons Two flat iron rings, formed into one piece, used to connect the studding-sail booms to the yards.

bowsprit A boom or mast extending forward from the stem (front) of a ship. It supports the foremast and the jibs.

brace A rope to swing yards and sails horizontally around the mast.

brig A two-masted ship rigged similarly to a frigate but lacking a mizzen-mast.

broadside The simultaneous firing of all guns on one side of a ship.

bulkhead A vertical partition in the hull that divides the vessel into compartments.

bulwark The portion of a ship's side that extends above the deck.

calavances   Small edible legumes.

canister   (Also *canister-shot*) Ammunition consisting of small bullets packed in tin cases. When fired from a cannon the cases open and the bullets spread in a destructive pattern.

cap   Short thick block of wood with two holes, one round and one square, used to hold two masts together lengthwise.

capstan   (Also *capstern*) A revolving cylinder, set on a vertical axis, used to heave up (weigh) anchors.

capuchin   Franciscan friar of an austere order that wore a distinctive cloak with a pointed hood.

carronade   A very short, large calibre naval gun, somewhat like a mortar.

catharpings   (Also *catharpins* or *catharpens*) Short ropes to brace the shrouds on the lower masts.

catheads   Two strong timber beams that project outward over a ship's bow from the forecastle. Used to suspend the anchor.

cob   (Also *cobb*) A blow or knock on the buttocks.

cochineal   A scarlet dye made from the dried bodies of a species of Mexican insect.

conn   (Also *con, cann, cun,* and *cond*) To direct the person at the helm to steer a ship.

cutter   A short, wide ship's boat fitted for rowing or sailing, used for carrying passengers and light stores.

davit   A timber, used as a crane, to hoist the flukes of the anchor without damaging the ship's side.

depredator   One who robs, despoils or pillages.

dirk   A short dagger such as used by a Scottish highlander, often worn by midshipmen.

enfilade   Cover the whole length of a target with guns.

felucca   A small Mediterranean vessel propelled by lateen (angled) sails or oars.

flukes The triangular blades at the ends of the arms of an anchor.

forecastle (Also *fo'c'sle*) A short raised deck at the bow of a ship.

frigate A fast, maneuverable three-masted man-of-war, carrying between 26 and 38 guns on a single gundeck.

garrison A body of troops stationed in a town for defensive purposes.

gig A light, narrow clinker-built ship's boat that may be rowed or sailed.

grape Multiple small cast-iron balls, sometimes in a canvas bag, used as shot in a cannon.

grapnel A small anchor, with four or five flutes and no stock, used for small boats or as a boarding hook.

grummet (Also *grommet*) A ring made from three turns of rope, used, for example, to fasten the upper edge of a sail to its stays.

gudgeon Iron clamp, bolted on the sternpost of a ship, to hang the rudder.

gunwale The upper edge of a ship's side.

hatchway An opening in a ship's deck through which one can descend into the ship or lower cargo.

haul-yards (Also *halliards* or *halyards*) Ropes and tackle used to hoist and lower sails, yards, and flags.

hawsers Small cables used, for example, to hoist up (sway) a topmast.

hove-to Brought (a vessel) to a standstill without anchoring.

jolly-boat A clinker-built ship's boat, wide and smaller than a cutter, usually hoisted at the stern of a vessel.

larboard Left side.

lee (Also *leeward*) The side turned away from the wind.

leeboard One of a pair of movable plates attached to a ship's hull to reduce downwind drift (leeway).

loom	The indistinct appearance of an object near the horizon. Also, the handle of an oar between the grip and the oar-lock.
lubberly	In the fashion of an inexperienced or clumsy sailor or a landlubber.
magazine	The compartment deep in a ship where the gunpowder is stored.
man-of-war	A vessel equipped for warfare or belonging to a recognized navy.
man-ropes	Small sets of ropes used for climbing a ship's side or negotiating a hatchway.
middies	Midshipmen.
midshipman	A young British naval officer, ranking below a lieutenant.
painter	A rope secured to the front (stem) of a boat. Used to tie it up (make it fast).
purser	The naval warrant officer who looks after the ship's provisions and "slops" (clothing sold to the sailors).
poop	The uppermost deck abaft.
port-fire	A device used for firing artillery.
post-boy	(Also *postillion*) A messenger on horseback or the rider of the front-left horse when two or more horses are pulling a carriage.
quarter	The rear half of a vessel.
quarter-master	A naval petty officer in charge of steering, signals, and stowing the hold.
quarterdeck	An upper deck, near the stern, reserved for superior officers, from which sailing activities are commanded.
rantipole	A wild, ill-behaved, scolding or quarrelsome person.
round	(Also *round shot*) Spherical cast-iron cannonballs.
running-rigging	The ropes (braces, sheets, and halliards) that are used to arrange the sails.

sally-port A landing place reserved for naval vessels; the opening in a ship's side used for entry.

saturnalia A time of uninhibited tumult and revelry. An orgy.

schuyt (Also *schuit*) A Dutch flat-bottomed riverboat.

scud Run before the wind with minimal sail.

sheet-anchor A back-up anchor, often the largest anchor onboard a ship, to be used in emergencies.

shrouds A large variety of ropes that support the masts.

skait (Usually spelled *skate*) A ray with a diamond-shaped body and long thin tail, often used for food.

sloop A light man-of-war.

steward The seaman who caters for the captain and officers' mess.

studding-sail (Also *stunsail*) A sail set on an extra yard at the outer edge of a square sail to catch more wind in a light air.

thoel (Usually spelled *thole*) A pin set vertically in the gunwale of a boat to serve as a part of an oar-lock.

train tackle The blocks that restrain the movement of a gun while loading.

vidette (Also *vedette*) A small vessel used for sentry or scouting purposes.

whiting A fish, commonly found off the European coast, that is often used as food.

xebeque (Also *zebec* or *chebec*) A small, three-masted vessel with a combination of lateen (angled) and square sails, used in the Mediterranean.

yawl A ship's boat with four or six oars. Smaller than a cutter but with a wide transom.

yards Long, stout poles hung horizontally from the masts to support the sails.